The Nearly Departed

THE
NEARLY
DEPARTED

Minnesota Ghost Stories & Legends

MICHAEL NORMAN

MINNESOTA HISTORICAL SOCIETY PRESS

www.mhspress.org

Excerpted quotations from *House of Spirits and Whispers* by Annie Wilder, published by Llewellyn Publications (© 2005 by Annie Wilder), are used with the author's permission.

Excerpted quotation from *A Boy from C-11: Case #9164* by Harvey Ronglien, published by Graham Megyeri Books (© 2006 by Harvey Ronglien) are used with the author's permission.

Earlier versions of "No Escape," "What Tunis Parkin Saw," "Frozen John," "Was It Mrs. Moriarity?" and "The Mad Priest" appeared in *Haunted Heartland* by Beth Scott and Michael Norman (Stanton and Lee, 1984); a longer account of the Minnesota State Capitol haunting appeared in *Haunted Homeland* by Michael Norman (Forge Books, 2006).

The Minnesota Historical Society Press is a member of the Association of American University Presses.

Manufactured in the United States of America

10 9 8 7 6 5 4 3 2 1

♾ The paper used in this publication meets the minimum requirements of the American National Standard for Information Sciences—Permanence for Printed Library Materials, ANSI Z39.48–1984.

International Standard Book Number
ISBN 13: 978-0-87351-717-1 (paper)
ISBN 10: 0-87351-717-2 (paper)

Library of Congress Cataloging-in-Publication Data
  Norman, Michael, 1947 June 29–
  The nearly departed : Minnesota ghost stories and legends / Michael Norman.
     p. cm.
  Includes bibliographical references and index.
     ISBN-13: 978-0-87351-717-1 (pbk. : alk. paper)
     ISBN-10: 0-87351-717-2 (pbk. : alk. paper)
  1. Ghosts—Minnesota. I. Title.
  BF1472.U6N69 2009
  133.109776—dc22

                                2009003189

This book is dedicated to my wonderful nieces and nephews:
Adam and Amelia Ball
Peter and Emma Lansworth

CONTENTS

PREFACE

"What ghosts really are, contrary to their bleak reputation,
is a symbol of hope. That is why we love ghost stories:
They help us believe that we—and those we love—survive
to illuminate the whole."
Edward Readicker-Henderson, travel writer

WHAT IS THE CONTINUING APPEAL OF THE GHOST STORY?
If we think of it as literature, then the ghost story is simply
a tale created by an imaginative writer who desires nothing more
than to provide a splendid fright. Once the book is closed or "The
End" rolls across the screen, the undead are safely tucked away . . .
until we next summon their vaporous, emaciated selves.

Ghosts in literature emerged from a time when our forebears
huddled around a fire and whispered words about fantastic presences in the shadows beyond that precious circle of light—weird
tales of the dead, walking. These storytellers discovered something,
some elemental appeal that struck a responsive chord among lis-
teners. Their stories were adapted and elaborated, handed down
through the generations, and spread from culture to culture, until
they became embedded in our literary and cultural traditions, the
principal subject matter in a multitude of folk narratives, novels,
short stories, films, and television programs. There has never been
a nation or a civilization without ghost stories.

Yet something more happens if we take another (creaking) step and ask what the enduring appeal is for the purportedly true stories of ghosts and hauntings—of visitations not penned by Dickens but planned postmortem by one's late Aunt Harriet.

Perhaps the allure owes itself to the fact that we have always been fascinated by what lies beyond: beyond the horizon, beneath the ocean's surface, atop the highest mountain, deep within the most impenetrable wilderness, past the stars. Any interest we have in the idea that ghosts or spirits or apparitions—or whatever you choose to call them—really do exist might arise, at least in part, from that most fundamental of human traits, the drive to explore and understand what lies beyond us and, in this instance, what awaits us beyond our physical demise.

Thus, if one believes at all in such things as ghosts, regardless of their provenance, then Edward Readicker-Henderson may be correct in saying that they serve as a means to deal with the one question all of us want to ask but seldom do. What becomes of us after death? Do we continue on in some manner, albeit not of flesh and blood? Or when death calls, as it must, is that the final tremble, the last we'll see of this world or any other? Does our consciousness end with our final breath of air?

The terrible joke here is that we will never know the answers to these questions until it is too late. For beyond death is either nothingness or a realm where some portion of us survives.

Many years ago, I began collecting and writing true ghost stories as a confirmed doubter, a skeptic who bridled at the notion of spectral entities hovering about us in some sort of time warp or parallel dimension, unable to reach the light. Tales of ghosties and ghoulies were delightfully chilling to me, yes, but they were ultimately fictions created to frighten small children and the faint of heart. They were direct descendants of those ancient fireside fables—or maybe the products of some sort of aberrant mental condition.

After interviewing hundreds of people who have told me about their brushes with the supernatural and after countless visits to haunted places—and one small personal experience—I am less of a skeptic today and more willing to consider the possibility, the *possi-*

bility, that something has happened when people report a haunting or an encounter with a ghost. What has exactly taken place I do not yet know or understand. What I do know is that we can't reject the millions of people in every nation and throughout the millennia who have reported encounters with ghosts and spirits.

We also cannot easily discount the deeply personal encounters in which the appearance of a ghost brings hope, such as the one described in a letter I received some years ago from John, a Vietnam veteran from Minnesota, who was nudged awake by something brushing against his cheek late one night in 1969, shortly after his return from Southeast Asia. He writes:

> I looked up to see a figure standing over me. It had apparently just touched my face, as it stepped back as if startled, pulling back its hand as if it had touched something hot. I'll describe the figure by saying that it looked like Spiderman in a black outfit. It was like a 3-dimensional shadow. The figure was of a slender person. I can remember facial features only vaguely, as if seeing them through a nylon stocking. . . . Although I considered myself to be a macho veteran just back from Vietnam, I took a deep breath and screamed my lungs out. The figure then turned and walked briskly into my closet.

John suspected that the ghost was his brother, who had been shot down in Laos the year before and whose fate was unknown. John has never again seen a ghost of any sort. How can his experience be explained? Was John asleep and this but a vivid dream? He says not. And the fact that his letter came years after the ghost's appearance adds weight to his rejection of the idea. Who can remember with such clarity something they dreamed twenty-six years ago? It is an event worth thinking about.

Some stories portend the survival of a part of the human psyche or, at the very least, an eerie convergence of death and the unexplained. Marge Van Gorp of Alexandria, Minnesota, recounts a situation involving a friend of hers who lived in a haunted house— footsteps in the attic, that sort of thing. What happened the night this friend's husband died is interesting. Ms. Van Gorp writes:

> Years prior to his death, [her friend's husband] had given [his wife]
> a beautiful musical teapot. Although it was wound up, it would
> never play music. She placed it on top of the cabinets between her
> kitchen and dining room. He died early one morning in the upstairs
> bedroom. As she walked down the stairs into the kitchen, the teapot
> played its melody. She was in such awe, and after listening to it, she
> rewound it and placed it back on its spot on the cabinet. The next
> morning at the hour of his death, and each morning thereafter until
> his funeral, the musical pot played its tune. She, too, died shortly
> thereafter and I do not know if it ever played again.

These kinds of ghost stories—or, more accurately, stories of the supernatural—are very interesting to consider. They do not feature screaming banshees, blood-spewing fireplaces, earth-secreting corpses, or swirling, moaning miasmas. Most true stories of the supernatural are not like that at all. They are really puzzles that present possible solutions, solutions that are, in the end, entirely unsatisfactory. And to me the factual basis for each story makes them even more chilling.

I have included both historical and contemporary stories in this book. The older stories are based on accounts written at the time, either in newspapers, letters, memoirs, or other documents. In many cases, however, I have visited the site of the historic haunting. The contemporary stories are based, in the main, on the first-person accounts of those who have had some involvement with the haunting. Though these are not all the ghost stories of Minnesota, they are stories in which the range of substantive information or the availability of individuals willing to go on the record with their experiences provided the authenticity I sought.

Some readers may find that few of the stories that follow have satisfactory conclusions. Most of these hauntings are specific to a time and a place and a person. Some are ongoing; others have apparently ended. Although the geographic location may have the reputation of being haunted, in the telling of the story I have relied upon interviews, witness statements, historical records, and, in many cases, visits to the sites at which the events occurred. Alas,

I did not meet a single ghost, I don't believe. I am not a psychic, a seer, or a ghost buster but rather a storyteller who presents these accounts for your consideration and entertainment. I'll leave it up to you to decide what the conclusions should be.

NOTE ON THE TEXT

In some stories pseudonyms are used to ensure the privacy of an individual. Those names are marked with an asterisk (*) the first time they are used. For purposes of clarity or continuity, some events portrayed in these stories have been modified. The author makes no personal claim or stipulation as to the authenticity of the events portrayed in this book. The ownership of some public buildings and properties mentioned in this book may have changed since publication. In all cases please respect private property and individual privacy.

The Nearly Departed

PEEK-A-BOO

*"I looked at him. He looked at me. And then he moved
sideways in a blur. Real people don't move that way."*
Nancy Bagshaw-Reasoner

Nancy Bagshaw-Reasoner hoped to make some extra income working a few afternoons a week at the Fitzgerald Theater's box office.
As an actor and sometime producer, Bagshaw-Reasoner loved being
around St. Paul's theatrical grandes dames in most any capacity, and
a steady, if modest, paycheck selling tickets certainly would help
pay the bills.

So it was that Bagshaw-Reasoner found herself on duty that
Wednesday afternoon in the unassuming Fitz box office. It was a
quiet afternoon in late fall, and the theater was without many upcoming bookings. Garrison Keillor's *A Prairie Home Companion* Saturday night radio program had ended its fall season and was on the
road. A few special events were scheduled—an author interview, an
early holiday staging—but not much was going on that needed the
attention of the box office.

Nancy answered the phone and handled the moderate walk-up
traffic but otherwise spent her time catching up on some reading.
The ticket booth is next to the cozy theater's lobby but accessed
through a separate outside door, around the corner from the box
office. Inside, past the box office, one can reach either the lobby

or the theater's business offices. A corrugated-metal security panel separates the theater lobby from the box office and business offices when the theater is closed, as it was then.

It was late afternoon and getting dark outside, of course. She started pulling together statistics on the day's modest sales, her final responsibility, so she could lock up right on time. The business offices were closed.

And then she saw the man.

He was looking into the small, rarely used box office window that looks out to the rear hallway, between the theater and staff offices.

She certainly didn't expect to see someone at that window—she hadn't heard anyone come in from outside.

She poked her head out the front box office window.

"I can help you over here!" she called out, looking down the dimly lit passageway.

She had caught only a quick glimpse of this man at the window before he seemed to back away, but it had been long enough for her to see his dark hair and that he appeared to have on a plaid shirt. His face was in shadow.

She waited expectantly and then glanced nervously at the side window a few feet to her right. No one was there, and no one was in the passageway.

She felt a queasiness stirring in her. The outside doorbell that the theater's management installed hadn't sounded, and she was certain no one else was around.

When it was obvious this shadow man wasn't going to show himself, she thought that she was mistaken. Maybe it was her own indistinct reflection off some surface, yet that didn't seem probable.

"Oh, well," she thought, "that was a little strange but . . . ."

She turned her attention back to the sales figures.

Abruptly, she again caught a movement at the side window. Was this guy back?

Now her slight unease grew to sharp anxiety. Had someone really gotten into the theater undetected? And was he now playing games with her? Perhaps it was someone intent on robbing her? Or worse.

She turned toward the window. Once more, he quickly ducked away.

Again, she leaned out the window and called out, "I can help you over here!"

"He must be down there, around that corner," she thought.

And again Bagshaw-Reasoner waited.

Now she was frightened. Perhaps someone was playing a prank, maybe one of the office staff. If so, it wasn't funny.

"Tom! Is that you? Get over here and stop doing that. You're scaring me!" she shouted. Tom was a friend on the management staff.

"I'm closing up the box office!" she called down the hallway. Leaning back in her chair, she hoped this prankster would reveal himself.

He did show himself, this man in the shadows, but not in the way she anticipated.

As she sat back, Bagshaw-Reasoner detected another slight movement to her right. Her nemesis had returned. He was watching her intently. The first two times he'd been at the window, she'd looked fully in his direction, but he had dodged aside. This time she shifted only her eyes to focus on him. He was a slender man who could have been anywhere from his late twenties to early forties in a plaid shirt, with thick brown hair and prominent sideburns. And, she thought, he looked very sad—especially his eyes. He was standing quite still, staring at her.

Then Nancy turned to face him.

The two stared at each other, and then, as if Bagshaw-Reasoner had suddenly been thrust into the middle of a Wile E. Coyote and Road Runner episode, this stranger in a plaid shirt moved laterally, in a blur.

"It was the scariest thing in the world," Bagshaw-Reasoner says of the man's bizarre exit. "He hadn't been transparent. There wasn't anything ghostly about him. He looked at me and went *whoosh*, sideways. If I could live through that, I think I can survive anything in the world. I almost had a heart attack."

Nancy Bagshaw-Reasoner had met Ben, the sometime ghost of the Fitzgerald Theater.

The century-old Fitzgerald Theater is St. Paul's oldest surviving legitimate theater. Opened as the Sam S. Shubert Theater in 1910, the playhouse was built as an homage to the late Sam S. by his show business tycoon brothers, J. J. and Lee Shubert.

One of the most elegant theaters anywhere in the country when it opened, the Shubert Theater was built for the ages.

The superstructure of steel and concrete has a solid Minnesota sandstone exterior. Originally, two thousand electric lights provided state-of-the-art illumination; a vertically movable stage enhanced productions; and sixteen dressing rooms could accommodate large traveling productions. A hotel through which patrons reached the theater made the Shubert a center of St. Paul's early twentieth-century vaudeville entertainment.

But with the advent of film sound in the early 1930s, however, live entertainment dwindled in popularity, as did the Shubert's fortunes. Foreign films became the mainstay from the late 1930s to the 1970s in the rechristened World Theater.

Minnesota Public Radio bought the deteriorating theater in 1980, and Garrison Keillor started broadcasting *A Prairie Home Companion* from there in 1986. In honor of the upcoming centenary of author and St. Paul native F. Scott Fitzgerald's birth, the theater was renamed in 1994. More recent, the theater was used as the setting for the filming of Robert Altman's *A Prairie Home Companion*. Concerts, live theater, lectures, and variety shows share the Fitzgerald with Garrison Keillor's schedule of radio broadcasts.

There may be more astonishing activity in the old theater than simply that which unfolds regularly on its compact stage.

For at least thirty years, Fitzgerald Theater former and current employees have said that the ghost of a man they know as Ben has startled them with his sudden appearances or has puzzled them with his trickster behavior. Although old theaters are expected to host a ghost or two, the close encounters people have had with

Ben—including Nancy Bagshaw-Reasoner's—make the Fitzgerald a distinctive addition to the roster of haunted playhouses.

No one knows for certain who this Ben might have been in life nor even if that was his name. Yet there are two theories as to his identity. One is that he was a former stagehand whose signature was found on a note discovered above the false auditorium ceiling during the 1980s remodeling. The other is that Ben was an employee many years ago who drank himself into a stupor and froze to death in an alley next to the theater, an alley that has since been covered and converted into an atrium used for audience access and storage.

Despite the paucity of documentation related to Ben's time on earth, many stories circulate about his time after death apparently interacting with folks who have worked at the venerable theater.

Understandably, other people's experiences with the Fitzgerald's ghost were a long way from Nancy Bagshaw-Reasoner's on that afternoon some eight years ago. As a relatively new employee, she was not familiar with the ghost stories.

All she knew was that she was terrified.

"I shuttered the window and ran into the business office," Bagshaw-Reasoner says. A door from the back of the box office leads into the theater's offices. "But then I thought, 'What good is that going to do? It can come through these walls.'"

She managed to get to a telephone and call her husband. She told him briefly what had happened and pleaded with him to get down there as fast as he could. He was scheduled to pick her up later, but at the moment she wanted him to get there right away and wait outside the main doors.

"I had to go back out of the business office, into the hall where I saw it go whoosh, and around to where the security alarm for the theater is. It locks all the doors and sets up the motion detector."

It was a tense few minutes for Bagshaw-Reasoner.

"I really thought I was going to die. I'm standing [in the business office], telling my husband it's here, it's somewhere in here now. And I just thought, oh, God . . . ."

Her husband pulled up in front several minutes later. She then tried to set the alarm. It wouldn't arm, however; one of the sensor lights was blinking "motion detected." She tried to calm down. She knew she couldn't leave the theater unlocked. She was ready to call her supervisor when, after a couple more attempts, she was successful.

Bagshaw-Reasoner told only her husband about her predicament that afternoon. But she wasn't going to work there alone anymore. She suggested to her box office supervisor that it would be safer for women not to work alone in the box office. She didn't disclose the real reason for her trepidation.

Nancy kept the story to herself until a few weeks later. She didn't have any choice about revealing it then, because she saw the furtive figure again, and this time she wasn't alone.

Jude Mitchell is the audience services supervisor at the Fitzgerald. She was with Nancy on that Saturday. It hadn't been an especially demanding shift on what can sometimes be a busy day of the week, so they'd spent most of their time chatting. "Having fun," Bagshaw-Reasoner remembers.

Nancy says that at one point both of them were standing, talking to each other. Mitchell was waiting for a computer printer to finish a job. Nancy was facing the side window where she'd seen the mystery man several weeks before.

"As I looked out, someone went by," Bagshaw-Reasoner says. "It was the same man I'd seen before."

Except this time he was wispy, floating.

She screamed and ran into the business office.

"He looked more ephemeral. But I saw his face, I saw his dark hair, and I saw his shirt, but the rest of him was a blur. He was swirling out into [the hallway] area."

Mitchell didn't see anyone.

She did notice that her companion's eyes had enlarged to almost cartoonish saucer eyes. It was unnerving, she says.

"I'm like, 'Yeah, right, Nancy,'" Mitchell remembers. She went back into the booth and resumed putting together ticket reports.

Nancy cautiously came back in but then cried out, "It's back again!"

This time when Mitchell looked out to the hallway, she saw a white, translucent form moving past.

"I picked him up out of the corner of my eye and he ran away. But he was standing there watching Nancy—like a wisp of white that moved off quickly into the gift shop area. By that time he had become a hazy form moving quickly."

Jude Mitchell had heard the stories and told Nancy that it was probably the resident ghost that they had just seen. Jude assured her colleague that her experience was not that unusual and that Ben did not seem to be evil or malicious.

Bagshaw-Reasoner seemed relieved, and then the story about her earlier confrontation tumbled out.

"I thought I'd been losing my mind," she says. "I didn't want to say anything, because I thought people would simply think I was nuts because I'm an actress."

It's difficult to pinpoint just when the stories of Ben the ghost originated. Most agree sightings increased during the 1980s. Some believe the theater's renovation may have stirred him up.

There are two hot spots at which most encounters with Ben—or his spirit brethren—have happened. One extends from the business offices to the hallway and inner lobby area near the box office, where Bagshaw-Reasoner saw the ghost. The other is an upper set of box seats on the left side of the auditorium.

According to Tom Campbell, the theater's production and facilities manager, members of a ballet company using the theater saw a man moving around the box seats when no one was up there.

On another occasion Ben may have been prowling about around the time a production of the British ghost play *The Woman in Black* was slated for a run.

"What was interesting about that show is that on preview night, actually all leading up to that show, we had weird sightings going on," Campbell says.

The play's director included scenes during which the title character, a ghost, walks down the aisle. But that was the only time the actress appeared off the stage. Yet something more seemed to be going on during the preview night performance.

"About halfway through the show, almost two-thirds of the audience, all in unison, looked up at the upper boxes [on house left], thinking something was going on up there."

Preview night audience members were puzzled over glimpsing an "actor" up there, but nothing came of it. Campbell says the actress playing the role was backstage at the time. No one was sitting in any of the balcony or box seat areas.

"There was nobody from the play up there," he confirms.

Regarding ghost sightings, Tom Campbell says the theater has been "unbelievably quiet" for some time. He has never had any sort of contact with Ben, even though he spends ten to fifteen hours a week alone in the building. He thinks Ben has "found his peace and moved on," though he has some doubts because of several recent changes in the part of the theater complex that houses the business offices, on the corner of Wabasha and East Exchange, a former hotel built at about the same time as the Shubert Theater. The entrance to the theater was originally through the hotel. The basement beneath was a German-style rathskeller at the time the hotel was there. It has been gutted with an eye toward future development, Campbell says. The five floors above the business offices have been converted into condominiums.

"You have to wonder if [Ben] had multiple spaces. Maybe now he's in this area," Campbell speculates. Perhaps Ben was connected to the hotel in some way rather than to the theater.

But Campbell has no reason to doubt that something mysterious has transpired in the theater.

"There were too many similarities in the way that the [sightings] were happening. The fact that it always happened in certain areas, the fact that it also seemed to be that if they saw anything or heard anything, it was a man. I don't know how I feel about believing in it, but I have to think that something was going on. If not a ghost, then some sort of spirit that lives in this space."

In the theater business office, directly behind the box office, one member of the business staff had a peculiar problem with an office chair.

The young man had been running envelopes through a postage meter. When he returned to his desk, his chair was missing.

"I looked all over," he says. "All the other chairs were pushed in because no one else was here. I couldn't find it anywhere."

Finally, he located it far from his office, behind the gift shop counter in the lobby.

Another box office staffer was on duty late one night following a performance. He was alone, finishing up some ticket accounting, when he had to use the restroom. He returned to the box office, but this time his chair was missing. He went back out looking for it and found it sitting in the middle of the inner lobby. He says it was like his chair had followed him to the bathroom.

Sometimes, staff members wonder if too many anomalies are being blamed on a ghost.

Jude Martin says, "There are those subtle things that happen, but then you think, 'Am I tired, and I don't remember that I did it? Or is [Ben] yanking my chain right now?'"

Another staff member thinks that every time there is a problem in the theater, the first impulse is to blame it on Ben. He notes that all theaters are "supposed to have ghosts," so it's natural that people would assume an old theater like the Fitzgerald is haunted. But what seems supernatural often turns out to be faulty wiring, noisy pipes, insufficient weatherproofing, or even practical jokes played by actors or crew members.

For years a Fitzgerald Theater stage light would sometimes be found shining when staff arrived in the morning. Whereas some thought it was a ghostly Ben turning it on, technicians discovered that when the lighting system was overhauled the problem went away.

Tom Campbell says that problems with the alarm system similar to what Nancy Bagshaw-Reasoner discovered—that the alarm seemed to show movement in the theater—were solved when the motion sensors were replaced and the unit was rewired.

But another former Fitzgerald staff member cannot be persuaded that his experiences there can be explained in any rational way.

Richard Rewey was the theater's house manager for many years. It was his job to supervise everything that took place in the front of the house during performances. He also filled in at other management jobs. He now works for the University of Minnesota.

The first time Rewey had a run-in with the unexplained came on a night as he waited for his wife to pick him up. He was the last one at the theater, standing next to the alarm panel near the door.

From somewhere behind him, he heard a man clearing his throat.

"It wasn't indistinct; it was very clear," Rewey says. "It went on for a good couple of seconds."

Rewey tried to sort it out in his mind, thinking perhaps he had imagined it.

Then he heard it again, several seconds of someone clearing his throat.

"It was coming from the inner lobby, which curves around the backside of the theater. I'm thinking someone is in the theater. I'm the last one here, and I've got to take care of it."

Rewey walked around the corner and into that inner lobby. He didn't see anyone in the relatively small space.

"Who's here?" he yelled.

He didn't get an answer.

Rewey came back and looked at the alarm panel. It was ready to arm, which meant it would detect any motion in the theater.

"I didn't know what the heck was going on," he says.

And then it came a third time, again as if someone was standing in the inner lobby only a few feet away from him. He was certain he was the only living being in the theater.

"I thought, 'Okay, that's enough.' I set the alarm and left."

"I stood outside and tried not to look back in, because I really didn't want to see anything in there."

Because of his own encounters, Rewey made a point of pulling together other people's ghostly encounters at the Fitzgerald.

He says that things happened most frequently to people when they were alone, or almost alone. He cites the case of a young woman who was late for a mandatory preshow ushers' meeting that Rewey had scheduled. She finally got to the theater and ran up a stairway to the meeting, pulling on her usher's jacket as she ran. Someone shouted down at her to hurry up. She later asked Rewey if that had been him. He said he'd been meeting with the other ushers. She blanched.

Rewey understands outsiders' difficulty in believing that these ghostly encounters have taken place.

"The thing that gives these stories credibility is that no one else is here," Rewey says. "But the thing that makes them lose their credibility is that no one else is here. It's difficult."

For instance, he routinely heard stories from ushers in the second balcony section who had seen a wall sconce dim and then brighten as if someone not quite diaphanous had just walked by. Or, he reasons, it could have been attributed to power fluctuations in an old building.

He says it's much easier to know you're not imagining things when someone else is there, as on a night when he and a colleague were locking up following a performance.

"The other house manager and I had closed the theater and shut the gate between the theater and the office space. We came back into the office, straightening up things, when we heard someone running his knuckles up and down the gate. We thought, 'Okay, it's time to go.'"

Richard Rewey's closest encounter with the Fitzgerald's ghost was up close and personal, and it again came after a nighttime performance.

As house manager, Rewey's duties included locking up the concession stand cash boxes inside the box office. On this night a few people remained in the theater, including production manager Tom Campbell and a couple of stagehands.

Rewey had taken the cash boxes in hand and opened the box office's back door when something caught his eye. He glanced over to where he'd seen the movement, next to a divider that separated two of the office cubicles.

"I saw the top half of a guy come through that space. He was wearing a blue plaid shirt and had gray hair. He melded into the divider and came out the back side of it."

The figure dissolved once he was through the room divider.

"Damn, it was something!" Rewey says. "It wasn't that I caught it out of the corner of my eye; it was something I vividly saw. It wasn't a trick of the light or anything like that."

Richard found Tom Campbell and told him, "I just saw Ben!"

"He was panicked," Campbell says. "I had to believe him. He's a straight shooter. I don't know if it was Ben or what it was, but he definitely had something happen to him that night."

Rewey's description of the man having gray hair differs from Nancy Bagshaw-Reasoner's, but the office lights were on at the time, whereas she saw him in shadow.

"And I just saw his top half. I didn't see any legs, just his shirt, head, and hair. I really didn't see any facial characteristics, but he definitely had gray hair."

The man was striding along with determination, as if he was on his way somewhere, Rewey says. That location is the old hotel entrance to the theater, and it's in the general area of where Ben has been seen.

Richard Rewey still thinks about those events and says he can't dismiss what he saw. He grew up with a ghost in his family's home—someone who regularly paced from the front door, through the house, into the kitchen, and then up the stairs.

"I've always believed in ghosts, although I have no idea what they are."

Neither Richard Rewey nor Tom Campbell put much credence into another oft-cited Fitzgerald ghost, a long-dead actress named Veronica.

"I don't know where that story came from," Rewey says.

Campbell jokingly says Garrison Keillor may be partly to blame for that.

"People make up good stories," he says. "I've sat through tours that Keillor has had [of the theater], and he'll just make up stuff. So people take it as the truth. Those stories then take on a life of their own."

Oddly, once individuals have had encounters with Ben, they are less likely to be worried or afraid of his sudden appearances.

Jude Martin says it was her natural curiosity to want to "have a Ben experience." Once she did with Nancy Bagshaw-Reasoner, she was far less apprehensive about any others in the future.

Richard Rewey says that, when he heard the throat clearing and someone's knuckles on the steel grate, "[I] was good and afraid. But I was also concerned about the theater because I was the last one to leave, and I thought there was someone in the damn theater."

So when Rewey saw the ghostly shape meld through the office divider, it wasn't entirely unexpected.

"It isn't like this bloody, gory creature is going to jump out and hack me to death. No, this is Ben, he's going to spook you, he's going to scare you, but that's all. I'm not afraid to walk around in the dark theater. I'd be expected to be surprised [by seeing Ben], but not afraid for my life."

Jude Martin adds, "No, it's not fear. It's knowing you might get surprised when you least expect it."

Nancy Bagshaw-Reasoner is now director of facilities at Metropolitan State University. She tries not to draw any major conclusions from her experiences with Ben. But she remains perplexed about what it was that she twice encountered. She has a near-photographic memory and can recall each detail.

"Was that his soul? Was there some agenda that he had? Was he somehow reaching out to me? I didn't have a sense of anything other than here was this sad man looking at me. That was the most dramatic element of it, other than the fact that it scared me to death! I thought maybe I should call an exorcist, maybe he's trapped here. You know, what do you do?"

What sticks with her the most is just how frightened she was when she realized it wasn't a flesh-and-blood human being she was dealing with. She had first been scared that this stranger was going to rob her, but that soon changed when he moved in such unnatural ways.

"I was thinking I had to get to a phone, call someone, call the police. And then when that thing moved like *whoosh,* I thought, oh my God, this isn't a police issue. Somebody call the Ghostbusters!"

Though her job with Metropolitan State University requires her to work in a modern office complex as a skilled communicator and high-level administrator, she often thinks back to her Fitzgerald work. Her keen memory helps keep the details sharp in her mind.

"You never forget it. I can picture it like it happened yesterday. It was such a strange, strange thing."

Strange indeed, but true.

SHADOWS ON THIRD AVENUE

*"I saw what looked like a leg . . . from the knee down,
the shoe and pant leg."*

Sam Rowan

A museum security guard was making his last rounds of the night.
The third floor was quiet and, as he had expected, deserted at this
late hour. The handful of visitors that day had long since gone
home.

Nevertheless, it was part of Sam Rowan's job to wend his way
through the museum's nine historic period rooms to make certain
no one had become so enchanted with the displays of American
and European décor that they'd lost track of time and become acci-
dentally locked inside or that they'd decided to spend a quiet night
in, for example, a grandly restored 1730 salon from the Hôtel de la
Bouexiere in Paris.

Rowan was leaving the Queen Anne Room when something
caught his eye.

Silhouetted in a contiguous doorway was a dark, indistinct figure—he had the impression it was a female—walking rapidly into
the room from the brightly lit corridor. The backlighting cast her
in deep shadow. Rowan himself was moving rather quickly through
his rounds and had stepped past her before it registered with him
what he'd just seen.

He hurried around the corner to the other door and then back through the doorway where he'd just seen her—to remind the person he assumed was a straggler that the museum's hours were almost over.

She wasn't there.

Impossible, he thought. He'd even heard the wooden floorboards groan under her weight.

A quick search confirmed what had been immediately obvious to Sam Rowan. He was the only living being in those rooms.

Since 1915 the esteemed Minneapolis Institute of Arts (MIA) has welcomed tens of thousands of visitors each year to its Whittier neighborhood home.

Considered one of the finest comprehensive art museums in the world, the MIA owns more than 100,000 treasured works of art from five millennia of history and most of the world's great civilizations. From Egyptian cartonnages to New Guinea yam masks to masterpieces by Rembrandt, Poussin, and Monet and contemporary works by artists as varied as Chuck Close, Frank Stella, and Ansel Adams, the MIA's collections are breathtaking in their diversity. Its notable achievements include extensive Asian, Native American, and modern art collections. Special exhibits are scheduled throughout the year. A 2006 addition designed by Michael Graves enlarged gallery space by one-third.

With its free tours, audio guides, numerous interactive learning stations, art library, and detailed directories, the MIA is "dedicated to bringing art to life for everyone."

But to at least some employees, more than art sometimes comes to life in the labyrinthine galleries and displays that comprise this Twin Cities museum.

For Sam Rowan it was his encounter with the "blurry, black shadow" coming through a door of the Queen Anne Room in September 1996 that persuaded him that not everything at the MIA could be characterized as a still-life. He had started work as a guard only a short time before. He might have wondered about the advisability of taking the job.

"I was pretty freaked out," he says of his encounter that night. "I told [my supervisor] about it, but it turns out he was one of the other guards who had almost the same experience as mine. . . . He was pretty nonchalant about it. He was like, 'Oh yeah, that happened to me a couple of years ago.'"

Each of the third-floor period rooms at the MIA depicts domestic furnishings and interiors from a number of different eras between the early sixteenth and the early nineteenth centuries. The Connecticut Room, for instance, represents the interior of a home in colonial America. Henry VIII would be at home in the Tudor Room, installed only a few years after the museum opened and its first period room. The English-themed Georgian Room displays British décor and design from the late eighteenth century.

The majority of the puzzling encounters at the museum seem to occur in or near these period rooms.

Sam Rowan remembers with clarity that late evening in September in the Queen Anne Room.

"I was making my rounds," he recalls. "I was going out one of the doors, and what I saw was [a person] about my height, five foot seven or so. It looked like kind of a free-standing shadow, a blurry, black figure coming in toward me, less than three feet away, walking toward me. I was walking pretty fast, so I really didn't stop. I was going to [say] we were just about to close. Of course, when I turned the corner, it was gone. I even heard the footsteps. I had the impression it was a female."

Rowan says the brightness cast from the hallway's overhead lights and from the hall's wall-mounted display cases kept whatever it was in shadow. His immediate reaction was that she wasn't anything more than an errant visitor who needed to be directed out of the museum.

Only there was no *she* to deal with.

The entire incident was brief, Rowan says, but long enough for him to believe that it was a person, or at least the shape of a living being, stepping into the Queen Anne Room.

"I'd say it was a ghost," Rowan admits.

He was apprehensive after the encounter and tried to avoid

those rooms for a while, especially after the museum closed for the night, but that's difficult to do when you're a museum security guard.

In time he became more curious about who or what he had seen than anything else. In time he had little compunction about working around the period rooms.

"I was pretty scared . . . for a little while, but now, actually, I feel comfortable. I like being up there. I don't feel threatened or uneasy. I enjoy it just fine. I decided if I see something, I see something. If I don't, I don't. Seeing something here at all is pretty rare."

The supervising guard to whom Rowan reported the encounter had his own run-in with a similar walking shadow.

It had occurred several years before, in the corridor only a few feet from where Sam Rowan saw the shadowy woman.

At one time a window in that hallway looked out on an interior courtyard. Remodeling has filled in that area with additional galleries, and an easily missed locked door now occupies the former window opening.

The guard was looking out this now-gone window at some courtyard activity below when he caught someone moving in the corridor walking toward him. He looked out the window for a few more seconds before turning to greet whomever it was approaching him. The hallway was empty. He was certain that someone had been there moments before.

Sam Rowan says he had his only other run-in with something he cannot easily explain several years later. It also provided him with some evidence that the first time had not been a fluke.

He remembers the second date quite clearly—March 11, 2005.

Although he maintains that the second experience was not as phenomenal as the first, others might disagree.

Rowan was again on his rounds, but this time he had just gone into the Northumberland Room, so named for its English country-estate furnishings.

"I saw what looked like another silhouette outline, but of just a leg from the knee down, the shoe and pant leg, maybe a little shorter than mine. But it looked like it was made out of shadow, dark not transparent, more detailed than the other thing [I saw]," he says.

The perambulating limb was striding along next to Rowan, keeping pace, totally synchronized. Yet while Rowan's steps echoed clearly on the wood floors, the other footfall made no sound.

"I didn't think anything of it, because subconsciously I thought it was probably just [my] shadow," Rowan says. "But after I left the room, I thought that didn't make sense, because the placement of where I saw [the leg] was right underneath the light. The shadow would have to have been cast from something."

Rowan retraced his steps. He stopped at about the point where the leg appeared and looked around at the light sources. The chandelier above his head cast a shadow downward, but not in a manner that would account for what he'd just seen. There were no bright sidelights.

Besides, Rowan concludes, shadows are flat against surfaces and definitely not free standing and most assuredly not three-dimensional. And under no circumstances do they march along . . . alone.

Lori Erickson is a development officer at the MIA and the resident expert on the ghost stories that circulate among the staff and visitors. She's taken it upon herself to track down the tales and attempt to separate fact from hearsay. A studio art major in college and an accomplished photographer who also blogs and creates videos, Erickson has never had a ghostly experience at the MIA—though she eagerly hopes to one day.

If she does, she will have plenty of company, as she has found.

One paranormal group conducted an investigation with compasses, thermometers, and tape recorders. They came to the conclusion that a male ghost lived in the vicinity of the Connecticut Room and the Tudor Room and was very possessive of that area. He hung around near the rooms' draperies and liked people. The group could not attach a name to the specter.

Unfortunately, holding any kind of investigation with electronic gear is very difficult in a modern museum such as the MIA, replete as they are with all manner of wireless communications and electronic surveillance devices, including video cameras and security motion sensors. Interference from the museum's own equipment would cast doubt on any paranormal group's findings should they use electronic gear of their own.

Sometimes, visitors are much more informal in their ghost studies. One group of curious visitors was discovered holding an unofficial séance in the Connecticut Room. The guards kept their eyes on them but did nothing to shoo them away.

Erickson believes the Connecticut Room may be the most haunted room in the MIA.

The same guard who discovered the séance told Erickson that once, when walking by the Connecticut Room, he saw a dark, shadowy figure lurking in the doorway. He also claimed to have found all the curtains on a four-poster bed drawn closed, when they are normally kept open. He assumed it was the work of a mischievous child. Perhaps it's the same child ghost who once pulled on a visitor's coat only to vanish right in front of the startled guest.

Erickson says the Connecticut Room seems to be one display that for one reason or another bothers people. She says the mother of one employee refused to set foot in it, while a former guard— who moonlighted as a bouncer and was a body builder—made it clear to others that he disliked working around the Connecticut Room.

But some of the other period rooms have had their own episodes.

On a morning in mid-2007, a guard turning on the lights in the Georgian Room heard a chair scrape back from the center table, as if someone had just stood up. People have also reported hearing children's laughter in the same room (a painting of children hangs above the fireplace in the room).

Not everything unexplained occurs in the period rooms, however. Erickson says a cleaning woman reported being locked in a bathroom in the new Target wing of the MIA before locks were installed on the doors.

The origin of any resident ghost at the MIA would be hard to establish. There has been only one documented death in the museum.

A workman died of a heart attack several years ago as he was installing a display in connection with the MIA's annual Art in Bloom exhibit. There doesn't seem to be any connection between the man's unfortunate death and the museum's ghost stories.

Some believe that physical objects can retain the living souls once associated with them or that various pieces of furniture can bring along their own ghosts.

At the MIA a large, disquieting oil painting of a woman, entitled *Mrs. T in Cream Silk, No. 2*, figures in one of the more famous, albeit doubtful, ghost tales there. The 1920 work is by George Wesley Bellows and hangs in an out-of-the-way corridor on the first floor.

Once, an unnamed guard fell asleep while working the late shift in the glassed-in communications center. He was supposed to have been monitoring the museum's many video cameras when he decided to take a short snooze.

He was brusquely awakened by an insistent tapping on the outside of the window. When he looked up, a wrinkled old woman decked out in a brocaded, cream-colored gown scowled and shook her finger at him, as if scolding him for his dereliction of duty. She then floated through the closed door, into the room, and vanished.

The guard recognized the woman as the subject of Bellows's painting.

Perhaps the stories of Mrs. T scolding a sleepy guard began in part because of the unsettling nature of the artwork itself.

In the nearly life-sized painting, a woman identified only as Mrs. T stares balefully out of the frame, her gray hair tucked under a lace head covering trimmed with small roses. Her gloved hands rest demurely in front of her, holding a dainty lady's fan and a small purse.

Not only does she have a bit of Charles Dickens's Miss Havisham about her, but the gaze from her brooding, deep-set eyes seems to follow, to watch, as one passes by. It is a technique that the artist used with particular skill in this portrait.

And yet the peculiar Mrs. T and her eyes do not in actuality move anywhere, at least not on a regular basis.

HEINY HANSON

"We human beings are so limited in what we can comprehend."
Dr. William Seabloom

Amy Merkle walked sleepily into the kitchen of her modest lakeside home. She hadn't been sleeping well for some time, and she could tell this was going to be another one of those nights.

Without turning on the lights, she poured cereal into a bowl and added a cup of milk. She took it with her and stared dreamily out the small window above the sink. An outdoor light on a nearby barn layered the yard in competing shades of light and shadow. Her gaze ranged past her home's wide wooden deck to the front yard and settled on an ancient basswood tree. She was worried about that tree.

Amy Merkle and her family loved this secluded, heavily wooded neighborhood on Shoreview's Turtle Lake. But her family had decided to make big changes. The small 1950s bungalow in which she stood would be coming down to make way for a new Frank Lloyd Wright–inspired masonry and glass home designed to take full advantage of the natural woodsy setting and unparalleled lake views.

Merkle knew they'd probably lose a giant silver maple from their yard in the new construction, but somehow, and in some way, the basswood just had to survive. A third of it had come down in a recent storm, yet it had seen too much community history to be chainsawed into oblivion.

Deep in the silence of her late-July postmidnight reverie, Amy stared across the softly lighted yard. Without being aware of it when it first appeared, she suddenly noticed a misty sphere rolling slowly along the ground.

"Wow!" she thought, keeping the thing in view. "That's just like you see on television."

The mist changed direction. That's when it really got her attention.

Gradually, the mist took the form of a man, though she couldn't see his face under his wide-brim hat. He had on a white dress shirt with the sleeves rolled up. Broad suspenders held up loose-fitting trousers. He was pacing, his head down, hands clasped behind his back; he appeared contemplative, like something was bothering him.

Amy wondered what it was that he seemed worried about. Why the pacing?

But then it hit her just what it was that she was looking at.

"Oh. My. God!" she shrieked.

She threw the bowl in the sink, ran back to the bedroom, and jumped in bed next to her startled husband.

"Kurt," she gasped, "I just saw a ghost."

Amy and Kurt, along with their five children, had lived on tranquil Turtle Lake for about a year and a half at the time, since June 1997. They loved the feeling of being up north yet only minutes from the city.

But from the moment they moved in, they thought about building a new house on the site. Seven people in a small bungalow was impractical for very long. Since Kurt owns a masonry business, they set about planning for a new home that would satisfy their family needs, blend in with the natural setting, and feature the use of masonry construction techniques that Kurt knew.

What they eventually built and moved into in May 1999 is a dramatic masonry home, extraordinarily spacious with hardwood floors, high beam ceilings, and striking uses of large windows to allow in as much light as possible and enhance the dramatic lake view and the wooded landscape. The Merkles were inspired by architect Wright's designs, including his use of some built-in furniture and a flat roof. Kurt was able to complete much of the work himself.

"This is a beautiful piece of property," says Amy, "almost like a park, so our goal was to preserve as much of it as we could. In fact, I took the entire perennial garden that was here and had it transplanted. Then when we moved into this [new] house, the landscaper used all of my flowers."

But on that July 1998 night when Amy Merkle saw the mysterious figure in her front yard, the couple was still in their old house. All Amy knew was that she had been astonished to see something transform itself into human form. She had no idea who it was or what his purpose might be, yet when she flew back into the bedroom and told her husband what she had just seen, he took the news quite calmly.

"Kurt is the one who wondered if [the ghost] had something to do with the original Hanson farm," Amy says.

Kurt Merkle was referring to George and Ruth Hanson. With their two adult children, the Hansons lived on and farmed a ten-acre parcel that included the Merkles' lot. From 1930 to 1947, the Hansons raised corn, chickens, and a few cows. It is not believed that either offspring ever married. On Christmas Eve 1947, they sold the property to a local dentist who tore down the Hansons' home and built a more contemporary rambler. Another family later owned the property, and it was from them that the Merkles bought the house and lot in June 1997.

Kurt Merkle's offhand comment led his wife, in time, to believe that she did indeed see a ghost on that late night, that the ghost was George and Ruth's son, Heiny Hanson, and that he showed up about a month before the bungalow's demolition for a very specific purpose: to let the Merkles know that he continued to care about what happened on the old Hanson homestead.

"I think Heiny was rather worried that his place was going to once again be ransacked or demolished, or the trees [taken out]," Amy says, "because once you live here you fall in love with the trees. I think it was a big worry. What are they going to do to the property?"

Amy did some sleuthing into the Hanson family's history.

"I asked one of the older neighbors if he'd ever heard of anything peculiar happening on our property. He said no. He didn't tell me this then, but he thought I was completely off my rocker," she laughs.

Her home's previous owners told her the same thing, that they'd had no sightings of reanimated landowners or their offspring.

Over the next few weeks the final preparations were made to take down the Merkles' old house. On the day it was flattened, there was almost a party atmosphere, according to Amy. Neighbors gathered to observe.

The Merkles' next-door neighbor, Doris Claes, learned the story of Amy's late-night encounter. Claes was a longtime resident of the neighborhood. Amy had been understandably reluctant to discuss her experience but had done so with Doris at her husband's urging.

Claes had a photograph of the Hanson family given to her by another neighbor, Dr. William Seabloom. She brought it out.

Amy looked at the old black-and-white image. Three men and two women are posing outside an older house, perhaps the Hansons' farm home, staring intently at the camera. An older woman in the middle is elderly and slightly stooped, yet she wears a slight smile on her weathered face. She has on an apron over an ankle-length dress. The other woman, also with the hint of a smile, is much younger and also conservatively attired in an ankle-length dress, though with a broad sash around her waist. Both have their hair pulled tightly back. She wears a pleasant smile.

Two of the men are somber, older men, wearing heavy three-piece suits and fedoras. One of the men sports a full white beard, his thumbs hitched in his suit coat pockets. The other is short and rotund.

But it's the third man in the photograph that caught Amy's interest. His age is hard to determine—certainly well under forty. He wears a broad-brim, high-peaked hat that looks vaguely western, a white shirt with buttoned sleeves too short for his lanky arms, and baggy trousers held up with suspenders.

She is certain he is the man she saw through her kitchen window that summer night—Heiny Hanson.

The photograph appears to show the Hanson family—mother, father, son, Heiny, and daughter, Eva. The other older man is unidentified.

"I think it was the house coming down, the destruction of the property," that brought him back, Amy says. Though the bungalow the Merkles lived in had never been occupied by the Hansons, the builder had suggested that the Merkles take out both the silver maple and the basswood trees, which were old enough to have been in the Hanson family's yard. In the end only the silver maple was lost.

Heiny's nighttime visit to the Merkles' old home was not the last peculiar episode the family had.

"It was after seeing Heiny that I felt something like a presence or had weird things happening," Amy says. "When my mom and dad stayed with the kids and we went out of town . . . my mother would thank [the kids] for making their beds and cleaning everything up, but they'd say, 'Grandma, we didn't make our beds.' Nobody had been in the house, but the beds got made."

At other times her parents were awakened in the night by loud noises. Her father would check around the house, but there wouldn't appear to be any ready explanation for what the couple heard.

Oddest of all, Heiny Hanson may have moved inside their new home.

Amy discovered that singular possibility late one night when she got up to look after one of her sons who had been sick. She'd been asleep in the first floor master bedroom when he buzzed her on the telephone's intercom system to say he wasn't feeling well. She got up, found an aspirin and medicated throat spray in the kitchen, poured a glass of water, and made her way down the staircase to her son's lower-level bedroom.

She gave her son the medicine and took his temperature. She made sure he was comfortable and headed back to bed.

Going back up the stairs, Amy noticed a shadow moving down the steps toward her at the same time. She stopped. The shadow stopped. Briefly confused, Amy thought it was her own silhouette but decided it was Kurt coming down the stairs, perhaps to look in on Brian himself.

"Kurt?" she called out.

"Yeah?" he replied . . . from the master bedroom.

It wasn't her husband on the steps.

"Here, I'm thinking, aren't shadows supposed to follow you? This one is meeting me," Amy says. "I screamed at the top of my lungs and ran up the stairs. I just remember bolting past that thing."

By the time she reached the bedroom, she had started to relax, a bit embarrassed at her own edginess. It had to be her own shadow, she thought. Yet how could it be? It wasn't connected to her in any manner and was coming *down the staircase* toward her.

Amy Merkle believes the shadow might very well have been Heiny Hanson.

"He must have been worried about what had happened to Brian that would get me up in the middle of the night to go downstairs with medicine," she says.

On another night, Amy figures, Heiny Hanson was looking out for her welfare once again. She was scheduled to fly out of the Twin Cities. Her husband had left some days before, and Amy was going to meet him.

"I stayed up all night, doing laundry, putting together doctors' notes, the caregivers' notes, making sure the house was clean," Amy recalls. It was about three in the morning, and the house was quiet as she continued organizing for the trip.

"I was in the kitchen writing out a note by hand when, all of a sudden, I heard a noise. My son's backpack had been on the bench in the service entry. I looked around the corner and saw it sitting in the middle of the service way carpet."

She put up her hands and said to no one in particular, but perhaps to Heiny, "I know it's getting late, but this is it, I promise. I'm going to bed."

Does Heiny have a sense of humor?

An incident in the family's garage may show Heiny's playfulness. One winter's day, Amy, talking to a relative on her cell phone's loudspeaker, pulled her large SUV into the heated garage, shut off the engine, and used the remote control to shut the garage door. The conversation went on until Amy finally said she had to go.

"The garage was completely dark," she says. "We have a big, long Escalade, and it just barely fits in that garage. As I was just about to the end, where you have to squeeze through to get by the bumper, the garage door went up. There's nobody home. The alarm is on. I'm just thinking, 'Wait, my ass is not that big!'"

Amy believes Heiny is attentive to her and her family because she has acknowledged his presence. The garage incident was humorous, she says, but at other times Heiny's sudden appearance has signaled his care or concern about what was going on in the household.

A few years have passed since Heiny Hanson last made his presence known to the Merkles. Perhaps he moves around the neighborhood, dropping in on folks who are experiencing difficulties. One particular neighbor had had a death in her family, and Amy learned that she was asking around the neighborhood whether anyone was having odd or unusual things happen in their homes, because she was!

Amy Merkle considers herself to be sensitive or attuned to mystical events.

"I think I'm very spiritual to begin with," she says. "And this just reaffirms that. . . . It does make me feel better. I think you're allowed to stay on earth watching over your loved ones once you pass on."

Some of what has happened to her may point to spirits from her own family who have stuck around to watch over her. Not long after she first saw Heiny Hanson, she caught the whiff of a wonderfully scented perfume. It was vaguely familiar, yet she could not recall its name. Later, she described it for her sister, who told her that it sounded like Windsong, a scent favored by their late grandmother.

About a year after the Merkles moved into their new house, Amy and Kurt were working in the kitchen when the robust odor of cigar smoke drifted through the room. No one in the family smoked. A week to the day later, Kurt received a box of cigars in the mail. They were addressed to his late stepfather as all of his mail was being forwarded to the Merkles.

Earlier in her life, Amy had narrowly escaped serious injuries in both a tractor accident on Kurt's family's farm and a 1983 automobile accident. In the first incident, she believes the intervention of a guardian angel or the spirit of her late father-in-law kept her from being run over by a tractor tire. In the 1983 incident, Amy, a trained respiratory therapist, believes she passed away for a brief time before being revived.

She fully accepts these kinds of interventions by entities most other people cannot see, let alone comprehend. To her they are a normal part of life.

"I think [these experiences] are a good way to show that things in the spirit world are not out to scare the bejesuses out of you," she says. "Heiny just wanted to say that this was my home and I'm concerned about it. Or maybe it was just that he was so happy with what we've done. . . . Maybe because Heiny was never married, maybe his love was for his farm and this piece of property."

Dr. William Seabloom lives across from the Merkles and grew up in the neighborhood. As a child he knew Heiny Hanson and his sister. Seabloom was the person who found the old photograph of the Hanson family and gave it to Doris Claes. He remembers Heiny as a pleasant person, always jolly whenever Seabloom spoke with him.

Seabloom is a widely known clinical social worker with a private practice in psychotherapy and consultation. He was surprised when the stories of Amy Merkle's encounters with Heiny first surfaced.

"I'd never known him to be around," Seabloom says of Heiny's ghost.

Yet Seabloom is open to the possibility that Heiny—and perhaps others—may indeed continue to exist, but on a different level.

"Amy didn't know Heiny, of course, and had no idea who it was," Seabloom says.

"We human beings are so limited in what we can comprehend. We tend, especially as Americans, to think we know it all. To have it all nailed down scientifically.

He points to other cultures such as Iceland—with its remarkable Ghost Centre in Stokkseyri and its interactive displays of twenty-four famous Icelandic ghost stories—that have a more open attitude about the supernatural.

Seabloom believes that arriving at the truth of any given situation, natural or supernatural, is much harder than it appears and that human beings are not capable of understanding everything they encounter.

And that includes ghostly sightings in his own neighborhood.

"What is this thing that she saw? If Heiny Hanson no longer exists physically, then what is this thing that she saw?" he wonders. "He was just like in the picture. He seemed to come back in a form that was familiar to him in life."

Seabloom says we can either dismiss, outright, claims of the supernatural, such as those about Heiny Hanson, or we can accept Amy Merkle's remarkable experiences. He understands the difficulty in comprehending on an intellectual level such astonishing events as the appearance of ghosts, but if we cannot do that, we must then deal with them in another way.

He says it is not too unlike religion.

"Religion is a mystery and is magic," he says. "We cannot understand it intellectually necessarily, [so] we must come to it on some other level of acceptance."

Perhaps in the end, it doesn't really matter at what level we approach the story of Heiny Hanson, a story which suggests that even in death there is no place like home.

A FINAL PARTING

"I had such a sense of that protection and of being reunited."
Maureen Hayter

It was long after dark on Albert Lea's Grove Avenue that last day of November 1942. Asleep in their tidy, two-story house were Maureen Hayter and her three children—two teen-aged girls and a boy, age four. Maureen's husband was Lieutenant Commander Hubert Montgomery Hayter, serving aboard the USS *New Orleans*. World War II neared its first anniversary. Of his whereabouts, the family knew only that he was somewhere in the Pacific.

Maureen Hayter hadn't seen her forty-one-year-old husband in months, nor had she received a letter from him in some time. She preferred to look upon that absence of correspondence without any resentment. During her sixteen-year marriage to the Annapolis graduate and career naval officer, Maureen had grown to understand that her husband's duties at sea often meant long absences from home. He had earlier served aboard the battleship *Arizona* and the destroyer *Yarborough* and, in 1939, had been named commander of the light minelayer USS *Ramsay*. He'd been assigned to the USS *New Orleans* in February 1941.

Maureen Hayter did not dwell on the dangers.

The *New Orleans* was a first-class ship, the lead vessel in her

33

heavy cruiser class, manned by skilled, battle-tested officers and sailors. They had been docked at Pearl Harbor when the Japanese attacked the previous December, but the ship had escaped with only minor damage even though her heavy guns could not be used; the ship's electrical power was being supplied from shore. Sailors had to rely on pistols, rifles, and machine guns to shoot at the swarming Japanese Zeros. During the ensuing months, the *New Orleans* and her crew had gone on to fight with distinction in the battles of Midway, the Coral Sea, and the Eastern Solomons.

So it was on this evening in November that the Hayter house on a street in small-town Minnesota was as quiet and as peaceful as it normally was on a late-fall night.

Abruptly, a fierce jolt forced Maureen upright in bed. She looked around, trying to figure out what had happened. Had something fallen, perhaps or collapsed in another room? She listened closely, but nothing else broke the silence. She looked in on the children; all three were deep asleep. A careful search of the downstairs produced nothing out of the ordinary.

She went back to bed and tried to settle down. And then her life changed forever. Suddenly, beside her was her husband, Hubert, bathed "in a heavy mist . . . his arms protectively about me," she later told author Dennis Bardens.

"I had such a sense of that protection and of being reunited."

But then she saw "a look of ineffable longing and of sadness" on his face.

She touched his cheek. It was cold. Then he was gone.

That's all she could remember the next morning. Though she rarely had dreams, she thought this must have been one of those occasions, brought on by her husband's long absence from home and her own anxiety in not having heard from him.

For the next several days, Maureen Hayter was "strengthened and buoyed" by her husband's loving presence. That contentment did not last, however. It gave way to uneasiness, a foreboding, as she reflected more on the coldness of his skin and the sorrow in his eyes—almost as if he were reaching out to her in comfort for a reason that was not yet clear to her.

And then the telegram arrived from the War Department. She hesitantly opened the envelope and read the inevitable words. Lieutenant Commander Hubert Montgomery Hayter had been killed in the line of duty while serving aboard the uss *New Orleans*.

Although details of the navy officer's death were sketchy owing to wartime restrictions, Maureen Hayter was able to learn that her husband had died in combat off Savo Island at Ironbottom Sound, near Tassafaronga on Guadalcanal.

History would record it as the battle of Tassafaronga, part of the legendary Guadalcanal campaign.

The particulars emerged later.

The uss *New Orleans* was part of a nine-ship naval force that tried to surprise eight Japanese naval destroyers attempting to deliver food and other supplies to their forces on Guadalcanal. The U.S. warships were able to sink one Japanese vessel, but the other enemy ships quickly recovered and opened fire with torpedoes; two hit the flagship uss *Minneapolis*. The *New Orleans* was just astern and had to veer away to avoid a collision. Tragically, the *New Orleans* crossed directly in front of a Japanese torpedo that struck near her bow, detonating gasoline tanks and the forward ammunition magazines. A 150-foot section of the *New Orleans* was severed, including the number one gun turret. That quarter of the ship veered sharply around to port, knocking several holes astern. The detached bow sank.

At the moment the torpedo struck the bow of the *New Orleans*, Lieutenant Commander Hayter was serving as the damage control officer. He was with his men at the central station battle position. Within minutes, asphyxiating gas filled the compartment. Hayter ordered everyone without gas masks to leave. He stayed at his post and gave up his own gas mask to an injured seaman. Hayter was fatally overcome by the lethal fumes.

For this exceptional act of valor, he was posthumously awarded the Navy Cross, the second-highest award for courage and the second-highest medal given by the U.S. Navy.

The U.S. Navy further honored Hayter when, on November 11, 1943, the uss *Hayter* was launched at Charleston Navy yard and commissioned at Charleston on March 16, 1944. Mrs. Maureen Hayter was present for the ceremonies.

The uss *Hayter* provided antisubmarine protection in the North Atlantic Ocean. Her most notable achievement may have come on January 16, 1945, when she found and sank the notorious German U-boat 248.

The uss *Hayter* remained in service throughout the war.

For Maureen Hayter the memory of that one extraordinary night with her husband's inexplicable visit meant far more than words could ever explain, even if those words seem to describe an improbable if not impossible event.

Lieutenant Commander Hubert Montgomery Hayter had died in battle on that very same evening—November 30, 1942.

Maureen Hayter knew in her heart that, as her husband faced death thousands of miles from home, his final thoughts were of her and of his children and that he was able to be with her.

To Mrs. Hayter it was her husband's "heroic spirit" that traveled all that distance "to reassure and sustain [her]."

She always thought of it as her devoted husband's final farewell.

NO ESCAPE

*"When the women found out the men had drowned, they came
to the mine and wanted to be with their loved ones."*
John R. Perpich, miner

The worst mining disaster in Minnesota history took the lives of forty-one men nearly nine decades ago at the Milford Mine, a manganese ore operation near Crosby. A surface cave-in near Foley Lake caused the tunnels and the main shaft to suddenly flood. Most of the miners drowned in the rapidly rising water or were crushed to death beneath lake mud and silt pushed through the tunnels. Just seven men escaped to tell the stories of their survival.

But theirs weren't the only stories told.

Months later, after all the victims' remains had been recovered, the mine reopened. And then began the whispered accounts of how the first men back into the mine heard the cries of their dead comrades' terrified spirits and saw their ghostly forms floating through the tunnels.

Fourteen-year-old Frank Hrvatin Jr. never forgot the day when the world as he knew it changed forever.

On that cold, blustery morning of February 5, 1924, he shivered in the dry house at the Milford Mine as he removed his street clothes and climbed into his slicker and waterproof boots. Because of a high water table on much of the Cuyuna Range, including Crow Wing County, the manganese mines were wet most of the time. The Milford workings extended from a main shaft to the east and west beneath Foley Lake, now named Milford Lake. For the most part the ground in the area was a mossy bog with standing water.

But young Frank didn't mind the conditions; he was just as happy to be working instead of going to school. He labored at the 165-foot level, shoveling dirt that remained after timber men erected the cribbing in newly opened drifts.

Meanwhile, at the bottom level of the 200-foot main shaft on that same February day, skip tender Clinton Harris manned the electric hoist that dumped ore from the ore cars into the bucket, or skip, which was then raised to the surface, emptied, and sent back down. Two skips were in use on that day, each counterbalancing the other.

Harris was substituting for Harvey Rice, the regular skip tender, who had called in sick.

Known first as the Ida Mae Mine, the Milford Mine is three miles north of Crosby, some one thousand feet from the northwest side of what was known then as Foley Lake.

The mine is part of the Cuyuna Range, discovered in 1895 by Cuyler Adams, and the last of the Minnesota iron ranges to be mined. The first ore was shipped from the Cuyuna Range in 1911.

At the Milford site some initial drilling began in 1912, but the main shaft wasn't sunk until 1917. Operations began in earnest in 1918, and full production was under way by late 1923 when the main shaft hit the 200-foot level.

At its height the mine produced 103,000 tons of manganese ore per year and employed scores of men from Crosby, Ironton, Aitkin, Trommald, Manganese, Cuyuna, and other Iron Range communities. Many of the men were newly arrived immigrants from Finland, Germany, Yugoslavia, Austria, Scotland, and Canada.

Frank Hrvatin Jr.; his father, Frank Hrvatin Sr.; and Clinton Harris were among the forty-eight men in the mine on that February afternoon in 1924.

The day had been a fairly typical, midwinter workday for the men when suddenly, at about 3:30 PM, a tremendous wind blasted through the mine, blowing the men's helmets off and snuffing out their carbide-gas mining lamps. Typically, the mine air was cool, and there was never a breeze. The in-rushing air was warm; there was some concern but no immediate alarm. Something had happened, of that they were certain, but no one knew quite what it was. Most everyone put their helmets back on, reignited their lamps, and went right back to work.

But then another powerful blast of tepid air, accompanied by what one survivor called a "strange booming noise," made it terrifyingly clear that not only had something gone dreadfully wrong but the entire underground work force was in imminent danger.

The electricity went out. Someone tripped the circuit breaker; the lights came on briefly, flickered a few times, and then died. The piercing emergency whistle screamed. Evacuate!

What the doomed men could not have known was that there had been a surface cave-in at a worked-out room on the mine's easternmost point. The cave-in opened a slender channel of mud that led directly to Foley Lake. Lake water quickly filled the crude canal and, mixing with lake mud and silt, flowed into the mine at the point of the cave-in.

Below the surface the stiff wind blasting through the opening at the site of the cave-in kept extinguishing the men's head lamps.

Young Frank Hrvatin heard the roar of water and mud and saw it all spilling down a tunnel.

"The lake is coming in! The lake is coming in!" he cried, running for safety himself.

Old Matt Kangas, a veteran miner, ran as hard as he could, but by the time he reached the ladder, he could barely climb. Frank got behind him, jumped between Kangas's legs, and boosted him up the ladder to survival, rung by rung.

The water, mud, and silt—a "slimy ooze," one survivor labeled it—rose in the main shaft as fast as the men could climb up the ladder.

Some of the miners trapped in the tunnels were crushed against the walls; others drowned when a wall of water overtook them. A few brave souls might have been able to save themselves, but they ran back looking for their trapped buddies.

It took just fifteen minutes for the 200-feet-deep mine to flood all the way to the surface.

From the hellish pit the last of the seven survivors staggered to safety, soaked to the waist and encased in mud. They fell exhausted and gasping for breath on the frozen ground where they were attended by coworkers who ran from the mine office and families from the nearby houses.

Miraculously, of the seven miners who made it to safety, not one suffered serious injuries, save for some bleeding from their mouths and ears because of the suddenly compressed mine air.

By nightfall, thirty-three women had become widows; eighty-eight children had lost their fathers.

The teenage Frank Hrvatin was one of the survivors and one of those children, and his mother was one of the widows. Young Frank stood by the shaft for hours, staring down into the black muck that swelled in the shaft a few feet below the surface. His father was buried down there—somewhere.

Clinton Harris, the skip tender from St. Mathias, died at the foot of the main shaft. He apparently chose to remain at his post next to the ladder, pulling on the whistle cord to warn miners at the upper levels. It blew for nearly five hours, even after silt had closed the shaft. Finally, workmen in the surface engine room disconnected the line to the whistle, silencing the last voice from the mine.

Within hours news of the disaster had reached to nearly all the communities on the Cuyuna Range. The Crosby village siren blew for hours, as did locomotive whistles, summoning families to the mine.

Some residents stood on the shore of Foley Lake and watched in silent horror as the water level went down, the ice on the surface sinking farther still as the frigid water below poured into the mine. A later survey found the water level had dropped a full four feet beneath the ice.

Other onlookers and family members gathered silently by the entrance to the shaft, trying to will away the inevitable—those miners who had not escaped would never come out of the mine alive.

New widows huddled, easing their pain by linking arms, their bright shawls shielding their heads and faces from the biting wind and thin, sharp flakes of snow.

One man who lost his brother-in-law said that when the women found out what had happened many of them wanted to jump in the mine to be with their loved ones.

By midnight, recovery operations were under way. In the sub-zero temperatures men took turns operating giant sump pumps that sucked out 12,000 gallons of water and slime each minute. Yet water continued to pour into the mine, filling the small drifts and cross-working.

The Crow Wing County mine inspector said he doubted that most of the bodies would ever be found.

For a while it seemed he might be right. Problems plagued the clean-up efforts. Pumping crews worked for twelve days to drain Foley Lake; it took three months to de-water the mine. Every time it rained, the water levels again rose in the mine. Heavy machinery was brought in to assist in the effort. A machine called a sand sucker cleared mud from the channel that had been created between Foley Lake and the sinkhole over the mine. Power failures were common.

Once the water was cleared, the heavy remaining mud was shoveled by hand from the blocked drifts, loaded into mine cars, and lifted to the surface.

The remains of the men were gradually located over the weeks and months of the recovery operation, but the last victim was not brought to the surface until nine months after the disaster, on November 2, 1924.

Yet not one man on the recovery teams complained or quit in despair. They were determined to find all the victims so that their families could give them suitable burials.

In time the Milford Mine reopened. There was no shortage of miners signing up to go underground again. Manganese was in great demand by the steel industry, and mine owners were guaranteeing steady work to every man who wanted it. Most did. And, of course, in almost every case mining was the only job the men knew.

But not a miner on the entire Cuyuna Range was prepared for the horror that lay in the bowels of the Milford Mine on opening day, according to Cuyuna Range lore.

Not only was there the lingering stench of decomposed flesh, but there was something even more gruesome. Miners said that at the base of the shaft, at the 200-foot level, the men's lamps shone upon the translucent form of Clinton Harris, the skip tender.

The ghost's bony fingers clutched the side rail of the ladder, his vacant eyes gazing upward. The whistle cord was still knotted around his waist.

The miners staggered back.

Suddenly, the phantom whistle screamed through the dark, winding tunnels.

The terrified men scrambled up the ladder. They didn't look back as they climbed toward the surface. Not a single one of them was said to have ever reentered the Milford Mine.

But in the end the Great Depression accomplished what the 1924 disaster could not; it forced the Milford Mine to close in 1932 when the demand for manganese iron ore declined.

Today, the mine is on public land but not easily accessible to the visitor. The shaft has filled in, but the opening has settled a few feet below surface level. Saplings grow from the depression. Near the old mine shaft, foundations for the water tower and pump house are visible. There is some indication of the location of the small houses miners' families rented for five dollars a month. They were torn down in the 1930s. Milford Lake is much deeper—an estimated thirty feet—than it was when it was drained in the 1920s, and it laps a short distance from the mine's second shaft, built after 1924.

A formal historic site to honor miners killed in the disaster has been proposed by Crow Wing County, which owns all of the land on which the mine was located. Plans for the Milford Mine Memorial Park include easier access to the site, a parking lot, boardwalks across the bog, interpretive walking trails, and possibly a canoe landing.

The county wants to ensure that no one ever forgets Minnesota's worst mining catastrophe.

Yet not all of the stories may be told in formal history books.

A county administrator who researched the Milford Mine trag-edy said the stories that stayed with him were those told by the miners who went back in after it reopened and saw the ghostly specters and heard the shriek of Clinton Harris's phantom whistle.

The survivors of the Milford Mine disaster are gone now, but their stories will live on, as may the ghosts of that selfless skip ten-der and the forty men who died with him.

6

OWATONNA

FORGET US NOT

"If there are such things as ghosts, then this is where they would be."
Harvey Ronglien

It was always so dark when it happened. That's what bothered Laurie Braunson.* Something was up there stirring around long before the sun came up.

At six o'clock on a winter weekday morning, the sunlight did not penetrate the murky interior at the Owatonna Fitness Center, situated in one of the old brick buildings at the city's vast West Hills municipal complex.

When she was an assigned lifeguard for the center's small pool at that early hour, Laurie was the first to arrive. She unlocked the heavy outside door, flipped on some lights, and then headed up the split-level staircase to the center's office. She had to pass the still-darkened exercise room. But that door stayed locked. She didn't want to look in there. That's where something moved every morning that she worked there.

So she unlocked the office door and then quickly headed back down the staircase to the swimming pool on the lower level, directly below the exercise room. She didn't like these lonely early mornings in the center. She got in a few warm-up laps in the pool, yes, but it also meant she'd be alone until people started showing up for the

6:00 AM swim lessons or individual swims, depending on the day. Later, she headed off to her high school classes. At that point she was usually more than happy to leave as soon as she could.

That's because someone seemed always to be there ahead of her, someone handling the weights in that still-closed exercise room. Laurie heard him, or rather she heard the steel weights noisily *clank* as if they were being readjusted or dropped on the floor.

And yet it was not possible.

"I knew I was alone," Laurie says. "The main door I unlocked was really noisy, so you could tell when anybody came in. But something was moving around upstairs in the weight room."

It was almost as if, Laurie says, someone who didn't know what they were doing was playing with the machines. The weights were all on manual machines that users individually adjusted themselves. Usually, the weights were carefully changed so that they didn't bang into one another.

"It was so spooky, creepy," Laurie recalls with a shudder. "It happened every time I went in the morning. I didn't go too often because it creeped me out so much. I did it a couple of times a month my sophomore and junior years."

By the time she was a senior, she told her supervisors she would not work the early morning hours.

As a young woman alone, Laurie was loathe to investigate. She really didn't want to see what she might see. She knew no one else was in the building when she got there, nor could anyone have gotten in without her hearing them.

"I didn't go up and check. I knew I would have heard someone coming in."

And it was far from the normal sounds one might associate with early mornings in an old building replete with exposed pipes running along the ceilings, painted brick walls, tiled floors, and a warren's nest of heavy old doors, innumerable rooms, and dark recesses.

Laurie Braunson spent seven years as a lifeguard and swimming teacher at the West Hills Fitness Center swimming pool. She grew up on a farm outside Owatonna, graduated from St. Olaf College, and now works as a biologist at the University of Minnesota. She plans on a career in medicine.

She is not a young woman who jumps at shadows or sees ghostly figures at every turn. In fact, she says that if the same thing had happened to someone else, she probably wouldn't believe them. But she says, "I can't deny my own experiences."

There's good reason for Laurie *not* to disown those frightening mornings. Ghost stories flourish at West Hills, a sprawling set of mostly brick buildings that today house Owatonna and Steele County offices, an arts center, the extensive fitness center, and other community, municipal, and nonprofit agencies.

But West Hills has a much longer history.

For over sixty years, from 1885 to 1945, the West Hills site was the Minnesota State Public School for Dependent and Neglected Children—the state orphanage.

Some 13,000 children passed through its doors over the sixty-year history of the institution. During the 1930s as many as five hundred children were housed there at any given time as wards of the state. Days-old infants were turned over to the school. Teenagers up to the age of eighteen who fell on hard times because of parental deaths or neglect ended up there. Siblings would be separated by adoption or indenture, many never to be reunited. The idea was to provide an interim home for children, but in reality most of the children stayed on because of low adoption rates in that era. Teenagers were often placed on indenture contracts with families until they turned eighteen. Others simply stayed at the orphanage, living in one of the sixteen cottages.

The state school was virtually self-sufficient. The original 160 acres grew to 329 acres and included a large farm operation with crops and domestic livestock, sixteen cottages (or dormitories) that housed the hundreds of boys and girls who lived there, a hospital, a power plant, and employee residences. A school provided a K–8 education; high-school-age teens attended the city high school.

On one corner of the campus is a touching children's cemetery where 198 children were interred, unclaimed by their parents. About 151 of the grave markers contain only the child's case number. Fifty of the graves are nameless or marked simply with a single word, such as "Baby." The average age of the children there is four years. Deaths came from various causes: diphtheria, a broken neck in a football game, and ruptured appendixes; one boy was gored to death by an elk the school owned while trying to retrieve a baseball in the animal's pasture.

By 1945, child welfare experts were changing the ways in which orphaned or abandoned children were treated. They were beginning to be placed in foster homes rather than in institutions. The Owatonna school closed in the mid-1940s. For the next twenty-five years, the buildings housed a state school that trained intellectually and developmentally disabled individuals. The city of Owatonna bought the entire complex for $200,000 in 1974 for use as city- and county-related offices and for other community and nonprofit organizations. The farmland became the city's industrial park. Several of the children's cottages remain and are used for offices. The former school, gymnasium, and hospital remain, as well. Some of the former children's cottages were converted into apartment buildings or private homes.

The orphanage's sprawling four-story Gothic administration building houses city offices. A substantial part of the first floor contains the remarkable Orphanage Museum, a vast collection of documents, photographs, and memorabilia designed to keep alive the history of the former state school.

Harvey Ronglien—himself a ward at the orphanage for eleven years—and his wife, Maxine, are the "architects and motivators" behind the creation of the Orphanage Museum and have worked tirelessly on behalf of keeping the memory of those abandoned children alive. Harvey is the official historian of the former state orphanage.

He knows that West Hills is a place that could well be haunted.

"If there are such things as ghosts, then this is where they would be," he acknowledges. "I've never experienced anything myself, but those who have swear by what happened . . . but they don't talk about it very much."

Perhaps a lingering presence by those who did not survive their orphanage years is not wholly unexpected. These youngsters often died without ever having experienced human kindness, as Harvey Ronglien wrote in his autobiography, *A Boy from C-11: Case #9164*: "As an adult, I came to realize the institutional environment did not provide certain needs a child craves. Although the environment made us physically strong, it left many of us emotionally deficient. Emotional starvation is inseparable from institutional life. Due to the size of the orphanage, individual attention was minimal. Consequently, the children suffered from lack of attention, appreciation, recognition and love needed for a healthy childhood. For many it left scars that would last a lifetime."

Laurie Braunson was not the only fitness center employee who knew that ordinary explanations for what took place would never suffice. When she reported the clanking weights to her supervisors, they'd acknowledge that other early morning lifeguards had had the same experience.

"I don't know if it happened to every lifeguard, but I knew it happened to several others," she says. Many of the fitness center lifeguards also worked at an area lake during the summer where they would exchange stories about the strange events at West Hills. "You couldn't logically explain it. I knew that the place was supposed to be haunted, so I assume this was part of all that."

Although she never saw what was producing the ominous clanking, Laurie found that others were not so fortunate.

A lifeguard friend of Laurie's sometimes worked the early shift. She, too, was disturbed by someone fooling around with the weight machines as she waited for swimmers in the pool area below. She handled it differently, determined to find out what was going on. One morning she quietly walked up the two flights of steps to the dark exercise weight room, pushed open the door, and stepped inside. Next to one of the weight machines was a pale young boy in worn pants and a baggy shirt. He was pulling down on the weights and then letting them go so they would slam against each other. He stopped when he heard her come in and looked at her. She dropped her flashlight and ran to the office, where she called another lifeguard. He came right over. They met by the outside front door. As they looked up the steps, a mist seemed to form in the hallway outside the exercise room. The couple went back outside to wait until more people showed up.

The child ghost wasn't menacing or threatening. He looked innocent, in fact. But his direct intense look was so distressing she left her job not long after.

After she heard about that episode, Laurie Braunson, too, decided enough was enough. "I think it was about that time that I quit, too. I was like, no, I didn't want to be there anymore."

And if that episode hadn't been enough, the encounter another lifeguard had in the pool area itself with what might have been the same boy, and again in the early hours, probably would have been. That lifeguard—a young man—was waiting for swimmers to arrive when the door suddenly opened and in came a young boy. He was alone and asked if he might be able to swim. He didn't appear to be with anyone, nor was he dressed for swimming. The lifeguard said that if he could find a swimsuit, then, sure, he could use the pool. The boy stared at him, turned around, and walked out the door.

The fitness center is not the only building in which Laurie Braunson thinks ghosts may walk. Next door is the former orphanage's school, now the Merrill building. Inside are several nonprofit agencies and the city's little theater. When Laurie worked at West Hills, a day care facility and offices were also there. She saw something in the window of that building late at night that was definitely not connected to anything currently there.

A family had rented the pool one evening for a birthday party celebration. Laurie finished up about ten o'clock and left for her car. As she walked by the Merrill building, she looked up at it.

"I don't even know why I did that, but I saw a really pale face looking out at me through the window. Whatever it was had moved the curtain aside. I did a double take, like did I really just see that? And then it disappeared, and the curtain was completely down. I don't know how it could have been anything else because the building was closed and dark. I can't really rationalize it. But I knew that something was out of place."

On a staircase in the same Merrill building, workers have detected cigar smoke although smoking is banned. At other times passersby have heard children singing or laughter coming from inside even though the building is closed and dark.

Laurie Braunson is unswerving in her recollection of those disturbing days at West Hills, yet she is reluctant to be too forthcoming. "I don't know if people will take me seriously if they find out I've had these experiences."

Most of all she is still looking for answers.

"Why do these things happen to only certain people and not everybody? Are some people sensitive to this or do other people just ignore it?"

Harvey Ronglien has grown used to hearing stories of visitors or employees who have heard children singing or crying . . . or have had doors bang open for no apparent reason . . . or have glimpsed a shuffling, older man in a baggy brown suit disappearing down the corridor. He himself points to a rocking chair in a corner of the museum and says that, when someone tried to take a picture of it, the camera refused to work. They could take pictures anywhere else without difficulty.

"There were a couple of janitors who quit a while back," Ronglien says, associating their departure with a scare they had, though they didn't go into detail. "Some people don't want [the campus] to be known as haunted. They'll just say some 'crazy things' have happened lately."

Many of those crazy things are precisely those that make some believe the old state orphanage remains haunted.

During the days of the state school, the massive administration building housed numerous orphanage services: a chapel, dining rooms, a small boy's cottage, teachers' rooms, and administrative offices.

Many of the West Hills ghost stories originate there.

One former head of the city's parks and recreation department dismissed others' claims of witnessing supernatural activity—until one night when he was working late and heard the door open for no apparent reason, followed immediately by a strong wind blowing through his office.

"He locked right up, [stopped for] a few drinks, and went home. From that point on you never told him there weren't ghosts," Ronglien says.

Ronglien knows of two other unexplained incidents.

Electricians were rewiring the building. Late one afternoon, they stuffed some wires into an electrical box in the basement and locked up for the night. The next morning all the wires had been yanked from the box.

Another parks and recreation director was putting baseball bats and balls away in a storage bin. As he dropped the balls into the bin, two of them came shooting out at him.

"He was stunned," Ronglien says. "He started again and darn if they didn't come back out."

Emergency calls to 911 have been reported as originating from a basement electrical room although no one is in the building and that space is kept locked. Police dispatchers have to check with the city offices because of these hang-ups.

It's on the partially used third floor of the old building, however, that some workers have been reluctant to tread. Some of the floor was used as dormitory-style housing for orphanage workers. In the same area was the infamous Tower Room where children were disciplined, sometimes at the end of a radiator bristle brush.

There are consistent cold spots on the third floor and the occasional shuffling of feet. A group of paranormal investigators claimed to have found the ghost of a young boy hiding in a closet. He was reluctant to leave because he had been beaten.

"These children were shunned by their families in life, and their very names, taken from them in death," a former orphanage resident once said to Harvey Ronglien.

Harvey Ronglien is right. If there are ghosts, then the West Hills buildings and grounds are where they walk, taking little steps, for they are most likely the young ones who passed without knowing family love or the compassion of another human being.

Perhaps that is what they seek even today.

7

WHAT TUNIS PARKIN SAW

*"I turned around to talk to him, but I didn't like
his appearance. So I left."*
Thomas McNamara

Tunis Parkin was the first person—but surely not the last—to see a
ghost in a Goodhue apple orchard near Holy Trinity Church. It was
a dubious honor. Parkin just happened to be in the right place at
the right time, or perhaps the wrong place at the wrong time.

Parkin was a Goodhue house painter whose artistry showed itself in the homes, barns, and windmills of the area. But on that
pleasant fall evening in 1922, Parkin laid aside his paintbrushes to
call upon the young lady who would one day become Mrs. Parkin. It
was after midnight when he started home, whistling as he walked.

As Parkin approached the orchard, the whistle died on his lips,
and his knees turned rubbery. Someone was following next to him.
From the corner of his eye, Parkin caught sight of a figure—tall,
silent, shrouded in mist—keeping apace stride for stride. It didn't
look human at all.

Maybe if he appeared indifferent it would go away, he thought.
So he shoved his hands in his pockets, cast his eyes heavenward,
and began walking faster.

So did the ghost.

Parkin slowed down.

So did the ghost. The thing stuck to him like a shadow.

Tunis Parkin broke into a run and didn't stop until he reached safety at the home of the town marshal, T. W. Taylor. He stammered out his harrowing tale. The marshal, brave and conscientious in the discharge of his duties, rushed to the orchard and made a diligent search. He found nothing of a supernatural nature.

As far as it is known, no one has inventoried the ghost stories unique to Goodhue County. If one was to complete such an inventory, Tunis Parkin's ghost story would certainly be a strong contender as the oldest and, in the end, most amusing encounter with the supernatural in that county if not in the entire state. According to at least one source, the events caused the "greatest commotion" of any ghost sighting in Minnesota as it "terrified most of the population of Goodhue."

Minneapolis Journal columnist Merle Potter was the first to break the Goodhue ghost story not long after it took place. He named names in recounting the events of those few weeks, and they all stood by their accounts—even Tunis Parkin.

But perhaps the story has become a classic because of that man's name, Tunis Parkin. There are few better names attached to an American ghost story than Tunis Parkin . . . even if the story itself turns out to be something less than meets the eye.

On the morning after Tunis Parkin's unplanned sprint to Marshal Taylor's house, every resident of the little community knew about the ghost. Most were skeptical of the story, saying that Parkin had probably seen his shadow in the moonlight. There had never been a murder or a suicide in Goodhue up to that time, and the townspeople were convinced that only violent and unnatural deaths precipitated a ghost.

So, they concluded, if there really *was* a ghost lurking about the apple orchard, it had to be a stranger to the community.

Yet the timid ladies of the town took no chances. If they had to be out after dark in that vicinity, they arranged to be escorted by a fearless male friend.

Thomas McNamara was not among those courageous gentlemen.

Two weeks after Tunis Parkin's ghost sighting, McNamara had his own run-in with the specter. He was returning home from a dance late at night. When he passed the apple orchard, a figure sidled up to him and began behaving exactly as it had with Parkin. McNamara panicked.

"I turned around to talk to him," McNamara says, "but I didn't like his appearance. So I left."

Tom Riley also met the ghost late one night at the edge of the graveyard a few blocks away. There, among the dark and silent tombstones, marched a pale form. Riley tore all the way to the main street, screaming that he'd seen Tunis Parkin's ghost.

Skeptics said Riley had seen Fred Frederickson's white cow.

One night, Margaret Clever, Florence Taylor, and Harriet "Pete" Hintz were passing the orchard arm in arm when a blood-curdling scream issued from the trees.

Harriet fainted.

Since she was given to frequent fainting spells, the townspeople disputed the women's report.

At eleven o'clock on another night, someone saw the ghost bobbing up and down among the trees, gyrating like an acrobat in a traveling circus. A quick search found Joyce Shelstad, a delivery boy from the grocery store, pulling himself hand over hand along the parish clothesline, sometimes dangling upside down. He had a lug of peaches to deliver. Finding no one at the parish house, young Mr. Shelstad was simply killing time in the fidgety ways peculiar to the young.

And on it went.

Whenever people gathered during the long dog days of summer, they spoke of what Tunis Parkin saw. And nearly every day brought reports of new and terrifying encounters.

Town Marshal T. W. Taylor decided it was time to act.

As chief official for the maintenance of law and order, Marshal Taylor knew it was up to him to rid the town of the bothersome being. His plan was simple: he and Tunis Parkin would hide in a thicket near the orchard and nab the ghost as it passed.

Parkin was less than enthusiastic.

But on the appointed night, he and the marshal scrunched low in the bushes, watching, waiting.

Tunis Parkin's enthusiasm had been tempered by the uncertainty of whether Marshal Taylor had the requisite ghost-hunting credentials. Thus, Parkin had alerted his friends to the planned spectral ambush. Parkin's friends in turn gathered up all the small artillery in the town and deployed themselves in the shrubbery directly opposite the ghost chasers.

The evening grew dark and quiet. A breeze stirred. Time itself seemed to stand still. For the first couple of hours, Parkin and Marshal Taylor sat side by side, the latter fixing his gaze upon the dark orchard.

Suddenly, a howl split the silence, an agonized cry like that of a wounded animal in pain.

The marshal was ready. He jumped up, groped his way through the maze of trees and found . . . the culprit: two gnarled limbs of a prized Baldwin apple tree scraping against each other produced the wild wailings when the wind disturbed them.

Tunis Parkin's armed friends crouching a few yards away heard the marshal stumbling through the brush and at first thought it was the ghost itself. Common sense—and good hunting safety— prevailed; they held their fire until they determined it was the law and not the ghost they'd sighted down their barrels.

In the gray dawn, Tunis Parkin and Marshal Taylor emerged from the bushes. The marshal, on cramped legs, hobbled down the street, muttering and wheezing as he went. Parkin loped along beside him, peering anxiously around every street corner for a glimpse of his associates. Finding them nowhere in sight, he decided they had crept away in the darkness.

The ghost evidently melted away too, frightened by the threat of fire power or the presence of the marshal in the bushes. Although Tunis Parkin whistled his way home from his girl's house every evening that fall—and perhaps for many more falls to come—he never again met the specter.

And yet one disturbing element in the Goodhue ghost story remains unanswered: Tunis Parkin *and* Thomas McNamara said it was a *being*—a tall, silent, shrouded figure—that kept pace with them near the apple orchard. Neither reportedly said anything about a *noise* accompanying the unexpected arrival.

Is it only a coincidence that on the night Marshal Taylor discovered the "wailing apple trees," the thing that mirrored Tunis Parkin and Thomas McNamara also decided to leave town?

Or is that old apple orchard ghost still lurking somewhere, waiting for a chance to reintroduce itself to a later-day Tunis Parkin on his way home from a date?

THE LYDIA MYSTERY

"The ground shoots upward . . . "
Jordan Independent, **August 28, 1940**

Seen from the rural Scott County highway that passes in front, the well-maintained, two-story farmhouse seems the essence of contentment in the lake-studded countryside near the crossroads community of Lydia. The house and several tidy outbuildings sit some distance away from the road, at the end of a hard-packed gravel driveway edged with young saplings. The broad lawn, sprinkled with pines and other trees, sweeps around a compact marsh dense with cattails and wildflowers. Off in the near distance, white-washed three-rail fencing encloses several small pastures.

It's hard to imagine that nearly seventy years ago a cornfield at this bucolic setting between Fish Lake and Lake Cynthia, a few miles south of Prior Lake, was the site of perhaps one of the most peculiar events ever reported in that part of the state: over a period of several weeks, large chunks of earth and stone exploded upward from the earth.

As extraordinary as that may sound, the phrase is not exaggerating what took place during August and September 1940. The *Jordan Independent* newspaper may have been the first to publicly disclose what was going on at that farm southwest of Lydia, then occupied by a widow and her five children.

On August 28, the newspaper ran photographs and a news story:

MANY ARE MYSTIFIED BY SOIL-BLOWING IN FISH LAKE CORNFIELD

Manifestations First Noticed on Monday, Aug. 19. Place Was Mecca Since. Hundreds of People Have Visited Mrs. Effie Snell Farm Past Ten Days and Wondered.

The story below the headline gave some details: "Since Monday of last week, the rumors had it, unaccountable spurts of soil and even of fair-sized stones have shot skyward from the black soil of the cornfield . . . north of the Snell farm buildings. The manifestation is described as resembling a geyser, only on a smaller scale but not of water."

On a single Sunday, the newspaper reads, "hundreds of cars [were] parked on the wide gravel road" and that "probably more than a thousand persons went there that day to look and listen, to ask questions, to ponder and wonder" about the strange phenomena. "On every day of the week, which has been a rainy week, people have visited the Snell place in droves."

A "considerable number" of the visitors "did themselves see these ground-spurts," the newspaper contends.

But what exactly was this curious event that everyone came to see?

The "mysterious and somewhat eerie ground-surface movements," as the Jordan newspaper marvels, seem to be precisely what the newspaper and several surviving witnesses say they were: numerous instances over a two-month period when clumps of dirt and good-sized rocks apparently erupted from the ground and then cascaded back down. The cornfield in which the eruptions took place is no longer planted but seems to have been about where the marsh is now, between the farmhouse and the county road.

Although rumors abounded that experts were going to investigate the eruptions as some sort of geological abnormality, it's not clear that any scientists ever visited the Snell farm, nor whether any scientific opinion was offered. Several surviving witnesses know of no such visit.

Others may have believed that Mrs. Snell's children were somehow involved. The earthly explosions seemed to take place when some or all of the five children were in or near the cornfield. One of the stones purportedly thrown up from the ground and pictured in the newspaper was so large, however, that the oldest Snell son, eighteen years old at the time, held it in both hands. Whether one or more of the smaller children could have produced the broad shower of dirt and stones reported seems questionable.

What other eyewitnesses suggest, however, is that on Effie Snell's property something far more ominous was taking place, perhaps supernatural. That's what Marvin Oldenburg thinks, for instance. He says what happened was thought by many people at the time to have been the work of a poltergeist.

"Maybe it's got a different name, but that's what I called it. A poltergeist," asserts Oldenburg, who is retired from farming now and in his eighties. The word *poltergeist* is German and means "noisy ghost." Poltergeists are said to be enigmatic spirits who signal their presence through the mysterious movement of objects or through the creation of puzzling sounds. Some believe their activity is often found in homes with teenage children. Most of the Snell children were teenagers.

Marvin Oldenburg still lives in the vicinity near Lydia in a striking hilltop home with breathtaking views of Fish Lake and the surrounding rolling hillsides, not far from the old Snell farmhouse. He worked a 133-acre spread inherited from his father, raising cows, sheep, and chickens and growing some grain—1948 was his best year for farming, he recalls.

But Oldenburg, a former Scott County commissioner, was a teenager in 1940 hauling raw milk he collected from small farms in the area up to Minneapolis for processing. He remembers with remarkable clarity that morning in 1940 when he made his regular milk stop at the Snell farm and saw it "rain dirt."

Even more curious, and another reason he attributes it all to something supernatural, is that the mystery eruptions seem to have subsided after the Snell children were confirmed in a local Lutheran church and began attending church services on a regular basis . . . which their late father, Fred Snell, had made his wife promise to do as he lay dying years before. She had broken her word on both promises.

To understand those peculiar events in the late summer and early fall of 1940, it's necessary to draw a picture of the world at large and of life in that part of Scott County's Spring Lake Township and in Lydia, the community nearest the Snell farm.

The nation was yet a year and a half away from the Japanese attack on Pearl Harbor and the start of World War II. Minnesota was in its eighty-second year of statehood; many adults had parents or grandparents with memories of life in territorial days.

Country life in Scott County was simple and austere. Small towns, family farms, and plainly designed rural churches with their attendant graveyards dotted the mostly rural landscape southwest of Minneapolis and St. Paul; both of those cities were a day's round-trip journey on narrow, unevenly paved two-lane roads. Many families still managed without electricity or telephone service. Farm children attended one-room schoolhouses. It was a time when the *Jordan Independent* could report, as it did in September 1940, that "School District No. 28 at Fish Lake will open for classes on Monday of next week for a term of 8 months. Miss Martha Franek of New Prague will be the new teacher in charge." High schools were in Prior Lake or Jordan.

Villages such as Lydia—today hardly more than a small cluster of houses and old storefronts at the intersection of Minnesota 13 and Scott County 10—were self-contained communities. A few small businesses met nearly all the needs of the local population: a country store with everything from groceries and gas to nails and veterinary supplies; a bank for their savings accounts; maybe a grain elevator; a café; and, of course, a tavern or two.

It was also a time when survival, especially in rural areas, was still precarious. Three months after the Lydia story unfolded, the deadly 1940 Armistice Day blizzard would strike Minnesota, including Scott County, and kill at least forty-nine people statewide.

It is not hard to imagine that in such rural surroundings an event that the Jordan newspaper termed "Lydia's 'Volcanic' Mystery" might create a commotion. And it did. Marvin Oldenburg and others say it was perhaps the most baffling thing they've seen in all their years.

At the time the mystery unfolded, the farm's owner was Mrs. Effie Snell, a widow whose husband, Fred Snell, had died young over a decade before. Mrs. Snell was left with five children to raise as best she could. The oldest boy was Marvin Oldenburg's good friend, eighteen-year-old Roland and the family member responsible for operating the modest forty-acre farm. According to a contemporary newspaper account, it had been two other Snell children, fourteen-year-old Ethel and thirteen-year-old Norman, who first noticed the "stone throwing."

Marvin Oldenburg and Roland Snell, whom Marvin called Chubby, though he was more muscular than fat, had been pals since childhood. They hunted deer and pheasant in the rolling, forested countryside and angled in nearby lakes. When his father died, Roland, who was not yet in his teens, assumed a man's responsibilities on the farm. Meanwhile, when he was old enough, Oldenburg took a job driving a truck carrying eight- and ten-gallon cans of raw milk between Lydia and Minneapolis. Although the Snells had just a half-dozen cows, Oldenburg stopped by on most days.

"A half a can, three-quarters of a can, not very much. But I picked it up every morning anyhow," remembers Oldenburg.

On one particular morning in late August 1940, as Oldenburg drove onto the Snell farm, Roland Snell rushed out to meet him. He confided to his friend that there was something funny going on at the farm. Roland explained that anytime he or his brothers and sisters walked into the cornfield between their house and the road, dirt and rocks started flying. No one had been physically injured, but Roland said the family was baffled.

Roland asked his friend if he had any extra time to see for himself and perhaps offer his opinion. Oldenburg said he always had a few extra minutes to spare.

Snell's three sisters and a brother went with them down to the cornfield—perhaps five to six acres in size, says Oldenburg—and walked into the corn rows a short way.

"Goddammit, here came the dirt," marvels Oldenburg. "I don't know who threw it or how it got out there, but it came . . . falling out of the sky. How it got up there I can't tell you. It was just coming down."

The other Snell children were walking behind Marvin Oldenburg when the first clumps of dirt flew at him. Oldenburg told Roland to stand next to him and the other four children to walk in front. The corn was ripening, but it was a thin crop, so there was good visibility through the rows, Oldenburg says.

Oldenburg says the dirt and rocks seemed to soar through an area about four corn rows wide. When more dirt clumps flew, he made certain all the Snells were in view and looked around for a cause. Oldenburg didn't spend a lot of time investigating the strange affair.

"I didn't want no more dirt down my neck," he says. "I looked around in the back, but there was nothing there. It couldn't have been a spout, because it was at least four rows of corn wide. Everybody got hit alike. The kids were in front. That I made them do the first time we walked in there. The further we got down there, the heavier the dirt got. It wasn't like just throwing a handful at you. It looked like if you had a shovel and it hit everybody at one time, all the time. I said . . . that's enough of that. I'm getting the hell out of here. I ain't hanging around."

Oldenburg drove on to Lydia to pick up another man, a pipe fitter named Charlie, who was going along with him to Minneapolis to buy supplies. On the way Oldenburg regaled him with his morning adventure at the Snell farm. His friend said he too would like to see what was going on. Oldenburg agreed to drive out with him to the Snells' after they got back from Minneapolis, which they did.

"Roland came out [of the farmhouse], and I said Charlie here wants to see the dirt fly. Roland said he'd take him out there," Oldenburg says. He also remembers stepping in the house that afternoon and feeling it shake.

Oldenburg, his buddy Charlie, and the Snells trooped down to the cornfield. Oldenburg made sure the Snells were in front of him, about ten feet away.

"Pretty soon here it comes over our backs. We always got it from the back end. Your hat was dirty; your shoulders got dirty. Nobody else was out there, no sir. It was a poor crop of corn, and the leaves were down. You could see all around you. There was nothing there."

And again Oldenburg wasn't able to pinpoint the precise location from which the clumps of dirt and rocks might have originated.

The men returned to Lydia, where Oldenburg stopped to buy gas and drop off his friend. Inside the station he found Herman Schultz, another friend of his. Oldenburg told him what had been going on. Schultz insisted on seeing the oddity for himself. Oldenburg balked at going out again but finally relented.

Roland Snell met them as they drove in.

"I said Herman here wants to see the high-flying dirt. We walked through the doggone corn again, and I told them that I wanted [everyone] ahead of us so we can watch everything they're doing. Chubby was walking along beside us. We walked in there a little way, and the dirt started flying. We walked a little farther in, and a little farther, and Herman said that's enough; let's get out of here."

It was during the pair's return trip to Lydia that Schultz said he might have an answer—albeit a very nonscientific one—as to why the Snell farm was facing such a vexing problem. He suggested that it might be the work of a poltergeist.

Schultz explained to Oldenburg that the Snells' late father, Fred, and the local pastor had gotten into some sort of disagreement. Snell pulled his children from a confirmation class and stopped the family from attending weekly services. But later, as Fred Snell lay dying, a neighbor persuaded him to allow the minister to visit, which he did. Snell then made his wife, Effie, promise that she would see that the children were confirmed and would attend church. But after her husband died, Mrs. Snell broke her promise. The children were not sent back to religious school, and the Snells did not attend church.

Herman Schultz told Oldenburg that he was with Fred Snell when he asked his wife to abide by his final wishes.

Schultz told Oldenburg he would go see the minister as soon as he got back and tell him what was taking place at the Snell farm. He thought by getting the pastor and the Snells back together he could put an end to the incidents.

"And that's what he did," says Oldenburg. He believes the pastor visited the Snells, and together they reconciled their differences. The children were confirmed, and the family resumed their regular church attendance. At some point shortly after that, the incidents of flying dirt seem to have died out.

But before the matter ended, sometime in late September 1940, there were other witnesses to the mysterious earth geyser, including Della Dorn Klingberg, who now lives in Prior Lake. In 1940, she attended Fish Lake School with her friend Delores Snell. That friendship brought Della into contact with the Lydia mystery.

It wasn't unusual for children of that era to occasionally stay with friends' families on school nights. Delores Snell had stayed with Della and her family on several occasions, and so it was that Delores reciprocated by inviting Della to spend a night at her house. It also happened to be when the Snells' cornfield eruptions were taking place.

"My folks had heard that something spooky was going on out there," says Klingberg, though she adds they didn't give their daughter any details.

So she went off to the Snell farm with her friend Delores. It wasn't long before something spooky did indeed put in an appearance.

"We were playing ball, and all at once the grandfather Snell yelled out 'Effie, the rocks are flying again!'" Klingberg says. A Snell grandparent was staying at the house at the time. "But I didn't pay any attention. Effie came out and said to us kids to come in the house; the rocks [were] flying."

She thought at first that it was the kids' grandfather who was throwing rocks, playing a game. "That's what I thought, but when it started, we were all called into the house. He came in, too."

But before she went inside, she watched wide-eyed as several columns of dirt erupted from the ground. The clumps of dirt would rise in the air and then break apart. It was an amazing sight, she says.

Once inside, the girls did their homework, played games, and ate supper. Not much was said about the earthen eruptions. When it grew dark, Della noticed that the Snells locked the doors by sliding wood two-by-fours into brackets on either side of the entryways. She thought that was odd, as most people rarely locked their doors in that era or had regular key locks. Her own family only used two-by-fours on the outside of barn doors.

As the girls were going upstairs for the night, Delores told her friend that if she heard any funny noises later on, she was not to get scared. Nothing would harm them.

Klingberg didn't know what kind of noises she was talking about. It didn't take long for her to find out.

"I don't know what time it was, but [the noise] sounded like a big bunch of dishes [breaking]. It was really loud . . . enough to wake me up."

Delores woke up, too, but repeated there was nothing to worry about. Della Klingberg did not sleep the rest of the night and hurried home right after breakfast.

Klingberg's parents asked her how the night had gone. Typical of a teen, she said "fine." Eventually, she confided to them that "there was something funny going on there." She told them about the children's grandfather warning them about the flying rocks, the doors being barricaded with two-by-fours, and then the sudden, loud racket that kept her awake.

Some days later, Della got another opportunity to witness the flying dirt. Her uncle had heard about the mystery and took Della along one day to see what all the commotion was about. She says a half-dozen cars were parked along the road, waiting for the show. Lucille and Norman Snell were near the cornfield, recalls Klingberg. Suddenly, a large clump of dirt soared into the air and then spread out "just like fireworks" before falling back down to earth. She says it happened several times.

Della Klingberg's memories of that night in the Snell home make her apprehensive. Even now, decades later, she maintains, "It would take a lot to get me to go back to that place."

Della went on to marry Elmer Klingberg, who had also grown up near Lydia. He and his family made their own attempt to see the erupting cornfield.

"We drove out there one day because we wanted to see it. There were so many cars we couldn't get near the place," says Elmer Klingberg. He never did see the exploding dirt.

Don Beuch is the unofficial Lydia historian and coauthor of a history of the community as reported in the local newspapers. His family has lived in the area for decades. He remembers his mother telling him about the Snell farm mystery.

"My mom was about twenty years old [at the time] and she [told me] that her mom and dad drove out there, and they saw all these cars and people. My grandpa told them to stay in the car. He walked up [to the field], but he didn't see anything. My understanding is that there were many people who went out there and didn't see anything, but there were also a lot of people who did. If kids walked out into the field, it would get worse."

Beuch notes that the old Snell house has changed hands a number of times over the years and has been remodeled extensively. He says he isn't aware of anyone who has lived there having any further incidents such as those reported in 1940.

According to the *Jordan Independent,* the last anyone saw of the "dirt geysers," as the newspaper termed the incidents, was on Saturday, September 21, 1940, adding that fall husking operations were taking place "without incident."

Marvin Oldenburg continued stopping each morning at the Snell farm to pick up a few gallons of milk. Oddly, he says the Snells never mentioned the mystery again, despite its local notoriety.

None of the witnesses still living knows for certain what, if any, conversation may have taken place between Mrs. Effie Snell and the Lutheran pastor after Herman Schultz told him about the incidents. Nor does it appear that any follow-up investigation was launched into the affair. As with many locally renowned events in those years before the Internet and twenty-four-hour cable news programs, the Lydia mystery seems to have soon faded from view, to live on only in the memories of a few living witnesses.

What is left then by way of explanation? Was it a sudden, inexplicable geological aberration? Perhaps a clever prank concocted by one or more of the five Snell children and foisted on unsuspecting visitors? Or could its origins have been the work of a poltergeist, as some thought?

As a practical matter, it is, of course, impossible to answer those questions with any measure of certainty given the time that has elapsed and the relative isolation and minimal documentation of the event. The handful of witnesses who remain are absolutely firm, however, in what they saw—large chunks of soil and rock erupting skyward without noticeable human intervention.

A geological explanation might point to a barely perceptible earthquake or long-dormant volcanic activity. Yet that seems doubtful.

An earthquake in 1860 did strike New Prague, about ten miles southwest of Lydia, with an estimated 4.7 magnitude, but that's the closest temblor known to date. The Minnesota Geological Survey contends the state "has one of the lowest occurrence levels of earthquakes in the United States," with fewer than twenty verified. Most were barely felt outside the immediate quake zone.

Marvin Oldenburg recalls the house shaking once when he stepped inside, and Della Klingberg refers to noises like dishes breaking. Might a tremor have produced both?

Since the newspaper terms the event a volcanic mystery, might we suspect activity linked to volcanoes slumbering somewhere beneath the surface? Again, that seems doubtful. Although there were active volcanoes in what is now Minnesota some 1,100 million years ago during the late Precambrian period, there seem to be no other instances of activity similar to that found in Lydia linked to volcanic instability.

There is some slim evidence that the cornfield in which the dirt and rocks were thrown up was not especially productive. Shirley Klingberg Stier, another witness who still lives in the area, says those few acres were peculiar.

"My brother picked corn in that field," says Stier. "He said the corn . . . was all twisted. It . . . grew that way. Other neighbors' corn grew normally, but in this field . . . [it] was twisted. He said he could hardly go through and pick it with the corn picker."

That view would seem to echo Marvin Oldenburg, who says it was a thin, poor crop of corn he saw during his several visits to the Snells. If at least part of the old cornfield is now a marsh, that might at least partly explain the poor growing conditions.

Historian Don Beuch and Elmer Klingberg wonder if another puzzling incident two years after the Snell farm episode was related to it in any way.

On a late night in February 1942, a log barn owned by the late Fred Snell's brother Louie Snell burned to the ground. It was about a mile due north of the Effie Snell farm. The fire "lit up the whole sky," one witness said. Neighbors three miles away could see the glow from the flames.

A barn suddenly burning down was not unusual in an era when kerosene lamps were still in use, especially in outbuildings. What puzzles Elmer Klingberg is what he says he found when he reached the scene with his father and two other men. The barn was gone, with only a few exterior logs left burning. But in the center of the smoldering ruins were blue flames about five feet around and rising from the ground like a beam of light. He didn't see anything under the flames except the scorched earth. The flames produced bright, vertical light extending upward into the night sky.

"I walked around that beam, and there was no heat to it," says Klingberg, who stayed several few feet away. "That's the funny part. It was in the center of the barn, a straight beam, not flared up, and as high as you can imagine."

Klingberg was a Scott County excavator for most of his life, yet there was nothing over the years to compare with the weird blue flame. "We all seen it," says Klingberg. "[The blue flames] stayed until morning. I don't know what it was."

With his years of studying Lydia area history, Don Beuch is equally baffled.

"In that area we don't have any natural gas [deposits] . . . I know of. We don't have geysers or any of that. . . . No one has ever found anything similar to it anywhere [in this area] that I'm aware of," says Beuch.

Perhaps we will never know what took place on those two farms nearly seventy years ago and therefore must be content to reflect on the events that some believed then—and believe to this day—were so strange and so mysterious as to be beyond human understanding.

THE CARETAKERS

*"I'm totally fine with ghosts being here . . . but it's one thing
to know they're here and another thing entirely to see them!"*
Stephanie Hall

The volunteer was at the main desk just inside the front door of the century-old stone edifice on Hiawatha Avenue that is the Pipestone County Museum. She had assisted a few visitors during her shift, but now it was quiet.

That's when *he* showed up.

The older man seemed to have come down the staircase that leads to the upper floors. She didn't really know, because suddenly he was just there, strolling through. The fellow was nice looking, well groomed, and clad in a pressed, though ill-fitting, suit and tie. He was pleasant and courteous, not unlike other retired gentlemen who stopped in occasionally to see the current exhibits or to carry out genealogical research.

But when he spoke, the volunteer soon knew something was amiss.

He smiled and introduced himself as Henry Abernathy. He was a barber in town, he told her, and a bachelor at that. He "lived upstairs," he added.

He looked around and then turned back toward her.

One more thing, he said, could he ask her to pass along a message?

That museum staff member who was wearing the new shoes, he was really quite pleased with her decision. He knew that the pair she had been wearing was quite uncomfortable.

Oh, and he liked her new haircut, as well.

With that out of the way, he nodded, smiled again, and ambled off through the door and down the hallway.

The volunteer followed after him, but by the time she got to the door, he was nowhere to be seen.

Ah! So the stories were true, not products of someone's imagination, after all.

The volunteer knew no one had ever lived upstairs. The building had been the Pipestone city hall before becoming a museum. The upper floors had been city offices. Now they were filled with historical exhibits and storage rooms.

Yet her visitor, the man who introduced himself as Henry Abernathy, was quite well known among the staff.

Some of them had seen him before. And now it had been her turn.

She had just spoken with the ghost of Henry Abernathy, one of several at the Pipestone County Museum.

Pipestone's Romanesque-style city hall has been a solid presence in the downtown district since it opened in 1896. Built of locally quarried rusty red Sioux quartzite for $8,000, the three-story monolith housed city offices until 1960, including the first public library, the fire department, the jail, and a meeting hall. It's been the Pipestone County Museum since 1967 and is listed on the National Register of Historic Places.

But staff members over the years have encountered enough fleeting ghosts, floating voices, and traipsing footsteps to believe that the museum is haunted. Indeed, it may well have the most documented hauntings of any museum in Minnesota. It is one of the few anywhere to have organized a special exhibit related to the topic, the 2007 exhibit, The Ghosts of Pipestone.

Stephanie Hall is the collections manager of the Pipestone museum and the unofficial curator of all things ghostly. Hall is perfectly suited to the job: she had her own encounter with what may have been the spirit of her late grandmother.

The museum itself has at least two ghosts: Mr. Abernathy, the aforementioned barber, and a young girl in a blue prairie dress. The nameless child is usually seen standing at the top of the staircase. No one knows why she is there, other than perhaps being attached to one of the museum's many donated artifacts.

Henry Abernathy is another matter.

"This building was never used as apartments, so he wouldn't have lived here. It is possible he lived in town and was a traveling barber because he traveled to different communities," Hall says.

There is no Henry Abernathy listed in any city directory nor in any other record Hall could find. But if he was a transient, he may not have had a permanent address.

Neither is there any clue as to why he "lives" in the museum, other than the possibility that he feels comfortable around the historical displays.

"He seems very friendly to everyone who's met him," Hall says. "The [volunteer worker] who spoke with him didn't know he was a ghost. She said he was very polite. For a few seconds she thought he was someone who had just wandered in, but when she followed him into the hallway and there was no one there . . . "

Stephanie Hall doesn't finish the thought.

The little girl in the blue prairie dress has been seen, but no one has spoken with her.

Hall is comfortable with ghost stories because she can add her own to the ones on file at the Pipestone museum. On the day Hall gave birth to her daughter, her own grandmother had a stroke. She died two weeks later without ever seeing her great-granddaughter. Hall says occasional odd reactions her infant daughter had were possible indications that her grandmother's spirit was there to see the newest family member.

"Babies do focus on things that we don't often see . . . but she would look over my shoulder and giggle and point and turn her head like someone was touching her. She seemed very engaged with 'whoever' was behind the couch when I nursed her."

Hall, her husband, and baby girl were living in Arizona at the time. She says whomever this guardian angel might have been moved with them to Pipestone. Her grandmother died in Worthington, so whether the "angel" is her or someone else, Hall says, "She's still in our house."

She says the family dog noticed something different in the nursery. She put her head down on the seat of a rocking chair as if someone was petting her. And Hall's daughter continued pointing and laughing and saying hi to empty space long after they moved to Minnesota.

"I'm perfectly content with [this spirit] being in my house," Hall says.

So when Stephanie Hall hears the ghost stories connected to her museum she is never surprised, even with a story as strange as the tale of the haunted shoes.

They are a pair of old and battered ankle-high leather galoshes with hard wooden soles. They seem to have been hand stitched. Hall says the museum has no information about how they came to be in their collection—they don't have a museum accession number or an indication of a donor's name. Museum staff believe they may have been European in origin.

They seem to have showed up one day . . . and they move.

During an exhibit of World War II memorabilia, the shoes were placed in an enclosed glass exhibit case with a German Nazi uniform. On a morning after the exhibit opened, a museum employee found the shoes sitting on the floor, outside the display case. They were put back in, but when the staff returned the next day, the shoes were again on the floor. They were placed elsewhere in the exhibit . . . and stayed put.

Stephanie Hall says a possible explanation was provided by a clairvoyant who visited the museum and saw the shoes.

"The psychic claimed they were made in a Nazi concentration

camp and had been owned by a [prisoner], but one who was a . . . go-between for the Nazis and the camp inmates. He would take money and articles of clothing from the Jews to protect them and then renege on his promises. So the man who owned the shoes was not a particularly nice man."

Hall could understand why the shoes might not feel comfortable next to a Nazi uniform.

The shoes are now stored on the museum's third floor when they're not on exhibit, well away from the German uniform, which is boxed up in Hall's office.

"The shoes haven't moved, so I assume they're perfectly content to stay where they are."

But the strange goings-on in the Pipestone museum are not limited to phantom barbers, ethereal little girls, and nomadic shoes. Other puzzling incidents have left staff members scratching their heads.

Incorporeal voices have been recorded and heard.

A group of paranormal investigators captured several of these voices on a digital tape recorder, voices that were not audible when the recording was made, Hall says.

For instance, one of the ghost hunters recorded an answer to a question, and on the recording another voice can be heard talking over hers. A short time later on in the recording, a male voice can be heard saying, "I'm sorry," as if apologizing for interrupting.

At one point their recording equipment stopped working. The investigators wondered what had happened. Once they got their equipment to work again, they played back a section that they had tried to record. A voice said, "You'll find out tomorrow," apparently in answer to their concern about the equipment not working.

Hall says other sections of the recording contained mocking laughter recorded near the mysterious shoes and what sounded like rhythmic tapping.

Sometimes mysterious voices are heard at the museum without the assistance of electronic equipment. A museum staff member had gone into a front closet—the old safe when the building was the city hall—to look for an item. As she crossed the threshold, she heard a group of men talking. She summoned a colleague over, and she, too, heard men's voices. It lasted only a few seconds. Both thought it sounded like a discussion, perhaps similar to one that might have taken place a century ago, when city business was being conducted in the room.

On a winter day in the early 1990s, an assistant museum director was working alone in the museum, sitting at his office desk during an especially nasty winter blizzard. Suddenly, he felt a tap on his shoulder. Then it seemed as if someone whispered in his ear that he should check the third-floor door to the roof. He did and found the door open and snow blowing into a storage area. Roof repair was being done, so he surmised that one of the roofers had left the door open. But who tapped him on the shoulder and put the thought into his head that he should check upstairs?

Museum workers say there is a sense that whoever or whatever resides more or less permanently in the museum wants to be told about any impending changes being planned for the museum, as if they are personally looking out for the building and its contents.

When a collection of vintage clothing was moved from the third floor to a collection room on the second floor, "the feeling in the entire museum was disturbed—very uncomfortable. We 'explained' what was being done and apologized, and the atmosphere changed almost immediately," remembers the museum's Elizabeth McCabe.

There may not have been spirits in the clothing, McCabe notes, but clothing carries "a lot of vibration or feelings from those who wore the clothes."

The clothing in the museum has been special to the owners—military uniforms, wedding dresses—so they hold many memories. "When they were disturbed by moving, the memories were disturbed as well," she says.

Perhaps that sense of ownership by the museum's supernatural tenants is the reason some staff members get the impression that their activities are being observed as they go about their daily routines.

At other times the fleeting sound of footsteps may indicate the presence of a potential helper, as in this 2003 incident reported by a museum assistant.

> I was helping out . . . for a few days. I was filing papers and hauling boxes and other things up to the attic. The first day, everything was going good until I started hauling the boxes. As I was walking up the stairs, I could hear someone following me, but I knew the other staff members were downstairs because I could hear them talking. The footsteps on the stairs behind me grew louder and louder so I hurried up the stairs so I could finish faster.
>
> On my second trip up the stairs, I could hear footsteps leading the way up to the attic. I tried to catch up to them, but no one was there. I was on my way down from the attic when I heard boxes moving around up there, as if someone was making room for me to set down my boxes. I swung open the door and no one was there. I knocked around the room and tried to find out what was making the noise, but my search turned up no one.
>
> I rushed back downstairs and the rest of the staff were still down there talking. I still wonder today who was just in front of me but never seen.

And then there's the rocking chair.

Museum volunteer Peggy O'Neill has taken numerous photographs inside the museum, some of which contain orb-like objects, which some contend are a sign of supernatural activity. But it's her photograph of the old, high-top rocking chair in the museum's permanent exhibit that captures attention. The picture appears to show someone sitting in it, his hand and arm resting atop the arm support.

That wouldn't be unusual, because of the museum's four permanent staff members, two have seen the rocker move of its own accord.

But Stephanie Hall is not one of those.

"I'm jealous because I never have [seen it rock]," Hall says. "But I think at the same time if I actually saw it rock I'd be really upset.

I always peek around the corner because I think I'm going to catch Henry [Abernathy] in it, that I'm going to catch it moving."

The chair is well away from anyone walking by and not close to any fan or air duct. Though the floor is somewhat uneven, Hall says, that wouldn't account for it rocking on some occasions and not others. If it rocked all the time, she could blame it on uneven flooring or some other natural factor.

"But sometimes it rocks when people are just looking at it," she says.

For all her days and nights in the Pipestone museum, Stephanie Hall has yet to see anything supernatural, even though she believes in ghosts and has no problem with them being around.

"I've been here many times by myself, and I've still never seen anything," she admits. "I've been here when it's dark and not seen anything."

That's fine with her because if something even remotely supernatural did show itself, Hall says, "it will scare me. Maybe they subconsciously know that, because I'm torn between seeing them and not seeing them. Maybe they know what I can handle."

And maybe what she cannot.

10

THE LEGEND OF ANN LAKE

"Haven't you heard? That camp is haunted."
Herbert Todd

Swan Molander tried to get comfortable on the rough-hewn floor. The heavy wool blankets he pulled up to his chin were barely enough to keep him warm. With two duck-hunting buddies, Molander had been out all day along the Ann River and onto Ann Lake, near Mora in Kanabec County. It had been a good hunt. The trio was bedded down in an abandoned logging camp building, near the Ann River Dam. A few feet away, also curled up on the floor trying to fall asleep, were a couple of acquaintances who'd also been hunting in the area.

Molander had just fallen asleep when he was jerked awake by a loud crash. His friend, Captain Seavey, was already sitting up and in the process of striking a wooden match. In its flickering light, the men saw that the door was standing wide open. Somehow, that heavy railroad tie they'd pushed against it had fallen away.

Molander and Seavey rolled out of their bedding, trod carefully the length of the floor to avoid the ties and debris strewn about, and looked out through the open doorway. Nothing stirred. They hefted the tie back against the door and returned to their three companions, all awake now and watching.

They talked it over for a few minutes, trying to figure out what had caused the tie to move as it did. It had been set firmly in place. There was no wind to speak of. And it was unlikely that one of the men had played a trick on the others—the crash awoke everyone nearly at once—and, besides, the floor was so littered with railroad ties and camp debris that a walk across it in the dark would have been foolhardy.

The next morning the mystery deepened. The horses they'd been using to pull a couple of supply wagons had somehow become untied from their small enclosure, called a hovel by loggers. Later, the men found two of the draft horses grazing a quarter mile away. A pony they had used to pull a buckboard wasn't discovered until days later; it had returned to its own barn near Knife Lake, several miles away.

Perhaps the men should have paid more attention to what one of them had said earlier in the day—that this lumber camp near the Ann River Dam was abandoned for a good reason: it was haunted.

Though these events may seem benign today, they caused a stir a century ago in the deep woods and young settlements of Kanabec County and were again detailed in a remembrance Swan Molander wrote a half century later. One of the earliest Mora settlers, he writes that the several days he spent at that logging camp in 1890 were the most puzzling he'd ever encountered, a decades-old mystery that remained unsolved.

Molander himself arrived in what later became the city of Mora in 1883. He was among the thirty or so individuals who steered the settlement toward cityhood over the ensuing years. He later served five terms as county auditor and wrote extensively on the region's early development before eventually retiring to St. Paul.

The Ann Lake experience unfolded because of Molander's passion for fall waterfowl hunting. Another Mora man, Stanton Seavey, knew that and invited Molander to go with him and his father on a duck hunt along the Ann River. At least once a year, in the fall, Stanton's father, Captain Seavey—who does not have a first name in the historical accounts—would come up to hunt with his son. The Captain lived in Pine City, not far away to the east.

This fall, the duck hunt had begun routinely enough.

Stanton had been told by several Native Americans that ducks were plentiful along the Ann River, west of Mora, flying in the direction of Ann Lake. So the men put together something of an expedition—Captain Seavey came over from Pine City with two draft horses, a water skiff, and a supply wagon. Stanton was taking care of a pony at the time, so he hitched it to a buckboard.

Together, Swan Molander, Stanton Seavey, and Captain Seavey set out along the Ann River, heading toward the dam at Ann Lake. Stanton and Molander drove the buckboard; Captain Seavey drove the supply wagon with the skiff secured in the back.

The men spent the day along the river before heading up onto the lake. Captain Seavey positioned himself at a point near the dam to watch for ducks that came in his direction. Molander and Stanton climbed aboard the skiff and paddled up the lake toward some rice beds. Molander let Stanton out about midway up the lake to wait for ducks.

The hunt was going well. "Ducks were piling up," Molander recalls, when darkness started to set in. He picked up Stanton and headed back toward the Ann Lake Dam. They saw a campfire near the dam and thought it was Captain Seavey, but they heard him call to them from the point where he'd been left off. They picked him up and made for the dam. There they found Herbert Todd, whom both Molander and Stanton Seavey knew from Mora, and a man introduced simply as Robinson. Herbert Todd said they'd been partridge shooting and duck hunting in the area. They'd seen the Molander outfit out on the water and thought they'd offer them a hot fire and a warm supper. The men gladly accepted.

They ate a traditional *booja* made of potatoes, onions, pork, several fresh ducks and partridges, salt, and pepper, scraped off the dishes, and lit their pipes.

"I see you brought no tent," Herbert Todd noted. "Where are you going to sleep tonight?"

"There's a perfectly good lumber camp over there," Stanton Seavey replied, nodding in the direction of the dam.

Todd and Robinson fell silent.

Captain Seavey looked thoughtfully at the men.

"Is there anything the matter?"

Herbert Todd hesitated before he said anything. He was an experienced woodsman, a hunter and trapper who'd spent his life in the wilderness of northeast Minnesota. He'd lived with the Ojibwe for a time, so he was always guarded when he spoke of the spirit world.

"Haven't you heard?" he said quietly. "That camp is haunted."

The other men shook their heads. Captain Seavey laughed. Swan Molander and the others wanted to hear what had happened.

"Well," Todd began, "during the last year the camp was used by loggers, the door would fly open in the night, dishes would rattle, and blankets would be pulled off the men in the bunks. No matter how they tied their horses, their halters would be untied in the morning. They had a hard time keeping enough men to finish the winter's work. The camp was never used after that."

Todd said that, since then, no logger or Ojibwe came close to that camp. They'd go miles out of their way to avoid it.

"The camp was bad medicine to the Indians," he added.

Molander believed what the man said.

Captain Seavey clearly did not.

"Well, I'll get the ghosts to do their best tricks. I know a few good knots myself! Let the ghosts try their hands at untying them!" the Captain said. He headed toward the old logging camp hovel where he staked their horses for the night.

"Are you really going to sleep in the camp?" Todd asked the Captain when he returned.

"I would not have cared very much whether I slept inside or outside, but after listening to your story, I certainly am going to sleep in the camp!" the Captain declared.

Todd and Robinson conferred briefly before reluctantly deciding to join their three companions in the old camp building.

The rough structure—Molander estimated it was some eighty feet long—was already starting to sag from years of neglect: cracked windows layered with dust; broken pottery, tables and chairs everywhere; not an oil lamp or candle to be found. Several dozen railroad ties lay strewn about the floor. At the far end of the room from where the men slept, a single door—minus its lock—was the only entrance. Before turning in for the night, they'd wedged one of the heavy railroad ties against it.

"Now let the ghosts slam that door if they can!" Captain Seavey laughed.

The men dragged their wool blanket bedding to a far corner. Molander, Stanton, and the Captain set up in one area. Todd and Robinson spread out a few feet away.

Captain Seavey set out his watch and wood matches on the floor beside him before crawling under his blankets. They wanted to get an early start before dawn for the morning shoot.

The events of that night were no closer to being solved after they found their horses missing the next morning. They'd rounded up the two draft horses, and Captain Seavey had rehitched them with tight knots. All five men went out on a morning hunt, but when they returned a few hours later, the horses had again vanished. They were found nearer camp this time.

Between the moving railroad tie and the unhitched horses, the men didn't have answers but were not ready to see an invisible hand behind it all.

"The easiest solution," Molander wrote later, "would be to say that someone played a prank." Not an unknown activity in hunting camps.

But then he ticks off the reasons why that solution doesn't seem sensible.

The door could only be opened from the inside—the railroad tie held it tightly shut. The five men were at the farthest end away from the door, nearly thirty yards, Molander reckons. Within seconds of hearing the rail tie smash onto the floor, they were all awake, and Captain Seavey had a match burning. Everyone was still wrapped in blankets.

Molander writes, "None of us five men could have got back to bed in time undiscovered. In fact, forty or fifty ties were scattered over the camp floor, which would have made it dangerous to walk in the dark, except with the greatest of caution."

And it would have taken a massive heave from outside to have moved the tie even in the slightest.

As for the horses, the small horse hovel was falling apart—only its walls and a few hitching racks remained.

"It would have been easy for anyone to reach the horses, but the ground was very soft and would have left foot imprints and there were none except tracks from the Captain's rubber boots," Molander writes. Captain Seavey had been the one responsible for tethering the animals. Molander didn't think it logical or even possible for him to have snuck out to untie the animals.

Molander suggests that, because the whole camp and especially the hovel smelled rather bad, the horses grew restless and jerked themselves loose. But then Captain Seavey told him that, with the knots he tied, the harder the horses pulled on them, the tighter they would become.

Could someone else have been lurking in the vicinity? Possibly, but despite some heavy logging, that entire region around Ann Lake was primarily wilderness then; the closest farm was several miles away, near the old Great Northern Railroad bridge at Mora.

The five men spent several more days duck hunting near Ann Lake Dam logging camp. They were not disturbed again, but according to Molander, they could not keep their horses tethered overnight. No matter what kind of knot the men used, the horses would be found untied and grazing elsewhere.

Is there an explanation? Swan Molander asked Herbert Todd if anything bad had happened back when the lumber camp was in use to trigger the weird incidents.

"There is a story that years ago a teamster had been found dead in the horse hovel," Todd replied.

A century later, the Ann Lake region where Molander, the Seaveys, Herbert Todd, and Robinson hunted is populated with year-round residents, summer cabins, and small resorts. It is still heavily wooded, though the virgin white pine that first attracted the lumbering companies is long gone. Hunting is still a favored pastime. Vanished as well are nearly all traces of the logging camps that once dotted the forests around Mora, though their locations are pinpointed on maps at the Mora Historical Society.

Though the location of Molander's haunted logging camp isn't known for certain, hunters occasionally stumble across the ruins of one of the old sites. If they should discover one near the Ann Lake Dam, perhaps the hunters will want to walk right on by. A night spent there may involve more mystery than they want to reckon with.

FROZEN JOHN

*"He then began to . . . fade away, somewhat like
smooth thinning out, and disappeared."*
Mr. Cosper, *Worthington Advance*

Nobles County's devastating blizzard of 1873 played such cruel
tricks.

Samuel Small was buying supplies in Worthington when the
storm blew in from the northwest. Nevertheless, he set off for his
Indian Lake Township home a few miles away. The storm blew in
too fast. He lost the track he was following, and his ox team became
mired in the chest-deep snow. Small abandoned the wagon team
and wandered off across the prairie. He would never know that he'd
gotten within a few dozen yards of his house but couldn't see it for
the blinding snow.

Searchers found him days later standing upright not far from
his home, frozen stiff as a plank, one hand grasping a wood fence
rail. He was coated in a sheet of ice. Evidently, death took him as he
tried to climb over the fence to reach a hay stack's meager shelter.

A Mrs. Blixt was worried that her husband couldn't find his way
home in the blizzard. He'd gone ice fishing earlier in the morning.
She left her children alone in the cabin and set off to find him.
Within minutes of leaving the front door, she became disoriented

in the freezing wall of white that enveloped her. She perished not far from her front doorstep. Her husband made it safely back.

A man named Taylor became separated from his three companions on their way home from the mill. He wandered for thirty-five miles before collapsing. Trappers found his body a year later in northern Seward Township. Three other members of his family also froze to death that winter.

But sometimes death was cheated out of its mission.

Miss Mary Jemerson and her students were trapped inside a log schoolhouse near Indian Lake for three days and two nights. They soon ran out of logs for the small stove and had to chop up the desks to feed the small fire. Snow blew through the cracks in the walls and around the doors. To keep everyone warm and their spirits up, Miss Jemerson marched the children around the stove. The only food was what remained in the children's lunch pails. Fortunately they were all rescued after the storm abated.

The winter of 1872–1873 remains one of the most brutal in Minnesota weather history. The state had been locked in snow and cold for two months even before the deadly January blizzard.

The first storm had arrived with a fury two months earlier, on November 13, with a three-day whiteout that dumped several feet of snow. A deep and dreadful winter had settled from the Canadian border south to Iowa. Many of the state's rail lines remained impassable until the spring thaw.

By January 7, 1873, residents in Nobles County had grown used to the snow and cold and adjusted their lives accordingly. The morning of the seventh dawned "beautiful and bright," one observer noted. Everyone thought it was a sure sign of a "January thaw."

But there were warning signs that everything was not as it seemed.

A schoolteacher in Worthington told anyone who would listen that his aneroid barometer had been falling steadily for nearly a full day, and had dropped lower than he had ever before seen.

By one o'clock on the afternoon of January 7, a towering wall of snow was bearing down from the northwest. Worthington townsfolk caught away from their own homes stayed where they were rather than risk walking even a few blocks to their houses. Farmers who had traveled to town stayed put, even if it meant leaving wives and children to fend for themselves back on the farm. When the blizzard finally passed, the lashing, forty-mile-an-hour winds had buried the county under even more snow and ice.

At least seventy people perished statewide during the January 1873 blizzard, including Samuel Small, Mrs. Blixt, and Mr. Taylor in Nobles County.

Yet the strangest death of all during that January storm may have been that of one John Weston, a farmer in Seward Township in northern Nobles County.

But unlike the other fatalities, his name became far more familiar in southwest Minnesota and for a time nationwide because of what happened after his passing—his ghost returned not once but twice to point the way toward his remains.

His story is one of the stranger ones in the annals of Minnesota's haunted history.

Back on that clear early morning of January 7, Weston evidently thought the day ahead would be fair and mild. He left his wife, Mary, and their young son and took an oxen sled east to chop wood near Graham Lakes, several small, interconnected lakes.

Weston was on his way home when he saw the storm building in the northwest. He was still a few miles away when the storm hit. Though he somehow made it back to his farm, he could not find the house. Later, searchers discovered two sets of sled tracks indicating Weston had twice driven in a circle before becoming disoriented and heading back east toward Graham Lakes. Somewhere along the steep banks of Jack Creek, he unhitched his oxen, and they wandered off.

Weston apparently had enough sense of bearing to walk southeast with the storm and toward what was then called Hersey but is now Brewster. He didn't make it.

A rescue party was assembled to find Weston even before the storm had finished its deadly business. The oxen were found strangled in their own yokes next to Jack Creek. The sled full of wood was also located. There was no trace of John Weston.

But that's not to say John Weston was nowhere to be seen.

His neighbor and good friend was a Mr. Cosper. With other men he had been among those searching for Weston when the blizzard had abated on the second day.

Unsuccessful, Cosper and the rest of the men returned home to feed their stock.

What happened next led to a notoriety for John Weston that certainly would have eluded him in life.

Cosper told *Worthington Advance* editor A. P. Miller what had happened just before dusk:

> I went into my stable after the bucket, intending to water my horses.
> I came out and turned the corner to go down the path when about
> half way down the slope to the well I was surprised to see John
> Weston coming up the path to meet me.
>
> He approached with his usual familiar smile, and his hands
> were tucked under the cape of his blue soldier overcoat, just as I
> had seen him approach many times.
>
> I called to him and said: "Hello Weston! Why, I thought you
> were lost in the storm."
>
> Weston replied: "I was, and you will find my body a mile and
> a half northwest of Hersey!"
>
> He then began to . . . fade away, somewhat like smoke thinning
> out, and disappeared.
>
> I had not time to realize what was occurring till it was over,
> and then I began to feel mighty queer.

Mighty strange, indeed.

Cosper's astonishing story spread rapidly over the next few days. New search parties were formed to look in the vicinity of Hersey, where the ghost said his body would be found. Still no luck, and so the searchers gave up until the spring thaw.

Not until April, after the snow had melted, was Weston's body finally located at the bottom of a deep slough . . . a mile and a half northwest of Hersey, just as the ghost had said. Snow had been very deep in that area. Authorities figured he'd made it nearly twelve miles through the blinding snow. But regrettably, hopelessly lost and no doubt exhausted from the exertion, he could go no further and fell face down, his fingers grasping a few blades of tall prairie grass sticking up through a snow bank. Even today, the desolate, expansive prairie is a formidable foe if a blizzard traps the unwary traveler.

There is a curious footnote to the story of John Weston. On the same night that his ghost visited his neighbor Cosper, Weston's ghost also called on his wife, Mary, but in a much more circumspect manner.

Mrs. Weston and her son had gone to bed when there was a loud pounding on the door. She awakened, but as the knocking was not repeated, she fell back asleep. Soon it started up again, only this time she called out to ask who it was and what the person wanted.

"Did you know that John was frozen to death?" The reply came in a voice that sounded to Mrs. Weston like that of her brother who lived nearby.

"Mother, did uncle say that pa was froze to death?" called out her son, who had also heard the man speak.

Mrs. Weston climbed out of bed and lit an oil lamp. She hurried to the front door. She moved aside the heavy wood timber that held the door shut, cracked it open, and carefully peered outside. There was nothing but rapidly accumulating snow.

She later said that, though the voice was eerily like that of her brother, she had been able to determine he had been home at the time. She thinks her husband mimicked her brother's voice so that his ghostly form would not alarm or frighten his family—a final tender act of the man with whom she had shared life on the Minnesota frontier.

THE LATE MRS. RANDALL

"The husband . . . was not the first one to whom the spirit
of the departed lady made [an] appearance."
Cottonwood County Citizen, **February 16, 1894**

The town is Storden. County of Cottonwood. State of Minnesota.

Latitude 44 degrees, 41 minutes north. Longitude 95 degrees, 31 minutes west. Elevation 1,141 feet. Minneapolis lies 155 miles to the northeast. Closer is Sioux Falls, South Dakota, 103 miles away to the southwest.

The town is about one-quarter of a square mile. Minnesota highways 5 and 30 intersect in the middle of town. The population is approximately 258, with a median age of about 45 years. Most citizens are Caucasian and trace their families back to German, Norwegian, and Irish ancestors.

Platted July 8, 1907. Incorporated June 7, 1912. The town and the township, also Storden, honor Nels Storden, the first settler.

The Chicago, St. Paul, Minneapolis, and Omaha Railroad once stopped at the depot. Now the state highways take folks into and out of town.

In 1875, Ole Christopherson offered up his farm as the post office, and so he became the postmaster. Later, the post office moved into Copenhagen, a speck on the map next to Storden. The two communities grew into each other long ago.

The countryside around Storden is rural, agricultural, and reasonably flat; the scenery, as you would expect it. This is farm country after all. Distances from Storden to, well, anywhere else are sometimes measured in hours and not in miles.

Weather can be unforgiving. Winter blizzards are brutal on the western Minnesota prairie. Spring and summer bring severe storms. An F5 tornado, which has winds from 261 to 318 miles per hour, struck fifteen miles from Storden in 1998, killing one person and injuring nineteen.

Yet as out of the way as Storden may seem, it has much to recommend itself: remarkably low housing costs and property taxes, no traffic congestion, plenty of wide-open spaces, and lots of activities at the region's consolidated Red Rock Central School District.

And there is time to wonder about something else—a rather curious ghost story.

Not that this ghost is one any newcomer—or longtime resident—is likely to have heard about, unless they are dedicated local historians, for it occurred over a century ago. But it was significant enough news in the early 1890s to have made the pages of Windom's *Cottonwood County Citizen* right there alongside a notice for the Women's Christian Temperance Union's semiannual meeting, some tongue-in-cheek speculation on whether or not Charley Chadderdon was Republican, and an advertisement announcing the opening of the new F. Stedman and Company Drug Store and its line of confections, soaps, perfumes, toiletries, and medications.

But with the headline "A Ghost Story," the story of a specter strolling about Storden trumps the WCTU any day.

The recipient of the ghostly visit was one John S. Randall, a Storden farmer who lived with his family near the intersection of today's County Highway 21 and 180th Street. He was a man "not much given to superstition," according to the newspaper. But then the editor seems to hedge his assertion by adding that the event which Randall related to him and that was the subject of the story "proves that there are some things happening on earth that are, to say the least, hard to understand."

Whether or not a few brief appearances by a ghost in rural

Minnesota a century ago proves anything regarding the supernatural is doubtful, but this case does make for an interesting story and does raise a few intriguing questions about the methodology the ghost chose in making itself known.

The identity of the ghost is known as well—John Randall's wife, Adeline V. Randall, who died on December 13, 1893. The farmer's late wife was interred in the "usual way," all agreed, which included, of course, being placed in a casket and buried under six feet of earth. Where she was buried isn't known.

Apparently, that was not enough to keep the late Adeline Randall from calling upon her husband, children . . . and two other men. Indeed, John Randall was not the first person to whom his wife said hello again some two months later, in early 1894.

Adeline, or her ghost, actually, first showed up quite unexpectedly in front of a man not identified by the newspaper. Evidently, he was a close friend of the family, for she gave him a very clear, very specific message for her husband.

She said he was to visit John, indicate that she had returned from the grave, and then tell him not to worry about her, to be kind to their children, and that she was faring quite well in the "disembodied world."

Her request must have been fulfilled, for John Randall included the incident in his subsequent interview with the newspaper.

A short time later, the Randall children were paid a visit in their home by their dear departed mother. Only the older children recognized her for some reason. This time she did not speak but rather offered only a "look of affection like a reflection of her earthly smile," Randall said.

Next came a curious addition to Adeline Randall's postmortem excursion, a visit with one John L. Hamery, identified as a "schoolteacher now at Wilder," a village southeast of Storden near Windom. Wilder's claim to fame is that the well-known Breck School had its beginnings in that village as the Breck Mission and Farm School. The school thrived in the 1890s. Wilder also had a one-room public school; it isn't known at which school Hamery may have taught nor what his connection to the Randall family might have been.

In any event, when the vaporous Adeline Randall called upon John Hamery, she reiterated her earlier request that her husband waste no time on concern about her but "set his mind at rest on her account."

Just why Adeline should think her husband was worrying about her condition is puzzling.

Does John Randall himself figure into his late wife's earthly visits?

Seemingly so.

Adeline did ultimately stop by to see him, he told the newspaper, but he evidently declined to discuss what she said or when she visited him.

It must have been quite an experience. Randall was so "unnerved," he said, that he was "almost unable to recognize the semblance" of his departed wife.

The ghost of the late Mrs. Randall, if indeed that is what these people had interaction with, certainly made a circuitous route to iterate the same message: "Do not fear, husband of mine, for I am well and beyond earthly sorrows."

But why did she not choose to issue the message only once and directly to her husband? The relationships among Mrs. Randall, John Hamery, and the first anonymous man she greeted are not recorded. One reason may be that she knew her husband would not take a visit from his dead spouse with composure—and who could blame him—and thus wanted to spare him the shock of her murky form.

Of course, we will never know the answers to these questions and can only engage in lively speculation about the motivations of this long-ago specter.

John Randall continued to live on the farm until at least 1917 and remarried some time after Adeline's death. He died in Minneapolis in 1922 and is buried at the Windom cemetery.

Perhaps in the end, all we can do is agree with the editor of the *Cottonwood County Citizen* who writes that "the story [John Randall] tells is verging on the marvellous [sic]."

Indeed.

INCIDENT ON HIGHWAY 11

"The 'ghosts' are supposedly poor souls from the
real-life Cook family massacre."
Steph Corneliussen

The hour was nearing midnight, but John Cook was still awake, reading by lamplight in his favorite chair. His wife, Deantha, lingered nearby finishing some housework. Upstairs, their three children were fast asleep. The Cook family led an arduous life, eking out their subsistence on the 1872 western Minnesota frontier, yet they tried to retain some sense of civilized normalcy.

John Cook was a Civil War naval veteran who had later worked as a government agent on the White Earth Reservation and traded furs with the Ojibwe, which he still did on occasion. He had staked a land claim near the village of Oak Lake, in Becker County's Audubon Township. No doubt he hoped that prosperity would be forthcoming. The Northern Pacific Railroad had built an Oak Lake depot the year before.

On the claim he planted crops and erected a house for his family—his wife and three children, eight-year-old Freddie, seven-year-old Mary, and little John, not quite two.

This night—April 26, 1872—John Cook had reason to be relaxed. Earlier in the day, he had bought a hundred muskrat pelts from an Ojibwe friend. They were now piled in an upstairs corner. The money he would get from their sale would be much-needed cash in hand. Little Freddie Cook had gotten so excited by his dad's friend's visit and the new pile of soft furs that he ran to tell his aunt Nellie Small, Deantha Cook's sister, who lived less than a mile away.

Unfortunately, other more disreputable souls also heard the news.

Based on later investigations, including statements from an alleged perpetrator, sometime before midnight on April 26, John Cook was shot to death in his chair, perhaps by someone standing outside a lighted window. The killers broke down the door and fatally struck Mrs. Cook over the head with several hatchet blows. Minutes later, the murderers clubbed the three children to death as they slept.

The muskrat furs were stolen, and the house was set afire to cover up the killings.

Mrs. Nellie Small's son discovered the still-smoldering ruins the next morning when he went over to get some fresh milk. He ran home to tell his mother, who rushed to the grisly scene. She found a few charred timbers still standing and what appeared to be pieces of bone in the embers; other human remains had fallen into the cellar.

Other neighbors soon arrived. They found only scattered bits of the Cook family's remains—children's small teeth, gold fillings, a set of false teeth, and charred bones—barely enough to fill a small pot. Some clothing fragments seemed to contain blood stains. There were no clues about how the family was killed, in what manner the fire occurred, nor who was to blame.

On an early foggy morning on Becker County Highway 11 during the summer of 1989, Norman Reeser* left his cabin on Pelican Lake, in the far northwestern corner of Otter Tail County, on a drive to Audubon, about twenty miles to the north.

It was slow going past Pike's Bay, along Big and Little Cormorant lakes, and through tiny Lake Center. Because of the poor visibility, Reeser kept the speed under forty miles per hour. Sometime after passing Little Cormorant Lake, Reeser was hunched over the steering wheel trying to see past the front of his car when a woman and a young boy suddenly appeared at the side of the road, walking directly onto the highway in front of him. Neither one looked in his direction.

Reeser hit the brakes, waiting for the impact of metal against flesh. But somehow they just as quickly seemed to be in the opposite lane walking on through the fog and then into the woods. Mother and child didn't look back at the horrified driver. He couldn't understand how he avoided hitting them—even at the speed he was traveling, the few feet that separated his car from the two people was too short a distance to have avoided striking them.

Yet there might be a reason he didn't hit them. They may have been ghosts.

At least that's what he told a reporter about the incident.

Norman Reeser was thoroughly traumatized by the incident when he stopped at an Audubon café a few minutes later. Two local men overheard him telling the waitress about the near miss he had had on County 11. That wasn't a real woman with her real little boy, the men confided in Reeser, those were the ghosts of Deantha Cook and her son Freddie, murdered on their farmstead nearly 120 years earlier.

Reeser told reporter Steph Corneliussen that, even though he didn't believe in ghosts, he knew they could not possibly have gotten across the road unscathed. Then there was the oddity of their taking no notice of the car speeding toward them. There had to be some sort of explanation, but he couldn't come up with one.

The legend in that part of Becker County is that the Cook family ghosts are sometimes seen in the woods of Audubon Township. Could this have been one of those occasions? If victims of bloody crimes sometimes rest uneasily in their graves, then surely this is a circumstance when spirits might prowl the countryside.

The Cook massacre created a sensation in 1872 Minnesota. An Ojibwe man known as Kahkahbesha, often translated as Bobolink, was eventually charged with the Cooks' murders. Two days after the murders, he sold a hundred muskrat pelts to a trader and was observed wearing a navy coat, similar to the type worn by John Cook, a navy veteran. He had also sold a woman's cloak, a gold watch and chain, a pencil, and a navy revolver, again something John Cook was known to have possessed. Further, it was shown he had been camping nearby at the time of the murders.

Minnesota governor Horace Austin dispatched two men to arrest Bobolink, which they eventually accomplished, with some difficulty, at Sandy Lake on May 20, 1872. The lawmen questioned him. He admitted having the incriminating possessions but denied involvement in the killings. He changed his story several times, however, at one point taking responsibility for killing John Cook but saying that he had been forced into it. He claimed a man named Mascaabeoson had masterminded the murders.

On January 15, 1873, Bobolink went on trial in a Detroit Lakes courtroom set up in a room over a billiard hall. Three days later, in deliberations that took just ninety minutes, the jury found him guilty of first-degree murder and sentenced him to death by hanging. He never made it to the gallows. On May 20, he died of "quick consumption" in the Ramsey County jail. Some suspect the authorities speeded his demise. He was interred in a secret location.

Neighbors buried the Cook family's remains at their farm site a few months after their murders. A plaque erected in 1923 by the Grand Army of the Republic marks the site.

Little is left to mark the lives of John, Deantha, Freddie, Mary, and John Jr. except the story of their terrible departure from this world . . . and their occasional reemergence from another.

14

MISTRESS MOLLY

"I believe there is something. I think it's an unrested spirit."
Tim Olmsted

The attentive young waiter leaned over the elegantly laid table, writing down the couple's dinner order. It was Saturday evening at the historic Forepaugh's Restaurant. A couple of other tables were also occupied in the aptly named 1940s Room on the restaurant's second floor.

Abruptly, there was a sharp tap on his shoulder. Annoyed that the couple at the table behind him would be so impolite as to interrupt him midway through another order, he quickly turned around.

"Yes, may I help you?" he asked the couple seated behind him.

They looked up at him quizzically and shook their heads. No, they were fine, thank you.

"I'm sorry, I thought you were trying to get my attention," the waiter apologized, taken aback at the oddity of it all.

"Everything is fine," the diner assured him, still not sure what the waiter meant by his comment.

Over the years that waiter, Tim Olmsted, had heard all the legendary ghost stories associated with the elegant Forepaugh's Restaurant, a three-story Victorian mansion on Exchange Street, but the incident that night had a singular impact on him.

"That made me a believer," Olmsted says. "It wasn't a twitch or an itch in my shoulder. It was someone trying to get my attention. I thought how rude. . . . I wanted to say, 'Wait until I take this order.' The people at the table behind me looked at me like they didn't know what I was talking about."

No one was walking through the dining room at the time, nor could it realistically have been the couple at the table behind him—they not only denied doing it but, as Olmsted soon realized, could not possibly have had enough time to lay a hand on him and return to their seats.

He finished writing the order and left the dining room, knowing that he now had his own brief yet perplexing encounter with Forepaugh's other side.

The documented history of this St. Paul landmark is straightforward.

Built for $10,000 in 1870 by pioneer St. Paul businessman Joseph Lybrandt Forepaugh, the lavish mansion has presided gracefully over the Irvine Park neighborhood, through good times and bad, for nearly a century and a half. In the 1870s a carriage house and barn were added, and the living space for the family, which included Joseph's wife, Mary, and two young daughters, was significantly expanded. Coupled with spacious grounds and picturesque gardens, the Forepaugh's refined home befitted the city's leading dry goods entrepreneur. Across the street his neighbor was Minnesota's first territorial governor, Alexander Ramsey.

Yet the history of the Forepaugh family itself is not a happy one.

By 1886, Joseph Forepaugh seemed to have begun exhibiting traces of severe depression, what his obituary just six years later would term "melancholia." He was "possessed of the idea that his financial affairs were going wrong." The newspaper added, however, that there didn't appear to be any legitimacy to his fears.

Nevertheless, he retired from his dry goods business to look after his real-estate holdings and investments, sold the mansion on Exchange Street and all its possessions rather than place them in storage, and took his family on an extended trip to Europe. The house was then purchased by General John Henry Hammond, who had served as chief of staff for General William Tecumseh Sherman. The Forepaugh family would never again live there.

The Forepaughs did return to St. Paul in 1889 and built a stately brick mansion at 302 Summit Avenue. From their new home on a bluff overlooking the city, the family could see their original Irvine Park address.

Less than three years later, however, Joseph Forepaugh's inner demons apparently won out. He took his own life, as recounted in his July 10, 1892, newspaper obituary:

> The dead body of Joseph L. Forepaugh, a wealthy and respected citizen of St. Paul was found at 11:15 yesterday morning lying beside a pond in the vicinity of the Selby Avenue bridge over the Milwaukee railroad tracks. A bullet wound in the head and the revolver still clasped in the dead man's hand clearly indicated suicide.

Forepaugh's depression had become so severe shortly before his death that his family had persuaded him again to leave his business interests and take a long rest on the Atlantic coastline. He never made the trip. The newspaper estimates his wealth at the time of his death at a half-million dollars—including real estate in the Seven Corners neighborhood, the house on Summit Avenue, a block of real estate on Fourth Street, and other smaller St. Paul holdings.

The original Forepaugh home on Exchange Street fell on hard times as the Irvine Park neighborhood declined during the ensuing decades. In the twentieth century, it was divided into apartments before being closed by the Housing and Redevelopment Authority.

A business group bought the mansion and after a million dollar restoration opened it in 1976 as an elegant eatery specializing in French cuisine. Through several changes of ownership, Forepaugh's has remained a prominent St. Paul restaurant. New owners in 2008 completed a grand refurbishing of the décor in the nine dining rooms. Period wallpaper, freshly painted ceilings, refurbished chandeliers, new carpeting, and burnished wooden floors give Forepaugh's a lighter, airier atmosphere. A main bar was expanded, and formerly closed-off doorways were reopened. The menu is now termed New American cuisine. A wine cellar has been expanded to feature a wider selection of wines.

Although the history of Forepaugh's is straightforward, the legends surrounding the place are something else again, especially since they don't always square with its known past.

And the legendary side of Forepaugh's is where its ghosts dwell.

Yes, Joseph Forepaugh and his family lived in the mansion for less than two decades; yes, he sold all of his possessions and moved away with his family for several years; yes, he later built a Summit Avenue mansion; and yes, saddest of all, he killed himself in the summer of 1892.

But the *reason* he sold the Exchange Street mansion and then took his own life a few years later is where documented history and legend diverge. According to the legend, Joseph Forepaugh had a mistress, a household maid named Molly, who lived with the Forepaugh family's other household staff in a third-floor servants' quarters. She committed suicide, the story goes, although the details of both her life and her death are obscure at best.

One version places her death in the early 1870s, while the Forepaughs still lived in the Exchange Street mansion. She tried unsuccessfully to hang herself from a chandelier in her third-floor quarters, and when the rope proved to be too long, she threw herself out the window, neatly completing the task. The reason for her suicide was her unrequited love for Joseph Forepaugh.

Another version of her suicide holds, however, that she died after Joseph Forepaugh shot himself in 1892, distraught over his death. If that is the case, the mystery is what became of Molly during that six-year gap between his taking leave of the Exchange Street address and his ultimate fate. If she died at the original mansion, then she apparently stayed with the new owners.

In truth, it is nearly impossible to verify details of the mysterious Molly's life, if indeed she existed at all; not even her last name has been hinted at. The indefinite doesn't seem to diminish either the quality or the quantity of ghostly activity reported over the past decades, however.

It is Molly's ghost—and perhaps that of old Joseph himself—that reputedly haunts Forepaugh's, particularly in the Sibley Room, carved out of the old servants' quarters on the third floor. The chandelier from which she tried to hang herself is said to be the one directly over one of the dining tables, in an alcove with windows offering a stunning view of the St. Paul skyline.

As a part-time Forepaugh's waiter for well over a decade, Tim Olmsted finds that he fields questions about the haunted side of Forepaugh's almost every night, even though the owners over the years have often turned down requests for interviews, séances, or exorcisms.

"This is a restaurant," they'll advise prospective ghost busters. Yet they've been known to allow customers to continue with informal attempts to contact the beyond if they're quiet about it and remain at their tables.

But in Tim Olmsted, an elementary teacher for the St. Paul school system, inquisitive customers will find someone who willingly shares the ghost stories . . . even details of his own discourteous tap on the shoulder.

"I believe there is something. I think it's an unrested spirit, that's what I believe," Olmsted says. "People will ask me if I believe in ghosts. No, I don't believe in ghosts, but I believe there are spirits—that there has to be something after this life. Understanding science, physics, energy . . . after a body [dies], the energy has to go somewhere. If science is right, then energy is continual. Imagine how much energy we carry. It has to go somewhere, so if it doesn't have anywhere to go, maybe it stays. We won't know until we pass away, but something has to happen."

Even years before the incident in the 1940s Room, however, Olmsted learned that Forepaugh's reputation for being haunted may have preceded its days as a restaurant.

Olmsted was teaching sixth grade in St. Paul and serving at Forepaugh's on weekends when he was invited to one of his student's homes for dinner. He gladly accepted.

The student's mother asked if it was true that he worked at Forepaugh's.

"Yes, I do," replied Olmsted.

"Well, do you know the place is haunted?" she asked.

"Oh, yes, that's an old story," Olmsted said casually. "We all know that. We don't call it haunted though. We say there are un-settled spirits."

"Well, my grandparents used to live in that house, and crazy things happened when they were there."

She explained that her grandparents had lived there after it had been subdivided into apartments. She told Olmsted that her grand-mother was once in the living room reading when the rocking chair she was in levitated and then dropped back to the floor. She was unhurt.

On another occasion the woman's grandfather said a long-dead army buddy showed up at the front door . . . in full military uni-form.

But Olmsted does not need to go back that far to recount his own personal knowledge of the place's haunted side.

Two regular customers—he calls them Jackie and Adolph—abandoned their favorite table on the restaurant's third floor after one strange night, he says.

"They always sat on the third floor, in [the Sibley Room]. They made jokes about the ghosts and what was going on. One particular night, it got freezing cold at the table they were sitting at. They said it just turned frigid and then went back to a normal temperature. They will not have dinner on the third floor anymore."

The couple described it as a sudden, deep, and numbing cold that lasted only a short time.

Then there was the problem of the wax candles.

At one time Forepaugh's used old-fashioned wax candles in the dining rooms and as a part of each table's centerpiece. At the end of each evening shift, waitstaff would extinguish the candles. The maître d' made his own rounds to confirm the candles were out. Olmsted says that on at least one occasion when all the staff had left and the maître d' was getting in his own car to leave he noticed a candle left alight in a third-floor window. He unlocked the building, went back upstairs, and blew it out. But when he got back into his car a few minutes later, the candle was again relit.

Olmsted says weird teasing wasn't unusual.

"There have been times when glasses . . . have shattered. Or the staff comes in the next day and finds the chairs are tipped upside down. All the tables, silver, china, everything is all strewn about."

One of the more well-known stories at Forepaugh's involves a nearly twenty-year-old photograph nicknamed the Ghost Bride, though the ghost and the bride are two separate entities.

In the photograph, a smiling bride and groom—Michelle and Robert—pose for a wedding day picture in a second-floor hallway.

The groom is on the left; his reflection seems to be visible in a mirror hanging on the wall, although the reflection is oddly angled. The bride, in a vintage 1940s ivory silk wedding gown with a Dior shawl collar, is to his left. They are standing in front of a lace-curtained window near a short flight of steps leading to a separate dining room.

But what startles those who see the picture is that behind the bride, and to her left, is an extended, disembodied arm clad in a tight, white sleeve that seems to be reaching out to her from the staircase. The arm's fingers are close to the bride's left arm, but the rest of the hand is hidden by the lace curtain. Only the arm from the elbow down to the wrist is visible—the upper arm and body are hidden by the stairwell's near wall.

And most bizarre of all, a portion of the arm appears to be *behind* the lace curtain. Yet that lace curtain is flat against the wall!

Whether the arm belongs to a man or to a woman, ghost or guest, is open to conjecture. Michelle, the bride in the photograph, says no one was standing next to her. Indeed, part of the arm does seem transparent. Some think it is Molly's ghostly arm. Others believe it is a man wearing a long-sleeve white dress shirt. Joseph Forepaugh?

Michelle and Robert were married outdoors on April 9, 1989, in Irvine Park, a "freezing cold" day, Michelle remembers. The wedding reception was at Forepaugh's.

The photograph was taken by her future sister-in-law, one of several photographers at the wedding. She was surprised when the photo showed up at Forepaugh's without her knowledge some time later.

"It's real," she says of the photograph, the original of which she owns. "It's definitely not a fake. We didn't see anyone else around us when the photo was taken."

She points out that no one in the wedding party except her was wearing something with long, white sleeves, as the arm in the photo seems to have on. The photographer didn't notice anything out of place until after the wedding photos were developed, Michelle notes, and neither did the newlyweds.

As to the arm's owner, Michelle does not think it's Molly. She believes the arm belongs to Joseph Forepaugh.

The partially visible hand is too large to be that of a woman, she thinks, and the sleeve is that of a man's white dress shirt. But others point out that a hearty nineteenth-century maid often wore starched white blouses and that her daily toil might have produced a pair of strong, sturdy hands.

Michelle has grown used to being called the Ghost Bride when people recognize her or when she stops by Forepaugh's to greet someone who has asked about her. But she did not want her last name used in this story. A copy of the photograph has been kept behind the Forepaugh's bar for those who are curious.

Waiter Tim Olmsted says there was a second photograph at one time, a Polaroid snapshot taken in the same second-floor dining room where Olmsted felt the tap on his shoulder. He says it appears to show a fogged mirror with a profanity written on it—either "fuck" or "shit," according to Olmsted, who says he saw the photo before it was stolen some time ago.

"If you turn the picture upside down, there is a silhouette of Mr. Forepaugh that's like the one hanging in the bar downstairs above the fireplace," he says. "Also in the right-hand corner there is an image of a lady that we believe is Molly."

Many of the ghost tales at Forepaugh's reach back more than thirty years, to its earliest days as a restaurant. Even then, guests reported eerie feelings in the Sibley Room, as if someone they could not see was watching them. That sentiment is not confined to the third floor—Michelle, the Ghost Bride, would not use the women's restroom on the second floor. She had the sensation there was someone else in the small room.

Other stories involve employees who have suddenly confronted a creepy situation.

A young waitress and two fellow employees were leaving after their night shift to attend a party for one of the bartenders. She'd inadvertently left a present for him locked in a storage closet under the first-floor staircase and excused herself to get it. She slipped her key into the closet lock when three loud knocks came from inside, rappings so strong they rattled the door. Her screams brought an assistant manager running. He unlocked the door. No one was inside.

"I've been screaming ever since," the waitress told reporter Sandra Peddie at the time of the incident. "It really was a frightening experience. I still wish it wouldn't have happened."

Another waitress who'd started working at Forepaugh's when it opened in 1976 but who remained skeptical of its haunted reputation told Peddie even an informal séance with a chilly ending didn't change her mind.

The séance was in the Sibley Room on the third floor. A group held hands around a large table. The ventilation systems were turned off; the windows were tightly closed. The minutes ticked by. Still nothing. Then a sudden gust of wind blew through the room, causing the table candles to flicker. A cold spot so intense that it caused one person to shiver and another to see her breath moved about the room before dissipating.

The group decided to take an interlude. Once reassembled at the table, they all noticed a strong, musty odor hanging in the air.

Waitress Susan Palmer said that a busboy setting tables in the Sibley Room returned to the downstairs kitchen for more supplies. He'd partially finished the setting. When he returned to the third floor, the silverware and dishes he had set out were gone, carefully put back into the pantry. He'd been working alone. A hostess turning on the lights up there saw the fleeting shadow of a man.

A carpet layer doing some work in June 1982 felt someone place a hand on his shoulder.

An early morning baker took a bathroom break. As she passed a door leading to the basement, she had noted it was closed. When she returned a few minutes later, the door was open. Suddenly, a white, wispy fog floated from one side of the doorway to the other.

Wine steward Bradley Conley says that on a late Wednesday night in the summer of 2008 he watched as a small, glowing yellow orb rose from behind the polished bar, paused for a few seconds, and then floated down around a bar stool and vanished.

In the summer of 1981, waitstaff heard a woman singing from the third floor when no one was up there. A waitress says neither she nor the other staff recognized the song. That summer was especially active because many of the staff heard the faint voice of a woman. Most assumed both incidents involved Molly. The strong aroma of violet perfume may also hint at her approach—legend has it that it was her favorite scent.

Despite what one may think, the stories about ghosts of Forepaugh's don't seem to have adversely affected staff over the years. One waitress says she and others thought the building had a "happy ghost," a puzzling compliment considering Joseph and Molly's grisly demises.

Has Tim Olmsted ever been nervous working there, even if the ghosts are a pleasant lot?

"No," he says but then adds, "Sometimes I have worried about 'meeting' someone on the steps when I have to turn off the lights or if someone forgets to turn off the air conditioning on the third floor."

Yet Olmsted never takes precautions about meeting someone on the staircase if he's working late, such as calling out to anything lurking unseen on the floors above.

But he has a practical reason for *not* talking to the ghosts.

"I wouldn't be working there anymore if I did!"

15

BULLETS CAN'T KILL THEM

"It's not fun to be in here alone at night.
I always think there's someone behind me."

Donna Bremer

The four nattily dressed gangsters weren't about to leave, not in the middle of a poker game. It didn't matter that it was well past midnight or that nearly everyone else had long ago stumbled home after a night in St. Paul's swanky Castle Royal nightclub, a city hotspot fashioned out of manmade caverns along the Mississippi River. There was no such thing as closing hours back in 1934, so if a few of the city's mobsters wanted to hang around till dawn, well, so be it. The lone employee left to clean up and lock the doors sure wasn't about to ask them to clear out.

So she waited in another room, out of sight down a narrow passageway, being very careful not to call attention to herself while this sinister quartet—at least a couple of them had Tommy guns propped against their chairs—finished their game. They were hunched around a table next to the fireplace, their suit coats neatly folded over the chair backs.

She'd heard them arguing and laughing for some time when suddenly the tenor of their voices changed. Louder, angrier they were. One of the men was screaming at another.

She crept down the passageway and peeked around the corner.

What she saw next nearly caused her to faint.

One of the men grabbed up his submachine gun and, in a quick burst of fire, ripped apart his three companions as if they were so much tissue paper. Blood splashed across the white linen tablecloths and splattered against the stucco walls. Chairs and tables tumbled to the floor as the victims were thrown backward, littering blood-stained cards and broken beer glasses across the hard terrazzo floor.

The frightened young woman shoved her fist into her mouth to stifle a scream and fled back down the passageway. She got to the nightclub office, picked up a telephone, and quickly dialed the police.

In a hoarse whisper she told the dispatcher what she had just seen at the Castle Royal. Then she ran out the front entry and waited for the police. And waited.

The cops were slow to arrive—not all that unusual in 1930s St. Paul—and when they did, they told her to wait where she was and they'd go in. She was happy to oblige. She hadn't seen anyone leave. Since there was no back entrance to the cave complex, the murderer was surely still inside.

The minutes stretched on. What was taking them so long? The restaurant wasn't that large. The place would be a mess; the killer, easy to corner.

Eventually, the cops came back out but with no one in handcuffs. She was taken back inside, down to the scene of the horrific shooting.

When she got there, she couldn't believe her eyes.

All was perfectly normal. No bodies. No blood. Every chair in place, each table upright, spread with fresh white linen tablecloths. The place was spotless.

The poor woman didn't know what to say. The cops did. They warned her that if she ever called in another false homicide, she'd be the one arrested and suggested that maybe she'd just fallen asleep and dreamed up the whole thing. Yeah, lady, that musta' been what happened, you got it?

She almost bought their story, nearly thinking that the whole episode had been sort of a bad dream, but as she turned to leave, her eye caught the one thing that told her the cops were lying—fresh bullet holes pockmarked the front of the fireplace.

That's the legend anyway, the infamous Castle Royal's contribution to the lore of St. Paul's wide-open gangster-welcoming era of the 1920s and 1930s.

But for those who work in or visit what are today the Wabasha Street Caves, that bloody massacre alleged to have taken place seventy-five years ago has an added, immediate significance.

"We think those murders may be the start of our hauntings."

The words are those of Cynthia Schreiner Smith, the chief tour guide and unofficial Wabasha Caves historian. Smith and the caves' owners, Steve and Donna Bremer, have pieced together the story through the accounts of people who worked at Castle Royal during its heyday and of individuals such as Bill Lehman Jr., whose parents built the nightclub.

Everything Smith and Donna Bremer have heard is enough to convince them that the murders took place, even though the identities of the perpetrator and the victims remain unknown and no bodies were ever found.

They point out that several bullet holes remain in the mantelpiece.

There's also the understandable link between such a cold-blooded killing and repeated encounters with nasty-looking ghosts in pinstriped suits . . . a primping dandy in the men's room . . . faint big band melodies accompanied by clinking glasses . . . and muffled voices coming from cold, dark corners.

If there are locations ripe for ghosts to gather, then this St. Paul landmark is one of them.

Cynthia Smith thinks there's a ready explanation for why no bodies were found and the crime scene was scrubbed. The St. Paul police were in on the cover-up and helped the gunman clean up the mess.

"Our best guess is that the bodies were dragged back to one of the unfinished caves where a hasty grave was dug in the soft sandstone floor. And that's probably where they remain to this day,"

Smith says. A cement floor was laid over the sandstone several decades later.

Adds Donna Bremer, "We've had people come in who swear they're buried in the back caves; cave five comes up frequently with ghost hunters and psychics."

Others speculate that the bodies were dragged to the nearby Mississippi River and dumped in.

"Back in the day, that's how they disposed of bodies," Smith adds.

In 1934, St. Paul was nearing the end of the so-called O'Connor system, named after the corrupt chief of police, John J. O'Connor. Gangsters roamed St. Paul unmolested as long as they kept their noses clean within city limits. Killers, kidnappers, and bank robbers like John Dillinger, Baby Face Nelson, Machine Gun Kelly, and even the Ma Barker gang called St. Paul home and included places like the Castle Royal nightclub among their hangouts, where they'd openly mingle with St. Paul's finest.

"The Castle Royal was a very expensive restaurant, very classy. A meal cost a dollar. With inflation that'd be about $100 today," notes Cynthia Smith. Part of the draw was the top-flight entertainment playing on the Castle Royal's bandstand, national bandleaders such as Tommy Dorsey, Glen Miller, Cab Calloway, and Harry James, among others. It was a "volatile mix," says Smith. "Eventually, you're going to have something happen."

The colorful history of the Wabasha Caves actually dates to the mid-nineteenth century, when they were carved out of the river bluffs to extract minerals. This particular complex has seven caverns that parallel each other and extend back about two hundred feet from the entrances.

By the turn of the twentieth century, French owners were using the caves for mushroom farming. The humid air and stable fifty-two-degree temperature mirrored successful mushroom growing in caverns beneath the streets of Paris.

When Bill Lehman and his wife took over ownership of the mushroom farm in 1915, friends encouraged them to open a restaurant where they could serve their fresh mushrooms. There is strong indication that the Lehmans operated a speakeasy during the 1920s. It wasn't until 1933, however, that the couple opened what an opening night advertisement says was "the world's most gorgeous underground nite club . . . featuring Juan King and his Castle Royal Orchestra."

Photographs from the era show a faux medieval stone façade with spires, parapets, and narrow, vertical windows. Portions of that façade remain. Inside, the three finished cylindrical caverns had curved stucco ceilings ending at intricately detailed wall brickwork, European-style hanging tapestries, Italian crystal chandeliers, and oriental rugs on the terrazzo floors. Diners ate at elegant tables decked out with white linen tablecloths and fine silverware.

The Castle Royal closed on the eve of World War II. In later years the caves were again used for mushroom growing and cheese storage. That's when a cement floor was added, perhaps hiding the gangsters' corpses forever.

Over the years the Castle Royal 2 Restaurant, a 1970s disco, and a teen nightclub all were tried there but without success.

The city of St. Paul was ready to fill in the caverns and board up the entrances when Steve and Donna Bremer bought the complex in 1992. The couple owns a construction company, which also has offices there. They've operated it as an entertainment, theatrical, and special events venue since that time.

"When people ask me if I'm afraid of our ghosts I say no, they're just having a party," Cynthia Smith explains lightly, even though three of the ghosts may be those machine-gunned gangsters.

She thinks the Wabasha Caves' ghosts are there because they don't know they're dead and therefore continue their revelry as if it's still 1935. The restaurant portion of the cavern looks much as it did in that era.

A psychic has said that at least three ghosts inhabit the caves; two of them like to sit at the sixty-foot polished bar in the cavern room next to the restaurant. That same psychic said she sensed that in a far back cave, number five, a Swedish girl had been raped.

Before the Bremers bought the caves, there were several years when the caves were boarded up. Transients and teens often broke in to sleep or hold parties.

The sexual assault the psychic alluded to might explain why people are sometimes uncomfortable standing in the entry way to cave five.

Says Smith, "They feel that someone doesn't want them there. We hear that from people on tours or people when they start working here. They'll say that right by the door there's someone who doesn't want them here. I sometimes feel it too."

The earliest reported ghost encounter was in the late 1970s when the caverns operated as Castle Royal 2. A waiter asked the owner if he had hired an actor to portray a gangster-era tough. No, said his boss. Well, replied the waiter, he'd just seen someone dressed in a pinstriped suit and straw boater in a back cavern. He'd even seemed to walk through a wall!

Donna Bremer says it wasn't long after they bought the business that the caves haunted legacy came to their attention.

"I like to joke that it wasn't on the seller's disclosure that the place was haunted," she says. "People stopped by all the time and asked if we'd seen any ghosts yet. No, I had to tell them. They'd say, oh this place is haunted all right!"

It wasn't long before Donna Bremer understood just what those visitors were talking about.

She heard voices coming from deeper within the caverns on a day when she and her two children were in the caverns cleaning out debris.

"Two men were talking. I thought it was my husband and the supervisor working [someplace in back]. We kept calling out, 'Steve, Steve, where are you?' but they weren't answering."

Donna was fearful that someone had broken in. She put her two children in the office, locked the door, and waited. About twenty minutes later Donna's husband and a construction supervisor pulled up outside.

They had just returned from lunch.

Donna told her husband that at least two men must be somewhere back in the caverns because she'd heard them talking. Steve didn't find anyone. He thought maybe she was hearing things.

"I told him the kids had heard the voices, too. They thought it was their dad. After that I became a little more aware that there could be things happening, but I'm certainly not into spirituality or anything like that."

Donna says an incident involving her son while the caves were still being remodeled persuaded her that more than an occasional voice might disturb the caves natural quiet. The twelve year old had accompanied his parents to work. While they were in the office, he bounced a tennis ball against the cave walls. That's what he was doing when he missed a bounce-back and the ball rolled near the open door to the men's room. As he retrieved the ball, he glanced inside. Standing at the sink with his back to the door was a man wearing a suit and fedora. He was looking into the mirror straightening his tie.

In an instant he had vanished.

"He came upstairs to the office and sat down, white as a sheet," Donna remembers. "I thought he might be getting the flu because he didn't look well."

The boy looked at his mom and said he'd just seen a ghost.

Startled by the boy's appearance and his statement, Donna tried to lighten things up by asking if he'd gotten the ghost's name.

Donna says he looked back at her and insisted he wasn't kidding . . . there had been a ghost standing at the men's room mirror.

The men's room area seems to be a center of ghostly activity. A deejay from the 1970s Castle Royal 2 told Cynthia Smith that he was in the bathroom washing his hands when he looked up to see a man in a pinstriped suit straightening his tie. The two nodded at each other. When the deejay finished washing his hands and looked back up to speak to the stranger, he'd vanished.

Same man? Seems reasonable to assume.

Smith shakes her head at both incidents.

"Can you imagine spending an eternity in the men's room washing your hands and straightening your tie?"

Donna Bremer says it's odd that there would be ghost sightings in that particular restroom. The Bremers built it in the 1990s. Before that it had been a doorway between what is today the dining room and the bar. The Castle Royal's original bar was in another room.

"For some reason [the ghosts] are drawn to that area; that alcove seems popular."

Cynthia Smith says one particular episode involving her husband, Bick Smith, who sometimes works there, and their daughter perplexes her.

They had all arrived on a Sunday to prepare for a group cave tour. Cynthia stopped in the office to check for telephone messages while her husband and daughter went on in to turn on the lights and set up for the tour.

One of their assignments was to unlatch the hooks that kept the restroom doors open, for better air circulation. They unlatched the men's room door; it floated shut. The pair went on into the fireplace room to switch on the lights. On their way back they found the men's room door latched open.

Cynthia says, "They came into the office and asked me if I'd opened the door again. I'd been on the phone! That was a very weird physical manifestation."

Another visitor once claimed he heard big band music as he stood in the alcove near the men's room, and once the same man saw a tuxedoed busboy emerge from a wall, check several table settings, and then vanish.

Cavern tours are usually given by actors costumed as gangsters. If the ghostly gangsters look the same, how does one tell them apart?

An actor portraying Baby Face Nelson circulated at one wedding reception to provide color and give mini-tours of the caves. A little boy who had been the ring bearer at the wedding ceremony took a particular shine to the actor and followed him around all afternoon.

About a month later the child's mother sent several photographs to Cynthia Smith. One pictured the boy next to a white mist. The mother wrote to Smith that she had showed her son the photo and asked him if he remembered the wedding and what fun he'd had with the gangster.

Oh yes, the child replied, he had fun with *both* of them . . . and then he pointed to the mist. The actor portraying Nelson was the only character gangster hired that day. Smith wonders what he had seen in that mist.

Several of the back caves are still filled with debris and old mushroom-growing tables. A couple of the caves are used only on ghost and gangster tours. In those, Smith sets up large historic photographs on easels. She has a superstition that if she hums songs from the big band era, the ghosts won't bother her. Before one tour she forgot to sing as she set up in cave six. When her tour got to that cave, she found one photograph turned upside down and backward.

"There's no way I got it wrong," she says. "The ghosts were letting me know they wanted to be sung to!"

She's heard faint big band music, glasses tinkling, and silverware dropped on plates. Her husband heard a clock chiming. There is no clock that chimes in the Wabasha Caves.

On another occasion Cynthia Smith was in a meeting with several other employees. As they sat along the bar, sipping root beers, she kept hold of her keys. She had a fear of losing them in the dimly lit cave rooms.

"It was getting close to the time to leave, so I put my keys down on the bar, looked at my wristwatch, and then back down to where I'd put my keys. They weren't there."

The group searched for nearly a half hour before discovering them under the bar, several feet away from where she had been sitting.

Then there are those incidents that Smith blames on a ghost she calls the grabber, perhaps one of the bar ghosts.

In one particular area Smith has felt someone grab the calf of her leg or her ankle. A couple of times it's been so tight that she's had to wrench her leg free. She says it's never been "malicious" or exceptionally hard but "just hard enough to let me know he's here."

Donna Bremer and Cynthia Smith are the first to acknowledge that it's not hard to let one's imagination run away in a place like the Wabasha Caves.

"It's a cave . . . it's echoey, not everything is a ghost, but there are a few things I can't explain," Smith says. It's those little unexplained incidents that can be the most troublesome. They tend to gnaw at you, never fully allowing you to accept or dismiss what you've seen or heard.

Those occasions on which the inexplicable takes place have seemed to become more infrequent.

"As the years have gone by, it seems to occur less and less," Smith says. "Whether it's because we're getting comfortable with them or if, one by one, they're moving on, I don't know."

Perhaps one day, the ghosts will let her know.

16

NIGHT CLERK

*"I know what the feeling is when people say
the hair stands up on the back of your neck."*
Kelley Freese, Palmer House Hotel

The job seemed perfect for the elementary schoolteacher looking to supplement her income over the summer. New owners at Sauk Centre's famed Palmer House Hotel needed a night clerk, and Jeanne Bellefeuille thought it sounded like a nice break from the classroom, something not too stressful—vacuuming, light dusting and cleaning, making sure clean silverware was set out in the dining room for the breakfast crowd, taking care of any late arrivals or guests needing assistance, and, mostly, just staying awake from midnight to 7 AM. The four-nights-a-week schedule was as much as she wanted with her children in various summer activities.

"Occasionally, we'd get people who were checked in and needed to get in their room, but for the most part I watched a lot of television and rolled a lot of silverware," Bellefeuille says of her temporary job. "I was great at the game show channel!"

Rarely did the hotel get any postmidnight customers looking for a room, so Bellefeuille's routine didn't alter too much from night to night.

She'd arrive just before midnight, and if the hotel's pub was empty, the barman cleaned up and left. On other nights, if there were customers, the bar might stay open until one or two in the morning.

Once the barman left, Bellefeuille made certain the hotel's doors were locked securely.

"I'm kind of a wuss," Bellefeuille admits.

She didn't want strangers walking in unannounced.

She'd get to the carpets right away, clean the lobby bathrooms, and then start rolling the hotel dining room's silverware into linen napkins while she watched television. The dusting waited until last, after dawn the following morning, because the sunlight helped identify any places she might have missed. The cook came on duty about then, and Bellefeuille left for home when the other staff arrived.

Though she didn't savor being alone all those hours, she knew the relatively anxiety-free job was temporary, something to do until she returned to Sauk Centre's Holy Family parochial school in August, where she was a veteran teacher. As long as she got her work done over the seven hours she was there, Bellefeuille's foremost task was to stand watch over the vintage hotel during the nighttime hours.

But standing watch came to include more than she ever anticipated because little by little Jeanne Bellefeuille grew to wonder if she ever in fact stood that watch *alone.*

The first indications that all was not right occurred very early on with a bitter cold that would sweep through the lobby, usually between three and four in the morning, even though 2002 was an especially hot summer.

"I could practically see my breath," Bellefeuille recalls of that chilly dip in the temperature.

Because of the hot weather, she typically wore shorts and a T-shirt to work during her first days on the job. But that wasn't nearly enough to keep her warm.

"I would grab the crocheted throws [in the lobby] and cover up in those and shiver anywhere from fifteen minutes to half an hour. Then it was fine, and I'd fold them up and put them back. But it would get icy, uncomfortably, unbearably cold."

After the third or fourth night, she brought more clothes, snuggled under the blankets, and got through it.

Then it was a lobby table lamp and a water faucet. Situated near a set of wide French doors in the lobby, the lamp clicked on nearly every morning and stayed lit for fifteen minutes or so before going off.

At about the same time on some mornings, a water faucet would put on something of a display.

"All of a sudden I heard water running, and I'd look in and say, 'Oh, there's really no one around . . . okayyy.'"

Bellefeuille attributed the erratic lamp to a short in the wiring or some other mechanical malfunction, despite the hotel's 1993 updating of its electrical system. But then in early August, after the lamp had gone on for its customary fifteen minutes before going off again, it blinked on again an hour later.

"That freaked me out," Bellefeuille says. "It had never gone on twice in one night before. I finally unplugged it and made a mental note that if it went on again, I was out of there."

The "series of coincidences," as Bellefeuille termed them, kept coming. Next it was the gas fireplace in the hotel's pub—she found it blazing away shortly after dawn one morning. The temperature outdoors was already near eighty degrees.

"I thought, oh, they could save money on energy bills if they'd just turn this fireplace off. I don't know how long it had been on because I was in the lobby [most of the night]."

She was reluctant to fiddle with the gas unit, so she dusted, wiped the windows, and left. That night she told hotel co-owner Kelley Freese that the fireplace thermostat may have malfunctioned because it had come on the previous night. Freese stared at her. She said that was impossible—it had been disconnected for the summer.

"Those little things I just thought of as unexplainable. I was never, ever frightened. I wasn't scared to come to work. It was, 'Well, okay, there's that light coming on again.' Then after it would [not come on] for weeks at a time, I'd think it was done. But then the light would go on again. That's why it was unsettling when it went on twice that one night because that had never happened to me before."

The parochial schoolteacher also drew upon her faith when dealing with these perplexing episodes.

"I'd guess in the midst of all this I'd say maybe a rosary a night!"

It all kept adding up. Moving silverware, for instance. That started early on when Bellefeuille organized her tasks so that she'd wrap and set out the silverware immediately after she finished vacuuming the dining room.

"I wanted to be finished . . . so I could shut the doors and be done," she says.

The procedure was to be straightforward: she wrapped the silverware in the starched linen napkins, set out and straightened each setting, organized the chairs at each table, and locked the room.

But it didn't always work out that way.

"A lot of times when I got to the door, I'd turn around and see a table where all the silverware had been turned around. I'm thinking, 'For crying out loud.' For the first few days I probably straightened silverware three or four times a night. I finally decided I'd wait and [wrap silverware] in the mornings . . . right before the cook came. I didn't want him to think I wasn't doing it. It was undoing itself! I just thought well, okay, the floor is uneven or something; that's just the way things are. I had to rationalize it! . . . It never occurred to me that there was a ghost, just a series of coincidences."

The night came, however, when an incident took place that could not be attributed to incongruous cold drafts, faulty wiring, crooked floors, or any other sort of quirky fluke.

That night Jeanne Bellefeuille may have met a ghost in the Palmer House Hotel.

It was about twenty minutes past midnight. The bartender and bar patrons had gone. The doors were locked. Bellefeuille pushed her vacuum cleaner through the pub's wide double doors but quickly drew back. A lone young man was inside, lounging near a table. He was nice looking, somewhere in his twenties, wearing jeans and a plain T-shirt. He wore a baseball-style cap.

He smiled at her.

"Can I still get a beer?"

Since 1901, Sauk Centre's Palmer House Hotel has anchored the downtown business district in that thriving central Minnesota community. Built by Ralph and Christena Palmer on the site of the earlier Sauk Centre House, the sturdy brick hotel on the corner of Main Street and Sinclair Lewis Avenue retains much of its turn-of-the-century architectural style and atmosphere. The spacious lobby's pressed-tin ceiling remains, as do the slender hanging brass ceiling lights. With old-fashioned lamps and large glass transoms above the gently arched windows allowing in enough illumination, the lobby atmosphere immediately suggests an earlier era. Polished wood tables, high-backed armchairs, and comfortable sofas allow for quiet conversations.

Copies of Nobel Prize–winning native son Sinclair Lewis's novels and other mementos of his life occupy several display cases. The Palmer House Hotel is the fictitious Minniemashie House in Lewis's seminal *Main Street* and is the American House in *Work of Art*, his novel about hotel keeping. Although set at a hotel in Connecticut, this latter novel draws from Lewis's experiences as a five-dollar-a-week substitute night clerk at the hotel for two weeks in the summer of 1902. He was a generally ineffectual employee who disdained the traveling salesmen atmosphere in the hotel, though he enjoyed the company of the Palmers' two children, Hazel and Carlisle. He would spin long stories to them during his twelve-hour night shift. A portion of his meager wage was withheld to pay for several items he broke, part of his "predictable and endearing incompetence," one biographer notes. During his Palmer House interlude, Lewis lived in one of the sleeping rooms.

After the Palmers sold the hotel, a series of owners managed to keep it open through the decades as lodgings for travelers arriving by train and later for salesmen needing a place to stay while calling on downtown customers. The building was extensively remodeled in the early 1990s, but declining business fortunes had forced it to close by 2002. In that year Brett and Kelley Freese bought it with two other local couples. The Freeses are now sole proprietors, the fifth owners in the hotel's history. The twenty suites have been extensively remodeled; many include Jacuzzi whirlpools and wireless Internet access. Turn-of-the-century antique décor is designed to

highlight the hotel's unique place in American history and literature. It is on the National Register of Historic Places.

When Jeanne Bellefeuille encountered that pleasant young man
in the pub, the Freeses had only recently taken possession. Kelley
Freese says there was no mention of the hotel being haunted when
the sale was being discussed.

As Bellefeuille occasionally told Freese about the oddities she
was encountering during her night shift, the new owner now and
then asked acquaintances around town if they'd heard any unusual
stories about the hotel. One day she mentioned some of the incidents to a local person.

"Well, Kelley, it's haunted," that individual confided in her. "Everybody knows it's haunted. Always has been."

Freese was surprised. She had no idea ghost stories were connected to the Palmer House, nor had she "spent any time thinking
about haunted places."

Jeanne Bellefeuille said the young man in the pub didn't seem threatening or ethereal, only polite and thirsty. Nonetheless, she was puzzled and more than a bit alarmed.

"My first thought was, 'Okay, how did he get in here?'" she says
thinking back on that night. As usual, she had earlier confirmed
that the exterior hotel doors were secured.

"I would never be here without making sure the doors were
locked. I'm also thinking: Who is this guy? Why is he here? And
how do I get to the phone to call for help?"

She remained calm and returned his politeness. "Technically,
yes, you can get a beer, but I don't have access to the cash register."

The bartender may have locked the taps before he left, she
added. "So, I don't know."

"Well, what kind of beer is good?"

Thinking a moment she said, "I like the one with the canoe
handle."

She had momentarily forgotten the name Leinenkugel's, which
features that design on its bottles.

"Well, I'll take one of those," he said.

She found the Leinenkugel's tap and pulled down the handle. Beer sputtered from the spigot.

"Well, we might be able to eke one out for you," she said.

She got a glass and filled it.

"How much is that," he asked, again smiling at her.

"I don't know. I'm just the night clerk. I pretty much vacuum and dust." She thought a moment and added, "How does two fifty sound?"

He pulled out a ten-dollar bill.

She looked at it and shook her head.

"Uh-oh, we have another problem. You'll have to drink three more beers because I don't have access to change. Do you have anything else?"

"I don't know," the stranger said, still courteous and accommodating. He dug in his front pocket and came up with five quarters.

"Oh, it's your lucky night," Bellefeuille smiled. "We're having a sale tonight. Beer is a dollar twenty-five."

He laughed, picked up his glass, and headed out the door into the lobby. He paused and turned around.

"It's okay if I take this up to my room, isn't it?"

Bellefeuille said sure.

At that point Bellefeuille felt a sense of relief and security. Obviously, he was an overnight guest. He didn't *get* in, he was already there. He had merely wandered downstairs for a late-night beer.

She put the five quarters in the reception desk, and then, curious about the man's identify, she checked the register. There was no computer system at that time, so guests' names were written in by hand.

No one was registered for the night. She wasn't unduly disturbed.

"It was summer and a slow week, so it was not unusual for someone to check in later in the evening and not have their names written down. I thought the bartender just didn't write it in."

She did make a mental note to tell Kelley Freese about serving the late-night beer. If the dollar twenty-five wasn't enough, she'd reimburse her for the rest.

The next evening, Bellefeuille told her boss about the visitor.

"She looked at me kind of funny," Bellefeuille remembers. "She checked the desk register and got the five quarters from the drawer."

"Who did they come from again?" Freese asked.

"That guy who's staying here," Bellefeuille replied.

"Okay. But there's nobody staying here."

"But there was a guy . . . "

"Well, what room was he in because I'll need to clean that room," Freese broke in. She did most of the housekeeping at that time.

Bellefeuille said she didn't know but thought it would be easy to find the one with the empty beer glass and the bed that's been slept in.

Kelley Freese said of the mysterious incident, "Jeanne watched him walk upstairs. I did the housekeeping 100 percent then, and we never did find a room that had been slept in, and we never did find the empty beer glass."

The only physical confirmation of the disappearing guest was the five quarters he paid Bellefeuille for the beer.

"I don't know where he went, but he went upstairs," Bellefeuille says. "I was okay with all of it as soon as I thought he was staying here. It never occurred to me that he wasn't [a guest]. So I wasn't afraid. I didn't spend the night saying, 'Oh my God, I hope whoever that was doesn't come down again.'"

She reasoned that he had gone into the pub while she was running the vacuum cleaner elsewhere.

Despite being unable to identify the man, Bellefeuille just calls the incident "a little odd. . . . I choose to believe it was a real person who just somehow got out of the building."

Yet the logic of a complete stranger somehow getting *into* the hotel after hours and then in some way sneaking *out* with a beer in his hand seems problematic.

He did appear real enough to Bellefeuille.

"I couldn't see through him," she laughs. "He had real money and was normal [looking]."

But Freese doesn't see how it could have been someone staying there without paperwork or anyone checking him in.

Kelley Freese had another reason for doubting it could have been a real person. It may not have been this young man's first visit.

As Bellefeuille detailed her story, not only did Freese wrestle with trying to figure out why there was no indication of him in any of the rooms but it also dawned on her that he may have been the same man she had glimpsed fleetingly not many days before.

It had been a quiet Wednesday afternoon, about two o'clock. The only guests were involved in a local children's theater production, and they were gone for the day. Freese was in the third-floor laundry room putting cleaning supplies in a maid's cart. She heard someone on the main staircase just down the hall.

"I could hear this clunk-clunk-clunk, footsteps, coming up," she recalls. "I stopped and listened because typically what someone will do is go to the first floor and call out my name. So I just listened to see who was looking for me."

She thought it might be one of the guests back early. She had a walkie-talkie if an employee needed to find her in the sprawling hotel, yet it had remained silent.

"Nobody is calling my name. Now the footsteps are up on the third floor, walking more briskly down the hall. I'm literally standing next to my maid's cart waiting to see who's going to come in the door."

Suddenly, a man strode by, snapped his head to look at her, and disappeared past the door. Not a word was exchanged. Freese didn't recognize him as anyone staying in the hotel.

She edged around the cart and looked out the doorway. The hallway was empty.

Thinking he'd ducked into a room, she opened each one on that end of the corridor. Nothing.

"I must be seeing things," she mumbled to herself as she returned to the laundry room.

But in truth she knew otherwise. She had heard someone walk

up the staircase; the footsteps had continued down the hall; she had seen a stranger walk by and had seen him look at her. No, she thought, she definitely had not been seeing things.

"I . . . had that creeping feeling. I also realized the minute he walked past the doorway that the footsteps stopped. And then there was the whole precursor . . . listening to the footsteps coming down the hall, watching him walk by. There was nowhere for him to go."

The hair stood up on the back of her neck.

Jeanne Bellefeuille's later run-in with the pub man led the two women to compare notes on his appearance.

Freese says, "We . . . absolutely described the same man, [except] when I saw him he had on a cap like when the kids wear baseball hats, backward."

By August, Jeanne Bellefeuille decided it was time to focus on preparing for the coming school year. To ease the transition, she offered to help find her replacement. She found one in her own family: her father, Jay Brisson, was retired and living in Sauk Centre. She thought the hotel work would "give him something to do."

Brisson followed his daughter through her duties for a couple of nights before starting out on his own.

"I think it was probably the first or second night. I thought I'd done pretty well, but in the morning I noticed there was water on the tile I'd washed. It should have been dried by that time. I thought what the heck, but I mopped it up again," says Brisson, a retired contractor from Wyoming.

"I had the same things with the silverware. We'd wrap the silverware and put it out on the side of the table . . . and then go around checking and one would be sideways."

Brisson had his own issues with the table lamp.

"You're sitting there, and all of a sudden the light would come on. I'd shut it off, and pretty soon it'd come on again. I finally pulled the plug!"

The cold swept in again for brief periods. Brisson had to "move around to get my circulation going," despite working up a sweat as he vacuumed during several of the hottest late summer nights.

He had his own troubles in the hotel's pub. Not only did the gas fireplace go on again one night, but the large-screen television did, as well.

"The bartender had left for the night and shut off the TV. I was mopping, and all of a sudden this racket came from the barroom. I thought: What the hell is that? Again all the doors were locked. I went in the pub, and the TV is blasting away. I got the remote, shut it off, and came back out [to finish mopping]. Again it comes on."

Brisson coped with the problem in the same way he and his daughter handled the capricious table lamp—he pulled the plug.

"I just figured, well, it's an old place and anything can happen."

The Bellefeuille family's connection with the preternatural side of the Palmer House Hotel did not end with Jeanne Bellefeuille and Jay Brisson.

Jeanne's daughter, Stephanie Bellefeuille, is a college student who has bartended in the hotel's pub. On a single night in July 2007, she had two encounters that made her—and later her mother—wonder if it was her family that was somehow attracting the attention of the hotel's other clientele.

"I am not a believer in ghosts at all," Stephanie Bellefeuille begins, and so her accounts of what took place that night are not edged in panic or wonderment but rather in a calm, just-the-facts-ma'am reflection on her extraordinary experience.

It was nearly closing time on a night when Stephanie was bartending. Two customers were left seated at the bar—a young man and his girlfriend. As Stephanie busied herself with cleaning up, the two patrons finished their drinks.

She heard a commotion.

"What was that?" the young man cried out.

Stephanie quickly turned around.

"What?" she asked.

He pointed to a bookshelf some twenty feet away from where he sat. He said a book had flown off the shelf. Stephanie saw a book lying on the floor several feet from the shelf.

"He freaked out," she recalls. Although she did not see the book leave the shelf on its short flight, she says the couple was seated too far from the shelf for one of them to have made it there and back to the stool. The pair quickly downed their drinks and left.

Alone now in the bar, Stephanie Bellefeuille turned up the background music, put the book back on the shelf, finished cleaning, and got ready to close up. She was at the end of the bar near the open double doors when she happened to glance across the lobby. A young boy of about ten was standing on the staircase.

"He was staring at me," she says. "It was like something out of a horror movie."

The child was a colorless gray, wrapped in a sort of haze. She could see through him to the wall beyond.

"I could hardly believe my eyes," she says. "I blinked and wondered if I was really seeing this or not."

Within what must have seemed an eternity, but was in reality only a few seconds, Stephanie decided she was most definitely seeing an apparition, let out a loud scream, and ran across the lobby—carefully avoiding a glance at the staircase—and into the hotel dining room where another employee was cleaning up.

As Stephanie stammered out her story, the clerk turned ashen. She had seen the same boy running around several times that night herself and was very upset by it.

"We hurriedly cleaned up, locked the doors, and got out," Stephanie says. The weirdest part of the evening was that the book incident and the sighting of the child took place within such a short span of time. The question left hanging, of course, was whether they were connected.

Although Stephanie Bellefeuille emphasizes that a flying book or the apparition of a small boy didn't win her over into a belief in ghosts, the young woman is clear, precise, and thoughtful about her recollection of the events on that late July evening. It was a night she'll never forget.

A little boy ghost is frequently encountered at the hotel, according to co-owner Kelley Freese. Curiously, Stephanie Bellefeuille's description of the boy as about ten years old is at odds with other witnesses who say the child is several years younger.

"He runs up and down the upstairs halls, giggling and laughing and playing with this little blue ball," Freese says. "Children especially see him and then tell their parents they had 'fun' playing with the little boy."

A couple visiting relatives in Sauk Centre once checked into the hotel with their little girl. One evening after they had been seated for dinner, their four year old asked if she could go play for a while with the boy on the staircase. The couple glanced at each other. No, they agreed, everyone had to eat first. Neither parent had seen a boy on the stairs.

On another occasion a local high-school barbershop quartet was performing in the main lobby. Tables had been set up for the audience. One couple attending the concert had a hard time keeping their preschool daughter seated in her chair. She kept running behind the lobby desk making a shushing sound, her fingers to her lips. She said she was trying to get the boy behind the desk to be quiet. He shouldn't be talking when someone is performing, she solemnly told her parents.

Kelley Freese has an idea that the child may be Lucius, who lived there when the Palmers were in residence, although the records are unclear as to whether he might have been a member of the Palmer family. Ralph and Christena Palmer had two children, Hazel and Carlisle, although Christena's mother and brother, George Brandnor, also worked for the Palmers.

In the fall of 2007, a visiting psychic told Freese that, when she walked through one particular part of the basement, the name Lucius came to her and that he was in the basement "taking care of the animals." A descendant of the Palmers once told Freese that there was indeed a boy named Lucius, a member of the original Palmer family, whose job it was to take care of the family's dogs—kenneled in the basement.

There are no records of a child having died at the hotel nor of any other documented deaths.

"I haven't heard him in a while," Freese says. "But I haven't night-clerked recently. I can't tell you the number of times when guests checked out in the morning and [compliment us] but then say some-body let their kid play in the hall last night and it kept us awake."

The Palmer House's reputation for ghostly activity is getting around. Several paranormal investigators have visited, and Freese has held paranormal conferences. She has not "initiated or insti-gated" any of the ghost stories associated with the place, she em-phasizes. There may be other specters lurking alongside happy little boys or beer-swilling young men to fill several of the hotel's suites.

"What I have found so fascinating is that through all of these different chance encounters I'm consistently told the same things [about the ghosts]—their names, their sex, a little bit of their his-tory, what rooms they're in, and what their roles in life were. That continues to amaze me, the consistency and accuracy over and over again."

A ghost bride stands on the third floor, at the top of the stair-case.

"I've not seen her in a long time," Freese says.

She says she'd glimpse the woman in a long, white wedding gown "out of the corner of my eye. I'd see this fabric flowing up the stairs and used to think I was out of my mind. But . . . people reas-sure me, no, no, Kelley, that's just her."

Another ghost who had a management role at the hotel in life can often give Freese a hard time. Psychics have told Freese the man does not like her nor the way she runs her business. When he's re-ally frustrated with her, she feels like he is physically on her back.

Freese has told him in no uncertain terms to leave her alone, but that works only temporarily. Psychics have tried to "get him to cross," but he won't.

Could that unpleasant ghost be the one who rearranges silver-ware, turns on lights, TVs, and fireplaces, and pulls the other pranks not uncommon at the hotel?

Perhaps.

But Kelley Freese seems to take her hotel ghosts in stride.

"They have personalities and moods no different than we do. Some are grouchy. Well, you meet crabby people in life, too."

UNFORTUNATE HERMAN

"There is no question about [the ghost]."

St. Cloud Journal Press

It must have been a grisly sight. The section hands found the pitifully mangled corpse alongside the Great Northern railroad tracks between Alexandria and Sauk Centre. As many as seven trains may have passed over what looked to be the remains of a middle-aged man.

From a very few personal items—a Minnesota Regiment lapel pin, an address book, a few letters, and a single photograph—the workmen were able to identify the victim as a Melrose man. His relatives there claimed his body and confirmed that the man's name was Herman. His last name has been lost to history. He had worked as a carpenter. The photograph, which helped identify the victim, was of his brother.

Evidently, Herman had set out by train from Evansville, perhaps where he was working at the time, with twenty dollars in his pocket to pay creditors in Alexandria or Brandon. No money was found on his body. Newspaper accounts of the incident don't indicate whether Herman had paid off any of his creditors.

Was Herman's death an accident? A suicide? Or might it have been foul play, perhaps at the hands of rail-riding hoboes? The fact that no money was found led to an immediate suspicion that Herman was a murder victim, yet authorities didn't identify a suspect or suspects.

From this seeming dead-end investigation, the matter might have faded into obscurity but for the following: reports soon circulated that the ghost of the dead carpenter was walking the very same section of track where his body had been found.

Herman's final chapter began in September 1903 when he boarded a Great Northern passenger train in Evansville for the short trip to Brandon, a small town a few miles southeast of Evansville, or to the city of Alexandria, about eighteen miles farther southeast. His family wasn't quite certain of his final destination. His home in Melrose would have been about thirty-five miles farther along the rail route.

No one really knows what happened between the time he boarded the train and when his remains were discovered alongside the tracks some three miles west of Sauk Centre. A St. Paul newspaper writing about poor Herman's demise dutifully notes that several trains had dragged the unfortunate victim roughly sixty rods (990 feet).

And then very soon afterward, Herman's ghost made its debut.

The first descriptions of the haunting came from five Great Northern section hands led by their foreman, a man named Fiala, who had been among those who discovered the corpse. They all claimed to have seen the ghost mutely walking along the right-of-way. They also said that, on other occasions, the unfortunate Herman walks "steadily down the railroad tracks until he comes to the place where his dead body was found and then [the ghost] suddenly vanishes into nothingness."

That at least is according to the St. Cloud newspaper that first carried an account of the nascent haunting. Fiala said his crew and another one close-by had all seen the pale figure. It must have been Herman, Fiala claimed, because the ghost was wearing the same clothes as the victim, right down to a jacket with a swatch of cloth missing. The foreman said he had cut it off to help family members identify the remains. The ghost always disappeared when the workmen tried to get close enough to speak.

The assumption was that the ghost was trying to reveal something about his horrible death, though what that might have been was lost on the railroaders because the ghost never murmured a word.

The strange story of the railway ghost made its way into several area newspapers, including the *Review,* a weekly in Osakis, on the southern shore of the lake that bears its name. The rail line ran through Osakis on its route from Alexandria to Sauk Centre and Melrose, so a man killed on one of the passenger trains traveling through the region evoked a great deal of interest.

But here the story takes an odd sidetrack.

Among readers of that Osakis newspaper story were a Mr. and Mrs. J. M. Madison, who then sent the tale on to their daughter, who bore the splendid name of Minnesota Madison.

Miss Madison worked for the Census Department in Washington, DC, but moonlighted as something of an authority in what she termed "psyclyre phenomena," an area of paranormal expertise evidently in vogue at the turn of the century. It apparently involved "reading" the intentions of ghosts over long distances.

In a letter to a friend back in Minnesota, and later published in the *Review,* Miss Madison contends that the ghost materialized along the tracks because it wanted to divulge something about its death—a common enough belief—and further, she writes, the ghost should be asked directly what it wants. In this way the ghost might reveal details of its death, or perhaps the identity of the murderers, if indeed Herman was slain.

Miss Madison's friend was one Lewis H. Vath, "principal of the Sauk Centre and St. Cloud business colleges." Though he may not have followed through on her directive, her letter did excite some interest by the Osakis village marshal. He assembled a posse and led them on a search to find the taciturn apparition. Alas, though they all claimed to "have seen the phantom" during the search, they failed in an attempt at direct communication with the thing.

The continuing disappointments in spirit communication did not make the sightings go away. In fact, an argument broke out between the *St. Cloud Journal-Press,* which first published reports of the ghost, and the *St. Cloud Times* and the *Sauk Centre Herald,* two newspapers that took a dim view of the spirit world in general and mocked any newspaper that would promote it. The *Times's* and *Herald's* scornful accounts of the searches forced the *Journal-Press* into the position of having to defend the existence of Herman's ghost.

The *Journal-Press* published an extensive interview with Fiala, the Great Northern section chief, describing his and his men's various encounters with the ghost of the late carpenter.

"Fiala says there is no question about [the ghost] and he avers that he is not afraid to take any party there in the night time," the *Journal-Press* huffed. "He never harmed poor Herman and is not afraid of his vengeance."

Fiala added that some two hundred people had seen the ghost. The newspaper boasted that even two Minneapolis police detectives had seen the specter for themselves . . . but failed in an attempt to arrest same.

For a ghost story that attracted so much attention at the turn of the twentieth century, it seems to have faded quickly from sight. No one stepped forward either to explain the haunting or to claim that Herman's ghost had revealed any important information. Apparently, no one was ever charged with his murder, if indeed that is what occurred in the first place.

So it may be that Herman's ghost still frequents that old railroad line, even now looking for someone he might choose to talk to.

18

SOMETHING STIRS

*"I'm not a real believer, but I think there are
things out there we don't understand."*
Thomas Rudd*

The white-columned neoclassical mansion looks out of place a few blocks off the small Minnesota community's main street, an ersatz piece of old southern comfort set down square in the middle of rural Minnesota.

The slender quartet of unadorned columns supports a covered front porch; a hipped roof and wide chimney add to its antebellum impression. The broad, neatly trimmed lawn might accommodate dozens of picnickers.

It could be someone's spacious home—in fact it once was—but a tall flagpole in the front, a formal covered entrance on one side, and a newer single-story attached multicar garage on the other, coupled with a long, curved driveway, hint at its business purpose.

In fact, this is one of the town's funeral homes.

But to say that this funeral home no longer accommodates private residents is not entirely accurate. On the second floor is a modest apartment that has been used over the years by various renters and, on occasion, the morticians working there. That's not unusual in small towns—the families of funeral directors often share space with the deceased.

Yet this place—a once popular community social hub when it was privately owned—is distinctive for another reason. An undertaker who resided in that two-bedroom apartment with his wife and child says that some of their experiences may indicate that a spirit, a presence, lingered there between the living and the dead.

Thomas and Belinda Rudd* moved into the apartment in December when she was pregnant with their first child. Thomas was a relatively recent University of Minnesota graduate in mortuary science. The apartment was provided gratis by the corporate owners of the funeral home.

Thomas had to sell the idea to his wife. She did not like the idea of living above a funeral home.

"It bothered my wife. I had to talk her into it. I thought we could save some money and become a part of the community. She thought the idea of living in an apartment was okay, but at the same time she never walked through the building to get to it."

The first-floor funeral home is laid out in such a way that the most direct route from the attached garage to the family's apartment goes by the embalming rooms.

"When my wife had to stay there by herself, she was uneasy and would have to have friends stay with her. She was always a little edgy. And then the fact that she was pregnant, she didn't want to be there by herself either."

Thomas thought the idea of getting acquainted with the town to see if they liked it was preferable to jumping right into buying a house. Without an investment in a house, or even paying rent on an apartment elsewhere, the couple could easily move to another city and another job. To make the job in the somewhat remote community even more attractive, his employers remodeled and updated the apartment for the couple.

Rudd learned that the imposing house had been on a farm until it was moved into town, most likely around the turn of the twentieth century. The four plain columns were an embellishment added after its move.

The mansion's longtime owner was a prominent businessman and community leader on whose family farm the house once stood.

He grew up in the house and lived there as an adult after it was moved to town. He was a successful Midwest wholesaler of merchandise sold in what were called variety stores, including the old Ben Franklin store chain.

The home's spacious rooms were used to display merchandise for visiting retailers, who would then choose which items to feature in their local stores. At night he hosted lavish parties for his clients and friends. Those visiting from long distances often stayed in one of the bedrooms, waited on by house servants, some of whom told Rudd about the house's colorful history when they attended funeral services there years later.

The town itself had something of a bawdy reputation during Prohibition because it didn't go dry. Stories are told about folks from towns and villages across Minnesota traveling there to drink.

When the businessman died, the house was in limbo for a few years, Rudd says, until it was purchased by an area banker. It has served as a funeral home since the 1980s.

Thomas Rudd is careful when he describes the eight months he and his wife spent in the apartment. There was nothing unusual the first four months, Rudd says, other than his wife's uneasiness, which he fully understood yet couldn't help her get beyond. He thought the apartment was adequate for the time being, at least until the baby arrived. He attributed some of his wife's unease to the impending birth and the ways in which their lives would change.

They decorated one bedroom as a nursery over the winter months. Belinda Rudd took a maternity leave, and their son was born in early April.

Thomas went back to work. He had to spend most of his time at a different funeral home in a nearby city owned by his company.

"He was a colicky baby," he says. "We didn't get much sleep; it seems we were up with him all the time, taking shifts and all of that. It was still cold out, so she didn't take him out very much."

Depending on his schedule, Rudd sometimes stayed home a couple of days during the week to help out.

But then it started, a few minor peculiarities at first. Rudd is circumspect when talking about their origins.

"I'm not sure when it [was], but our son was still an infant. Belinda told me that she saw . . . different lights flickering; lamps would flicker."

He thought it might have been caused by power surges or some old wiring. He had done some rewiring, but much of the electrical system was fairly old.

Belinda was cooking one day, and a bag of chocolate chips she was using seemed to open up; a couple of chips fell out onto the counter. When she told her husband about it, he attributed it to the cellophane's loosening. She thought it was more than that.

He didn't find anything out of the ordinary.

That was when Belinda Rudd saw the apparition.

It was two o'clock in the morning. Belinda had gotten up because the baby was fussing. She was in a favorite nursery rocker when she glanced toward the doorway. Looking back at her was a man standing in shadow. He appeared to be passing by in the hallway, on his way into another room.

She woke up Thomas, who was asleep in the bedroom.

"She didn't scream; it didn't startle her. She was scared more like when you freeze, like she wanted to make sure of what she'd seen."

Belinda told him there was someone walking around in the apartment and then proceeded to describe the man. Though he was doubtful there was anyone there, Thomas agreed to look around. It was in vain. He thought the stress of being a new mother may have contributed to the incident.

Yet, even as he was skeptical of his wife's concerns, he wasn't entirely certain something truly unexplainable wasn't going on there.

"The only thing that happened to me was when I left the apartment and then came back and the lights were on when we could have sworn we'd shut them off, or I'd find the TV set on. I'd think I'd turned off the TV, and then later I'd find it on in the middle of the night. I was certain I'd turned it off because I would have remembered if I left it on, especially at night. Or maybe I was just being absentminded."

But then some of the baby's toys began behaving oddly.

"Good dog, Clifford."

That's the catchphrase played by a small recorder inside the book *Clifford the Big Red Dog* that the Rudds bought for the nursery. Sometimes they'd hear it being recited in the middle of the night. Baby toys that play a tune when they are squeezed suddenly began playing, as well. The couple heard the music coming from the baby's room after they'd gone to bed.

"We dismissed it as low batteries," Thomas Rudd says, "but most of the toys were new. We'd be sleeping and hear a toy [start up]. Like that kid's book *Clifford the Big Red Dog*. You push the button on the page that correlates with a picture. It would say "Good dog, Clifford" or "Yeah!" or something like that. Well, that one just kept going off."

That's when Rudd couldn't help rethinking his wife's beliefs.

"When you started putting this piece with that piece, then I was thinking, okay, now what's going on here. Then of course my wife is trying to convince me of what she's seen."

Despite Belinda's misgivings and, increasingly, Thomas's disquiet, they stayed in the apartment above the funeral home.

"I thought, let's keep this up," Thomas Rudd remembers. "But then summer came around; our son was growing up; and we wanted to get a house."

The couple found one they liked and agreed to terms. Their closing date was set, but the previous homeowners said the Rudds could move furniture into the empty garage if they liked, which they did.

"We were waiting to close. We hadn't taken our beds over, so we were still sleeping in the apartment."

Not for long.

On what would prove to be their last night in the apartment, the couple went to bed as usual.

Their bed started vibrating.

"The last straw," Thomas Rudd calls it.

It was not violent but insistent enough to awaken them; the headboard of the queen-sized bed shuddered against the wall.

Thomas and Belinda sat up and looked at one another, each

one assuring the other that, yes, they'd both felt it. It stopped. The couple went in to check on their little boy. He was sleeping.

"I told her it was probably a train going by," Rudd says. He didn't really believe that, but he got up to look out the window anyway. The freight tracks are within eyeshot of the window. The streets and the train tracks were quiet.

He knew there was another, even bigger problem with his assumption. Only the bed was shaking. Nothing else in the bedroom was affected. A long, heavy freight train would make the entire room, the house, shudder.

Then it happened again—a rapid quaking of their headboard, just forceful enough for them to sit up again and look around. It was like someone had grabbed hold of the headboard and was there shaking it.

"We sat frozen, going, 'Okay, is this going to keep up all night?' but that's when it subsided. We were half asleep but awake enough to try and piece it all together. It wasn't worth getting out of bed and saying we're getting out of here now. We ended up trying to fall back asleep."

The next morning Belinda made her decision.

She told her husband she would not stay there another night. He knew she was also concerned for their young son's welfare.

"Yes, definitely," Thomas Rudd says when he thinks about whether the bed-shaking incident, as brief as it was, moved him to place credence in what his wife had been telling him for several months, to move from skepticism to at least a partial acknowledgment that something was amiss—that maybe there was something inexplicable happening around them.

"I'm not a real believer, but I think there are things out there we don't understand. . . . Once I dismissed the train, I thought that, with bringing our son home, that might have brought something into the house, some activity. Maybe it was watching over our son. In the back of my mind I wondered if part of him being colicky was that he saw things or something maybe was getting him upset. It seemed to be focused around [the baby] since nothing happened until we brought him home."

For the first couple of nights after they moved into their new home, Thomas thought maybe even a new house wasn't going to help.

The baby's toys would not stay quiet. One would start playing its simple melody. Or up popped that mechanical voice "Good dog, Clifford"—over and over again.

"We got nervous, like okay what's going on now. It happened only a few times, but I had to literally take the toy and put it into a closet, or in the garage, because it just would not stop [playing]. I didn't want to take time in the middle of the night to get out a screwdriver to take the batteries out."

That's what he attributes it to—low batteries. But he doesn't sound convinced.

Several years have passed since the family's eight months in their funeral home apartment. That's enough time to gain some perspective on what took place. But Thomas Rudd still does not have an entirely satisfactory solution.

He wasn't able to find any traumatic events in the building's human history, no murders, no suicides. He knows other individuals who have since lived uneventfully in the apartment. But that doesn't mean he has forgotten that time. He has studied other cases of supernatural phenomena—apparitions, recordings of past events, poltergeists—so as to better understand what took place.

"We've told mostly friends and relatives about it. They're inquisitive. I've told some coworkers [at the funeral home], and they kind of blow it off as nothing. Of course, I'm downplaying it, too, because I don't want to sound to them like someone who believes in this kind of thing."

Even though he may play down what took place during those months, Thomas Rudd is definite about one thing.

"I know what I experienced. It's not *The Amityville Horror,* or even a major experience. I don't think any of these things ever are. They are more subtle."

But they were of enough consequence that a young mortician and his family could not ignore what may have been an unseen presence hanging about the local funeral parlor.

THE LUTEFISK GHOST

"Is it possible for a place to seal in the energies that have been here?"
Reverend Terje Hausken

On that frightfully cold January night, the Reverend Terje Hausken waited patiently for the young teens in his confirmation class to settle down. They were seated at long cafeteria-style tables in an ad hoc classroom tucked into a corner of the drafty country church basement. With his usual patience and good humor, Hausken smoothly encouraged the youngsters to stop their chatter and center on his lesson that night on Lutheran liturgy.

The first few minutes ticked by as Hausken, a solidly built, jovial pastor in his late fifties, weaved together biblical teaching and personal stories that kept the students engaged. Confirmation classes on winter nights could be challenging, but his years of pastoral care had prepared him well for most eventualities.

Except for what happened next.

A low, rasping moan—it *seemed* human the pastor says—started rising from somewhere on the floor above them, from within the darkened church proper. The entire class, and Hausken, fell silent.

"It lasted about fifteen seconds," he says. "Kind of guttural, like 'Oooooo.' It was eerie; I'll have to say that. An eerie sound, yes. And we could tell it was off in the distance."

Although the pastor had spent many evenings in his rural

143

church, nothing he had ever encountered there, nothing that he had any familiarity with, equaled that sudden disturbing groan from inside his church.

"It almost did sound human," he admits. "I feel funny saying it *was* human, but it *sounded* human."

No sooner had the moaning died away and the class settled back down than it started up again and once more gripped the attention of everyone there.

Situated on a slight rise in the landscape amid endless fields of corn and soybeans in west-central Goodhue County, the Vang Lutheran Church, ELCA, traces its history to a simple wood-frame church built in 1862. The Norwegian word *vang* means a field or lawn and is taken from the Vang/Valdres region of Norway from which many of the early Vang parishioners originated.

The present church, designed by Olof Hanson, the first deaf architect in the United States, was finished in 1897. Vang now serves over five hundred parishioners from local townships and from as far away as Northfield.

Painted a dazzling white with a soaring corner bell tower, the Vang church is the quintessential Minnesota country parish. But Hanson's design flourishes belie its humble location and modest building cost of $5,933.03—including land and architect's fee.

Hanson's gently arched stained-glass windows allow natural light to fill the interior, while the bell tower above the main entryway is visible for miles. A more recent low-slung addition does not detract from the original structure's singular appearance.

Inside the church the polished wood pews spread across the floor in three sections, while a wide balcony with even more pews curves around the perimeter. Near the altar is a striking Hinners Model 10 pipe organ that parishioners bought for $1,020 in 1906. Its original hand bellows were replaced by electric bellows in 1935.

Terje Hausken was still an interim pastor at Vang during the time he taught the confirmation class, "edging toward retirement."

"This is a good congregation," Hausken says. "We have a lot of fun on Sundays!"

A Norwegian by birth, Hausken was about five years old when he moved to the United States with his parents in the early 1950s. The family lived in New York for a year before moving on to Minnesota.

After completing seminary, Hausken was a youth pastor in Edina and served churches in St. Paul and Pine Island, among many others. For most of his ecclesiastical career, he specialized in divorce counseling and church mediation; he's the author of several books on the subjects and once had a mediation practice with an attorney. Yet Hausken has always stayed close to his pastoral roots by serving various church congregations wherever he has lived.

When he arrived at Vang, Terje Hausken didn't know that the church already had a reputation for haunting.

He came to learn that parishioners had been reporting odd noises and unexpected incidents for many years. Then he discovered that there is the legend of a ghost photograph that was allegedly taken inside the church sometime in the 1930s. It is said to picture an apparition. The claim has been included in several books. But Hausken has never seen the photo, nor does he know of anyone who has. Several parishioners, some of whom have been members of the congregation for over half a century, know nothing of such a photograph. It may be an urban legend or, as Hausken says in this case, a rural legend.

But what Terje Hausken and those young teens heard that night was most decidedly real, nothing legendary about it.

"It wasn't the wind," Hausken asserts. "I can't do a good imitation of [what we heard], but you know how the wind sounds; you can tell it's that."

Further, Hausken says the deep "moan," as other people that night described it, "was definitely in the building; no question about that. We heard it twice. It stopped and then started again about ten minutes later."

One girl was so upset she began to cry.

Hausken said the noise seemed to originate from somewhere above where the class was sitting, in the general direction of the left, rear corner of the church; above that space is an attic that opens off the balcony.

Jim Sviggum is an adult member of the parish who was assisting the pastor at the confirmation class that night. The Sviggums have attended Vang church for decades. Jim Sviggum says he clearly heard the "weird" and "eerie" noise, as he calls it, and that he had never heard anything like it before. He has been in and out of the church all his life.

Neither could Hausken compare it to anything he'd heard there, though he's often there at night and alone for much of the time.

Hausken is careful in assessing what he thinks it might have been. It was not human, he says, but it "sounded human."

"Buildings do make funny noises," Hausken adds cautiously. "But all I can say is, and I don't know structurally what this building is capable of, but all I know is it wasn't the wind. I know that. It wasn't even windy outside."

Rather than puzzling over the incident, Hausken takes a light-hearted approach.

"I know that if they were spirits, which they *aren't*, but if they were spirits they wouldn't hurt me anyway. Besides I hope they're Norwegian, so I can talk to them!"

Hausken remains fluent in the language.

His ease in handling such a strange affair is clear, too, in what happened after the second time he and the class heard the sound.

"I told them that I hated to do this, but we had to go up into the sanctuary because we had to use the hymnals since we were working on the creed . . . the worship service itself. They asked, 'Do we have to?' but I told them there was nothing wrong."

But one young teen decided he'd have some fun, Hausken says. The boy quietly left the group and headed upstairs. The rest of the class trooped up the steps and opened the door to the church, whereupon the boy leaped out from behind crying, "Boo!" at the same time.

"Those kids were really mad at him," Hausken laughs. "They started punching him, and I [joked] that they should hit him as hard as they could."

For his part, the youngster who played the joke, Tyler Under-dahl, says he thought the noise might have been the furnace kicking on. At other times, the pipe organ's air pump will make funny noises, but Hausken says it wasn't turned on that evening. Hausken, Sviggum, his son Peter Sviggum, and others don't think that what they heard could be attributed to anything mechanical.

It turns out that odd events are nothing new for the Vang congregation.

Stories have circulated for years that people, especially women and men working in the kitchen before the annual fall dinner, have heard voices or unusual sounds there; some members of the congregation have refused to enter the church at night or stay there alone when the church starts emptying out.

Bev Sviggum, Jim's mother and a member of the congregation for over sixty years, says she was in the church countless times "when I still drove." Despite being by herself, she "never felt alone."

"I always thought there was somebody with me. I thought it was probably God, that it wasn't a ghost. But then I heard some noises, and I kind of figured God wouldn't make noises."

A stairway that has since been taken out seemed to be the center of the out-of-place noises Bev Sviggum heard.

"There were more noises from in there than anywhere else," she says. "It was a kind of a squishing movement, like a person was going up the stairs. But the main thing was, if I was up here alone, I never felt like I was alone."

Bernice Stenhaug, another longtime member, says she's heard lots of unusual noises there, but more so during the daytime when she was a volunteer cleaning the church. Sometimes people will want an escort to their cars in the parking lot, she says, after hearing about the church ghost.

"We were here a while back, and someone heard something. Wind? I don't know. I've just gotten used to it."

Amusingly, the strangest incidents have occurred around the time of the annual fall dinner—a lutefisk gala—the second Wednesday of each October. In fact, Reverend Hausken says jokingly that any worrisome noises or unexplained incidents at Vang should be attributed to "the lutefisk ghost."

But Bev Sviggum says it's more than the typical joking over the nutritional benefits of this traditional Norwegian dish.

"[Lutefisk] cookers that we put in one place we'd find some-where else," Bev says. "But then maybe someone else did come in and move them. I can't swear they didn't. But they weren't where I'd left them. Then we'd argue about where we'd left it."

Silverware, dishes, pots, and pans would be moved around as well.

Finally, Bev says smiling, she and her coworkers decided "we'd just put the ghost in charge of it all" until the day of the dinner. They figured the ghost would chase away anyone looking to disrupt the lutefisk feed, which attracts upward of 1,200 people each fall.

Hausken isn't ready to dismiss the kitchen mischief as people simply forgetting where they put things. He has been told stories of oddball happenings around the time of the fall dinner by quite a few parishioners.

"I've heard it from others . . . that things would get significantly moved around, where it's obvious someone has come in and moved items. I've heard that quite a bit."

Hausken and Bev Sviggum admit it's possible an anonymous parishioner may have been the culprit. Or, as Hausken is known to joke with his parishioners, the lutefisk itself might be responsible for temporary memory failure.

"With those lutefisk fumes, people really aren't responsible, you know, they get delirious!"

Terje Hausken, born in Norway, has never eaten lutefisk. But, he adds diplomatically, "I'm told this lutefisk is the best around."

If there is a ghost—or perhaps a poltergeist—in Vang Lutheran Church, a possible candidate could be the church's pastor in the 1890s.

His name was C. A. Mellby. He served Vang from 1892 to 1898. But what makes several parishioners, and Terje Hausken, think it could well be Reverend Mellby is what happened in 1895.

Reverend Mellby was given a leave of absence to study in Europe. While he was gone, the congregation voted to build a new church—the present one designed by Olof Hanson—about a mile north of the original church location. The Vang Church cemetery is still at the first site.

The new church was built without Mellby's knowledge, a violation of church procedure at the time. There is speculation that several influential church members on the north end of the church boundaries thought the church was too far away from them. Some church members on the south end of the district were so upset they switched congregations.

No one knows what was said when Mellby returned, but he soon resigned to take a teaching position at St. Olaf College, where he remained for fifty years. He did return once to Vang to preach on the occasion of the church's eighty-fifth anniversary.

But it is believed Reverend Mellby was very angry with the congregation's decision and that it is his spirit that haunts the church.

"It's that old Norwegian minister, I'm telling you that!" Terje Hausken says with a grin.

Bev Sviggum agrees. She definitely thinks there's a presence of some sort in the church.

"I think it's the pastor. He's kind of watching out for us."

Vang Lutheran Church is neither spooky nor forlorn. The church and its bucolic surroundings could be the centerpiece of a Grant Wood painting. Dozens of families can trace their church roots back for generations; there is a sincere affection for their country parish and its history.

For his part, Reverend Terje Hausken takes a benevolent and open-minded attitude toward his church's unusual ghost stories.

"This is not against our faith or anything like that. We sometimes can't explain what we hear or what we see, but that's why they call it mysteries. You wonder what that is. If this is what a haunting is, then they don't scare me because the stories that I hear are comforting stories, very animated stories. In history there is such a connectedness that I think it's important that we remember these stories well. They connect us to our past, and that's important. They are charming; they lend character to a place. They pique people's interest. . . . They're certainly not scary, not frightening."

But Terje Hausken keeps open the possibility that there are more things than stories circulating at Vang Lutheran Church.

In a cautious, ecclesiastical manner, he says, "I don't believe in ghosts . . . I don't *think*."

A COSMIC RESORT

*"It may have been more disturbing if she'd
walked through a wall, but probably not."*
Eric Rhinerson

The bartender simply wanted a nice cup of hot coffee at the end
of his evening shift. He walked across the empty dining room and
around a corner to the kitchen. He stopped short. A woman he didn't
recognize stood next to the coffee pot a few feet away. She wore a
long, pleated skirt, a full apron, and, curiously enough, a bonnet.
She glanced his way and smiled pleasantly, almost as if she were
greeting a friend or at least someone with whom she was familiar.

She wasn't startled in the least bit, but Eric Rhinerson certainly
was. The lady vanished.

"I forgot about the coffee," says Rhinerson.

Shaken by the incident, Rhinerson went back to sit down on a
bar stool. Sharon Gammell was there. The pair had been chatting
before Rhinerson left to get the coffee. She was his boss, the owner
of Thayer's Bed-and-Breakfast, a century-old inn in Annandale. She
noticed Rhinerson didn't have the coffee he'd gone for and that he
seemed a bit pale.

"What, did you see a ghost?" Gammell asked.

He paused. "I think so."

She laughed.

"Well, it's about time!"

The year was 1996. Eric Rhinerson had taken the part-time weekend job at Thayer's about six months earlier, while he finished his degree at nearby St. Cloud State University.

The inn is a circa 1890s Annandale landmark built during the heyday of passenger rail travel. A registered national historic place, Thayer's is now a lovingly restored B&B that still manages to maintain its charming Victorian interior and unique exterior design. Sharon Gammell and her late husband, Warren, bought the former railroad hotel in 1993.

Although Eric Rhinerson was astonished at the ghost's unexpected appearance, perhaps he should not have been. Soon after taking the job, he learned that along with tending bar came countless tales of unexpected appearances by more than a few former owners and guests whose time on earth had long since passed but who still frequented the hotel's long, quiet hallways and period rooms.

Rhinerson was skeptical of those stories.

At first.

It didn't seem to matter either that owner Sharon Gammell was a psychic herself who, along with several employees, told him all about the ghosts of Thayer's. How was it possible that the supernatural resided side-by-side with modern, casually attired vacationers?

But then Rhinerson started "seeing things out of the corner" of his eyes, as he puts it. Yet those occasional incidents might be put off to working late nights in an old hotel with myriad dusky crannies and corners, dim lighting, and hardwood floors that can groan under anyone's weight. It was always eerie when the lights were turned low, but then again it was an old building. . . .

Then came that night when he decided a cup of coffee would be just the right thing to keep him going for a few more hours.

"It may have been more disturbing if she'd walked through a wall, but probably not," he acknowledges.

Rhinerson and Gammell believe the woman standing near the coffeepot was Caroline Thayer, Mrs. Augustus Thayer. Caroline and Augustus—or Gus, as he was better known—built the hotel in 1895.

Rhinerson had seen one photograph in the hotel of a much older Caroline Thayer, so it wasn't the physical resemblance that necessarily led him to conclude that he'd seen a woman who'd been dead for decades, rather it was the bearing, the self-assuredness she exuded.

"She didn't need to say hello. This was her place. [She] was definitely aware of where she was and what was going on. She was very much at home," says Rhinerson.

Perhaps if Caroline Thayer has decided to linger awhile, she's chosen for herself a younger incarnation from those years when her life was intimately connected to ensuring the comfort of her hotel guests.

Owner Sharon Gammell remembers well the encounter Rhinerson had that night and how astonished he was by the experience. "It took a bit to cool him off," says Gammell.

Seeing Caroline Thayer for those fleeting moments persuaded Rhinerson that many of the stories told about Thayer's were quite possibly correct. He understood all the other little things that he'd noticed in the preceding few months.

"After seeing [Caroline] . . . I had a new perspective on every story in the place. Suddenly, the things I saw out of the corner of my eye moving up and down the stairs that I'd doubted before I suddenly paid more attention to."

He describes some of those other sensations as "more or less a presence . . . that someone was standing next to you . . . the feeling of being in a very busy room. You know there are people there, but you can't quite see them."

He also sensed near-constant movement on the open staircase in the main lobby, a few feet from the cozy bar area. (Thayer's no longer has a public bar.)

"There was always the sensation of traffic there. It wasn't uncommon to see orbs of light moving back and forth, streaking across the room. They weren't things you wondered if you saw; you know you saw them."

Usually, he says, these orbs or streaks of light moved quietly back and forth, but now and again they'd shoot across a room, especially the spacious dining room adjacent to the bar. Other employees told him that the top floor also seemed to be a hot spot for the odd, streaking light spheres. There are guest rooms and storage closets on that third floor.

Rhinerson faced it all with equanimity. He was never anxious or alarmed that he was being "attacked" or that something was attempting to "zero in" on him.

"And the thing that was very strange was the sensation that there was a rotating clientele [among the ghosts]. It didn't seem that it was always the same energy there. On certain nights you felt that the building was having a party."

On other evenings, Rhinerson says there was little if any activity. Both the tangible and intangible seemed to be fast asleep.

Sometimes overnight visitors sought solace in the cozy bar after a close encounter with one of the resident specters. Once, just before closing, a guest came down looking upset, a bit pale. The young woman asked for a drink. It was Rhinerson's turn to ask the routine Thayer's question: Had she seen a ghost? It turned out she had. She had awakened to see a man standing and staring at her near the foot of her bed. But it wasn't an intruder intent on doing harm, for he soon faded away. She decided a nightcap served by a nice, young three-dimensional bartender would be just the remedy for the disquieting encounter.

Though most of Eric Rhinerson's experiences were quite benign, on a few rare occasions he suspected that something a bit more aggressive might have been loose in there. One came on an evening while chatting with a couple of lingering bar patrons. It was the closest he came to being truly frightened.

"I suddenly felt like someone had just kicked me in the chest. . . . I was almost having a minor convulsion. The breath was just pulled right out of me."

Gasping for air, he leaned so far forward that he almost fell off the stool on which he was sitting. The two customers stared at him. One of them said it looked like a "streak of light" had "flown" directly through Rhinerson's chest.

"I have no idea what it was to this day," says Rhinerson, who now owns a furniture repair and restoration business in southern Minnesota. "It was not just a little physical sensation, of being creeped out, but a tangible sensation like someone had taken a ball peen hammer and hit me in the breast bone. I didn't see what went through me. I just felt it."

Rhinerson says the sudden, jolting shock was like being "dunked in cold water" or stepping in front of a high-pressure fire hose without realizing it was turned on. Strangely, he doesn't think that it—whatever it was—had been aware of him sitting behind the bar.

"It came through me and kept right on going about its business. . . . I don't know that it was even looking at me. It's just like I was sitting in its flight path."

Even though he was cold and shaken, Rhinerson finished his shift but left when the last customer did. "It was one of the few times I cracked open a beer behind the bar," he admits.

After that, and even though the bar could remain open until 1:00 AM, Rhinerson says that if all the customers had gone before the official closing time, so did he.

The first time Sharon Gammell stepped inside the old hotel back in 1993, she didn't need to be told that it was haunted. From earliest childhood Gammell says she has developed her own psychic abilities and, along with them, a conviction that the supernatural is more common than one might otherwise believe.

"People are psychic. Period," says the diminutive, vivacious redhead with a penchant for colorful attire. "Whether you use it or not, you've got that ability. I choose to use mine. I have since I was a little kid."

A veteran Twin Cities restaurateur, Gammell, with her now-deceased husband, Warren, had been looking for a business opportunity that was not a restaurant. They scouted locations in Minneapolis, St. Paul, southern Minnesota, and even as far north as Duluth before a Sunday newspaper ad listing that the historic Annandale hotel was for sale caught their eyes. They had to take out a map to see that the small city was about an hour northwest of the Twin Cities in western Wright County. They were intrigued enough to schedule a visit with the owner.

"We walked in, but it didn't look anything like it does now. The place was a mess," says Gammell.

Nevertheless, the couple was smitten. She thought that a faithful renovation could return the hotel to its halcyon days of the late nineteenth and early twentieth centuries. But Gammell says that in order to carry out her ambition she needed some additional support and understanding from an unlikely quarter. And so she struck up a conversation with the ghosts that she was certain inhabited Thayer's.

"There were a bunch of them here, and they weren't very happy. I told Warren to talk to the owner while I went upstairs. . . . I said [to the ghosts], 'Here's how it will play out. If we buy this building, I expect you will honor my guests, and then we will honor you. We have to have a working arrangement, or it can't be done.'"

Apparently, Gammell's heart-to-heart with the resident spirits was successful. Over the next three years Sharon and Warren began an ultimately successful, painstaking restoration of the hotel's exterior, interior, *and* reputation.

"I actually had one guy come in and say he only wanted to rent a room for two hours. I had to say, 'No sir, that's not what we do here anymore,'" Gammell says, laughing.

Tragically, Warren Gammell would not live to see the hotel's rebirth. Three years after the couple bought the hotel, in 1996, Warren was killed by a drunken driver. The question then became whether or not Sharon would go on alone to finish the restoration and operate the business.

She stayed.

Gammell's research indicated that in its first years the hotel had been a fashionable destination for travelers from as far away as Chicago and New York. The old Soo Line Railroad helped finance the hotel's construction and even advertised the hotel and the community of Annandale to prospective vacationers in eastern cities. Today, trains still rumble through several times a day across West Elm Street (Highway 55), but they carry freight instead of smartly dressed travelers.

Gammell describes Caroline Thayer as the "chief cook and bottle washer" when she and her husband operated the hotel. Menus from that era featured gourmet dinners with fine beef dishes and even oyster stew.

"They were focusing on [those with money] and those who had time to recreate. That was surprising to me. They catered to an up-scale crowd," says Gammell.

Gus and Caroline Thayer owned the business for several decades before selling it to their daughter. The hotel eventually passed out of the family but continued in business as a hotel and restaurant. Nevertheless, as passenger rail travel declined so did the hotel's fortunes. It closed for a few years in the late 1960s and early 1970s. Unlike other small-town hotels, however, Thayer's was not remodeled into apartments or bulldozed into oblivion during redevelopment efforts. A partial restoration was undertaken in the 1980s. The hotel's location on Highway 55, a still-busy route between the Twin Cities and North Dakota, helped keep it going, as did its 1978 inclusion on the National Register of Historic Places.

Situated amid summer gardens and ponds on nearly an acre of land a few blocks from downtown Annandale, Thayer's architecture looks as if it would be at home on a dusty street in the Old West. The three-story balloon-frame building has a cream exterior with teal and light purple accents. Distinctive upper galleries, or balconies, on each floor stretch across its width; chairs on each provide a way to watch the passing scenes. A wide front porch a few feet from the street has steps flanked by a pair of stone lions, suggesting those found at the New York Public Library, and a solid oak front door. A small plaque announces the hotel's designation as a national historic place. White lace curtains grace the windows.

Inside, the pressed-tin ceilings and walls and much of the original woodwork remain; the mid-1980s renovation moved the main staircase from a side wall to the center of the lobby.

Through the wide front doors, a front parlor has comfortable antique settees, rockers, side chairs, and tables. The vintage bar where Eric Rhinerson worked extends off the parlor while the guests' dining room is reached through a broad archway. The walls are chocka-block with old paintings, photographs, and knick-knack shelves.

Each of the eleven guest suites come with ghost stories attached.

"It's a great building," says Sharon Gammell. "It has so much character how could someone not take care of it?"

In the years after her husband died, however, Sharon may not have known just how hard it was going to be to care for it.

In 2001, a third-floor water pipe burst. The damage was so severe that Gammell had to close for a year so repairs could be made.

Then disaster struck again just two weeks before the scheduled reopening. Heat from one of the guest room's saunas triggered the hotel's sprinkler system, turning the staircase into a veritable waterfall. Gammell blamed the problem on a sensor set to activate the sprinklers at a temperature below that which is found in a heated sauna. Waterlogged ceilings sagged so low that Victorian chandeliers dipped to eye level. Carpeting had to be torn out and replaced; thousands of dollars in antiques were ruined.

Again, Thayer's was closed, but finally, in 2003, the repairs and restoration were complete.

Keeping the business going was a challenge during those years, says Gammell, because Thayer's was and is a destination establishment that caters to geographically diverse customers.

"A very loyal clientele had built up," notes Gammell. "But if you close the doors, they have to find somewhere else to go."

Fortunately, during the time Thayer's was closed while undergoing repair, the ghosts—and their stories—did not leave for a quieter venue. Gammell says that after she and her husband bought the hotel and she had her own candid tête-à-tête with the ghosts the couple heard more stories of odd events reported over the years.

One young staff member tried to sneak in a cigarette break using the kitchen's large walk-in cooler. The door suddenly slammed shut. He couldn't push it open, even though it was not supposed to be lockable. It took him some time to attract another employee's attention.

Gammell smiles and says the ghosts made their point—the young man was not supposed to be smoking on the job.

Skeptical guests are quite often the subject of ghostly pranks.

Gammell cites one incident involving a group of six couples who had come for a weekend stay. They'd been joking all weekend that no ghosts had made their presence known to them and teasingly suggested the owner was making up the stories. The couples went out for late-evening cocktails. When they returned, according to Gammell, no members of the group could get their keys to work in the front door. After several fruitless attempts, one woman suggested to her friends that if the place was indeed haunted, maybe they should just ask a ghost to open the door. Although she felt a little silly doing it, she asked aloud that the door be opened. It swung open.

"They were kind of freaked out," says Gammell. "We've had a number of people with incidents like that."

One of her favorite stories involves a couple who got married at Thayer's several years ago. Their best man was also staying there. He dismissed the ghost stories as so much hokum.

"We had everything for the wedding all set to go. We were out in the garden, and there's no best man," says Gammell, who also is licensed to officiate at marriages. "We couldn't find the best man. Ten minutes later, he comes charging out, and we get through the wedding, and everything's fine."

Gammell didn't learn why the best man was late until six months later when the newlyweds returned to spend a weekend. The friend who had been the best man was going to stay there as well, but he hadn't arrived yet. As they waited for him, the couple confided to Gammell that on their wedding day he had gotten locked in his room.

"It's hard to lock those doors from the inside. He couldn't get out for the wedding. Finally, he said, 'Okay, can you just open the door?'"

The door opened. Gammell figures he acknowledged the ghosts, and they complied.

When the man finally arrived to spend the weekend, he was good natured about the earlier incident but made it clear he was *not* going to stay in that room again.

On another occasion, an employee who had spent five years working at Thayer's complained to Sharon that she'd never seen one of the ghosts. She was disappointed. Sharon suggested that she simply make the request that one of them manifest itself.

Two weeks passed, and it was a quiet Monday after a busy weekend. All the guests had checked out, and Sharon Gammell and the employee were putting everything back in order. Sharon was in her main-floor office doing paper work; the employee was in the kitchen.

"SHARON!!!"

Gammell hustled out into the dining room as the woman came charging through the kitchen door. She claimed a man dressed in a work shirt and jeans had materialized out of the kitchen wall and walked right past her.

It turned out that the woman had taken up Sharon's suggestion.

"Well, he certainly let her see him," smiles Gammell.

Even though Gammell says "there's nothing worse than an unhappy ghost," she is unshakable in her belief that, although the spirits at Thayer's may be prankish or sometimes display odd senses of humor, they are not harmful.

"I think there's a misconception about ghosts that they're all stuck here and unhappy," says Gammell. She says ghosts are like the living—if they enjoy a particular location, they're apt to return, or even hang about.

For eternity.

"We've got people who probably stayed here, had a good time, and now come back to visit. Or maybe you come back because you heard someone made a change in the decorations," says Gammell.

Eric Rhinerson agrees. "I heard Sharon once describe Thayer's as a 'cosmic resort.'"

The biggest misunderstanding about a haunted place such as her own, says Gammell, is "that it's scary. That it's bad. That it's going to hurt them. That ghosts are something other than what they are. I think a lot of people come expecting to get scared. They like that Hollywood horror flick thing."

Seeing a ghost is highly unusual, Gammell says.

Of Eric Rhinerson's experience, Gammell calls it "the holy grail of ghost hunting. I don't guarantee you're going to see one. Seeing a ghost is almost impossible. The chances of that happening are a bazillion to one. I just happen to have it here a lot; apparently, they find this a cool place. But still it's not that usual."

Gammell says she doesn't literally talk to the ghosts. It's an "information exchange," she explains, with her words and ideas communicated to a spirit in a kind of thought process. She in turn gets information back from them in the same manner.

"The ghosts we have here are not energy repetition, which is one kind of ghost that you'll get. You're not seeing a *ghost;* you're seeing a *memory.* You're having the interaction with it here. . . . I interact with them all the time, so it's not different for me. But I think for other people it would be. I've had ghosts around me my whole life. I think it's odd that other people have a problem with it."

Gammell doesn't particularly care what terminology is used to describe the supernatural.

"We use the word 'ghost,' and they don't care, and I don't care. It's a whole lot easier . . . than to say this is a ghost, this is a poltergeist, this is a spirit, and so forth. We say 'ghost,' and they are perfectly fine with that."

Quite a few known—and unknown—lodger ghosts keep company with the living at this Annandale inn. The most prominent include Augustus "Gus" and Caroline Thayer—she of the sudden appearance to Eric Rhinerson. But there's also a former workman named Sam, a little girl who watches silently from the staircase when there's a weekend murder mystery dinner, and an alluring young woman who used to work at the hotel . . . in one capacity or another. She doesn't say much more, but Sharon thinks the meaning is quite clear. The hotel once had a seedy reputation.

Gammell says the spirit of her late husband, Warren, lingers there. Many of the spirits at Thayer's are nameless or perhaps just passing through on their way elsewhere.

Ghost animals hang about Thayer's, as well. They include several cats and a dog-wolf hybrid that upsets Tennessee, one of Gammell's

Maine Coon cats. Tennessee stands his ground when the ghost dog is on the prowl.

Gammell says builder Gus Thayer is most frequently in residence. Gus sometimes acts as a mediator if one of the ghosts disturbs the peaceful coexistence Gammell encourages between the ghosts and her guests at the inn.

There was the ghost of a crabby, anonymous grandmother, for instance. She favored relaxing afternoons lounging in a rocking chair. But then grandmother got very disturbed during some minor room remodeling. Gammell says the rocking chair the old woman loved swung back and forth all evening long.

Gammell got upset that the old woman was upset and finally gave her an ultimatum: either she had to stop with the chair or she could leave; she was unsettling some of the guests. About a week later, Gus "told" Gammell that he'd had a talk with the cranky woman and that she'd agreed to stop the irksome rocking.

Perhaps the oddest ghost story concerns a beginner ghost named Nels, an old codger who apparently came to stay when his photograph was hung in the spacious dining room.

Nels's was among several old family photos that had belonged to a young woman who was Sharon Gammell's personal assistant. The woman didn't want them herself because they didn't fit with her home's more contemporary furnishings. Gammell had agreed to hang them at Thayer's, alongside the dozens of other vintage gilt-framed photographs. One of the photographs was of a stern-faced man named Nels, the personal assistant's great-grandfather.

Gammell finished hanging the pictures, including that of Nels, shortly before a weekend murder mystery dinner. Among the guests was a Rochester couple that had been among those locked out months before. The couple was still not persuaded that ghosts rambled about the premises, despite a brief, malodorous episode in their room shortly after they arrived for the mystery dinner. The couple complained that one of the resident Main Coon cats must have had an accident because there was a distinctly disgusting odor in their room. Sharon checked the room but found nothing to account for the smell.

She thought the ghosts might be making mischief and told them to change the smell to something more pleasant. The nasty odor went away.

The mystery dinner proceeded without a hitch but with no obvious signs of the supernatural. The guests were disappointed, especially the Rochester guests. They were still waiting for an actual ghost sighting.

The next morning, a Sunday, Gammell and her staff noticed the couple didn't come down for breakfast. A staff member sent to check on them came back down to say the couple's room was empty. Apparently, they had left sometime during the night.

Later, Gammell found a message awaiting her on the answering machine. It was the wife. She'd left it early that morning after they'd gotten back to Rochester. She told Gammell to call her as soon as possible and added that she and her husband were fine.

Gammell finally connected with the woman, who then proceeded to explain their hasty departure.

The air conditioning was keeping the room comfortable on the humid August night. Suddenly, the room became ice cold and the lights went on. At about the same moment, a full male apparition appeared standing near the foot of the bed. The man looked at them, doffed his hat, and then vanished. The lights went off, and the room warmed up. The couple got out of bed, packed their suitcases, and drove home.

Gammell offered her profuse apologies and urged the couple to return at a later date.

Gammell soon learned the unexpected visitor had been Nels, the ghostly great-grandfather. He'd done it because the couple continued to make fun of Sharon and his great-granddaughter.

"He'd never haunted before," says Gammell. "I said that's fine, but he'd have to figure out another way [to haunt the hotel]."

The Rochester couple did eventually return to Thayer's but not to stay in their former room. When a photograph of Nels was shown to them, they both agreed that he had been their late-night visitor.

Guests who don't want surprising nighttime encounters might be well advised to take Sharon Gammell's advice.

"I say that if they don't want ghosts in their room, make it clear that it is out of bounds, off limits . . . that they don't want to be disturbed."

In other words, talk to the ghosts. Whether you believe in them or not.

21

TAYLORS FALLS

LOST IN TIME

"*I believe it is possible that there could be an-other dimension, so I keep an open mind.*"

Don Lawrence

For Becky Risler, working at a Taylors Falls bed-and-breakfast comes with its own unique and surprising rewards, like finding the imprint of a human body on a bed's fresh quilt and pillow . . . when no one living had been in that guest suite.

To say that she was startled by the rumpled bedding is not an exaggeration. She shouldn't have been, for stories abound that this B&B is haunted.

These periodic ghostly interludes are not all that unusual at the Old Jail Bed-and-Breakfast in Taylors Falls, the oldest licensed such establishment in Minnesota. But material traces like this are more infrequent.

"It was so physically obvious. It's something I didn't expect, and I certainly hadn't seen it on any of the other beds," Risler says of that winter morning in 2006.

She discovered the ghostprint the morning after she made up a twin bed in the guest room, straightened the antique quilt, smoothed out the feather pillows, and left, locking the door behind her. Everything was nice and neat and ready for guests, though no one was booked in immediately.

164

"The next morning I went back in to dust, and there was the impression. A body had lain on the bed," she recalls. The pillow also bore an indentation of what looked like someone's head. "I evened part of it out just to see if the down comforter [underneath] had gotten wrinkled somehow, but it smoothed out perfectly."

No one else was in the building at the time.

Risler is an assistant to proprietor Don Lawrence, who has owned the Old Jail B&B for several years. She may be the most sensitive to these mostly sociable ghosts, but she is hardly alone in noticing their presence. Lawrence himself can hear some of the ghostly activity, but he says he hasn't seen anything. Interestingly, he says that's not true of his granddaughter. Lawrence remembers an occasion when his own family was at the inn for a picnic. His preschool-age granddaughter ran inside the B&B's main building but came scooting back out seconds later. She cried that there was "a little boy ghost" inside. She wouldn't go back in unless someone was with her. No one had discussed ghost stories in her presence.

And then there are the brief, albeit intriguing, comments guests sometimes jot down in the journals kept in each of the four suites:

The ghost is friendly—just make peace with the spirit before you retire.

We threw the ugly [stuffed toy] cat that was on the bed into a basket in the corner—the next morning it was on the floor under the basket!

The door blew open with no wind. Knocking.

An old jail lock hanging on the wall swayed back and forth.

Curious noises early in the morning.

2 AM There was a light knock, knock, knock at the door.

All are small incidents, certainly, but not surprising given the colorful history of this notable hostelry perched on Angel Hill in old Taylors Falls, overlooking the picturesque upper St. Croix River.

The Old Jail Bed-and-Breakfast complex comprises two locally historic buildings—the original one-room town jail and a former saloon known as the Schottmuller Building.

The 1884 hoosegow now is the comfortable Old Jail Cottage, perhaps the most distinctive hotel room anywhere in the state, complete with the original iron-barred windows and front door. Fortunately, the original cells are long gone in favor of a loft bedroom, a wood-burning Franklin stove, and a full kitchen. The occasional ghost is optional.

The jail was a temporary home for local reprobates until the city sold it in 1923, after which it was used as a garage and an icehouse. Taylors Falls historian Helen White remodeled it for use as a B&B in 1981.

Next door is the older three-story Schottmuller Building with two guest suites. White restored it, as well, in creating the Old Jail B&B. Owner Don Lawrence uses one floor as his private apartment.

The Schottmuller property has an equally intriguing history. In 1869, Joseph and Frank Schottmuller erected a single-story stone saloon to go along with their brewery farther up Angel Hill. A cave connecting the two was used to cool the beer. A short time later, they purchased a two-story livery stable from the Chisago House Hotel and hoisted it atop the saloon. Over the years, the new three-story building housed several businesses on the first floor, most notably the Cave Saloon, while the families maintained a residence on the top floors.

For some time in the late nineteenth century, the building moved out of the Schottmuller family's hands and became known as the Holt Building, with a meat market and other stores leasing space on the lower level. The upstairs was used as a boardinghouse for lumbermen and later as a residence for new generations of Schottmullers, who bought back the building in 1904.

The newest owner, Don Lawrence, lives on the second floor of the Schottmuller building, between two guest suites, surrounded by a fascinating collection of Americana, including a barber chair, an antique gas pump, and vintage deep-sea diving gear.

"It doesn't bother me if there is a presence here. And they don't seem to bother anyone else. I think you just need to communicate one way or another with them. I hear things like footsteps upstairs, but I haven't had any visual contact at all. I've gone up there, but there's nobody."

The ghosts in this small hotel are not those of horror novels. They are welcoming presences, according to Becky Risler, who discovered them the first time she stayed overnight.

"I don't know if it was because I was new here and they could sense me or what. Don had started to change things upstairs in the Overlook Suite. It seemed they were very, very active in that early winter of 2006. I was going upstairs into the back bedroom, and I felt a presence. It wasn't spooky but like you knew someone was there. It was an enveloping, comforting feeling. I didn't feel afraid, because I sensed that someone was watching over me. So that's the kind of ghost she is. She's not mean or vicious or anything else."

She?

Risler and Lawrence believe the inn's foremost ghost is female and quite likely Etta Hovey Schottmuller, wife of Frank J. Schott-muller, the son of one of the original building owners and the man who reacquired it in 1904. Frank, Etta, and their family opened a general mercantile on the bottom floor and lived on the upper floors. The family's life together was plagued by tragedy. The couple had four boys, none of whom lived past middle age. Frank E. died at age two from eating sulfur kitchen matches. Etta died in 1917, just fifteen years after her marriage to Frank. She left behind her husband to raise their three surviving sons, ages five, six, and eleven.

Little Frank may be the boy ghost that some children, including Don Lawrence's granddaughter, have seen in the Schottmuller building. Once, an inn employee found her son chattering away with someone only he could see. Invisible playmates are not uncommon among children, so perhaps this was such a case. Or perhaps not.

Stories circulate, however, about at least two other deaths in the Schottmuller building. A paucity of records makes it nearly impossible to verify such speculation.

"That's the town rumor," Risler says. "The little boy did die here, so that's why I think he's here. I think Etta is here because of him."

The case for a ghostly Etta is strengthened because most of the unexplained sounds and incidents take place on the inn's upper floors, once the Schottmuller home. If so, she is still taking care of her house and reacting to the changes new owners make. She would be sad, too, in having left her boys to grow up without a mother.

Etta also makes her feelings known, according to Risler.

One recent winter day, after the Christmas decorations were taken down, Risler could feel a change in the atmosphere, especially in the Overlook Suite, with its stunning view of the St. Croix River. She thinks melancholia over the end of the holiday season may have set in with Etta and Frank.

"I could feel her presence at the end of the bed, and I sensed just a terrible, terrible sadness," Risler said.

But later, during that same winter, the mood seemed to brighten. That suite became "very, very active," Risler says. She heard someone singing softly, what seemed to be a child jumping off the beds or chairs and onto the floor, and century-old floorboards groaning as someone walked across the suite. Risler thought the ghosts were very close at hand.

"Sometimes when we went upstairs into the kitchen and the bedroom you'd feel a big, cold cylinder of air," Risler remembers. She said it was like walking into an icy circle, or a tube of frigid air. Soon it would pass.

Risler reveals little apprehension in knowing that she, more often than not, is the one who figures out that the spirits are at hand. In fact, she welcomes their presence.

"I told [the ghosts], 'It's just fine you're here. We don't want you to go. It's your place, too, but you can go if you want to. We're taking care of it now.' But I'd like to know for sure who they are."

Risler grew up with what she calls an ESP-like bond with her mother. "I've always been able to see things like spirits. I enjoy when the [ghosts] here do things. I tell them there's nothing you guys can do to scare me. Some things are a little stranger than others, but it's something you have to be open to. Anything is possible."

As with many haunted places, the ghostly activity seems to be more frequent when remodeling projects are under way or when certain visitors make these house spirits wary. Several paranormal investigators felt uncomfortable during their visit in 2006. Risler wonders if it was because the ghosts themselves were uneasy because someone was intentionally looking for them and they didn't want to be bothered.

"They come and go," Risler says. "They'll be very active for certain stretches of time. They get stirred up when furniture gets brought in or we paint, really when anything gets changed. It's like they have to check everything out."

One couple staying in the Old Jail Suite had the alarming experience of waking up to a large piece of furniture's having been moved several feet sometime during the night. It was a tall, upright secretary with breakable knickknacks that had been taken off the top and put inside. A magazine rack that must be moved if the secretary is rearranged was still in place.

"We all saw that the secretary had been moved, and it's a tough piece of furniture to move because it's set on bricks and takes two people. . . . The couple didn't hear anything. It was weird. The woman was terrified, just sitting on the couch wrapped in a blanket," Risler says. She had gotten up to use the bathroom during the night and found the secretary sitting in a new position.

Another overnight couple sitting on the couch in the Old Jail Suite saw a woman in a long black dress standing on the suite's balcony, gazing down at them, with one hand resting on the balcony rail. Their description of the woman was similar to a photograph of Etta Schottmuller.

Owner Don Lawrence says ghosts weren't part of the discussion when he bought the inn, because "sometimes that scares buyers away." But he's okay with their ramblings anyway.

He doesn't generally discuss the ghost stories when taking reservations or speaking with potential guests. It's a mixed blessing. He mentions one couple that might have passed on staying overnight if they had known about the ghosts. At the same time, he adds, the prospect of encountering a ghost might attract other guests.

"A lot of people are interested in it and get excited. I believe it is possible that there could be another dimension, so I keep an open mind, but I haven't had any concrete evidence myself."

That doesn't mean he neglects to look for proof, as when he shows off the suites.

"Whenever I walk into a unit now, if I'm showing it to somebody, I look at the bed. People have talked about impressions of people on the beds. I don't like that, because it looks like I was lying down!"

Lawrence says the long and colorful history of the jail and the Schottmuller Building is packed with evidence that former residents may be lingering there still. He points to the days when raucous loggers and other rivermen stayed in the small sleeping rooms, each room crowded with several beds. Their brawling ways might have resulted in more than one fatal quarrel.

Lawrence also wants to explore inside the original Schottmuller cave, but that would involve hauling away tons of rubble and debris.

A cave exploration might be useful for nascent ghost hunters as well: in addition to the storage of beer, local legend says the cave was used by a long-ago Taylors Falls undertaker to preserve bodies in the era before refrigeration . . .

DUST to DUST

"Things can happen in an old house."
Ethel Thorlacius

The homesteader came home drunk. Again. His wife heard him stumble through the door, much as he had done on too many other late nights. But enough was enough. She'd been worried sick at his absence. It was deep in a Minnesota winter, and nighttime travel on horseback or afoot across the frozen prairie was treacherous and possibly deadly. No, this time she'd had it. She decided to punish him in a way that he wouldn't likely forget anytime soon.

He could not sleep with her that night, she told him, and pointed the way up a ladder into the unheated storage loft of their rough-hewn farm home. There is no record of whether he protested the abrupt treatment, or even whether she had to help him climb the ladder, but according to those who know the story, in the end it didn't really matter. His fate was sealed in ways neither he nor his wife ever anticipated.

Without any sort of roof insulation above the loft and probably with little more than the clothes on his back for warmth, that nameless homesteader didn't have much of a chance against the subzero temperatures outside. His wife found him frozen to death the next morning.

And though his family no doubt wept over his untimely death—

and his failings as a husband and as a father—and then buried him in the earth, this was not to be the end of him. According to some in northwestern Minnesota's Marshall County, that pioneer farmer made at least a couple of appearances long after his body had turned to dust.

Marshall County historian Ethel Thorlacius says the farmer's reappearance is one of the more interesting ghost stories in her region of the state.

"In later years, the house was empty and eventually sold to a neighbor a few miles away," she notes. It was moved to another farm and attached to the barn, where it was used to store feed and grain.

The abandoned house was not unlike hundreds of others scattered across northern farmlands, homes that had once held generations of families but were now reduced to an existence as cheap, makeshift storage buildings with their windows gone or boarded over and their doors ajar or missing completely. The sights and sounds of the families they once held have been reduced to only vague and distant memories, if even that much, except in the house where one particularly drunk farmer froze to death. There his ghost would not rest.

"That farm held two generations," Thorlacius says of the place where the old house was moved, "and oftentimes the grandfather and grandson would find themselves working together."

The grandson had allergies to the grain dust, which made work difficult, according to Thorlacius. But nevertheless, he was expected to do his share of the chores.

So on that one particular day when grandpa hollered out for his grandson to come and help shovel the grain in that old house-barn, the boy diffidently moved to obey the old man. His father and brother were also close by and must have heard the call, so perhaps they'd get there first to help out, he reasoned.

The minutes ticked by until finally the youngster quietly peeked around the corner of the door of the old house and into what might have once been a living room but in which now hung a cloud of grain dust.

Through the dust, the young man saw his grandfather a few

feet away shoveling the grain as he had expected. But instead of his father and brother nearby, he saw someone else. A man, a stranger to the boy, stood beside his grandfather, shovel in hand, swinging it back and forth to clear away the grain, nearly mirroring the grandfather's actions. When the young man blinked and looked back, his grandfather was very much alone. His peculiar assistant was nowhere to be seen.

Ethel Thorlacius heard the story directly from the young man, though he didn't tell anyone right away about what happened.

"He eventually did when he was older," she says.

But that was not to be the end of it. Thorlacius says there was a second odd incident.

The two families lived in different houses on the farm. One day, the young man's father—the grandfather's son—was at work doing some remodeling on the house he lived in with his own family. He was cutting a doorway through one of the walls and into a room in order to create a bit more living space.

As he set down the saw after roughing out the opening, he glanced into the room beyond.

There was a man standing in the next room looking back at him.

He certainly looked real enough, what with his black coat and slouch hat and knee-high black leather boots. He was so real, in fact, that the farmer started to speak, thinking he had a visitor, when suddenly whoever or whatever it was vanished.

Thorlacius thinks it was the same ghost that had visited the man's son, the old homesteader whose angry wife had sent him to his death. And she believes she knows why the ghost didn't stick around the second time. "Perhaps he was afraid he would be asked to do some work again!"

"From what I understand, [the incidents] did occur," Thorlacius says, ever the cautious historian, even though she got the stories directly from the two men involved. But she certainly thinks it's possible that the long-gone homesteader returned because, as she adds, "Things can happen in an old house."

Stories of a reanimated homesteader are not the only bizarre occurrences in that part of Minnesota bordered to the west by the Red River and North Dakota.

A few eerie encounters with puzzling lights in the sky—including one reported by a deputy sheriff—have given Marshall County a reputation among those who pursue unsolved mysteries.

On a late August night in 1979, Deputy Sheriff Val Johnson radioed then-sheriff Dennis Brekke that he needed immediate assistance on a county road near Stephen, Minnesota. By the time the sheriff got there, Johnson was in an ambulance en route to an area hospital. His patrol car was sitting askew on the highway. The windshield was fractured; a headlight was shattered; and two radio antennas were bent. There were several dents in the hood. One of the red lights atop the cruiser had a small hole in it.

Johnson later told his boss that the last thing he remembered was driving toward a very bright light that seemed to be floating in the sky about a mile away. He estimated he woke up about forty minutes later and radioed for help.

Experts told Sheriff Brekke that something had struck the deputy sheriff's cruiser and, further, that the object had been traveling at an accelerated rate of speed. The air force told him that they had no planes in the area, nor were there other reports of unusual lights in the sky.

Deputy Johnson reportedly encountered a good deal of razzing after the incident, but a Grafton, North Dakota, couple came forward with their own unusual story from that same night. The husband and wife had been en route to their rural home when a blindingly bright flash of light arose in the eastern sky, in the general vicinity of Stephen. Grafton is a short distance southwest of Stephen. Though they didn't want to tell anyone about the incident, they did eventually provide a written statement describing what they saw.

Deputy Val Johnson's Ford LTD cruiser—with its original 1979 damages intact—and the Grafton couple's testimonial are on exhibit in the Marshall County Historical Society Museum in Warren.

PHANTOMS OF THE PARAMOUNT

*"In fact, I look for the ghost quite a bit. If I hear a noise,
I'll look in that direction."*

Scott Anderson

Scott Anderson considered the job in front of him. Even though he was a chief administrator at Austin's historic Paramount Theatre, he often had to roll up his sleeves to pitch in where necessary. Today it was sanding and sealing an equipment rack in the sound booth at the rear of the theater. He looked up at the high ceiling lights in the auditorium, which were really too dim to work by, so he hauled the framework out into the lobby to work on it there.

He slipped a Steely Dan CD into the theater's sound system.

"I kind of like loud music," says Anderson, the Paramount's operations director and one of its longtime guiding lights. "I had it cranked up pretty loud, so I could hear it."

But he then noticed something odd was going on with the Steely Dan recording. The volume had been slowly turned down.

"I could still hear the music, but it wasn't nearly as loud. I wondered what happened."

Anderson wiped off his hands and went back into the sound booth.

The sound board has sliders that move up and down so that an operator can set each audio input at a specific point. Although several other sliders remained where Anderson had locked them into place, he says the CD volume control had been "definitely moved" to make the music softer.

But he has an idea of what happened.

"However he did this, he turned it down. He didn't turn it off, just turned it down to a level he thought was more reasonable."

"He" did this?

Yes, "he" did.

Scott Anderson is, of course, talking about a ghost in the ornate old theater.

He believes the unsolicited Steely Dan critic is an elusive phantom that may be the ghost of Karl Lindstaedt, the theater's original owner, an infrequent, albeit persistent and mild-mannered, spirit.

For Scott Anderson there have been enough curious incidents at the Paramount—coupled with his own personal encounter with a ghost earlier in his life—to persuade him that specters are around us, including the one sheltered at Austin's splendidly restored movie palace.

The Spanish colonial revival Paramount is the crown jewel of Austin's thriving arts community. Built on the site of an earlier theater destroyed in a tornado, the Paramount opened its doors to first-run movies and vaudeville performers on September 14, 1929. It was Austin's first all-talking motion picture house (several others were showing silent films). Back then, adult tickets were fifty cents, and children's were a dime. Vaudeville acts complemented the early talkies through the 1930s.

Famed Minneapolis architects Ellerbe and Associates designed the Paramount as a 914-seat atmospheric theater—in this case a motif intended to transport the audience to a romantic Spanish courtyard, complete with baroque faux balconies, the plentiful use of plaster swirls, and black wrought-iron highlights.

Overhead, the theater's high azure ceiling simulates an evening sky: as the house lights dim, twinkling star lights and projected clouds complete the illusion. In 1943, the design and color scheme were changed to a Normandy style, with blue, peach, and teal accents around paintings of medieval knights on horseback.

The exterior's baroque-style façade was patterned after the Church of Jesus in Rome.

But by the mid-1970s old movie palaces like the Paramount were falling victim to the new entertainment venues—television and sleek multiplexes. The theater closed as a movie house on April 30, 1975. For a few years in the late 1970s and 1980s, it was a bar and nightclub.

But in 1987, the Austin Area Commission for the Arts took on the formidable task of restoring the Paramount to its earlier grandeur.

The theater has been restored to a near-perfect replication of its first few decades, right down to the exquisite ceiling stencils reproduced by Blooming Prairie artist John Durfey. A new seating arrangement allows for 623 patrons.

The lobby has the look and feel of the original 1930s movie palace. The checkerboard tiled floor and patterned carpet replicate the originals, while the stenciled dark-wood beams add to a coziness not found in modern multiplexes. An ornate birdbath sits inside a curved alcove. Several display cabinets hold photographs and memorabilia from the Paramount's storied past. From the lobby one enters the auditorium through a draped proscenium arch and broad double doors.

The building's exterior has been refurbished, and a red, white, and teal neon marquee with "Paramount" writ large has replaced the original, which was removed during a street widening. In 2007, the final piece of the restoration was put in place, a stone spire at the roof's peak; the original was destroyed by lightning in a 1945 Halloween day storm. On the exterior walls singular tiled circles, or mandalas, representing the cosmos are enclosed in two bands of patterned glazed ceramic tile that delineate each of the building's several stories.

Today, the Paramount is the only atmospheric theater in Minnesota outside of the Twin Cities still used for its intended purpose, hosting over eighty theater, music, and business events each year. It's one of the few Spanish colonial revival buildings in Minnesota and the only one in Mower County. It's listed on the National Register of Historic Places.

"Atmospheric theaters are so cool," Scott Anderson says with obvious satisfaction. "This theater has a personality of its own; people from all walks of life come together to experience it."

Sometimes visitors might see more of the theater's historic legacy than they think possible, especially during those times when Anderson thinks the resident ghost is out and about.

"I look for the ghost quite a bit. If I hear a noise, I'll look in that direction. I don't know if you can communicate with them, but it would be very interesting to see him. I've had a number of experiences with ghosts, not a lot, but I would love to encounter this one. I'm pretty sure there are one or two here, friendly; we've had no terrible experiences. It doesn't scare me at all, but in fact some people can't be here by themselves. . . . They just won't do it."

Even when Steely Dan's music suddenly became softer, Anderson didn't shy away from a hoped-for encounter.

"I was sort of hoping I'd see him. I started looking around for him because somebody turned it down. . . . I didn't do it!"

Anderson says a local television station tried to repeat the incident in a 2006 Halloween feature. The TV crew tied a monofilament line to the switch and manually tugged at it.

The Paramount ghost isn't old by haunting standards. Reports first surfaced when the theater was a nightclub thirty years ago.

"When we started to restore the theater, a man from town who used to work here during the bar era came by and told us a number of stories about ghost experiences," says Anderson. "That's when we first heard about it. I've never heard of anything before that era, so I think he appeared when it was a bar."

Most of the stories from that period are anecdotal, except for one in which Anderson was directly involved.

The longtime Austin resident is also a musician. In the 1970s and 1980s, he played in a band. During a gig at the Paramount during its bar years, his band performed one number during which they wore "goofy" masks to parody the song. As they usually did at the end of their show, band members asked the audience for some written feedback about what they liked and did not like during the performance. Most of the comments were straightforward, except for several audience members who had an odd reaction to the song during which they wore the masks.

The band was complimented on the funny masks, but a few people thought the "masked man" peering out of an alcove above the stage proscenium arch was "freaky."

There is a small window-like niche directly above center stage— purely an architectural embellishment. No one was up there that night, nor is the space ever used.

"I was on stage at the time, so I didn't see it, but apparently people in the audience saw it," says Anderson.

A friend of Anderson's also claims to have seen a photograph of one balcony decorated for the holidays in which there is a translucent human figure next to a small Christmas tree.

"I haven't seen the photo, but I'd love to get my hands on it. I certainly believe him."

In another incident a manager during the bar era was cleaning up late one night. She was alone when she heard someone walking toward her across a creaking wood floor that was installed over the old theater seats. She turned around to see who it was. A bar stool was spinning at the far end.

"There are stories that people would leave for a brief time and come back, and the blenders in the bar would be on," adds Anderson. "Or they'd leave the building at night . . . and come back, and the marquee would be lighted. There'd be no way they'd leave [the sign] on inadvertently, because it's so bright out there. They just wouldn't do that."

He speculates that the ghost may be the Paramount's original owner, Karl Lindstaedt, and that he first showed up because he didn't like the fact that his theater had been closed down and converted into a bar. No one has approached Anderson with ghost stories from that earlier period between 1929 and 1975.

"Up until that Steely Dan experience, I always thought he liked the fact that it's a theater again. He had been resting in peace until I woke him up with that really loud music," laughs Anderson.

But another incident during the summer of 2006 makes Anderson wonder if perhaps there aren't *two* ghosts at the Paramount or maybe merely that Lindstaedt finds amusing ways to make his presence known.

It all began with a visit by two older ladies, cousins, whose shared great-grandfather was George Dorn, one of the early film projectionists at the Paramount. The women had never lived in Austin and were visiting the city to see where Grandfather Dorn had spent a share of his working life. They'd heard stories about his years in Austin and knew that the theater had been restored. Anderson was delighted to meet the ladies and give them a tour so they could take photos, one with a 35MM camera and the other with a newer digital model.

The three were talking and reminiscing and went into the auditorium. Anderson turned down the house lights and started up the cloud projector and the twinkling stars so they could get a sense of what their great-grandfather would have seen before each movie began.

Anderson darkened the house and brought up the romantic night sky with its myriad stars and rolling clouds. The only other light was from the decorative neon above the proscenium arch. Both women were snapping photos of the enchanted nighttime effect when one of them called out to Anderson.

"There's a moon in this photo!" she said, looking at the small screen of her digital camera and then toward the ceiling.

"It looked just like the moon," says Anderson of the image. "Even the clouds are on this side of the moon, like at night. It even has a crater texture to it. They wondered how that could have happened. I said it can't. There aren't any other light sources in the room. I said to them the ghost made it happen. I was serious. That was the only explanation I had."

The photograph plainly depicts a flawlessly proportioned moon floating above the proscenium arch, with clouds scudding across its face. The effect is startling.

"I formulated the theory afterward that it was their great-grandfather giving them a sign through this photo," says Anderson, adding the name George Dorn to that of Karl Lindstaedt as candidates for the ghosts of the Paramount. "Every time I talk about it, I get chills. A moon belongs in that kind of night sky, but . . . it's not there."

Karl Lindstaedt or George Dorn, both would seem to have reasons to linger in the theater they knew so well. Lindstaedt was well known in Minnesota's early twentieth-century entertainment business. He was acquainted with many of the vaudeville performers who played in Austin and other Minnesota cities. A photograph of Lindstaedt with comedians Bud Abbott and Lou Costello is on display in the lobby.

If there is a person suitable for keeping tabs on a haunted theater, it may well be Scott Anderson. Even before his days at the Paramount, he had encountered the unknown in the form of one of the more frequently reported disturbances attributed to ghostly phenomena—disembodied footsteps.

The setting was an older rental farmhouse outside Austin during the 1970s. Anderson and his wife lived there with several friends.

The time was late evening.

Everyone except Anderson and his wife had gone to town. They had put their dogs in the kitchen for the night and gone to bed but were not yet asleep.

Suddenly, through the open bedroom door, they heard heavy, purposeful footfalls coming up the staircase. They called out, but no one answered.

Anderson clearly remembers that night.

"Thump. Thump. Thump," Anderson says. "Very deliberate, very slow, but like he's trying to make noise. And we were thinking, 'What the heck is happening?' We didn't move because we didn't know what we could do."

The footfalls got to the top of the staircase and thumped down to their open bedroom door. Neither Anderson nor his wife could see anyone.

"But we could feel a presence in the doorway. It was palpable but not visible. Then it left and went back down the stairs. I could hear a person walking. But it went downstairs much quicker."

Anderson hopped out of bed, and reacting as if it might have been someone playing a bizarre prank, he grabbed a hunting knife and set off after the prowler.

"All the time I'm thinking this is a spirit; this isn't a live person. I thought [the knife] isn't going to do me much good!"

A house search turned up nothing. Yet the raucous behavior of their two dogs locked in the kitchen persuaded him that something had been walking about.

"The dogs were barking frantically, turning around, barking in the air. They knew something was there, but they couldn't see it or tell where it was. They didn't know where to bark, so they were kind of freaking out."

Anderson and his wife sat at the kitchen table talking about the episode until their friends got home. They recounted the episode, speculating anew about who or what it might have been. Anderson's buddy thought it might have been one of the previous owners who objects to riding dirt bikes around the yard and a nearby farm field, which Anderson and his friends did on a regular basis.

"Just then the yard light, and all the lights in the house, dimmed right when he said that," he recalls, still taken aback at the episode.

Scott Anderson thinks it was the ghost's way of saying, "Yup, that's right."

GETTING BILLED

*"As we walked by the till counter, an oar
came flying out of the corner."*
Sue Samuelson's diary entry

May 10, 2004. Karen was at the table doing paperwork when she heard the candy machine handle turn. Reese's Pieces were in the catch tray when she went to look. She was the only one in the store. She called me right away. . . .

June 14, 2004. Karen was working on a flower arrangement at the worktable and saw a small, shadowed figure standing by the basement door. She stared for about two seconds until she didn't see it anymore. Whatever!

October 26, 2004. Sue heard a knock at the door. It was Rose. . . . She said 'Are you open?' Sue said 'Sure.' Rose said the door was locked. Sue said no it wasn't, the knob turned really easy. Rose said it was locked solid, tight! We laughed. Oh, Bill . . . .

P.S. Bill locked out two other women today, too. And then he let some men in. Funny!

November 7, 2004. Sue, Mona and Pam were here. Sue was giving them a tour of the mill. As we walked by the till counter, an oar came flying out of the corner, between Pam and Mona. Needless to say they didn't want to finish the tour.

May 16, 2006. Sue came to work—and by the door was a strong

odor of cigar smoke. Went out and back in a couple of times and
the smell lingered. Bill was a cigar smoker.

These notes are drawn from the diary of a haunting that contains
occasional entries on peculiar events, both large and small, that
have characterized life in a country store which specializes in home
décor and gifts and that is situated in a comfortably refurbished
old feed mill in Norwood Young America, about thirty-five miles
west of the Twin Cities.

Owner Sue Samuelson's informal journal tracks the incidents
that have led her to believe the mill's manager during the 1930s
hasn't quite left the premises.

Samuelson operates the Mill House inside a cream-colored
building under a bright red tin roof along the town's Third Avenue
Southeast. A covered front deck overflows with hanging baskets,
antique tubs, painted milk cans, flower arrangements, and con-
tainer plants. On the porch's corner, wide steps lead up to the deck;
a newer pergola frames the side deck extension below a fading exterior sign reading "Howe's Feed Mill, Purina Chows," a reminder of
one of the mill's earlier incarnations.

Inside, even more antiques, crafts, and country furnishings vie
for space on pine tables and shelving or in glass front cabinets. The
original hardwood fir floor complements the open beam ceiling
and rustic cut-timber walls. A broad staircase with wide handrails
leads to an open second-floor balcony with more crafts and wares.
A separately owned floral shop, the Flower Mill, takes up a third of
the main floor.

A stone archway leads to a rear expansion into a connected former warehouse that has been remodeled into a coffee shop and
café and an additional sales space.

The Mill House is on one of the oldest business locations in
Carver County. A store was there as early as the 1850s. An 1862 fire
destroyed the original structure, but a new milling operation was
built after the Civil War by the Ackerman Brothers. By the 1930s, it
was Farmers Elevator and Coal. Later, a local rural co-op owned the
building and operated it as a farmers' supply outlet.

When Sue Samuelson and her partners bought the place in 2002, it had been closed for five years.

"I didn't want to see it disappear," says Samuelson, who lives nearby and knows something of the historic nature of the mill. "The city wanted to tear it down, and we didn't want them to do that."

During the remodeling Samuelson and her contractor-husband found 140-year-old floor studs.

With the mill's long history, it might seem problematic to identify just who or what might be haunting the place, but for Samuelson a name quickly attached itself to the ghost—Bill, the mill manager in the early to mid-1930s.

"His family came by because they heard we had a ghost inside. We started describing what he does, and they said that 'sounds like grandpa' because he was such a prankster," Samuelson says.

She concedes that "it might not be him" and that she's never seen him, but she continues to call the ghost Bill because of what she says the ghost does, especially pulling pranks.

The targets of such pranks "get Billed."

But whether it's Bill or there's some other explanation entirely, there is little doubt that there have been an uncommon number and variety of weird goings-on.

It all started shortly after the shop opened. Samuelson won't soon forget those incidents.

"Karen [Hallquist, owner of the florist business] had a briefcase, and every day it would . . . go flying off the counter. One day she was outside and came back in, and it was off the counter. Even with its Velcro pockets, everything was out on the floor. Now this was the first week that we were open. We thought it was a pretty strange thing."

Karen Hallquist says the incidents took place on the spot where Bill's original rolltop desk had stood.

"I always put my briefcase on either a chair or the countertop or something else in this area. I'd walk away, and I'd come back, and it would be on the floor."

Sue Samuelson says she was with customers a few times when they all heard something hit the floor. Each time, she suspected it was the briefcase, and when a customer was concerned about the crash, she'd simply smile and say there was nothing to worry about, that something must have fallen over.

Karen Hallquist says the briefcase incidents were the "real attention getters," the indications that life in their small businesses was going to be anything but normal.

"By the time it hit the floor about the seventh time, we were, like, why is that doing this. It was a big briefcase, it was heavy."

She still carries a big briefcase, but now she usually sets it directly on the floor.

Early on, Samuelson started a scrapbook documenting the restoration of the old mill. She took several photographs that appear to show orbs of light and, in one case, a mist in which she picks out a face.

"I was here on a Sunday by myself shooting pictures. There's a chin and the eyes, and he's got a hat on. His hand is coming up, and he's tipping his hat."

On another occasion, Samuelson and her camera were documenting the installation of new wiring and building insulation when something "streaked through the air" within camera range.

Karen Hallquist has come the closest to actually seeing something very, very out of place. The incident happened on a June day in 2004 while she worked on a floral arrangement.

"It was over by the stairway," she remembers. Those stairs lead down to the basement. "I glanced up once and then away, but I thought, What was that? It was short, like a little person standing there."

The shadowy figure lingered for a very few seconds before it vanished.

Hallquist and Samuelson are both disinclined to be in the shop after closing hours, although on many days one or the other must work late to finish paperwork or deal with inventory.

Samuelson says, "It's not easy being here late at night by myself. I turn the music up really loud or put a movie in the computer. . . . I've had some kids, my daughter and her friends, who want to stay here overnight, but I've said no. I don't want to push it."

Both Samuelson and Hallquist have brought their dogs to work with them if they have happened to work late. But even with her beagle for company, Hallquist won't venture too far from her own office.

"I won't go upstairs. Or into the basement, either," Hallquist says.

The candy machine incident recorded in the store diary was disquieting for her. It's the old-fashioned apparatus in which one puts coins and turns a handle and candy falls down a chute into a small tray. Hallquist was alone in her office when she heard the distinct "click-click-click" of the machine's handle, as if someone was turning it. Hallquist found the tray filled with Reese's Pieces.

Hallquist called Samuelson. They agreed she'd gotten Billed.

Sometimes, days or weeks have gone by without an incident. After Karen Hallquist saw the figure on the stairs, it was several months before another of Samuelson's diary entries.

That next episode played out about midmorning during a late October weekday.

A customer banged on the front door. Samuelson walked over and opened the door. The woman at the door asked if the store was open. Samuelson assured her that it was. The puzzled customer pointed out that the door was locked and the dead bolt was in place. The door couldn't be opened from the outside, yet Samuelson had unlocked it earlier that morning.

That sort of problem is typical of what happens, Samuelson says, something not malicious but more in the category of pranks.

Yet a few times, the activity, if not malicious, has certainly been aggressive, as when two of Samuelson's friends visited from Detroit Lakes and she showed them around the store.

"As we walked around the [cash register's counter], an old rowboat oar came flying off the wall and went right between them. Scared them to death. They didn't want to finish the tour."

Samuelson suspects Bill made his presence known because earlier she had told her friends about the resident ghost.

"The whole time one of them was driving out here, she was saying, 'I don't want to see him. I don't want to see him.' Well, then he threw the oar at her!"

Bill the ghost's fondness for startling visitors with flying merchandise once extended to a visit by the Avon lady.

"I was meeting with her downstairs," Samuelson says, "and a plaque came up off the wall, floated for a few seconds, and then dropped to the floor. It just lifted and dropped."

The Avon woman's jaw dropped. Samuelson remained unruffled.

"We try not to scare people because I want them to come back. So we kind of downplay stuff."

Another employee had a sugar and creamer set fly off a cabinet next to her.

The mischief making extends to the electrical system and a video recorder in Samuelson's small balcony-level office.

During the remodeling, the building's wiring was replaced and circuit breakers were installed. Yet Samuelson still found that the lights could behave oddly.

In July 2005, Karen Hallquist and another employee locked up for the night, leaving but a single nightlight on. Samuelson and her husband, Pat, returned to town later that night and drove by the store. All the lights were on. She thought perhaps Hallquist was working late. She was not. She came by later, noticed the lights were on, stopped, and turned them off.

Days later, Samuelson again saw the store lights on as she drove by after dark. She had worked that day and had turned them off.

"That's a lot . . . to turn on," Samuelson says.

Especially curious is Samuelson's diary entry for May 5, 2006.

Karen Hallquist, two other employees, and Samuelson arrived at work to hear a "whirring" noise coming from the office upstairs. When they investigated, they found the video recorder was in the process of rewinding a copy of Steven Spielberg's *The Goonies*. The cassette recorder itself was set on channel 3, which is necessary to watch video recordings. Usually, it's set on a local channel so Samuelson can watch television while she works at her desk.

"Nobody had watched any movies," Samuelson remembers. "We do that on Saturdays, but this was a Thursday. So maybe Bill was watching movies all night?"

Then there is the matter of the missing knives. Nearly a dozen of them. Gone.

"They are the ones we use for cutting flowers," Samuelson says. "We haven't found them yet. They're big, white-handled things."

Will they find a stash of knives one day?

"I don't know," flower shop manager Karen Hallquist laughs. "We clean out down here all the time; we look under the counters with a flashlight and so forth. We just don't know where they go."

A child's teddy bear that's been around the store for some time has figured in a couple of amusing getting-Billed episodes.

Karen Hallquist was at her worktable when she got up to fetch something from her office. When she returned a few minutes later, the teddy bear was propped up in her chair.

But what happened to a sensible local contractor was even more impish.

The man had been hired to install stairs that would connect all three floors, the basement included. He was on the main floor; his two carpenters were working separately, one in the basement and the other on the second floor. The staircase had not yet been put in place.

The contractor cut a length of wood and carried it over to a pile of finished boards nearby. He returned to the table saw and found the teddy bear sitting on it. He shrugged and put the bear back on a shelf.

When it happened again, he shouted to his assistants: "Dammit, you guys! Stop doing that!"

The men denied any involvement.

"He got Billed!" Hallquist notes playfully.

Pat Samuelson, Sue's husband, is a man who didn't believe in things he could not see. A tile contractor by trade, he did much of the finishing work at the Mill House. An incident in which he tried to move water pipes away from a basement wall, in order to protect them from winter freeze, caused him to reconsider whether or not there was something strange going on.

He successfully moved the pipes inward but could not find the source of some dripping water that was coming through the ceiling above the water pipes. He adjusted the faucets several times but to no avail. He finally discovered a large coffee urn that was sitting directly over a small hole in the floor above. The spigot had been

opened, allowing the soapy water inside—it was being cleaned after a party the night before—to drain out onto the floor and down
through the small crack. Both Sue Samuelson and her husband are
at a loss to explain how the handle had been opened.

Pat Samuelson shakes his head over that incident.

"I don't know. It's all adding up a little bit, you know. It sure was
real strange. I'm a believer."

A local man assisting Pat Samuelson with a project got Billed
when he laid down a tool to work briefly in another area. When
he returned, the tool had vanished. After a search they found it
covered with sawdust in the back warehouse, which was still under
reconstruction.

Sue Samuelson seems captivated yet resigned to never quite fig-
uring out the odd intrigues she and the others have encountered at
the Mill House.

"Karen and I are desensitized to it now. I don't pay it much attention, unless I get frustrated with something. Then I get mad," she
says. "A woman wanted to come and do a psychic thing, and I said
no. What we have we can deal with. We don't want more, because
if this property dates back to the 1860s, who knows what you're
going to get? I don't want to stir up any more activity than what we
have."

Samuelson has asked a few people if anything unusual had occurred there before she opened her business, but they haven't mentioned anything.

"Some people are really interested, but I haven't had anybody
go, 'Oh, that can't be true.' We have one of the old mill owners who
visits all the time. He kind of laughs."

Have they ever considered trying to cleanse the building of any
lingering revenant?

Not really.

"When my briefcase fell, we'd joke and say, 'Stop it, Bill! Knock
it off!'" Karen Hallquist laughs. "We'd yell at him. But I don't think
we've ever said, 'Bill, go home,' or anything like that."

The ghost of that old mill manager might be there to stay.

THE LOVELORN FARMER

"He's never hurt me or tormented me or anything. I figure
as long as I don't actually see him I'll be perfectly okay."
Tina Kockler

In a leafy grove of mature oaks on a hillock a few miles outside
Elmore, a solid old farmhouse with weathered gray siding has attracted its share of attention over the years, but not always for the
most desirable reasons.

Tina Kockler knew all about the Cordell place when she moved
in on Halloween day 2002.

That the house was sometimes on the market for years before
anyone bought it.

That no one lived there for very long.

That the real-estate agent showing her the property warily asked
if she had "heard the stories about this house."

That even Tina Kockler's own grandmother couldn't believe she
was going to live there.

That everyone knew this house was haunted.

And though Tina Kockler now has enough stories of her own
to fill several Halloween evenings, she is still there in her rambling
five-bedroom 1930s-era home, which sits on five spacious acres
and looks a bit foreboding on even the sunniest days. In the house,
where the only sound may come from the infrequent pickup on the

lonely country road out front or from the wind rustling century-old oak trees . . . or from the scrape of footfalls as her resident ghost paces across the front porch.

"I like it out here," says Kockler, a cheerful Fairmont beautician and barber. "I've got too much time invested in it now. I'm getting it fixed up the way it should be. It's a big, old house, and it needs a lot of work because it's been neglected through the years. Nobody has stayed long enough to do anything. It doesn't bother me. It's nice and quiet. Yeah, I like it out here just fine."

"Out here" means at the crossroads of two Faribault County roads within eyesight of the Iowa border, in a part of Minnesota where, in the summer, lush farm fields stretch for as far as the eye can see, where the roads are straight as a furrow, and where clusters of leafy trees in the distance suggest a farmhouse may be embraced within these prairie windbreaks.

Set far back from the blacktop road, Tina Kockler's home is at the end of a packed-dirt driveway that curves past a weathered red barn with wagon-wide double doors and a steeply sloping roof capped by twin cupolas, each with its own ancient weather vane.

The solid two-story house has a gambrel roof, two enclosed back porches, and old wooden storm windows. A satellite dish and a modern two-car garage attached to the house via a breezeway seem oddly out of place.

It looks like a home built to withstand the extreme weather that often churns across this part of the state—a sturdy home.

And that's exactly what folks in this part of the county say it is because the man who built it seventy-five years ago wanted a sturdy, fine-looking home for him, and for the schoolteacher he loved.

His name was Lee Cordell, a bachelor farmer somewhere in his sixties when he set to work building his dream home. He meant it for the much-younger teacher he was dating. Perhaps he thought the relationship had gone further than she did, or perhaps he didn't make his intentions clear to her. He planned to ask for her hand in marriage.

Or maybe she was just humoring an old man by being nice to him.

Whatever the case, Cordell finished the house and was ready to move in when he brought the schoolteacher over and showed it to her. He allowed as how he hoped that after they got married they would fill the five bedrooms with lots of children.

But if Lee Cordell thought she would be pleased with his rather offbeat proposal, well, she must have broken his heart instead.

She laughed, told him he was crazy. Said there was absolutely no way she was going to have a bunch of kids with a man his age. Why, just the idea of it was foolish, just plain foolish!

She walked out on him, quit her teaching job at the East Chain School, and left the region.

Lee Cordell was a man changed. He moved into his big, beautiful, and empty new home and became a virtual recluse, a hermit whom neighbors or townspeople in Elmore saw only every once in a great while.

For nearly thirty years the old man lived alone with his memories of what might have been.

Then one day, neighbors found his body sprawled against the woodpile on the cellar's dirt floor. No autopsy was performed—he was in his nineties, folks guessed—since his death appeared to be from natural causes.

Though Lee Cordell has been dead for nearly fifty years, there may be something of him left in the house he built for the insensitive schoolmarm.

When Tina Kockler bought the Cordell place in 2002, it came with years of accumulated tales about its haunted history.

A nurse lived there with her truck-driving husband and their children. When dad was on the road, the nights were the worst for mom and the kids. The little ones crawled into bed with her when the footfalls in vacant rooms got to be too much, or the inexplicable noises, or the water running from somewhere. They moved out after six months.

Another young family lived there. Apparently, dad wasn't bothered, but mom and the children knew someone else already lived there. They didn't stay long, either.

The housekeeper for another family quit when pictures flew

off the walls and furniture somehow got rearranged in the house.

Kockler knew all those stories and more, having grown up in the area. But it was a good, solid house and one that she could afford. She wasn't sure how she would react to living there, however, especially when the real-estate agent told her about its past. She was venturing into the unknown. Were the stories true or just idle gossip? It was frightening.

Today, she displays a mixture of tolerance and acceptance of life in the haunted Cordell place, for that is definitely what it is.

"He's never hurt me or tormented me or anything. I figure as long as I don't actually see him I'll be perfectly okay."

He? Him? Kockler's frequent use of those pronouns makes it clear that the late Mr. Cordell is a familiar presence in her life. And though she hasn't seen him, that's about all that hasn't happened to her.

Kockler's introduction to the strangeness of the Cordell place came on the first night she slept there, on the day after Halloween. Kockler and her then boyfriend dragged a mattress into a first floor bedroom. She turned down the wall dimmer switch as far as it would go without the room becoming completely dark and settled in. Suddenly, the light brightened and then settled back down.

"I thought, 'You've got to be kidding me. It's true!'" she says.

For the next five months Tina Kockler and her boyfriend became acutely aware of what everyone said about the house.

Once the couple moved upstairs, the windows started rattling. There's nothing unusual about that in an old country farmhouse . . . except that on these occasions there was no wind and no trees nearby to brush against them.

"It was loud enough you couldn't talk to the person next to you. It went on for about a week. Like there was someone pounding on the window glass. It would always start about a half hour after I went to bed."

Exasperated, Kockler locked each window tight. That seemed to stop the clatter. Perhaps it was just old unsecured windows.

That wouldn't explain, however, what seemed to Kockler to be the nighttime visits of a phantom plumber. There was a half bath upstairs, nonfunctional when she moved in but now remodeled. Her bedroom was not far away.

"Every night it seemed like he would go into the bathroom, take the back off the toilet, and start tinkering around inside, in the tank. You could hear that distinct sound—the sliding of the lid off, the sliding of it back on."

Kockler had to turn off the water in the pipes leading to the sink before they began the bathroom's remodeling. Yet when the remodeling began, the water had been turned back on.

During the same nocturnal visits, Kockler says it seemed that someone was tinkering with the electric baseboard heat in the bathroom as well, tapping on it in several places. Again, the fixtures were old. So perhaps . . . ?

Yet what was that perfect, circular light Tina Kockler watched zoom across her bedroom, arcing from a window to a sitting room outside her bedroom door?

"It looked like a flashlight going dim, but it had a bright circle in the middle. It flew in a perfectly straight line from the window out to that room. Probably five minutes later, it flew back across the ceiling . . . and out the window. It was a swift movement, so if you weren't paying attention, you might not have seen it, but it was a good-sized ball [of light]."

She tried unsuccessfully to figure out its source. No passing cars have caused that kind of light to appear in her home—at least not in all the years since then—nor was there anything in the room that might account for it.

"I've never seen it since."

So maybe it was something mechanical?

But then what was it banging on that closet wall? And who was it that came in her kitchen door late that one night?

The closet in question is in a spare bedroom that shares a wall with the sitting room outside Kockler's upstairs bedroom. There was a pounding on the wall as if somebody was locked in the closet and couldn't get out, rattling the door handle, banging on the walls.

"I'm not going to get up in the middle of the night and check it out. But the next morning I did," says Kockler.

What she found was that the closet door was open—it's normally kept closed. It was, she says, as if somebody was finally able to open the door.

Sometimes, the nightly footfalls are the most upsetting, and they are noticeable on the hardwood floors in most of the rooms, as on the late night when she thought her boyfriend had gotten home.

Kockler was still awake. Her boyfriend always came into the house through the kitchen door at the side of the house. And that's what he seemed to be doing then.

"I heard the door open, and I heard it close. I heard him come through the kitchen, then the living room, and up the stairs. I'm sitting in bed waiting for him to turn the corner, but there was nobody there. There was nobody there."

She repeats that last phrase twice, laughing nervously and shaking her head.

Her boyfriend didn't get home for another hour.

Most of the activity Kockler encountered took place from the day she moved in on October 31, 2002, through the following March, when her boyfriend moved out. Unbeknownst to her, he was a relative of Lee Cordell. She thinks that fact may have played a role in the strange goings-on.

"My boyfriend was petrified of it, which I was surprised at. I worked part time at a bar, and I'd get home from work late, and every single light would be on upstairs and down. I was at work one day, and he said the couch moved on him. He was on the couch, and it slid out about six inches and then back in. The TV remote control moved at one point. He had set it down to go into another room, and when he came back, the remote was on the other side of the living room."

The house was quiet for nearly a year after he left, Kockler says. But then the puzzling incidents slowly started up again.

"But it's not nearly as active as it was the first months there," she adds.

But even that diminished activity doesn't mean the ghost has finally given up the farm. He may simply have cut down the number of appearances to an occasional checkup every now and then.

She knows he is around because she'll hear those familiar footfalls.

He seems to like a small, open porch off the living room. It's a part of the house's exterior that has been waiting for remodeling. The floorboards out there are terrible, she says. When her dog bounces around on it, she knows he's out there. Yet when her dog is nowhere near it, she'll notice something else.

"You can hear someone walking around on it. I've heard that numerous times. I've gotten up and run over to the window to see, but nobody is on the porch. It sounds like my dog jumping on it, but my dog is on the other side of the yard."

Kockler has had two different dogs during her years there. The first, a Rottweiler, would not set foot in the house though he was an indoor dog. Even with the kitchen door open, the dog sat on the back steps and refused to come in. She got a second dog as a puppy and raised him in the house. He is comfortable there, she says.

She's heard something similar to the porch walking when she's been upstairs in her bedroom.

"It's like a person standing on a loose board, rocking back and forth. I tried to figure it out for two days. I was trying to get something to make that noise, and I couldn't do it. Even walking around I couldn't get it. . . . You'd have to walk around and hit it just the right way. To this day I still can't figure out what would have caused it."

If Tina Kockler can't sleep at night, she'll often come downstairs and curl up on the sofa. She might watch television for a while—ESPN is a favorite channel—or perhaps flip on a table lamp and simply enjoy the silence of a country night.

Except when it isn't quiet, that is, as on the night she thought a couple plastic totes she had in the kitchen had been thrown across the floor.

"I got up right away to see if they'd moved, but I'd moved them around so much I couldn't tell. It was dead quiet in the house, and it happened only about ten feet from where I was lying. It was very distinct."

Tina Kockler's sister stays overnight from time to time. She isn't immune to the disturbances.

She thought that an old chair in an upstairs room was being dragged across the floor when it wasn't or that what for all the world sounded like a book was being dropped in an upstairs hallway. That particular incident echoed through the whole upstairs because whatever it was slammed against the hardwood floors.

Kockler emphasizes that she has never seen a ghost in her home, but that doesn't stop others from thinking they have. There was one report that a person driving by the house one early evening saw a filmy woman walking along the top roofline. Kockler wonders if that might be the schoolteacher returned to ask forgiveness for her brusque leave-taking.

A group of paranormal specialists, including a medium, visited Kockler's home at her invitation. They scrutinized the house with video cameras and digital tape recorders. In a spare bedroom the group got the phrase "go away" on a recorder, and in the cellar they got the phrase "help us." These electronic voice phenomena were not heard aloud by anyone present, Kockler says. Later, she and one of the mediums stayed just a few minutes in the cellar. They both got a "creepy feeling," according to Kockler.

The paranormal group identified two ghosts in the house, a man and a woman. The medium said the woman's name might be Luella, but she wasn't certain. Neither ghost was dangerous, they told Kockler. They were just . . . there.

Of course, Tina Kockler has faced skepticism from those who hear stories about the Cordell place.

"Some are really intrigued by it, but others think it's baloney. I always tell them I never believed in it either until I moved into the house. My boyfriend now doesn't like to talk about it. But one night shortly after he moved in, we were watching TV when we heard something above us, someone walking around or something sliding. It happened about five or six times. He muted the TV and asked if I'd heard that. I kind of laughed and said, 'Yeah.' He will admit that that caught his attention."

A group of her friends showed up shortly after she moved in. They wanted to hear the ghost. Kockler and the women gathered upstairs and quieted down.

"Sure enough, [the noises] started up. They all gasped. I actually had to escort them all the way out to their cars. They didn't want to leave by themselves. They're believers!"

Over the past several years, Tina has extensively renovated the home's interior. New walls have been built over the existing studs, and bathrooms have been modernized. She has plans for continuing the renovation. She thinks those changes may be one reason life is much quieter these days.

"He must like what we're doing because he's never done anything definite in all that time. A noise at most. Every now and then you'll hear something, like a book drop, something to that effect, usually at night. Maybe he'll leave when it's all remodeled."

But otherwise her plans are specific.

"I plan on staying there. Yes."

With or without her bachelor-farmer ghost.

26

THE WATCHERS

"I never believed in ghosts until I lived there."
Erica Johnson

A comfortable if slightly dilapidated rental house on a modern, working dairy farm outside Harmony may host three ghosts, including the spirits of two children buried nearby along a narrow stream.

Not far away, in an isolated rural farmhouse, a cheerful little girl in a dusty blue dress and white pinafore skips into the dining room, though she long ago departed this earth.

Again not far away, in a newly occupied house on Elm Street, a family found an impish presence on Halloween day they hadn't anticipated.

These three homes in south-central Fillmore County near Harmony are the settings for three singular stories of individuals dealing with events they never thought possible. Each had watchers from an incorporeal world living among them.

It was summer and well past midnight in the rental house on a dairy farm near Harmony. A young woman was in bed and restless, trying to get some sleep in a sweltering upstairs bedroom. A whirring electric fan created a small and warm breeze.

The bedroom door swung open. She got up, closed the door, and turned off the fan.

"That must have caused it," she thought.

Once more the door opened. Again, she closed it. Back in bed, she rolled over to look at the time on her bedside alarm clock—2:04 AM.

Again, it was the door.

"What the heck?" she wondered.

She turned the fan back on, tried to sleep, and tried to ignore the door, which would not stay shut. Still uncomfortable, she looked at the clock. It read 4:14 AM.

"I haven't been laying here for two hours," she muttered to herself, sitting up on the edge of the bed and reaching for her cell phone. Its screen glowed 2:14 AM.

How could her bedside clock have moved forward two hours? It didn't seem possible.

Doors that didn't stay put? Clocks that changed time?

That was enough.

She pulled on her clothes and headed to her parents' home, which was a short walk away on the same farmstead. That's where she spent the rest of the night, unsure of what was going on in her house, which she was renting from her parents, but willing to make one clear admission to herself: she was scared.

She told her parents about the clock and the doors. They were skeptical. They said it was the breeze from the fan that blew the door open, that she had probably fallen asleep and didn't notice the hours go by. She begged to differ.

"It freaked me out," she says today. "I'd never experienced anything like that before. I never believed in ghosts until I lived there. Never have. And now I do."

The woman is Erica Johnson, a vivacious Harmony real-estate agent in business there with her mother. She moved into what was known as the Albert Weber house in May 2006. She knows houses. She knows all about old houses. She grew up in one and knows that odd noises—squeaky doors, rattling window frames, and creaky floors—are nothing unusual.

She said that what she experienced within weeks of moving into the Weber house was very different.

Even before the disconcerting episode with time-shifting clocks and recalcitrant doors, there were the quiet footfalls in the upstairs hallway. It wasn't enough to alarm her or make her pack up and move out. Maybe there was a simple explanation. And after all it was a convenient place to live for a time, on her family's farm. Plus, she usually had a roommate with which to share the miscellaneous household chores and expenses.

From that point forward, for over a year, Erica Johnson says she lived warily with her ghost . . . or ghosts.

Although she says she's not sure who the ghost is, she has found some strong candidates.

Albert Weber was a local farmer who lived in that house near the turn of the twentieth century and is said to have died of a heart attack in the front yard. Weber's earlier brick home once stood where a pasture is today. His two young daughters died of diphtheria. They are buried next to a creek that runs through the property.

Some of what Johnson went through had the sort of childish playfulness one might associate with children, whereas the footfalls seemed to be those of an older man. The girls lived in the brick home torn down long ago.

"It could be Albert Weber," she says. "He lived here. He passed away before his wife. He could be hanging around [waiting] for his wife and doesn't know she's passed on, too."

Erica told her roommate at the time about the incident with the bedroom door. The young man's reaction surprised her.

He confided that once he'd been sitting in the living room with his feet resting on an oversized exercise ball. Suddenly, he felt something tugging the ball away from him. He moved his feet off and watched as the ball rolled away, spun around, and then came back to him.

Johnson says, "It's like it plays games with you. If you're watching TV, you'll hear the water turn on either in the bathroom or in the kitchen. I'll get up to shut it off, and it's already been turned off.

Or I'll come home—it doesn't do this anymore—but for a long time I'd come home and the hot water would be on in the bathroom sink. It had been on for such a long time that the sink basin would be so hot you couldn't touch it."

Johnson learned that a family who had rented the house some years before had had the same problem. The mother in the family thought it might have been her young children playing in the sink. She would shut off the faucet but then find it back on sometime later. Johnson learned that the mother was "creeped out" when she lived there.

The house itself sits on a small rise at the end of a long, narrow drive that cuts through a cornfield. A spare house on a large working farm, it is architecturally unremarkable: white, utilitarian aluminum siding—with discordant light green siding under the eaves—a tacked-on carport, and small, bare windows. Antique lightning rods form processions along the peaked rooflines. A two-story addition long ago doubled the interior size by adding a living room and extra bedrooms; an old side porch got enclosed somewhere along the line. The entire structure seems to have been built more for functional expediency than for beauty.

Inside lingers a musty odor of stale carpeting and windows kept tightly shut against the elements. Some doorways have been closed off, and several windows have been realigned. The signs are apparent that the place shelters those in transition. There is sadness there, a sense that its better times have long since passed.

It is a house in which the unseen would not be the unexpected.

Whatever it was in Erica Johnson's house, it had a thing for doors.

One incident involved a later roommate and a door that opens off the kitchen and onto a narrow, enclosed staircase that leads to the upstairs bedrooms.

"Molly and I were both upstairs getting ready for work. She went down the steps and couldn't get the door open. It hasn't been locked for years. There's no key to it."

Johnson, too, shoved against the door. It would not budge.

Somehow, the door had been locked tight. She called her father from her cell phone; he had to pry the door off its hinges to get the women out.

"We don't know how, but it locked. For as long as my parents have owned the house, there's never been a key to it. Now we have the lock taped over."

All the closets are in the upstairs hallway. The doors are left open to avoid the persistent mustiness from permeating her clothes. That didn't work.

"It always shut my closet door," she says.

She did lock one door, the one to her bedroom.

"I sleep with my doors locked to my room. I've learned that if I lock my door, it stays out of my room at night. They don't come in."

Johnson says doors swinging open became commonplace. She might be talking to a friend in the kitchen, and one of the cabinet doors would open. One day, she was cleaning the house, and the door to the basement swung open. On colder days it might have been doors to rooms she kept closed to preserve heat.

"But you don't see anyone open it. He'll shut it and do it again. It's like he does stuff to bug you or annoy you. Like, I'll do laundry, and he'll throw my clean clothes on the floor or off the dryer. Sometimes it's the detergent."

On another occasion when Johnson and some friends were watching late-night television, they all heard a loud crash in the basement. No one wanted to go down and find out what happened. Later the next day, Johnson got up her nerve. She found all sorts of items that had been on several basement shelves tossed on the floor. It was as if someone had swept them clean.

As the months passed, Johnson says the activity became less pronounced; sometimes weeks would go by in relative quiet, except for what she terms the "pacing around upstairs."

Erica Johnson takes a sort of don't see, don't flee attitude.

"I've never seen it, nor have my roommates. Never heard it talk or anything like that. . . . I'm used to it. I don't want to see it. I laugh when people are over here and he does something and they get creeped out. It's not like where you'll come home and all your furniture is pushed up against the wall."

Erica Johnson faces something of a dilemma as a real-estate agent. She has thought about her own personal experiences should she ever be faced with the prospect of selling a house she thought to be haunted.

There is a debate in real-estate circles about the necessity of disclosing that a particular house is reputedly haunted. Johnson says sellers are not required to disclose a property's ghostly reputation. She does cite a case, however, in which a family bought a house specifically because it was supposed to be haunted but then decided it wasn't. The family ended up suing the real-estate company for claiming that it was haunted.

That may not be an issue for the Weber place. Erica Johnson and her father are remodeling another house that she plans to live in. Plans call for the Weber house to be taken down and a new house to be built on the site.

That may not mean the haunting will be forgotten—or even over.

"It would be fun to figure out who the ghost is," Johnson says. "But I don't want to do anything that's not right and get him mad."

There's one thing she will definitely *not* do—strike up a conversation with the ghost.

"I'm afraid it'll answer me back!"

Sylvia Johansson* remembers that it was a Saturday. As with most Saturdays on the farm, Johansson helped review the farm account books and caught up with paperwork she brought home from her banking job in the small Iowa city south of Harmony.

She was tightly focused on the work spread out before her when something startled her. She was not sure what it was, but some movement from across the room caused her to look up.

A little girl, perhaps six or seven years of age, came skipping merrily through the kitchen doorway. The child stopped when she noticed Johansson and gave her a big smile. She smiled back.

"Oh, my," Johansson muttered, her eyes widening. Long, silky brown hair capped with a bright red bow framed the child's sweet, smiling face. She wore a crisp, white pinafore over a calf-length, dusty blue dress with small, white flecks. On her feet was a pair of high-top, brown laced boots with pointed toes.

Johansson thought she looked like she had stepped off the pages of a Laura Ingalls Wilder story.

The girl stared placidly for a few more seconds, smiled broadly again, and skipped on into the dining room.

Johansson followed her around the corner. There was no sign of her.

For a few moments Johansson wondered if one of her children's friends had come over to play, but that thought quickly faded. Her kids were upstairs, and she knew of no child like the one she'd just seen, certainly not one who looked as if she belonged on a prairie homesteader's claim.

Sylvia Johansson had known for several years that the farm-house in which she lived with her husband and five children abounded with several ghosts, but this one, this merry little girl ghost, was someone new. In time Johansson and her family would see her again, learn more about her, and eventually even think they had a solid lead on her identity.

"She was absolutely real," Johansson says. "She was there. She wasn't transparent at all. She was solid. She smiled right at me . . . and I smiled at her!"

The child disappeared so quickly that Johansson knew she could be added to the other two ghosts already in residence. She immediately shared the sighting with her children, who all knew their house was out of the ordinary. They were intrigued by their mother's latest ghost adventure.

But shortly after, that same little girl tried to become acquainted with one of Johansson's daughters. It did not go well.

"My daughter saw her a few days later, but she was terrified because she was so real."

After that, she thought back to several other times in recent months when she thought she'd seen a child taking a quick look around a corner at her or ducking through a doorway down the hall.

"I kept thinking it was my kids. But after that, I wondered if all the peeking going on numerous times was [by] this little girl."

Johansson thought the ghost was checking her out before making a more direct approach.

It made more sense to Johansson when another one of her daughters got up to use the bathroom during the night but instead hurried into her mother's room. She whispered that there was a girl kneeling in the hallway next to a small chair which held a doll.

The mysterious child might have been connected to an episode one morning after Johansson had piled her children into the car for the ride to school. She had forgotten something and hurried back into the house to find it. As soon as she got inside, she heard two girls talking from somewhere upstairs.

"I thought [a TV or radio] was on. . . . It was just two little girls chattering away like there was no tomorrow. I can't tell you what they were saying, just the way two little girls chitter-chatter."

She went upstairs, walked all around, but the girls' voices had fallen silent.

There was another Saturday encounter, as well, when Johansson was in the kitchen washing the inside windows. She was balancing on a chair, trying to wipe the last streak off a window, when she thought one of her daughters came into the room and leaned on the back of the chair.

"I turned around to talk to her. She wasn't there. But I know I saw in the corner of my eye a little girl by the chair."

By this time, after years of living in her haunted house, all Johansson could do was shrug her shoulders—and finish the windows.

The farm that Sylvia Johansson, her husband, Frank,* and their children have lived on for over thirty years is south of Harmony, a short distance across the Iowa border. She grew up in Harmony, and the stories emanating from her experiences living in that haunted farmhouse are known to many. She's reluctant, however, to become too public about the events because it all sounds "sort of crazy," she says. "Sometimes, I don't know how you tie it all together."

Before Sylvia and her husband married, her husband-to-be had bought the house and acreage. The house itself sits in a tree-studded windbreak surrounded by a wide lawn.

Even before they were married, while Frank worked the land and fixed up the house, Sylvia helped out with some of the chores, including mowing the lawn.

That's when she thinks she had her first encounter with the farm's ghosts.

"Every time I got to one corner of the yard at the back of the house, I thought someone was watching me. It didn't happen anywhere else in the yard. And every time I'd turn and look, especially at this one upstairs bedroom window in the corner of the house, it seems there was a man [in the window] who would step away the moment I looked up. He was peering out at me."

She told her husband about it and on a few occasions went into the house to check around. But she gave that up after a while. Not only did she never find anyone or anything out of place, but it also made her nervous.

"I didn't want to be alone in the house."

It didn't take long for Sylvia Johansson to think that seeing a man look out at her from a bedroom window might be the least of her concerns.

On the very first night Sylvia spent in the house, she found herself alone because her husband was taking night classes.

She was watching television in the living room when their dog started barking frantically. Johansson is not a timid woman, but she was alone in a relatively isolated farmhouse with only a single wall-mounted kitchen telephone. She got up out of her chair and headed for the kitchen. The lights were on, but there were no curtains yet on the windows.

"I didn't want to go in because I knew if someone was outside, they would see me. So I went upstairs and looked out from up there."

When she looked across the yard in the moonlight, she saw a man standing near a tree.

"I was scared, but I couldn't get to the phone because I thought he would see me."

She looked out periodically until the man seemed to have gone and the dog had stopped barking. The rest of the night passed quietly.

In time Johansson grew to believe that, although the person outside in the moonlight seemed real enough, it was probably one of the ghosts.

The farm had changed ownership only once between the time it was established about a century ago and when the Johanssons bought it. Three of the original family's children—two boys and a girl—apparently never married and lived on the farm into adulthood. They all died there as well. Those are the ghosts Johansson believes are the close watchers in her house.

In that original family one younger son died, possibly of complications from an especially virulent flu.

"He knew he was going to die because he wrote a letter about it. I found it in the attic," Johansson says. "I found the envelope with the letter [inside]. It was about how he wasn't going to live. It was sad."

She put it away in a cabinet thinking that if any descendant of the family ever stopped by, she would give it to them. But then the letter disappeared.

"To this day I can't find it. You doubt yourself after a while. . . . Did I really find that letter? But I did because I stood right there and read it. "

The family's daughter met a grim death when she was in her forties.

"I've been told that on a Sunday she went out to get milk and never came back."

The family later discovered her body at the bottom of an open septic tank.

"Some speculated she jumped. Others said she fell," Johansson says.

After her encounters with the man in the window and under the tree and after seeing the little girl skipping from the kitchen into the dining room, Johansson grew curious about what the earlier residents looked like. She asked around the neighborhood. An older man showed up one day with a confirmation photograph of the daughter.

"It was the girl I saw," Johansson says, "only she was older [in the photo]. Her hair was pulled back. Oh yes, it was her. When I saw the picture, I knew it was."

Johansson also discovered that the children's father loved to play the fiddle. He'd gather all the children in the dining room when he played, and they would dance and sing along as he played. The girl had been skipping happily into that same dining room.

Johansson thinks that the girl returned at an age she preferred, the years when she was a carefree daughter who loved her daddy's fiddle playing.

But it's another adult son in that first family, and the circumstances of his death, that Johansson thinks about more often.

He died of an apparent heart attack. Johansson says when his family discovered him in the yard, they threw a long black coat over his body. No one quite seems to know why, whether it was to await the authorities or because they didn't know what to do with him.

It is this man that Johansson associates with the figure in the window and the man outside in the nighttime.

Over the years Johansson has studied ghostly phenomena on her own and has developed a theory about his movements.

"Sometimes, [ghosts] observe you. But once they accept you, they come a little closer. I wondered if the man I saw in the yard could be the man who died out there, and [I told him] that I meant no harm. He then came back into the house."

Her view is that the man's ghost had always been in the house, though he left at some point after the Johanssons moved in, lingered outside in the yard, and is now back inside.

For Sylvia Johansson there have been many incidents that reveal this ghost's comfort in mingling with the family.

"At different times I'd see that man in the dark clothes upstairs, going from my bedroom to the attic [door]. It's only a short distance."

The bedroom is the same one in which Johansson saw someone staring out the window as she mowed the grass.

When Johansson's youngest daughter was about twelve years old, she got a scare when she assumed it was her dad walking up the stairs behind her.

"She heard footsteps behind her," Johansson says. "But when she went into her room, she turned to see a strange man walking by her door and on down the hall."

The girl fled back down the staircase and wouldn't go upstairs alone for over a year, Johansson says. "She was really afraid, but I'd tell her that if they were going to hurt you, they would have hurt us a long time ago."

If Frank Johansson had to be out late, his wife and the children would usually be in bed when he got home. Usually, Johansson heard him come into the house and then up the steps and into the bedroom. But on several occasions after she had heard what she assumed was her husband come in the house and then up the steps, there'd be nothing more. It clearly wasn't her husband—he would arrive home later.

The same sort of thing occurred when Johansson mistakenly thought her husband had come into the house to work on some farm accounting at the kitchen table.

"Many times, he'd come in to do his work, but I wouldn't know he was in the house, but then I thought I'd hear him in the kitchen chair. I'd go in, and he's not there. But I knew somebody had sat in that chair."

Does the younger son in that original family—he who died of influenza—make an occasional appearance?

Johansson's oldest daughter was washing the dishes one evening. She glanced up at the window over the sink. There was the reflection of a man standing behind her, the left sleeve of his white T-shirt rolled up to hold a pack of cigarettes. She stumbled backward, and he was gone.

In that same area of the kitchen, Johansson's son thought someone had come in behind him and turned around to see who it was. As he did so, a drawer next to the sink slid open. Just as if someone had come in to get something out of it.

Sylvia Johansson says most of her friends and colleagues are intrigued by all that's gone on in her house over the years.

"The thing they can't get over is that I'm not afraid of it. But what's there to be afraid of? They don't hurt me."

She says there have been too many incidents that she can't rationally explain to attribute all or even some of it to other causes. Her take on the supernatural is that ghosts exist all around but that only certain people "let them in."

They are the watchers who wait.

The observer in Sandee Hoiness Pates's house may have been the owner's mother, who died there.

Sandee Pates and her husband, John, lived in Eden Prairie when they decided to retire to Florida. Their home sold well before their new Florida home was built. The couple decided to rent a home close to Harmony so that they could be near her elderly parents.

They found a perfect rental home about twenty minutes from Harmony. They moved into the very old house on the small town's Elm Street, on Halloween day 2000.

"The movers laughed when we gave them the street name and they realized it was Halloween, but when they found out that our son's name was Jason, they stopped laughing," Pates remembers.

The Pates didn't find Freddy Krueger in the attic, but they did stumble on a houseful of anomalies that they attributed to Casper because, as Pates says, "No harm was done, and he left us with some amusing stories."

What was entertaining to the Pateses might have been disconcerting to others, especially when they found out that the mother of the man who owned the house had died there. They might have been disconcerting, too, because many of the incidents seemed in line with a caring mother fussing over her home, even after death.

Sandee Pates says she was hooked on watching a particular morning television show while she got ready for work, whereas her husband preferred a certain morning radio show. The couple discovered their favorite stations would be changed to other programs.

Often, the door to the unattached garage stood open in the morning after one or the other of them had shut it the night before. Did someone else in town have the same garage remote control frequency? The home's owner, who lived just a few blocks away and had grown up in the Pateses' house, said he had the frequency changed because he was having that same problem.

If it was a finicky mom, she definitely had her eye on the monthly electric bill.

"We would leave particular lights on in the house before we went out for the evening. When we returned, they would be off."

In the dining area an antique chandelier hung over the table and chairs. Sandee heard the crystals tinkle without, she says, "any noticeable air movement."

Then again, perhaps *someone* noticed that speck of dust.

One day an electrician installed a new computer cable connection in their upstairs office. He had to make several trips between the computer and an electrical connection in the attic. In the process he collected a considerable amount of insulation on his clothing and shoes. When he was finished, he left a trail of insulation down the stairs and out the front door. Sandee Pates vacuumed it all up, and that, she thought, was that.

The next morning fresh pieces of insulation were scattered on the wooden edges of each step but not on the carpet runner.

Mother had an eye on keeping her old place secure, as well. The Pateses' front and back doors had key locks, but the back entrance also had a slide-bolt lock. They normally used the back door to get to their garage.

"After one outing we returned," Sandee Pates says, "and could not get in the back door."

The slide-bolt was engaged.

Sandee and her husband lived in the house for just nine months, but it was long enough to give them a lifetime of haunted memories.

DOORWAY to the OTHER SIDE

"From the beginning, the old house spoke to me in many ways."
Annie Wilder*

Annie Wilder has found that living in one of Minnesota's most haunted private homes brings nearly daily reminders that supernatural activity can occur when one least expects it. In a house rife with ghosts, she knows that even a twilight stroll can wind up with an unexpected ending.

Annie and her friend Jonathan* decided to take a walk along one of the inviting footpaths that edge the Mississippi River in Hastings. It was a pleasantly comfortable summer night, and she thought it would be a nice way to show the new man in her life something of the lovely old river town in which she lives.

When the couple got back to her 1880s-era Victorian mansion in the city's historic silk-stocking district and climbed the steps of the wide front porch, it seemed a spirit or two may have come calling during their absence. The comfortable porch chairs had been changed around—they were now pulled closer together, into a more intimate conversation grouping.

She put it back into the array she favored and tried to put it out of her mind.

It didn't work.

The next morning, when Annie glanced outside to the porch,

the chairs were bunched back together again in the same snug arrangement in which she had found them the previous night.

Later, Annie did what she often does when confronted with a
mystery in what she terms her "energetically unusual" home—she
telephoned a psychic friend with some questions.

"Was this Leon acting up again?" Annie asked the psychic.

That would be Leon Kuechenmeister,* who lived in the house
for three decades. He died six months before Annie moved in. She
says that he is one of the resident ghosts.

The psychic was able to reach Leon. According to the psychic,
Leon denied having anything to do with moving the furniture.

Annie followed up. Could it be another spirit in the house?

No, the mischief with the furniture had not been connected to
any one of the twenty-odd ghosts Annie has contended with in her
house. It had been the work of a spirit connected to Annie's new
boyfriend. Unbeknownst to him, and to Annie, he had brought his
own personal spirit. Apparently, the visiting spirit thought this new
relationship needed some otherworldly input.

What better way to introduce people to the many ghosts in one's
house than by holding haunted tea parties? That's what Annie Wilder
does, on occasion, in her home of fourteen rooms, four porches,
and her host of ghosts, including the four-legged kind. Sometimes,
the guests are not always those explicitly invited.

A Girl Scout leader and several of her troop members were
scheduled to attend one of the tea parties and then tour the home
while Annie shared her ghost stories. The scout leader stopped by a
few days before the tea party to pick up a copy of Annie's memoir
of her years in this spirit-laden mansion, *House of Spirits and Whispers*. Annie suggested a quick tour, which she gladly accepted.

When Annie led her into the old-fashioned summer kitchen at
the rear of the house, the visitor suddenly gasped and jumped back.
She stammered that she had just seen a black cat with a white bib
shoot from behind the door and then abruptly vanish.

Annie smiled and calmed her down. That was simply the ghost
of her own cat. He had died of old age earlier that summer. She had

been lonesome for him earlier in the day because it was on just this kind of warm September day that he loved to sleep in a sunny window. She had spoken aloud of her loneliness and asked that if the cat's spirit was still around, she'd like to see him or at least know of his continued presence. Apparently, he had chosen this unorthodox way of making his inaugural appearance.

The clock glowed 5:21 AM. Annie Wilder's adult daughter, Molly,* sat up in bed, wiping the sleep from her eyes. Somewhere in the house came the voice of a woman, her words indistinct, muffled by occasional sobs. It sounded like she was speaking with someone, but she could only hear one side of the conversation.

"It's so sad. But it's just so sad . . . ," the bodiless voice kept repeating over and over.

Molly thought at first it was her mother speaking with someone on the telephone. She quickly nixed that idea—the house was still dark.

Ah, well then, she reasoned, just another ghost. She knew her mom's very first ghost experience in the house was hearing the voice of just such a woman having another one-sided conversation, that it had taken place in the room Molly was now using as her bedroom, and that her mom had actually seen a grief-stricken woman at the foot of her bed.

Added to all that, Molly was listening to this odd exchange on her mother's birthday. The ghosts had been quiet for some time, so perhaps this might be a sort of gift to demonstrate that little has changed in this century-old home—an envoy from the spirit world might come calling at the most inconvenient hours.

Annie Wilder says her sprawling Hastings house chose her as much as she chose it some fifteen years ago. It is full of remarkable stories, ghostly and otherwise: stories of house spirits, family spirits, and others who have revealed themselves to her over the years, stories of the psychics and the friends who have helped Annie understand the nature of those spirits, and stories of the amazing—and sometimes startling—ways in which she became acquainted with her unseen tenants.

In the years since the publication of her popular memoir, her story of a life filled with brushes with the spirit world continues to the present day, though the ghosts and spirits that filled her home are far less in evidence now than they once were.

Her house is a looming presence on a postage stamp–sized corner lot. Long but rather narrow, the mansion has faced changing fortunes over the decades. Several early prominent Hastings families lived there during its early years. In more recent times it was broken up into a duplex and, later, a triplex, which is what it was when Annie bought it in the early 1990s.

The once-grand mansion was in poor shape: exterior paint was peeling; the roof was in desperate need of repair; the interior had been chopped up into makeshift apartments, complete with temporary walls; and hideous color choices covered many of the interior surfaces. Outside, the small yard was denuded of trees, save for three skimpy Chinese elms on the boulevard. No one had attempted any flower gardening in a very long time. An old carriage driveway led to a sagging garage. All in all, the old manse was in desperate need of some tender care.

Enter Annie Wilder.

The first impression Annie had of her home-to-be was that it seemed "unloved and spooky." When the real-estate agent showed it to her, she was alternately wary and hopeful.

"Why hadn't anyone bought this house?" she wondered.

It was listed well below market value. The real-estate agent suggested something might be wrong with it. He also told her an old man had recently died there.

Annie says that one of the things that immediately struck her was that "time had stood still inside the old house." Not only had the place been subdivided into three apartments—two downstairs, one upstairs—but the worn furniture in each, the 1940s-era kitchens with red linoleum countertops and the generally gloomy interior, gave it the feel of something old and worn out. Fortunately, the remodeling into apartments had not destroyed the house's architectural integrity, even though several walls had been added.

The full walk-up attic had been used to hang laundry. The dark, dank basement would have given pause to even the bravest of souls.

Annie Wilder knew she could not make an immediate decision about purchasing the place. Although she was attracted by its possibilities—and its low selling price—she knew that if she moved in, she would have to deal with something else. Ghosts.

"Although the old house may have been unloved, as soon as I stepped inside, I knew it wasn't unprotected. I felt like we were being watched, as if something was alert, aware of our presence," she writes in her memoir of her first visit.

The publishing executive has a heightened sense of an unseen world around us that comes naturally to her. Her mother can see and hear spirits, and her Irish grandmother and her great-grandmother were both psychic. Her father is a dowser, an individual able to locate water and electrical lines. Annie terms herself psychic and intuitive; she has the ability to sense ghosts, to understand and quite often see the spirits that abide in a particular place.

On that day she first toured the property, Annie and the real-estate agent had been told by the home's owner to enter through the back door into what was then an apartment in which a longtime tenant, the late Leon Kuechenmeister, had lived with his wife.

As far as Annie was concerned, he had never really left.

"He was watching us that day, too, silent and heavy as the air, bound to earth and his former home," she writes.

She could detect his presence through a "ghostly smell . . . a distinct musty-sweet odor." The scent was apparent whenever spirit activity was imminent.

She didn't know what to make of Leon's presence. It was not especially comforting. He didn't seem evil, she says, but definitely ominous. He was watching her, equally uncertain what to make of this young woman who was looking through his house. It had been his place for decades, and now someone else was nosing about.

She thought about the purchase for several days, as much to make certain she wasn't rushing into a financial decision that she would later regret as to consider the prospect of buying a house full of ghosts. She decided to go ahead and make an offer, which was accepted. She soon moved in with her two teen-age children.

"[The house] spoke to my imagination. I had looked at so many houses that didn't have any allure at all, not even one unusual or charming feature. This house was filled with intrigue and possibility—lost grandeur, forgotten beauty, and stories and secrets, I was sure of it, hidden away in its unexpected twists and turns," she says.

She has remodeled the grand old home back into a single-family dwelling, refurbished the rooms, repaired the exterior, and updated it throughout.

As it turns out, Annie says, it was filled with spirits. She has heard or met most of them during the ensuing years. *Leon Kuechenmeister,* the elderly tenant who died in the house, lived in the rear downstairs apartment; his ghost still visits on occasion, and it was his presence Annie felt on that first visit. *Julia, Betinna, and Katrina Hartnett,** three spirit sisters attached to an old door Annie found in the basement that now hangs in her living room, may have lived in the mansion at the turn of the twentieth century. *Melancholy Woman,* who sits forlornly at the foot of her bed, may have been the voice Annie heard on the first night she spent in the house and the voice her daughter heard more recently. *Marie* is a departed servant who favors the basement. Another three nameless ghosts, two young men and an old lady, were convinced to go to the light by a psychic.

There is another ghost who is not so benign, a leering, ominous presence that Annie calls *Dark Man.* He unnerves Annie, who writes of his sudden appearance:

There was a spirit right beside my bed. The spirit was male, around six feet tall with swarthy skin and long, oily black hair that hung in his face. Actually, everything about him seemed oily—his hair, his skin, even his clothes. He was dressed all in black. He was about two feet away from my bed, leaning up against the attic door, with his arms crossed over his chest and one leg crossed over the other. He had a smirky smile on his face and was looking straight at me. His vibe wasn't exactly evil, but it definitely wasn't bright and sunny, either. And his demeanor was almost provocatively familiar. I didn't take my eyes off him—I was too afraid to. I had just started to say a prayer of protection when Dark Man disappeared. Even the way he left was disturbing. Instead of just vanishing instantly, the way Leon, Petros and the sad-woman apparition had, Dark Man took a few seconds to blink out. It seemed deliberately willful. It was almost as if he were making sure that I was aware he could leave— or come back—whenever he wanted to.

Annie Wilder has not seen Dark Man in some time. She was able to communicate with him when a psychic visited.

"She asked Leon if Dark Man was a threat," Annie says. "He said he wasn't. Leon said Dark Man was here before the house was and he likes the area. He liked the energy of the house and the people who live in it."

The psychic requested to speak with Dark Man directly, Annie remembers. Dark Man is what Annie calls him, but they wanted to know what his real name had been.

"He said people who knew him by his real name have long since left this earth and it is of no consequence," Annie says. "Now if you're cynical, you could say that was a way to get around checking it, but in the context of everything [Dark Man] said it totally made sense to me. . . . He likes the drama of being called Dark Man, and he's going to stick with it."

Dark Man told the psychic something else, something that might unnerve the faint of heart. He was, he says, "always watching things that go on in this house."

He was surprised that Annie saw him that night in her bedroom.

"That made me laugh, too," Annie says. "That resonated because it's like, yes, I was probably in that twilight zone since I'd been asleep. So he probably wasn't expecting that I could see him. But it never occurred to me that he wasn't a spirit even though he looked like a flesh and blood person."

Although Annie Wilder identifies about twenty ghosts in and about her house, no one is quite sure of the exact number—they seem to come and go quite a bit.

One of the first psychics Annie consulted said it was a "very haunted house."

"She asked me if I had trouble with the pipes in the house," Annie says. "I said I did. And then she told me that's how they're communicating."

The psychic said there were three spirits—an old man, a young man, and a young woman. She said the woman ghost liked the top landing of the house's open staircase. Another ghost preferred standing on the front porch watching people and cars go by. Annie learned from a neighbor that this may be the ghost of a tenant who had lived in one of the apartments and who died on the front porch. The man used to love watching the world go by on the street.

Another psychic said a ghost looked out an upstairs window quite a bit.

Annie wasn't pleased when another team of psychics told her that one of the ghosts there was mentally ill. Although one of the early owners was committed to a mental hospital and died there, Annie believes that if a mentally ill ghost were among those in the house, she would be more aware of it. "I'd have more problems."

"These are the kind of connections that make living here interesting. It's like a big, living mystery, a puzzle," she says.

From the beginning, Annie says, the ghosts communicated through pounding on the walls, occasional appearances, and whispers.

The whispers are "not anything that I've ever heard. It's not pipe noises," she insists.

When a crew of paranormal investigators showed up two years ago, the whispers were quite evident.

"One of the guys heard it and got freaked out."

Annie writes: "[The whispers] actually woke me up. Since I was scared in that [bedroom] to begin with, even when nothing happened, I was petrified. Like the woman's voice I had heard when we first moved in, the whispers seemed to be almost coyly indecipherable, discernable for a syllable or two before fading out, then swirling back loud enough to be heard and almost understood, only to disappear again. I looked around my room, fully expecting to see someone. This time I wasn't sure it was a ghost."

In fact, Annie's father came over to bleed the old radiators in the house hoping to clear up the strange whispering. It didn't. She still heard the whispers coming from the water pipes and radiator in her bedroom. It only happened in the back bedroom. In time Annie's daughter heard the whispers downstairs in the basement laundry room, and the words became more and more distinct.

Annie's decision to update the dangerously old electrical wiring in her house led to a startling discovery and her understanding of one reason why Leon Kuechenmeister was still hanging around. She had briefly sighted him after she first moved in, and it seemed he was continuing to communicate with her through pounding on the walls.

She had asked three electricians for estimates on the wiring project. Whereas the first two made do with looking around the main floors, the last one also wanted to see the basement. Within minutes of going down the old steps, he was calling out Annie's name. She found him at the top of the steps saying there was a hiding place downstairs. Although she was a bit concerned about this stranger beckoning her to accompany him to the basement, her curiosity got the best of her. She grabbed a cordless telephone and followed him down.

He pointed to a small crawl space hidden behind some boards. He edged in the opening and brought out a length of pipe. Inside were two cans welded together lengthwise. A plastic coffee can lid was affixed to one end. She took it, removed the lid, and pulled out a stack of papers, envelopes, and folders. One of the envelopes was addressed to Leon Kuechenmeister. Two cough drop tins were filled with old coins, including a nineteenth-century silver dollar.

It was obvious that the envelopes were stuffed with money.

Hidden treasure?

It seemed to be, and then it struck Annie that this may have been the reason Leon was there. He was trying to lead her to the money he had apparently squirreled away.

Annie later determined the cans contained $4,800, mostly in hundred-dollar bills. She returned it to Leon's surviving family members.

"There was never any doubt in my mind about giving the money back," Annie writes. "Inspired partly by altruism and partly by fear, my decision was based both on the belief that the valuables truly belonged to Leon's family and the prospect of what every night for the rest of my life would be like if I kept the money."

Although Leon—an "unhappy old man," Annie says—did linger, his appearances became more infrequent. Annie also found that the discovery of the hidden treasure and Leon's in-person visit calmed her, lessening her fear of this former tenant.

"I thanked Leon for choosing us, as I had already done many times. But this time was different. I wasn't afraid of him anymore. And if he ever had been, maybe he wasn't afraid of me anymore, either. The energetic transfer of ownership of the old house was complete."

Annie thinks Leon comes and goes now. He isn't stuck here forever.

"I don't think he's earthbound now. I think he was earthbound before we found the money and gave it back to his family, but now I think . . . that he feels a very strong responsibility to protect this house. . . . One of his roles is to make sure nothing that shouldn't be here sticks around."

A psychic told Annie Wilder that Leon thought of the house as a "bus station for spirits."

"Spirits come through here, but he doesn't like that," Annie says of her most permanent guest. "From what I know of him [when he was alive], he was set in his ways, very conservative, a traditional male of his era. So he doesn't like to have an out-of-control situation in his house."

Even as a spirit, Leon Kuechenmeister feels a sense of ownership, a sense of entitlement to control who comes and goes. He'll always be connected to this Hastings mansion. And in his own manner and in his own way of showing it, perhaps Leon trusts that Annie Wilder will be too.

28

THE NANNY

"In these old places there is an old energy. Sometimes, it's good energy; sometimes it's bad energy."
Elizabeth Hudson*

New owners renovating old houses may want to take into account the sensibilities of former tenants—especially those who reside there unseen.

Case in point: A splendid American foursquare residence on a busy corner a few blocks from St. Paul's Grand Avenue. Built a century ago by a prominent St. Paul metals dealer, the home has had only three owners. The Hudson* family lives there now. They know firsthand how refurbishing an older home can trigger all sorts of unexpected surprises, including a midnight appearance by the ghost of the original owner's favorite nanny.

It all began within a week of the Hudson family's moving in, shortly after they commenced some painting and interior remodeling projects.

"That's when we really started noticing things," says Elizabeth Hudson, who with her husband, James,* bought this classic home in the early 1990s.

"We'd hear footsteps at night. If I was in bed, I could hear them up on the third floor and then in the second floor hallway. We would get up because it was like somebody was in the house."

Over the next several years, they grew accustomed to countless peculiar events that in time became an integral part of their daily routine.

One day it might be discovering all the kitchen cupboard doors standing open. On another it was coming across their family pictures, overturned. Or they'd find other pictures that had slipped off the walls.

Elizabeth's sister lived for a time in the third floor's small efficiency apartment while she attended school in St. Paul. A rocking chair in a corner of the room pitched back and forth.

"Those were the sorts of things we first noticed," she says. Small, some might say inconsequential, incidents that taken alone hardly signify a ghost at work.

That was only the beginning.

At least once a week, Elizabeth Hudson says, they would be awakened from a sound sleep by more than simple footfalls.

"Some nights it was a baby crying. When we moved in, [my daughter] was only two years old. . . . I would get up, but she'd be fast asleep. But it was a baby crying [I heard]. On other nights it would be a party, music. We'd hear old-time music, and there'd be muffled voices. We'd go downstairs [to look], and of course, there'd be nothing."

All of that was merely a prelude to a nighttime visit by the ghostly nanny.

Although they grew up elsewhere, Elizabeth, a North Dakotan, and James, a native of Owatonna, are confirmed St. Paulites, both with degrees from the William Mitchell Law School. Their first, smaller house was on Goodrich Avenue.

After their daughter was born, the family needed something larger. They bought the 1908 foursquare because they were taken with its generous floor space and the sturdy, classic design infused with interesting Victorian flourishes.

There were also practical concerns.

"We looked for a long time," Elizabeth Hudson says. "We wanted an older house with a good-sized kitchen, more than one bathroom, and closets in the bedrooms. It took a while to find that."

Built by a businessman who specialized in metal fabrication, including metal boat docks, the house in the Summit Hill neighborhood is typical, boxy-looking foursquare architecture—two and a half stories with touches of the craftsman and prairie styles. Each of the first two floors features four large rooms; a gabled top half-floor was converted early on into a small separate living space. In the front a broad, open front porch with wide steps overlooks the tidy front yard and busy city street.

Inside, the first floor has a living room and dining room on one side and a kitchen and a den and office on the other. Fine woodwork, original built-ins, and arched doorways between the airy rooms are also typical of the foursquare style. A wide stairway winds to the second-floor bedrooms and a central bathroom. Another staircase leads from the second floor to the half-floor loft apartment space above.

An older but distinctive addition by the original owner was the installation of seamless stainless-steel kitchen furnishings in a 1949 remodeling. Even the kitchen drawers are stainless steel.

But it is that earliest family's use of a nanny for their many children during the early twentieth century—and perhaps that anonymous young woman's continued presence there—that really sets the house apart from its neighbors. Descendants of that first family lived in the house until the 1980s.

"We think the ghost was that family's nanny," Elizabeth says. For nearly seven years she and her family lived with this benevolent ghost. Though they sought alternative explanations, she says, the activity began to tell its own story.

Elizabeth Hudson learned about the ghost in a roundabout way from her own children's nanny that she employed at the time, Jessica,* who also worked part time at a day care center. One evening during a rainstorm, the father of one of the day care children gave her a ride to the Hudson family home. He was surprised to see that Jessica worked at his grandparents' former home. He wondered if they knew about the ghost.

Hudson later tried without success to get additional details about the ghost from him. All he revealed was that his family thought it was the nanny employed by his grandparents, but some members of the family didn't like to talk about it. He was curious as to whether the Hudsons had encountered her.

Oh, yes, they certainly had . . . in a close and personal way.

About two o'clock in the morning, both Elizabeth and her husband were fast asleep, with their cat, Leonard, curled up at the foot of their bed. Suddenly, the cat let out a howl and bolted from the room, awakening the couple.

Then they heard footfalls outside their open bedroom door.

"James and I are both wide awake," Elizabeth recalls. "We didn't see anything; we just heard these footsteps coming closer."

Whomever it was stopped right outside their doorway, softly illuminated by a nightlight.

"For me it was like somebody shot a jolt of electricity into the room. It was a weird feeling," she says.

Her husband got out of bed and cautiously looked out into the hallway. He was astounded at what he saw.

She was out there, a young, plain-looking woman in a long green dress with a tight bodice, standing a few feet away, but turned away from him in a three-quarter profile. Her long brown hair was pulled straight back and tied. She seemed to be gazing at someone or something.

She was gone in a few seconds.

"He came back into the room, but he couldn't even speak for a minute," Elizabeth says. Her husband had been the resident skeptic.

His description was clear and concise but mixed with wonder at what he had just witnessed. She wasn't in a haze, wasn't vaporous in the least bit. She looked to be a three-dimensional person of flesh and blood standing in the hallway, only it could not possibly be.

"I was thinking I'm the one who was not so skeptical [about ghosts]. I ran out there, and of course, I didn't see anything. And we can't hear anything. Everything was back to normal in an instant."

Neither one has seen the woman they call Mary since that night, but that's not to say she has disappeared.

This watchful nanny may have shown up a few months later when the Hudsons started a major repainting of their home's exterior.

As many as ten men set to work stripping all the old paint off the house. Elizabeth Hudson says she understood that the original owner put a fresh coat of white paint on the house every year, whether it needed it or not. Much of that old paint was lead based and required a long and arduous process to safely remove it from the house.

For two days in a row, Elizabeth was met by a puzzled contractor telling her that their radios were going haywire. As the crew worked on the house's exterior, several radios around the perimeter were tuned to their favorite stations, or so the crew thought. The contractor claimed that all the radios would switch to what he termed "ragtime" music. The men turned them back to the original stations, but soon the music would return to that turn-of-the-century music.

The painting crew witnessed an even stranger episode once they began repainting the house. Each day at about three o'clock in the afternoon, a young woman showed up at the corner across the street, staring at the Hudson home as it was repainted.

The mystery woman would stand there for only a very short time. They never saw her arrive; they never saw her leave. It struck them as odd because her attire seemed so out of place on those hot summer days. The contractor wondered if Elizabeth had any idea of who it might be.

She asked what she looked like.

"Well," he said, "she's in her twenties with brown hair kind of pulled back, and even though it was very warm, she had on a long green dress."

"Every day that's who they'd see, exactly the same as James described the woman he saw," she marvels.

Over time Elizabeth learned from contemporary family members that one nanny in particular, during the 1910s and 1920s, was a favorite. She stayed on with the family when the man she was engaged to died in World War I.

Following a visit to the Hudson home, a psychic friend told Elizabeth that the ghost was indeed Mary, the family nanny; she was distraught that a child in her care had died when she left the infant alone to attend a party downstairs at the owner's invitation.

A particular attentiveness to the needs of small children in the house may help explain a few other episodes. Elizabeth said there would be times when she would suddenly awaken at night to discover one of her own children in need of her attention.

Jessica, the nanny Elizabeth employed at one time, had a baby when she worked there. Once, she profusely thanked Elizabeth for "pulling" her out of bed to check on the infant. The baby had rolled onto her stomach and was turning blue. Elizabeth told her that it had not been her who woke her up.

Elizabeth's children seemed to sense the presence of the nanny, as well. Both her son and her daughter told her on different occasions they were happy that their "ghost nanny" was with them on trips away from the house. "She's taking care of me," Elizabeth quoted her three-year-old son as saying at the time.

"We've never had the sense that this [haunting] was anything bad at all," Elizabeth Hudson says of those years with Mary. "I think now she is okay with us, that the kids are going to be okay." The ghost was never threatening. No one was ever harmed in any way. The ghost nanny was looking after the children in some sense, perhaps atoning for her own negligence.

"She was a very benevolent presence. There wasn't a time when we were really frightened, though that incident where we heard her and James saw her was pretty startling."

After the larger home remodeling projects were finished, the ghost's presence "gradually started tapering off," Elizabeth says. She hasn't noticed much activity in several years.

"At the end, it would be things like lights being switched on when we would be in the room. She would usually turn them on and not off for some reason."

The last significant event the Hudsons attribute to Mary occurred when a man hired to clean was struck in the shoulder by an antique mirror that flew off the wall and then shattered against the floor. "He was a bit freaked out by that. I had heavy-duty hangars on it," Elizabeth says.

The Hudsons are comfortable living in a home with such a remarkable history. Elizabeth is equally calm in recounting its haunted history and eager to learn even more about Mary, "the family ghost," whose presence may go back much further than she realized at first. She believes there may have been ghostly episodes in the house before her family moved in, ones that have not been shared with anyone outside the home's founding family.

"This is what we experienced. In these old places there is an old energy. Sometimes, it's good energy; sometimes it's bad energy, whether you want to call it a ghost or some remnant energy left from someone or something a long way back."

She knows she can never fully explain it, nor is there a rational explanation. But it's been quite enough to know that home remodeling can have all sorts of unintended consequences.

WAS IT MRS. MORIARITY?

*"The rocking chair was going back and forth
as if someone were having a good time."*
Dick Gibbons

The pleased young homeowner leaned back in the comfortable armchair in the library of his St. Paul home. He was already accustomed to the pleasure of having his own special hideaway in which he could spend time with his hundreds of books.

An English teacher, Dick Gibbons reflected on his good fortune as he picked up the novel he was reading, needing to spend time with the fictional characters he tried to bring to life in the classroom. This room, his library, was his private place. It was one of the unique features that first persuaded him and his wife, Valjean, to buy the two-story brick house a few months earlier.

During the evening, if Valjean was away, Dick liked to settle into his favorite chair and read, as on this particular May night in the mid-1960s. His yellow Labrador was snoozing on the floor beside him.

Unexpectedly, since there was no sound, save for the occasional car passing on Goodrich Avenue, the dog raised her head and whimpered. Dick glanced down. The lab stared at something in the adjoining living room. When she growled a second time, Dick put down his book. He patted her on the head, got up from the chair, and led her into the next room. The light from his reading lamp in the library barely penetrated the darkness of the living room.

Dick remembered well what he saw there.

"The rocking chair was going back and forth as if someone were having a good time," he says.

Dick suddenly felt clammy and very nervous. All the blood seemed to rush to his head.

He didn't want to trust his eyes, at least not at first.

He steadied himself and then reached around the corner to switch on the living room chandelier.

The chair still rocked.

For some reason Dick looked at his watch and timed the chair's movements. It rocked for precisely one minute, then fifteen seconds more . . . and then abruptly stopped.

Dick Gibbons had no idea how long the chair had been moving before he noticed it. He took the Lab by the collar and tried to lead her over to the rocking chair, but she dug her claws into the carpeting, stiffened her legs, and stayed right where she was.

Yet she never took her eyes from the rocker.

A few seconds later, she abruptly turned her head toward the adjacent dining room as if following something with her eyes. She bolted from Dick's grasp and trotted into the dining room and on toward the kitchen. At the foot of a stairway leading to the upper floor, she stopped, sniffed at the air, and looked up the steps. Dick followed her gaze but didn't see anything unusual.

Thus did Dick Gibbons's attitude toward the supernatural change for good. In his words, he later confided, "The rocking chair episode changed me from a mocking skeptic to a believer."

Valjean Gibbons also changed her views.

One afternoon six weeks after her husband's strange evening, Valjean was home alone, finishing a painting project. She went down into the basement to fetch a can of paint. The lid was stuck fast, and, try as she might to pry it open, she could not.

Finally, she decided to get a bigger screwdriver from a toolbox in the kitchen. When she got back to the basement, however, the lid from the paint can was gone. The can itself had not been moved.

Valjean later told her husband that someone must have taken the paint can lid. But there was no one else in the house. The couple gave the basement and then the house a thorough going over. The lid was never found.

In the summer of that year, she again found herself working alone when the crash of breaking glass sent her running to the cellar. Two stacks of wooden storm windows were piled on the floor. Her husband had propped the windows against a wall at the beginning of the summer. Now they had fallen, in the opposite direction from the way they had been stacked. The glass was cracked in only two of the windows.

That there was something odd going on in the Gibbonses' house did not come as a surprise to others in the neighborhood. For instance, they had a difficult time finding babysitters. None of the girls on the block ever seemed to be available. Dick suspected it was because they knew the house was haunted.

The couple researched the home's history, hoping to find a clue to the perplexing events. A family named Moriarity had built the house during World War I. The place had remained in the family until the Gibbonses bought it.

Neighbors said old Mrs. Moriarity lived alone for some time before moving to a nursing home. The couple also learned that the elderly woman claimed to have awakened one night to find a man crouching near her bed, staring down at her.

She said it was a ghost.

Skeptics said she had either dreamed up the incident or imagined the entire business. Others thought a burglar might have broken in.

Regrettably, the Gibbonses were never able to attach a name to the ghost in their house. They concluded it must have been a member of the Moriarity family who resented outsiders in the house. Or perhaps it was Mrs. Moriarity herself stopping in to visit with the people who bought her house.

In any event, the ghost—named Moriarity or not—must have been satisfied with Dick and Valjean Gibbons. It left the house, never to return.

30

MOOSE LAKE

SALLY COFFEE

"As far as I know, the ghost is still there
waiting for someone to take a drink."
Walter Lower

The Coffee family must have been a nasty piece of business.

In the early days of Moose Lake, it seems like nothing but bad luck, mayhem, and bloodletting followed whenever that bunch showed up. And more often than not, one of the men in the family was usually somewhere in the middle of the chaos.

The seedy clan had settled on the southeast side of Crosses' Lake. It later became Coffee Lake, of course named after this infamous family. Theirs was a hardscrabble existence. Since there were no roads in the area, they got to Moose Lake by walking down the old Soo Line railroad tracks, now a part of the Willard Munger Trail.

No one knows exactly when the Coffees showed up; records suggest two of the Coffee boys—Bill and Jim Jr.—attended the first town school for a time in the 1870s. The Coffees were at least partly Native American, so they may have followed one of the old trails up from southern Minnesota that ended at the many lakes in the area. For centuries Native Americans had come up those pathways each summer to fish, hunt, and pick wild blueberries along the lakeshores.

The old man was Jim Coffee. His wife was Sally. Hers was a

dreadful fate, but we'll get to that in a moment. The boys, Bill and Jim Jr., may have been the meanest of the bunch.

Not all of the Coffee men ended up on the giving end of the bloodshed, like the shooting at the Moose Lake Hotel. A Coffee was involved in that, but not to his benefit. A hardened gambler by the name of Jacobson was playing poker with one of the Coffee off-spring when an argument about the deal turned nasty. Jacobson reached behind him and grabbed an iron poker from alongside the woodstove. With it he smashed in the Coffee lad's skull.

More often than not, it was the Coffees who were the assailants. The notorious 1888 murder of Moose Lake saloon keeper D. C. Clemmens came at the hands of the Coffee clan. It had been illegal from the earliest days of white settlement for U.S. merchants to trade liquor to Native Americans. Canadian traders in early Minnesota were under no such constraints. Later, local, county, and state law banned saloons from all liquor sales to Native Americans, and in the early years of Minnesota statehood, such sales were even a crime punishable by death.

Clemmens skirted those laws any chance he got. Authorities had more than once told him to stop the practice. One day in 1888, U.S. marshals showed up at his saloon to warn him once more to stop selling liquor to Native Americans. The law must have been especially persuasive this time, for Clemmens got the message, much to his eventual regret.

Some Coffees and a few of their friends showed up a short while later. But because the Coffees were part Native American, Clemmens turned them away.

That did not sit well with the boys. They stomped out of the saloon, vowing they'd get even. Clemmens, knowing that the family was as good as its word, closed down the tavern and locked himself in his room on the second floor. Later that night, the Coffees came storming back into town armed with .44-40 caliber rifles and from the middle of what is now Highway 61 riddled the saloon with bullets. Clemmens was killed in the volley.

Then there was the pitiful fate of mother Sally Coffee and the ghost story it has given rise to.

Not much is known about the woman other than that she seemed to fit right in with her wicked brood, which seemed less like a family and more like a band of dangerous misfits. Yet that is no justification for what happened to her.

Despite all the laws against it, Jim Coffee Jr. had been in Moose Lake drinking heavily on a late fall day in 1889. Sally Coffee was in town at the same time. Whether she was drinking with her son or involved in some other perhaps nefarious activity isn't certain.

But mother and son must have been together at some point during the day because they had a terrible argument. Whatever it was about, the fight made Jim Jr. livid. He took off out of town down the railroad tracks.

Sally Coffee left town a few minutes later.

Now the rest of the story is based on circumstantial evidence, but it seems that mother and son met up on the Soo Line railroad trestle over the Moose River south of the town. The argument continued until its terrible conclusion: Jim Jr. raised the rifle he carried with him and shot his mother between the eyes. Her body was left on the trestle, sprawled across the tracks.

An engineer on the Soo Line saw the body and reported it to town officials. Railroad workers loaded the body onto a section car and brought it into town.

Because of his very public quarrel with his mother, Jim Jr. was quickly arrested. He denied killing her. No witness ever came forward, nor was there any evidence linking him to the crime. She had been shot with a large caliber rifle like the ones the Coffees carried, but so did many other men at the time. Neither Jim Coffee Jr. nor anyone else was ever charged with the crime.

Today, the trestle on which Sally's body was discovered crosses the Moose River as a part of the Willard Munger State Trail, just off Highway 61 on the edge of Moose Lake. The asphalted, arrow-straight trail is bordered with neatly trimmed grass and profuse wildflowers. The only sound is the occasional red-wing blackbird or the soft gurgling of the river as it tumbles over scattered rocks. Under the trestle's gray, weathered floorboards, the narrow river gently flows into a broad marsh surrounded by dense woods. The old timbers creak as one walks across them

A detailed map at a parking lot just off the highway, which leads to the trail—and the trestle—provides a guide to the popular recreational route.

There is nothing at the trestle to indicate the horrible event of a century ago, except for this: Years later, when the trail was still the Soo Line track, engineers claimed they would see a black-haired woman standing on the trestle, squarely in the middle of the tracks. She held her arms out, as if in supplication, as if begging for her life. The engineer could never stop in time to avoid hitting her, but it was no matter. The train passed right through.

And some say she stands there still.

Moose Lake may have more than one ghost lingering about.

Motorists driving on Highway 73 on the south side of the city pay little attention to the long, steep hill that sweeps by a medium-security prison, the local hospital, and a number of businesses and on into Moose Lake. But once upon a time, that road was a main artery between the logging at Sand Lake and the old Fox and Wisdom Sawmill, located about where the Riverside Arena is today.

During the winter huge sledges carried heavy loads of thick white-pine logs destined for the mill. The draft horses pulling the load raced down the hill to keep their loads from overtaking them. There were no such things as brakes on those logging sleds.

A drunken man's accidental death at the bottom of the hill gave rise to another legendary Moose Lake ghost, joining Sally Coffee in startling unsuspecting passersby, according to historian Walter Lower.

The Fox and Wisdom mill opened on the Moose River in 1882 and operated for just seven years before closing down and moving its operations to Willow River. It's not clear when the unfortunate nameless carpenter was killed, but it was sometime during those years.

The man lived near Sand Lake but worked in Moose Lake. He had a strong fondness for even stronger whisky. His nightly route home took him along what was known locally as the Mercy Hospital road, including the steep hill often traversed by the logging wagons. He usually gripped a whisky bottle in one hand, especially on a Minnesota winter night.

The man knew many of the teamsters driving the log sledges and sometimes shared his bottle with them if he could catch a ride.

On one particular December night, the man was stumbling along even more inebriated than usual. A sledge bound for Fox and Wisdom suddenly appeared at the top of the hill with a sizable load of logs. The carpenter recognized the driver and stopped in the middle of the road, drunkenly grinning from ear to ear and waving his half-empty bottle high in the air.

But it was too late.

The sledge had already started hurtling down the hill, the driver barely retaining control. The man was too drunk to move out of the way, and the team of horses was moving too fast—logs piled high on the sled behind them—to stop in time. He was struck in the head by a pole in the horse's rigging and died instantly.

An old logger told historian Walter Lower that the man's ghost continued to appear for many years, standing at the bottom of the hill, whisky bottle raised high, waiting for one of the teamsters to stop and take a swig. It was speculated that if one of them did, the ghost of the dead man could rest. The teamsters who saw the ghost were always tempted to try *these* spirits but never did.

Lower writes that, as far as he knew, the ghost was still on that hill, waiting for a more amenable traveler to join him in one final toast.

OLD EARL

"My husband and I love old houses, but there's no way I can go through that again. I don't even want to try. It's not worth it."
Laura McHenry*

The troubles began when she heard someone open the front door.

"Hello!"

Only a hollow echo in the otherwise empty house returned her greeting.

"Hello!" she repeated. "Hello!"

Again, silence.

The young college coed put down the dishes she had been wiping off in the kitchen and headed toward the living room. It was a nice fall day outside the big old house she shared with a roommate a few blocks from the Winona State University campus. She wasn't too worried—it was probably a friend from school—yet it *was* odd. She wasn't expecting anyone, and besides, they rarely used the front door.

The door was standing open. She looked out onto the screened-in porch, all the while calling out hellos.

Clearly, no one was out there.

More to assuage her own slight unease than anything else, she pushed the door firmly closed and then gave the doorknob a couple of tugs to make sure it was tightly shut.

Well, that was weird, she thought to herself.

Yet before she finally moved out of the house two years later, the young woman would come to believe that self-opening doors might have been the least bizzare event she would come upon.

Today, Laura McHenry is a successful Wisconsin magazine editor, but in 1984, she was beginning her sophomore year as a theater major at Winona State. That's when she was introduced to the disquiet that living in a haunted house can bring. McHenry and another theater student, Michael Klaers, had taken up residence in what was known around campus as the theater house, a fully furnished, spacious Victorian-era pile on Wabasha Street, about five blocks from campus. Especially attractive was the rent of about $300 a month, unusually reasonable, even by 1980s standards.

"It was nice," McHenry, a native of Mahtomedi, says of her college residence, "but the people there before us were giving us crap, saying it was haunted."

Those theater students from the year before had chosen McHenry and Klaers as their successors and as the reluctant recipients of the old house's ghost stories.

When she moved in that fall, McHenry hadn't paid much attention to the tales. The semester had begun, and both McHenry and Klaers were focused on their classes, the demanding schedules theater majors have with play productions and, on occasion, at least some semblance of a social life.

Klaers took an upstairs bedroom; McHenry took the single bedroom on the main floor.

"We decided to make sure that we stayed connected with the whole roommate thing, like what's going on in the house, paying bills and stuff, by having dinner together once a week," McHenry says. "So we picked a night that we'd have dinner, and that was good. But with theater schedules you're hardly ever home, so [outside the dinners] we didn't see each other very often."

When McHenry was home alone, she started noticing what she terms strange things, beginning with the self-opening front door. For the most part she tried to keep thoughts of those episodes out of her mind.

"I'd go and do my work," she says. "It happened for a month or so, shortly after we moved in. I would hear someone enter the house. The outside door would be open. I'd say hello, hello. Nobody would be there."

And that's about when the whistling began.

"A tune," she recalls. "A musical tune. I'm hearing this whistling, but I'm not seeing anything. It was coming from between the living room and the front room."

The incidents were hardly daily occurrences. Sometimes days or weeks would go by quietly. But it was frequent enough that she overcame some initial reluctance and confided in Klaers at dinner one night.

"He said the same things had been happening to him!"

For his part Michael Klaers remembers the house as nice but "very strange."

Although he shared the house with McHenry during their sophomore year, Klaers stayed in the house for three more years because he was on a five-year plan; he had a rigorous second major in mathematics.

"There were a lot of door openings and closings," he says. Once, he was sitting in the living room with a friend when the side door leading out to the driveway banged open.

"Earl, will you please close the door!" he called out. The door swung shut. "That was amazing. Maybe it was a gust of wind, but it closed when I told it to."

Earl was the name McHenry and Klaers attached to their shadowy tenant. The home had once belonged to a prominent local man who had died in it years before. His two daughters, quite elderly when the two students lived there, inherited the place and rented it out to college undergraduates.

"All of the old man's furnishings and belongings were still inside," Klaers says. There were four-poster beds in the bedrooms, Persian rugs, and bookcases sagging with old books, and the kitchen had all of his old utensils.

One of the two upstairs bedrooms was permanently locked. It was their understanding that the old man's daughters had filled it with their father's bric-a-brac because they didn't want to throw it out, yet had nowhere else to store it.

In addition to coming fully furnished, the house had most of its original woodwork, several original stained glass windows, and ornate doorknobs throughout. On the main floor was an old-fashioned parlor at the front, with a living room, dining room, bedroom, and kitchen completing the first-floor's plan. Upstairs was the single, usable bedroom, which Klaers had, along with a single bathroom.

The dank basement was filled with old family personal effects and a good deal of rubbish.

Outside, the house was painted a nice shade of green and featured two large porches, front and rear, over a fieldstone foundation. The driveway extended along the house on the left; a set of concrete steps led up from the driveway to the main entry. From late spring to fall, the tree-shaded lot kept the house pleasantly cool.

"I was amazed [the owners] would let college kids stay there." "It even came with a nice boat!" he jokes.

Klaers says that a decrepit old motor launch with a small pilot house sat on a trailer with one flat tire out in the backyard. The housemates held *Gilligan's Island* parties onboard. "It was a very popular house for parties," Klaers laughs.

Klaers, who is now a nationally known theatrical lighting designer based in Santa Barbara, California, didn't notice a connection between the odd incidents and any parties the housemates held, onboard the boat or elsewhere.

At the dinner during which Laura McHenry and Michael Klaers shared their experiences, the pair were far from worried or frightened.

"We kind of made a joke about it," McHenry says. "Then we thought, well, maybe it really was haunted. When these weird things happened, they didn't occur like once a week . . . maybe every three months. Those months in between it's, like, okay, that must be done now. But then something else would happen. But you would talk yourself into not leaving [the house]."

Klaers agrees.

"We never felt any of it was malicious. It seemed to go in spurts. We'd hear things for a while, and then it would all die down," he says.

Klaers also heard the same melodic whistling McHenry did, except "it seemed to move around the house" when he heard it. As with most of the early incidents, either Klaers or McHenry was usually alone when they took place.

Every so often objects appeared to have been moved after one of them had left a room.

"It's not that you would see the objects moving or anything, but they'd be out of place. Then you'd think, oh, well, maybe I moved them, or Michael," McHenry says.

It seemed to be a way for the two to rationalize what seemed impossible.

On other occasions, Klaers says, some of the behavior was more annoying than anything else.

A stereo unit switched on in the early morning hours, tuned to a station the pair never listened to. It was "annoying music, loud and fast like heavy metal," Klaers says. He would climb out of bed and make his way downstairs. There were no remotes—they weren't that common in 1984—so he opened the cabinet doors and pressed a button to switch off the unit.

"We took it as part of living in the house," Klaers says. "It wasn't that big a deal."

They were college students after all, so both of them said their priorities were classes, keeping their cars running, and "having parties" . . . perhaps not necessarily in that order!

Living in a house one believes is haunted is not always serious business.

"We became famous for living in this weird house, this haunted house," Klaers says. Quite often, friends would drop over so they could see for themselves. Michael tried to be obliging, even if it meant creating something special for the occasion.

On one evening, a friend of Michael's insisted on experiencing something scary. So Klaers turned off all the lights, lit a candle, and started talking about the house, a kind of informal séance, he calls it.

Before long his friend had to use the bathroom, which was upstairs. It was later at night and dark, but most of the lights were off. Klaers knew his friend was nervous about finding his way up to the bathroom but didn't want to show it by actually turning on any lights.

Now, Klaers, whose specialty was in technical theater, had installed music speakers throughout the house, including one in the lone bathroom. They could be individually controlled from the main stereo unit. Klaers waited until his friend was in the bathroom, adjusted the speaker system so only the bathroom speaker would be on, turned the volume as high as it would go, and hit the on switch. Music blasted into the bathroom.

Klaers heard a scream that drowned out even the music and then angry words from upstairs:

"I just peed all over your walls!"

The first year passed with those minor, peculiar incidents occurring irregularly but, McHenry says, "Whatever it was was getting more bold," with more instances of the door opening, footsteps coming inside, and the roommates not finding anyone around.

"It started out tame and then progressively got worse," she adds. Yet it was far from being serious enough for one or both to contemplate moving out.

For their second full year in the Wabasha Street house, Klaers and McHenry decided a third roommate might help defray household expenses. Another theater major, Rebecca DeWitt,* moved into the front room, which they closed off into a bedroom.

Today, DeWitt is a paralegal in southern Wisconsin. She has a clear recollection of her years in that "beautiful, historic" house. She says strange "little stuff' got to be rather "common place."

The house and its grand appearance were lovely, she says, but there was something very odd about it.

"I didn't like to be in the house alone," she says. "One time I remember just ducking in to change my clothes and then leaving right away."

Laura McHenry says several episodes told her that their unseen but far from unnoticed tenant was becoming more presumptuous, as happened at a dinner party one night with friends.

"It was after dinner. I was sitting on the couch in the living room area with my boyfriend," McHenry says. "Mike was sitting across from us with his girlfriend. We had invited another couple. I drained a glass of wine and put it on the floor when all of a sudden the other couple's eyes widened. They said my glass had gone under the couch. I said okay, bent down, and grabbed the glass."

The other couples screamed when she reached under the couch.

They told her the wine glass had not just rolled under the couch but had risen in the air, turned on its side, and then slid under the furniture.

"Like someone had picked it up, turned it, and slid it under the couch," she says. "They were all astonished. And I said, 'Yewwww, I just stuck my hand under there!' I'll never forget that."

On another occasion a late-night study session ended with McHenry and DeWitt "scared stiff," in their words.

It was perhaps three or four in the morning. Michael Klaers was still at the college theater—it was tech week for the next production—and McHenry and DeWitt were studying, getting ready for final exams. The girls were at the spacious dining room table, Laura poring over her textbooks, Rebecca DeWitt using a new, portable electric typewriter to work on a term paper.

McHenry excused herself to use the bathroom. She remembers what happened next as if it were yesterday.

"I'm up in the bathroom, and all of a sudden the light goes off, and I heard this roar at the same moment. It wasn't coming from [any one point]. It was all around me, everywhere. It was loud and all encompassing at the same time. Then the light came back on. I didn't finish what I was doing."

It didn't end there.

McHenry then heard Rebecca screaming in the dining room. She raced down and found her friend sitting rigid in the chair.

"I couldn't move," DeWitt says. "I was so petrified I couldn't speak."

Finally, DeWitt was able to blurt out what had happened. The typewriter's return carriage zinged to one side, and white sparks erupted from the tabletop. She turned to unplug the typewriter thinking it had shorted out, but it was already unplugged.

The "fireworks sparklers in slow motion," as DeWitt calls them, seemed to be coming from the middle of the table, flying into the air and then floating back down to settle on the plastic tablecloth that covered the table.

"She's motioning with her hands and just couldn't stop," McHenry says. "I asked her if the lights had gone out. She said no. I asked if she heard that roar. No. But there were these fireworks coming out of the middle of the table."

When the two women calmed down, they started looking around for the causes of both episodes. They plugged the typewriter back in—DeWitt says she never unplugged it in the first place—and it worked just fine. They looked at the chandelier thinking a bulb may have exploded throwing glass down on the table. All the bulbs were fine.

The tablecloth showed no signs of burn marks, nor was there any evidence of burns on the other items—books, papers, notebooks—piled on the table.

"It was just weird, so totally weird I can't tell you," McHenry says, shaking her head. "We sat there and talked about it for a long, long time. But at least we were together. I said I wasn't going to the bathroom again unless she came with me. It's four in the morning. What are you going to do? Not go to sleep again? I don't know if we were keeping the spirit up or what, but it wasn't very happy with us."

As frightening as it had been, both women weren't terribly surprised at the incident.

Says DeWitt, "It all didn't seem that unbelievable [with] everything that was going on at the house."

In the spring of Laura McHenry's junior year, an encounter with the house's resident ghost proved so disconcerting, so upsetting, that she had to escape it.

It was before six in the morning. She was sound asleep in her main-floor bedroom. In the darkness she awoke with a jolt. Someone had plopped down on the end of her bed. She squinted in the dim light. No one was there.

"I closed my eyes and immediately started to freak out. Things were obviously getting worse. I just lay there, rigid, hoping that whoever it was would get up and move away."

It did not.

Whatever—or whoever—had chosen this method to frighten the young woman succeeded. An then it started bouncing up and down on the mattress.

"I had the blanket up over my head. I could not move. Every muscle in my body was tense. The whole bed was bouncing, and I was bouncing along with it under the covers."

After what must have seemed like an eternity, it all suddenly stopped. McHenry lay there and waited. And waited. She had the courage to finally look out from under the blanket.

"I threw off those covers, put on whatever clothes I had laying on the floor, and ran out of that house so fast."

She sprinted all the way to the college commons because she knew it opened at 6:00 AM. When the doors were unlocked a few minutes later, she was the first one in. She sat there until her first class started later that morning. Several friends stopped by to chat because it was unusual for her to be there so early in the morning and because she was still visibly shaken.

McHenry finished the academic year still in the house but moved out early the next fall quarter. DeWitt and Klaers stayed until they graduated.

Says McHenry, "Nothing really happened after that bed bouncing, but I remember I spent more time at the theater. I made sure that Mike was there after that. I had boyfriends at the time, too! But I'd had enough . . . and I moved out. The first year was fairly tame with just the doors and the whistling. The second year when Rebecca moved in and Mike and I were there, that's when most of this stuff happened . . . over about a two-year period."

For her part Rebecca DeWitt believes it's possible that a place can be haunted.

"I think there are ghosts out there. Was this one? I don't know. We all tried finding an explanation for it but couldn't."

All three roommates got used to the activities in the house and agree that no one was ever hurt or injured while they lived there.

Klaers stayed a total of four years in the theater house. Except for witnessing the gyrating wine glass and periodic door openings, much of Klaers's knowledge of all that had gone on came from Laura and Rebecca. He says Laura "was really freaked out by the bed shaking incident" and "took it as a given" that it happened. Based on all that he had personally seen and experienced, he has no reason to doubt his roommates' genuineness.

"It did seem to go in spurts," he says. Neither did there seem to be a particular pattern. "We'd hear things for a while, and then it would die down."

Yet at the end of it all, Laura McHenry seemed to have received most of the unwanted attention. Why didn't she leave?

"The rent was cheap. I was a college student. I'm big and strong. I'm in the theater half the time anyway. And you have roommates. When you're twenty, it's not that big a deal," she explains.

And the main episodes were so infrequent that the roommates could almost have forgotten what had gone on—but not quite.

Today, she has sharp memories of her Winona college years, memories that have shaped her attitude toward life. And the afterlife.

"There are certainly things out there that we're not fully cognizant of. I guess I've always had that faith. . . . I don't know if [living in that house] really changed my views. The worst part of it was that you don't really understand it, so it can really freak you out. But if you don't dwell on it and instead think, well, that stuff happens, there's something out there that I don't know yet but someday I will, you can just move on."

There may be one other risk to avoid if moving into a haunted house. Beware if it's advertised as fully furnished. If there is a ghost in residence, it may really not like someone else using its things.

Laura McHenry was sleeping in Earl's bedroom.

In Earl's bed.

Surrounded by Earl's old furniture.

"Maybe that's why he didn't like me there," she shrugs.

THE MAD PRIEST

"My beloved Bishop, I pray you, cast off my chains so that I may return to St. Mary's to finish the work I have started."

**Father Laurence M. Lesches, St. Peter Hospital
for the Dangerous Insane**

Motes of dust danced in a shaft of gray early morning light from a high window of the empty chapel at old St. Mary's College. The morning was Bishop Patrick R. Heffron's favorite time of day, when it was new and fresh and full of promise. Yet on this day as he celebrated Mass he felt apprehensive. There were no recent problems for the bishop of the Winona diocese, and the founder of St. Mary's three years earlier, nor did this date—August 27, 1915—bear any particular significance. He thought perhaps it was the heat, which was already oppressive, his vestments hanging heavy upon his shoulders and sweat beading on his forehead.

Bishop Heffron had just raised the chalice when he heard a door latch click behind him. Rarely did anyone ever join him in Mass at this hour. He listened for footsteps but heard none. He spun around. Father Lesches, one of the college tutors and a man with whom the bishop had had many disagreements, was standing just inside the doorway, glaring back at the bishop.

Father Lesches advanced toward the altar. He raised a five-shot Smith & Wesson revolver and fired directly at Bishop Heffron.

The first bullet went wide of its mark. A second shot tore into Bishop Heffron's thigh. The priest marched down the center aisle, never taking his eyes from the bishop.

He fired a third time, hitting the altar's tabernacle. Pausing briefly within just a few feet of his intended victim, Lesches took direct aim at the bishop's heart, but Heffron, who was shouting that Father Lesches had an "unworthy soul" as the shots rang out, twisted away and threw up his arm. That desperate act saved the bishop's life for it deflected the bullet into his right chest.

Bishop Heffron slumped against the altar, seriously wounded but alive. A pool of blood gathered on the floor beneath his feet. A blood-stained Mass card lay nearby.

Father Lesches fled down a nearby staircase and out a door back to his room in St. Mary's Hall. Bishop Heffron staggered down the aisle after him.

Father Thomas Narmoyle, who was working elsewhere in the building, heard the shots and rushed to the bishop's side. Heffron told the young priest what had transpired. Father Narmoyle called the authorities.

Remarkably, Bishop Heffron had the stamina and presence of mind to tidy up the altar and then struggled to his residence across campus. He was then taken to the Winona hospital.

Within minutes the city police were on the campus and found Father Laurence Michael Lesches in his campus quarters, room 135 of St. Mary's Hall. He did not resist arrest. The revolver lay in an open suitcase on his bed and a shotgun was found in the priest's steamer trunk.

He told the police that he shot Bishop Heffron because the bishop had called the priest unfit for the religious life and better suited for farm work.

Authorities charged Father Lesches with assault in the first degree.

At the hospital, officers questioned Bishop Heffron, who had been put under the care of Dr. William J. Mayo, summoned from his Rochester office by college officials. It was common knowledge that, although the bishop and the priest had known each other for seventeen years, they had never gotten along. The bishop was a visionary committed to education. He was respected and generally well liked but would brook no disobedience. He dealt ruthlessly with associates who flouted his orders or failed to meet his standards.

The bishop believed that Father Lesches failed both of these standards. An arrogant, abrasive man in whom the arts of diplomacy and negotiation were wholly lacking, Father Lesches had few friends.

Bishop Heffron told the police that, in his last meeting with Father Lesches, the priest had begged again for his own parish. At the age of fifty-five, he wanted the security of settling in one community.

The bishop was unmoved.

"I told him that he was too emotionally unstable to handle such an assignment," he told authorities. "I have believed that for years and again I suggested that he consider farm work which would not require close, personal relationships."

On December 1, 1915, Winona Court judge George W. Granger called his court to order. The proceedings of the *State of Minnesota v. L. M. Lesches* lasted two days.

Bishop Heffron, fully recovered from his wounds, was the state's chief witness. He testified that Father Lesches was mentally disturbed, unable to distinguish between right and wrong at the moment of the shooting and unable to judge the effect of his act.

Other witnesses supported the bishop's statement.

Court-appointed defense attorneys also pleaded their client's disturbed mental state. The priest's personal physician, Dr. Arthur Sweeny, was the final witness for the defense. He testified that Father Lesches was a paranoiac and a potentially dangerous man to be at large.

The jury returned its verdict in less than an hour: acquittal on grounds of insanity, with the recommendation that the defendant be committed to a mental institution. The next day, Judge Granger ordered that Father Lesches be transported to the State Hospital for the Dangerous Insane in St. Peter.

Though embittered by the sentence, the priest nevertheless showed trust in his physicians and, in time, cooperated with them in his care. By 1919, a proposal was in the works to deport Father Lesches to his native France. Bishop Heffron nixed the idea.

Several years later, the doctors pronounced the priest in sound mental and physical health and recommended that he be released. But Bishop Francis W. Kelley, the successor to Bishop Heffron, refused to sign the necessary papers.

Laurence Michael Lesches remained at the St. Peter mental hospital for the rest of his life. He died there at the age of eighty-four on January 10, 1943. His remains were interred in St. Mary's Cemetery, a few miles from campus.

Bishop Patrick Heffron died of cancer in 1927. He was sixty-eight.

The tragic confrontation between Bishop Heffron and Father Lesches has given rise to the most persistent ghost story in Winona, the haunting of Heffron Hall at what is today's St. Mary's University.

A four-story, fully remodeled residence hall with ninety-three rooms for men and women, Heffron Hall was built in 1920 as the second building on campus. But it seems that its notoriety stems as much from the stories and legends connected with it as for its academic history.

Even before Father Lesches's passing in 1943, a mysterious death on May 15, 1931, was deemed a bizarre coincidence by some, while others saw it as Father Lesches exacting revenge from afar.

A nun cleaning rooms found the charred remains of Father Edward W. Lynch sprawled across his bed allegedly in the simulated form of a cross—the bed forming the vertical part and the body forming the horizontal beam. The corpse was lying face upward, a burned Bible close by. Nothing else in the room had caught fire or was even singed.

The coroner later ruled that the priest had been electrocuted earlier that morning while reading his Bible in bed. The priest apparently reached up to turn off a faulty bed light when 110 volts of electricity shot through his body. But electrical experts said that that amount of voltage would not have been sufficient to completely burn Lynch's body.

What made some suspect a supernatural link was that Father Lynch had been a close friend of Bishop Heffron and an adamant foe of Father Lesches. The two priests had had numerous arguments. On one occasion Father Lesches went so far as to predict that Father Lynch would go to hell because of his interest in athletics.

Father Lesches frequently quoted his favorite biblical passage and more than once had directed it to Father Lynch. It was said that the Bible next to Father Lynch's body was open to that single unscorched passage: "And the Lord shall come again to the sounding of trumpets."

A short time after Father Lynch's unexplained death, three college priests were killed in a plane crash.

For the nearly seven decades that have passed since Father Lesches's death, students living in Heffron Hall have known about the ghost of Heffron Hall, and some have reported their own encounters with the unexplained. For others, the stories are used to entertain incoming freshmen.

Late-night footsteps and tap-tap-tappings—Father Lesches used a black gold-headed cane—unusual drafts, and cold spots linger on the third floor, especially near the supposed ghost room. Papers lift from the hallway bulletin boards when no breeze is stirring, and women students sometimes suffer identical nightmares on the same night.

A third-floor resident walking along the dimly lit corridor heard footsteps come up behind him. He turned around, and no one was there. He hurried back to his room and slammed and locked the door. The footsteps stopped outside. Someone knocked. He opened the door.

A figure in a dark cloak stood before him, his face hidden in the shadows of the cowl.

"What do you want, Father?" the student asked, thinking it was a resident priest.

"I want . . . *you*," he uttered.

The fit young man drew back his fist and landed a roundhouse right to the thing's jaw . . . and promptly broke several bones in his hand. His roommate, who claimed to have seen the hooded visitor's face, said it looked like it was made of clay.

School disciplinary records for that day noted that a student had broken his hand in a fight in the cafeteria. But no one on campus was known to have suffered a broken jaw, which surely would have been the case if the cloaked figure had been real.

A student who lived on the fourth floor of Heffron Hall is said to have tried to walk down the staircase to the floor below but was held back by an invisible force.

In 1957, an explosion ripped apart a number of large metal trunks in a fourth-floor Heffron Hall storage room. The blast was never fully explained.

Several freshmen decided they were going to contact the ghost directly and organized a séance in one of their rooms on the third floor. They sat on the floor and lit several candles. Moments later, three of the candles were snuffed out simultaneously. The others remained lit. They quickly abandoned their effort.

A scientific investigation by the campus newspaper some years ago seemed to find anomalies on the third floor of Heffron. Five people—two photographers, a temperature recorder, a time keeper, and a wind recorder—used high-speed film, infrared cameras, sensitive barometers, tape recorders, and other scientific equipment to determine if there were any physical changes occurring in the building. The survey was under the supervision of legendary professor Robert Kairis, the adviser to the *Nexus* newspaper and a member of the History Department.

The team spent two nights in the hall. They found that, just before two o'clock each morning, the instruments showed a temperature drop of between ten and fifteen degrees in the seven-hundred-foot-long hall corridor. Oddly, the temperature drops were not consistent but seemed to occur in random spots along the hallway.

Father Lesches died between one thirty and two o'clock in the morning.

Separating fact from myth in the Heffron Hall story is the most difficult task of all. The facts are fairly straightforward and well documented—the confrontation between Bishop Heffron and Father Lesches and the mysterious death of Father Lynch—but the legends that have grown up around them are nearly impossible to verify. Indeed, most appear to have no basis in fact. Yet they continue to circulate on campus and have just enough of the authentic for many to believe that a ghost does inhabit Heffron Hall . . . and that it might rear its wispy self when they least expect it.

THE BOY IN THE RED CAP

*"I'm still skeptical, but I'm open to the possibility that there's
more to [ghosts] than anyone can reasonably explain to me."*
Greg Kneser

The pleasantly warm early fall day promised to be another typical morning on the leafy hilltop St. Olaf College campus on the outskirts of Northfield. Housing director Greg Kneser had settled in at his desk when his secretary told him that two students wanted to see him.

"What do they need?" he asked.

The two women would not say. But, the secretary added, they were very upset and insisted on speaking with Kneser right away.

"Okay, send them in," he shrugged.

When they had sat down, Kneser noticed that one had a fresh gash across her forehead.

They seemed nervous, obviously upset about something. Kneser tried to put them at ease and asked how he could be of help.

"We want to see the ghost file," one of them said.

Kneser didn't know what they were talking about.

"You want to see what?"

"We want to see your ghost file."

"What do you mean, a ghost file? I don't think we have one," Kneser replied.

"No, no, we *know* you have a file on ghosts at the college, and we want to see it."

Kneser was puzzled. He'd been on campus nearly two years and had never heard of or seen such a file around the office nor heard something like that mentioned. He told the young women that.

They were not mollified.

"Well, we understand that the dean of students' office keeps a file on ghosts and that it's secret. They won't show it to anyone, but we want to see it."

Kneser grew more perplexed by the minute, but he wanted to find a solution to their disquiet.

"I really don't know what you're talking about, but there are people in the office who have been here longer than I have. Maybe they know something about a ghost file," he offered.

Kneser walked down the hall to the office of the dean of students, the late Dan Cybyske, and asked him about this so-called ghost file.

Cybyske laughed. He asked Kneser if the students said it was a couple of inches thick and so secret the college was required to deny its existence. Kneser was astonished that Cybyske knew what they were talking about.

"So do we have a file like that?" Kneser asked.

Cybyske said absolutely not. The St. Olaf ghost file was nothing more than an urban legend. When told, the students were disappointed to hear it, though not entirely persuaded.

"We know you're required to deny that it even exists," one woman said.

Kneser knew none of this was going to be solved until he learned what brought the women to his office.

"Look, you're here. Obviously, you're upset about something," he said sympathetically. "Why do you want to see it? Maybe I can help you out."

They looked at each other and nodded, as if in agreement to confide in him. They then carefully laid out a story of their chilling experience in Thorson Hall, a campus residence hall. It was a story so amazing that on that morning in 1992 Greg Kneser took it upon himself to turn myth into reality by creating a St. Olaf ghost file—a document that may be distinctive in the annals of American college life.

Kneser is now the vice president for student life and dean of students at picturesque St. Olaf College, founded in 1874 by Norwegian Lutheran immigrants and known worldwide for its music programs, math and science curricula, and global education initiatives. Its three thousand students choose from forty-three majors or from myriad concentrations and preprofessional programs.

From that morning's conversation nearly twenty years ago, however, when he was director of housing, Greg Kneser has shaped an entirely unique chapter in "Ole" history—the very real possibility that he has collected more ghost stories at St. Olaf than have been documented at any other college campus in the nation.

They include the repeated appearances in Thorson Hall of the ghost of a young man wearing a red baseball cap, an English professor who died long ago but who was seen sorting through books in Rolvaag Library, eerie occurrences in the theater building, and ghostlike activity in several other residence halls.

Kneser has spoken with thousands of students over the years, many of whom have related their own ghost stories to the affable administrator, who has a reputation for being easy to talk to and open-minded.

"What I've done [with the ghost stories] is more about entertainment and folklore," he says, noting he is not an academically trained historian and would characterize himself as a skeptic, although his viewpoint has become less rigid over the years.

"When I got into this, I absolutely did not believe any of it. But as I've heard stories that defy any rational explanation, I'm someone who is still skeptical, but I'm open to the possibility that there's more to [ghosts] than anyone can reasonably explain to me."

The story Greg Kneser heard from the two women in late September 1992 would be the first entry in his ghost file. This is what they told him.

Teresa* and Amanda* were sophomores at St. Olaf who had befriended one another as freshmen. Now they were roommates in a first-floor room on the north end of Thorson Hall, a sprawling four-story stone Gothic-looking dormitory on the northeast edge of campus. It was early fall, so they had been on campus only a short time.

Thorson's resident assistants organized a bonfire behind the hall so that everyone could get better acquainted. The nice fall evening brought everyone out of their rooms to visit around the blazing fire, including Teresa and Amanda. From the bonfire pit behind the hall, the building takes on an almost fortress-like appearance with its dark gray cut-stone façade, a plethora of rectangular windows, and numerous heavy doors.

The two roommates' dorm room window looked out toward the bonfire. As they walked out, they looked back toward their room. The light was on. They briefly quizzed each other and agreed that the light had been turned off.

When they glanced back to make sure it was indeed their room, a shadowy figure was framed in their window. Thinking someone had gotten into their room, they went back inside and made their way cautiously down the hallway. They tried their doorknob, which was locked, as they thought it would be. Once inside, they found the light still on but no sign that anyone else had been inside.

"They couldn't figure out why the light had been on or why they'd seen a person standing in the window," Kneser says.

Amanda and Teresa decided against mentioning the episode to anybody, perhaps dismissing it as a fluke.

Added to the mix in their first weeks were persistent issues with electrical problems in their room—flickering lights and a stereo and CD player that seemed defective. But they knew it was an old building with old wiring, which could have accounted for the problems.

The days passed and the women settled into their room, making easy friendships with other residents in that part of Thorson Hall. They had built bunk beds to allow for more floor space. Amanda took the top bunk, and Teresa was in the bottom bed.

Teresa was the one who saw him first, the young man in a red baseball cap. Early one morning, Teresa's screams sent her roommate sitting bolt upright.

"What's going on?" Amanda said sleepily.

"There's some guy in our room," Teresa said.

"Where? Is he still there?"

Teresa said she didn't know—she was hiding under the sheets.

Amanda leaned over the bed frame and peered through the dim light. She didn't see anyone.

The women got out of bed, checked the door (locked), and looked in the closets (empty but for clothes).

Teresa said she had awakened and looked across the room. A young man of college age was sitting on the floor. He had on a red baseball cap. She screamed and he vanished.

Amanda downplayed the incident, attributing it to perhaps something Teresa had for dinner the night before—or simply a bad dream.

But Teresa was adamant. It had not been a dream. She had been as wide awake as she was at that moment, talking with her skeptical roommate.

Over the course of the next few weeks, Teresa repeatedly saw this young man in their room, usually late at night. One night, he might be playing solitaire and, on another, sitting at their desk. Each time it happened, Teresa kicked her roommate's mattress from below to wake her up. Amanda never saw him.

"These women were the closest of friends," Kneser says, "but they didn't talk to other people about this. The one is thinking, 'I'm crazy, I'm seeing ghosts,' and the other is thinking her best friend is crazy, she's seeing ghosts. It is causing some strain on their friendship for obvious reasons."

St. Olaf College has a four-day fall vacation in October, and that fall, Teresa went home and Amanda opted to stay in her Thorson Hall room over the extended weekend. She also decided that it would be more convenient to sleep in the lower bunk.

Campus buildings are usually quiet over the short holiday since most students leave campus. The women of Thorson Hall's north wing, where Amanda and Teresa stayed, regularly walked in and out of each other's rooms to borrow clothes or maybe check on available snacks. There was a general open-door policy where knocking first didn't come into play very often.

Thus it was on a morning during the break that Amanda stood at the mirror brushing her teeth when a friend from down the corridor stuck her head in the door.

"Who was the guy in here last night?" she asked.

"Nobody was here last night," Amanda said. "I was tired, so I studied some and went to bed early."

"No really, I came in the room, and there was a guy sitting on the edge of your bed with a red baseball cap on. Who was he?"

The women had told no one of seeing a guy in a baseball cap. It seemed that someone from outside had now confirmed Teresa's story.

A no-longer-skeptical Amanda told Teresa the story when she got back.

"This is what I've been trying to tell you! This is what I've been seeing in the room, a young guy in a red baseball cap sitting there," Teresa said.

A week later, Amanda learned the truth for herself.

Teresa, now back in her lower bunk, woke up to Amanda's screams with such a start that she banged her head against one of the iron bars holding the lofted mattress and cut her forehead.

Amanda sputtered that she'd just seen the boy across the room. Teresa didn't see him, but she was reassured in knowing that both of them had actually seen the ghostly intruder.

It was on the following morning that the two shaken women showed up in Kneser's office demanding to see the ghost file so they could figure out whom the ghost might be and why he was there.

"They wanted to know what happened in that room, what was going on in this place," Kneser recalls. "They wanted to know what they could do about it. I said I knew a lot of stuff, but I didn't know how to get rid of a ghost."

Teresa and Amanda eventually talked with then dean Dan Cybyske, who told them the next time they had a problem with the ghost to tell him he's not welcome and that he should leave them alone.

A few weeks later, the lights in their room flickered, as they had done several times before. One of them spoke up to tell the ghost he was not welcome and ought to leave them alone. They had no more problems.

A short time later, the women's story took on added significance when Greg Kneser learned from Dan Cybyske that the haunting of the young women's Thorson Hall room may have been rooted in a real-life tragedy on the St. Olaf campus.

On Halloween night of 1986, five adventurous young St. Olaf men surreptitiously broke into an abandoned natural cave on the northeast corner of the campus, behind Ellingson Hall. The cave had been used as a brewery as far back as the 1880s and later as a cheese factory. The college had used it for storage until it was sealed off in the late 1970s. Most people on campus didn't know the caves were even there or had forgotten all about them.

But that was not the case with the five students, who burrowed through a nearly forgotten eighteen-inch-high entrance that had been partially filled in years before. Fifteen feet down the narrow tunnel, they reached the interior cave rooms. On the far end of one of the rooms, the boys broke through a masonry wall and started tunneling into a high bank of wet sand. They didn't realize the tunnel passed under an air shaft that had been filled with sand. The air shaft collapsed into the tunnel, burying one of the young men under a massive mound of sand and debris. His friends tried unsuccessfully to save him. It took rescuers several hours to recover his body.

Several months later, college and city officials filled in the cave and any remaining air pockets and graded and then relandscaped the hillside.

Dan Cybyske told Kneser that the young man who died had lived in the same room the two young women occupied. That part of Thorson Hall had housed men at the time he was enrolled. Kneser later learned the young man favored a red baseball cap, the same color as that of his high school athletic teams.

The connection between the dead student and the haunting of Thorson Hall seemed too close to be a coincidence for Kneser.

"We hear about things happening in that little area of the building around where he lived," Kneser says, though in the twenty-five years since the tragic cave-in, the room numbers have been changed, and there have been some minor building alterations. "We're talking about a very distinct area in the north end of the building: a bathroom and about six rooms."

Most of the stories involve brief, sudden encounters. A student walking down the hall will see, out of the corner of her eye, someone leaning against the wall. Or a student may be talking to someone in a room with the door open when it will seem as if someone has walked by, but when they look, the hallway will be empty. One student was brushing her teeth when she saw a young man's face reflected in the mirror.

Alison Vandenberg is a Twin Cities publishing executive, a 1996 St. Olaf graduate, and the recipient of a brief but memorable visit by what may have been the red cap ghost of Thorson Hall.

"I'm a pretty skeptical person," Vandenberg says, "and still don't entirely believe the encounter that I [had]."

Yet she is clear, concise, and unhesitating in describing what happened during her sophomore year in her first-floor room of Thorson Hall.

"I woke up in the middle of the night and saw a figure crouched by my phone, looking up at me."

He was wearing a red cap.

Alison yelled to her roommate that someone had broken into their room.

"I then looked back, and he was gone," she says.

Remarkably, she assumed she was dreaming and went back to sleep. Her roommate saw nothing.

Later, when she told friends about it, she learned about the ghost with the red hat. She had never before heard about the ghost.

"It gave me the chills," Vandenberg admits.

The ghost's brief appearance in her room wasn't the only mystery she and her roommate had that year. A stereo unit's radio settings swirled through the dial, seemingly of their own accord. Books and bric-a-brac fell off tables without provocation.

She says the room was not comfortable. Overall, there was the feeling of a presence in the room, a sense that there was another, albeit unseen, third person living there with them.

Several times during the course of the year, Alison and her roommate would be so scared that they stayed in friends' rooms for the night.

Meanwhile, Greg Kneser is careful not to be misled by students who create their own encounters with the red cap ghost, because they may want attention.

"The stories that really make me scratch my head are told by people who are really reluctant to tell them, like [Amanda and Teresa] who came into my office. They had a practical problem that they wanted solved. They weren't sleeping well; one of them had a gash on her head. They wanted somebody to take care of their problem. It wasn't like they were seeking attention at all. They hadn't told anybody about it, but it was causing a relationship problem between them. That was it."

She was already running a bit late to her scheduled 11:00 PM study session with friends at St. Olaf's imposing Rolvaag Memorial Library. Hustling under the stone arches and through the main doors, the student headed for the center stairwell into the stone edifice's labyrinth of different levels. The library was expanded at different times, making the floors various heights, each accessible by different doors.

She skipped down the winding center stairwell until she got to the floor where she'd agreed to meet her friends. As she reached the landing, she stopped short. An elderly lady was bent over a library cart that had been pushed up against the wrought-iron railing. She seemed upset, grumbling to herself as she furiously moved books around on the cart.

"Can I help you with something?" the young woman asked, concerned that the woman seemed distressed. Even more peculiar, she wore an out-of-date, dowdy dress. And what was she doing there at such a late hour?

The old woman merely scowled, shook her head, and mumbled something the student could not understand. She went back to sorting through the books on the cart.

"Okay, whatever," the young woman said, as much to herself as to this troubled stranger.

The girl continued on down the hallway to find her friends, still not sure what that had been all about. As she passed down the hall, she glanced at the photo gallery of distinguished faculty, established by the college years ago, which lined that floor of Rolvaag Library. Deceased St. Olaf faculty and staff with thirty-five years or more of service were honored with a photograph and inscription.

The student stopped short. She was suddenly caught by one particular photograph, a stern, dark-haired woman in sensible plastic glasses, dressed in what looked like a light wool dress with a white shawl collar. A large broach was pinned at the neckline. The inscription below the photograph read: "Charlotte Jacobson, Professor of English, Librarian, 1931–1974."

The student's eyes widened in astonishment . . . and recognition. This was the lady at the stairwell, of that she was certain.

She turned around and scurried back to the center stairs. The library cart was still there and still piled with books, but the dowdy old lady was nowhere in sight.

"That's the story that's the most captivating to me. It's my favorite of all the St. Olaf stories because it defies all reasonable explanation," Greg Kneser says of Charlotte Jacobson's brief appearance that late night in Rolvaag Library.

The story came to him in a roundabout manner. The woman who had seen Professor Jacobson attended one of Kneser's ghost story nights that he holds each October at various residence halls. This student had waited in the back of the room until he was ready to leave.

"She was very reluctant, kind of shy about it," Kneser says.

What she told Kneser captivated him.

"She didn't make any grand claims. She said it wasn't like [Jacobson] disappeared in front of her or that she could see through her like it was a ghost, but she said the lady in the picture was the lady in the stairwell."

Kneser had never heard a ghost story connected with Rolvaag Library, nor did he know Charlotte Jacobson. He promised the student he would do some digging. That's when the story of Charlotte Jacobson became even more intriguing.

A few days later, Kneser stopped in to see the head librarian, a close friend of his.

"Is your library haunted?" Kneser asked candidly.

The librarian laughed.

"I don't think so," he replied.

Kneser told him of the young woman's nighttime encounter.

The librarian did not know Charlotte Jacobson, but he told Kneser that another library staff member—a woman who had worked in Rolvaag Library for over thirty years—might know something about the late Professor Jacobson.

Kneser talked with the veteran librarian and then showed her the landing where the library book cart had been and where the student had had the brief meeting.

"Oh, my God!" the librarian said.

"What?" Kneser asked.

"That's what she did!"

"What do you mean?" Kneser urged.

"Charlotte, Charlotte Jacobson, that's what she did," the librarian told him. "It annoyed her to no end that people couldn't get books shelved right!"

After Jacobson retired in 1974, she came back to the library, walked among the bookshelves, grumbling, and took it upon herself to reorganize books wherever she found them out of order, including, presumably, those piled on a stray book cart.

"What this student saw twelve years after Jacobson died was her doing just that, arranging books," Kneser marvels. "The student had no idea who Charlotte Jacobson was or what her story or history had been."

Since that night, another student has reported a book of English poetry flying off a shelf and hitting her hand and her cell phone tumbling out of her pocket to land five feet away. Perhaps a more playful Charlotte.

The haunting of Thorson Hall and Professor Jacobson's singular sighting in Rolvaag Library can be traced to specific individuals who may have reasons for lingering on the St. Olaf campus. The young man who died in the cave-in loved the St. Olaf campus and the friends he made there, according to one of his buddies, who was quoted by a journalist after the tragedy. Charlotte Jacobson spent virtually her entire professional career on the campus. Two other St. Olaf ghost stories also may have originated with historical figures.

Ytterboe Hall, on the western edge of campus, was the site of reported poltergeist activity in the early 1970s. What a student witness described as "1940s-era dance music" played quietly at late hours from somewhere close to her room. She found the source: an unplugged radio somehow secreted in the wall of her room. Another student said a "force" blew across her room, causing the posters on her wall to fall to the floor and roll up. A ghost there might make sense. There has been a documented death in Ytterboe Hall, the man for whom the hall is named. He was the head resident in 1903 when a scarlet fever epidemic swept campus. Ytterboe volunteered to fumigate the hall with formaldehyde but contracted poisoning from the substance. He died in his hall apartment in February 1904.

The pioneer St. Olaf drama teacher Elizabeth Washington Kelsey reputedly haunts the speech and theater building. She died in 1953 following a thirty-year career teaching drama and as an instructor in spoken English. Her portrait hangs in the theater lobby.

A sound technician claimed that when he stopped a tape with a composition for an upcoming production, the piano portion kept playing. From his vantage point in the light booth, he looked out on stage. At a piano sat an elderly woman with 1920s-era bobbed hair and round, rimless spectacles. She quickly stopped, looked up at him, and walked slowly off the stage.

Laurie Braunson,* who had the eerie encounter with a phantom weightlifter in Owatonna's West Hills fitness center, says that, when she was a student at St. Olaf, she stopped in the theater one night with three friends because they heard it was haunted. A lighting technician was adjusting lights in the theater, but otherwise they were alone.

Braunson says that, as the group walked up the staircase toward the lobby, Professor Kelsey's portrait seemed to be shimmering.

"There was nothing else . . . we could see, but the painting was glowing. Her face was taking up most of the painting. It was a real close-up."

The students ran to find the technician. They asked him to turn on the lobby lights, which he did. The painting portrays Professor Kelsey sitting in a chair, "kind of prim and proper and toward the back of the painting," Braunson says. "It's not a close-up at all."

"I don't know what happened, but all of us saw [it glowing]."

St. Olaf undergraduates often work during the summer assisting with camps, conferences, and special programs. That's what Genevieve* was doing during the summer of 2001 as the Hilleboe Hall supervisor. She was living in the hall, as well. Hilleboe and Kittelsby (known as HillKit) halls are two connected residence halls on the southwest edge of the campus.

But at about seven o'clock on a summer night—certainly not the witching hour, as she notes—an incident occurred that has left her searching for a logical explanation. She described it for Greg Kneser.

Genevieve was lounging in her room, trying to stay cool on a stifling hot early summer evening when piano music came from the lounge next door. A small child's voice was singing along, a young girl, it seemed. Odd. No one was staying on her floor at the time, and she hadn't heard the outside door open, which she normally could from her room.

She listened for a few minutes. The music stopped. The child skipped lightly down the hallway outside her door, singing to herself—*lah-la-lah-la-lah*. Gen pulled on a robe, opened her door, and looked down the hallway, expecting to see the child or at the least to hear a door slamming as she left.

Instead, the hallway was silent and empty.

The child could not have made it out the front door or even to the door that leads to the hall's basement. Genevieve checked the front doors, which were still locked. No cars were parked in the drive; no one was walking by.

Gen was puzzled and a little alarmed. She couldn't imagine someone trying to play a trick on her—the child's voice seemed authentic, and the light footsteps running by her room were childlike—but she returned to the hallway and opened several rooms along the child's route, anticipating, perhaps finding someone hiding in one of them.

In five of the rooms, water streamed from the faucets.

Her occasional bewildered *hmmm* changed to a strangled whimper.

Genevieve turned off the faucets, grabbed her toothbrush, and ran to Mohn Hall where the main summer conference staff was headquartered and where she stayed for a time after the close encounter, as she terms it.

How did a little girl get into a locked dorm all by herself and disappear? For that, Genevieve had no answer. Neither was there a reason for a little girl to haunt Hilleboe Hall. None ever lived there. She tried to think of every possible logical reason, but nothing seemed probable. And just to make sure she wasn't the one being haunted, Genevieve did her thinking from behind a locked door that night.

Does a young woman in a white dress wander the second and third floors of the north end of a residence hall named after St. Olaf's first female graduate, Agnes Mellby?

During the mid-1990s these women's residence rooms had small vanity tables with mirrors attached. One night, a student whose room was in the north end fell asleep while studying. She awoke to see a woman dressed in white sitting at the vanity and staring into the mirror. The student gasped, and the woman vanished.

A curious parallel to that story came six years later.

Greg Kneser was telling the various St. Olaf ghost tales to a roomful of students and had wrapped up for the night when a student stopped him. She apologized if what she was about to say sounded stupid, but she wanted to tell him what had happened to her in Mellby Hall. She had told only her roommate about it.

She had returned to her room and was chatting with her roommate, who was sitting on her lower bunk when she looked up at her own bed, lofted above the other. On her bed lounged a young college-age woman, but in a white dress that reached below her knees and wearing heavy black pumps on her feet. Her hair was pulled tightly back from her forehead.

She seemed to be listening in on the conversation the two women were having.

The student who saw her thought perhaps someone was visiting and didn't say anything right away . . . until the reclining woman vanished.

As a Lutheran college's vice president, dean—and collector of ghost stories—Greg Kneser is sometimes asked how he squares apparent hauntings with his religious beliefs.

They seemed incompatible to him at first.

"It's fun to tell these stories, to have a good time with them. It helps me to connect students to the history of the college . . . but it was troublesome to me that they just didn't line up with my theology."

Kneser eventually spoke to his own pastor about the discrepancy between religious beliefs and alleged hauntings.

His pastor said he didn't see a theological problem with ghosts. The Bible talks about ghosts, he continued, noting that there's nothing specific that says they couldn't exist.

"That helped me have a more open mind about it," Kneser says. "There are some things I'm going to know about; there are some things I'm never going to understand. And this is just one of those things I'm never going to understand. I'm okay with that. It's one of those possibilities you might find out about in the hereafter, but for now I'm going to worry about something else today."

ANOTHER FIFTEEN FRIGHTS

If you're looking for more ghostly sites around the state of Minnesota, here are fifteen additional places thought to be haunted by one entity or another. No guarantees, but if you don't go looking you'll never know what it is you *might* have . . . *unearthed.*

DULUTH

Who is the little girl in the long, frilly coat volunteers glimpsed in Duluth's **St. Louis County Heritage and Arts Center?** In a fourth-floor storage room, museum volunteers have seen her for just a few seconds, always staring wistfully upward toward a high shelf. The sightings went on for some time. Eventually, staff members were assigned to rearrange the objects on that shelf and found what she may have been looking for. On the highest shelf was a toy baby carriage. They moved it to a lower shelf. It is still there. So may be the little girl.

Elsewhere, in the **Depot Museum,** a paranormal group captured "orbs" in several photographs taken inside the museum and unidentified voices on tape recordings. Most mysterious of all was a video image of a gray, shadowy figure floating alongside the old Northland passenger rail car, one of several dozen classic rail coaches in the museum. From the vantage point of the camera inside the coach, the figure would have to have been nine feet tall or five feet off the ground. The figure twice passed by the windows. Executive Director Ken Buehler says the eerie form was "amazing."

FALCON HEIGHTS

Historian Kurt Leichtle lived at the **Gibbs Museum of Pioneer and Dakotah Life** for two months and never saw the ghost of little Willy Gibbs, yet he wonders about all those burglar alarms going off in the middle of the night. He had to make the trip over to the Gibbs house museum on Larpenteur Avenue just north of St. Paul each time, once arriving to find several squad cars and a police dog. An officer told Leichtle he was certain he had seen an outside door-knob turn as he was inspecting the house. Heman and Jane DeBow Gibbs's son Willy was eight years old when he died of pneumonia from smoke inhalation after helping fight a grass fire in the neighborhood. For over sixty years museum staff have felt Willy's presence. He plays pranks like moving artifacts from room to room. Sometimes he has appeared late in the day or early evening. In most cases a staff person senses that someone is nearby or hears footsteps or an out-of-place sound. One tour guide heard the tinny tinkling of bells from the hired hands' room. Willy's sepia photograph hangs in the museum.

LUVERNE

Eccentric and colorful Herman Jochim built Luverne's art deco **Palace Theatre** on North Freeman in 1915 as one of the finest showplaces in southwest Minnesota. With his wife, Maude, playing the organ for silent pictures, Herman's typical theater bill might include the latest Hollywood film or traveling vaudeville entertainers. Today, a visit to what some call the gem of Luverne might include clues that the Jochims have not left the building. In the theater's balcony Herman's favorite seat never quite gets folded up. Props for live shows are inexplicably moved or misplaced. A sudden distracting clank filters down from the old projection booth in an otherwise hushed auditorium. A subdued melody from Maude Jochim's Geneva console organ may startle a night janitor making his solitary rounds. And Herman Jochim's funeral in the Palace Theatre itself makes this legendary haunting even more intriguing.

The Jochims loved the theater, and its exceptional condition today under the city's ownership is a testament to their attentive management. Who can blame them for keeping watch over this jewel?

MINNEAPOLIS

The execution was efficient—and swift. Convicted killer John Moshik swung from a fifth-floor gallows at Minneapolis's **City Hall** on March 18, 1898, the only man ever hanged there. Despite pleading insanity, Moshik was convicted by a jury and sentenced to die. He had mortally wounded railroad conductor John Lemke when Lemke refused to go along with a robbery scheme. Lemke identified Moshik as the perpetrator before he died.

Moshik's ghost may be responsible for some of the strange incidents reported in the century-old Richardson Romanesque building at 350 South Fifth Street. Paintings have fallen off walls, and lights mysteriously blink on and off. Other ghosts may be of the half-dozen suicides who jumped from the interior bridges of the county center, opened in 1974.

The city hall's night crew has an embarrassment of riches when it comes to places ghosts might lurk: a labyrinth of dungeon-like rooms in the basement, winding spiral staircases, out-of-the-way attics, and lofty, dimly lit meeting rooms.

A cleaning woman taking the service elevator heard someone sneeze behind her as she passed the fifteenth floor. She was alone. The same woman saw a lady and a gentleman seated in the cafeteria. She wore a hoop skirt and held a parasol; he had on a gray suit and a top hat. The cafeteria was closed for the night. Another maintenance man heard his name called when no one was around. He also wondered who rattled a door from the inside that he'd just locked.

The building is on the National Register of Historic Places.

From the comedy of the Marx Brothers and Jack Benny to Broadway spectacles such as *The Lion King* and *Wicked,* the **Orpheum Theater** has been a downtown Minneapolis entertainment landmark for nearly ninety years. According to legend another performance sometimes occurs backstage—the sudden appearance of a misshapen male ghost.

Opened on October 16, 1921, as the Hennepin Orpheum Theatre, the million-dollar theater drew top vaudeville performers from the colorful Martin Beck's Orpheum Circuit for a top ticket price of forty-seven cents. Audiences saw the likes of George Jessel, "Dainty June" Havoc, Smith and Dale, and even Fanny Brice. Six years later, as vaudeville waned with the coming of talking pictures, the Orpheum turned into a movie palace. *Gone with the Wind* had its Twin Cities premiere there in 1940. The theater was later owned by Ted Mann before being purchased by the Minneapolis Community Development Agency from singer Bob Dylan and his brother. A ten-million-dollar restoration began in 1993, which restored much of the theater's original architectural highlights, including the original dark Victorian color scheme, an art deco marquee, and a one-ton crystal chandelier hanging from the domed ceiling.

The phantom of this Orpheum is a fleeting figure whose legendary sightings are few. He is said to have been a working man killed during the complex construction of the theater in 1921. His misshapen form is due to his fatal, horrific accident. He appears only infrequently to tell his tale of woe and then vanishes before any questions can be asked of him.

It was a Greyhound bus station, an animal slaughterhouse, and a children's playground. All those previous lives present an infinite number of possibilities for what may haunt Minneapolis's famed music venue **First Avenue** and its adjacent nightspot, 7th Street Entry. Those earlier uses of the building and land have been cited by writers and employees as the basis for intermittent sightings of the ghost of a young woman said to have died of a drug overdose when it was a bus station and of occasional poltergeist activity.

A former bar manager checking the women's bathroom after a late-night concert saw just such a young woman in one of the stalls, hanging by her neck. The manager was shaken at the thought that a patron had committed suicide, until she looked back to see empty space where the body had been. It may have been the same ghost who walked out of 7th Street Entry, smiling at two employees as she passed. Barefoot and dressed in an army jacket and jeans, the nameless ghost strolled into First Avenue and vanished.

Other stories involve suddenly airborne objects hurtling across the dance floor—dishes, ash trays, and bottles, even the odd set of headphones or a microphone. Another person claimed to have heard braying sheep in the basement. An out-of-control lighting system supposedly plagued the crew filming Prince's *Purple Rain* in 1983. Perhaps the strangest story is from a former employee who told music journalist Jim Walsh of the night a lone balloon circled the dance floor, rose to drift by the women's bathroom, and then floated down to settle at the employees' table, accompanied by a sudden blast of cold air. It was, the witness said, as if "someone was leading it by a string."

MOORHEAD

Prospective college students searching the Internet sites of Minnesota campuses will find the usual mix of academic information, snapshots of residential campus life, invitations to contact an admissions office for a personal tour, and perhaps even photographs and descriptions of campus buildings. **Minnesota State University—Moorhead** has a colorful website filled with just those sorts of highlights. But Moorhead may be the only Minnesota college campus that includes a resident ghost as a campus attraction.

The brick, vine-covered **Weld Hall** is the oldest building on campus and is now the home of the English Department, the television production center, and the Masters of Liberal Arts program. Weld was among the second wave of buildings to be erected on the campus, between 1908 and 1921. With Comstock Hall it completed what is now the mall.

A striking auditorium is still used in Weld Hall, and it is there that legend—and Moorhead State's website—says the ghost resides. Sightings are rare. Origins of the spirit are even scarcer, although the most common belief is that he may be the ghost of a construction worker killed during the building's construction, presumably not related to the Minneapolis Orpheum's carpenter ghost. A former Moorhead State president whose father-in-law supervised the Weld Hall construction around 1916 debunked the theory, telling a newspaper reporter that neither he nor his wife had ever heard of a death during the construction. A paranormal expert came up with inconclusive results during a visit to Weld Hall several years ago. And so this ghost's true identity remains a mystery.

ONAMIA

Archeologists have found evidence of settlement along the shore of Mille Lacs Lake from as early as 3000 BCE, and copper tools are in evidence from 1000 BCE. The Dakota, who came to the region in the sixteenth century, were predominant when Daniel Greysolon, Sieur du Lhut, explored the region in 1679. By the early eighteenth century, however, the Ojibwe had started moving westward from their homes along Lake Superior, in search of better fur-trapping prospects. By 1745, they had gained control of Mille Lacs Lake. Today, the Mille Lacs Band of Ojibwe live on a 3,500-acre reservation. The **Mille Lacs Indian Museum and Trading Post** holds one of the most extensive collections of Ojibwe-related historical and contemporary objects in the nation. Jodell Meyer, an administrator at the museum, has heard one man say that the museum's site is a pathway to and from the spirit world, and Meyer has discovered support for that belief. A former site manager was taking a cell phone call near the outer windows late on a Friday night. It was the only place his cell phone could get reception. He heard an audio-video program begin in a back room—something triggered only by motion. He was alone. A visitor saw a Thanksgiving table setting in the old trading post house where no display was set up. The same man saw a ghost woman in the basement of the trading post. A visitor standing at an outdoor information kiosk felt the hairs on his neck stand upright, and then a hand grasped his shoulder before he could run away. (He is the one who speculated that the museum is a pathway to the spirit world.)

Ojibwe medicine men bless the museum when new site managers take over. "Native culture believes that spirits are all around us at all times and once in a while make their presence known," Meyer says. The spirit helpers surround us and help us make our life's journey.

PIPESTONE

For 3,000 years people have been coming here—the Iowa and the Oto, the Sioux and the Mandan, and the Ponca, Sauk, and Fox. All have come to quarry catlinite, the precious red stone that Native American tribes use to make pipes, effigies, and other items associated with their traditions. Today, the National Park Service administers the **Pipestone National Monument** as one of the last vestiges of tallgrass prairie and to protect the quarrying operations, which are still carried out by Native American craftspeople. Those who work there and those who quarry the sacred pipestone will also tell you it is a spiritual place where the incessant winds, along about twilight, sometimes carry other than natural sounds—native songs, drumming, and the rustle of moccasined feet along the ancient Circle Trail. Ranger David Rambow says it is an "important and spiritual place" for native people. "Many people come here looking for answers along the trails around the Monument." According to legend the Pipestone monument lies at the precise juncture of energy lines, known as ley lines, which are also found at England's Stonehenge and in Sedona, Arizona, lines that have protected Pipestone from deadly weather systems. One tornado bearing down on Pipestone allegedly split in two before reaching the city and then joined back up and headed for Ihlen and Jasper.

Is the **Calumet Hotel** the most haunted building in Pipestone? The Pipestone Museum may compete for the title, but the 120-year-old Calumet could easily stake its claim. Built of distinctive Sioux quartzite from nearby quarries, the thirty-eight-room inn has a history colorful enough to make any visitor believe the past may be brushing past you unseen. The telephone in room 207 seems to ring the desk, even when no one has checked into that room. A woman in a bright red dress flits surreptitiously down the hallway. A quiet man in a stylish dark wool suit lounges in the dining room. Cleaning women on the third floor have their carts messed with, by something.

ROCHESTER

There may be other haunted highway intersections in Minnesota, but none may compare with Rochester's **U.S. Highways 52 South and 14 East Interchange** and what happened there to Stan Sauder one morning in the fall of 2007. Cars exiting the southbound lane of Highway 52 onto Civic Center Drive Northwest take a cloverleaf around and under Highway 52. They are usually headed to downtown businesses or to their jobs at one of the Mayo Clinic–related health facilities, as was Sauder that particular midmorning. He normally parked in an employees lot and took a shuttle to his office. On this day he was going to try and park closer to work. So at about 9:30 AM, the Mayo Clinic media services engineer from Pine Island signaled his turn at the cloverleaf with U.S. 14 to head east on Civic Center Drive.

That's when he saw her, an attractive middle-aged woman with blonde hair, wearing a loose-fitting white dress that fluttered in the light breeze. She stood stock-still on the inside grassy median of the southeast cloverleaf. Her arms hung loosely at her sides.

"It was the strangest, most bizarre thing that's ever happened to me," Sauder says. "She was on the inside of the curve. There was nowhere for her to have walked over there. There are no sidewalks. It's a very high traffic area. You'd even have to climb over a fence to get there from the bike path. . . . I thought, 'What on earth is this woman doing just standing there.'"

More disturbingly for Sauder, she made eye contact with him as he kept her in sight when he rounded the curve. For nearly half a minute she followed his progress around the cloverleaf. After he took a few seconds to look for oncoming eastbound traffic on Civic Center Drive, he looked back in her direction. She had vanished.

"It is virtually impossible that she crossed the street without getting hit. There's so much traffic," Sauder says, "and there was nowhere for her to hide."

There was no parked vehicle nearby. She didn't seem upset or distraught. She seemed peaceful.

"Today, whenever I'm at that intersection, I try to figure out how she could have gotten there. I look all the time. I know that she was there, but what was it I saw? What does it mean?"

Is it possible this was a woman who wandered onto the inner cloverleaf from elsewhere? Perhaps. Is it probable? No. Though he does not say so specifically, it is clear Stan Sauder does not think this ethereal woman in white was a living being.

ROSEAU COUNTY

The Windigo stories at **Roseau Lakebed** have been associated with that ancient site not because the Windigo originated there but because its legendary appearances came about in the general vicinity. In particular, this malevolent spirit was seen many times around, but never in, the vanished Ojibwe village at Ross, where its sudden appearance foreshadowed death. Later, the Jesse Nelson farm was located at the village site. Oddly, the creature was habitually seen during broad daylight. Local historians Hazel Wahlberg and Jake Nelson unearthed three instances of the Windigo's appearance.

On their way to school one morning, two children—Jesse and Edna Nelson—came across the Windigo in the road. They said it was nearly eight feet tall and dressed all in shimmering white. A young Ojibwe man died unexpectedly soon thereafter.

The Mickinocks were a well-known family in the Ross area. Old Mrs. Mickinock—a revered grandmother to many in the village—died after her daughter saw the Windigo striding across the prairie near her home.

Grandmother Mickinock's daughter, Anna, was tending a fire to dry the meat from a moose her husband killed. She got sick after drinking water from a nearby swamp and knew that death was near. Jake Nelson saw the Windigo three days later, and by the following morning Anna Mickinock was dead.

A will-o'-the-wisp—often thought of as having supernatural origins—was a common sight in some muskeg near a stand of willows about a quarter of a mile from the village. The mysterious dancing light was produced by a gas rising out of the muskeg. But when people tried to catch it, they always failed.

A plaque marks the Ross site.

ST. CLOUD

Nearly thirty years have passed since the last report of the high-heeled ghost at **St. Cloud State University**'s historic **Riverview Hall,** and with the building's recent renovations, this wandering wisp may never again take her nightly rambles. The 1911 two-story yellow brick Georgian revival edifice on the banks of the Mississippi River is the university's oldest classroom building. Listed on the National Register of Historic Places, Riverview Hall once housed the St. Cloud Model School, where undergraduates did their practice teaching with children in kindergarten through sixth grade.

Professor John Bovee says he heard the clicking of high heels coming down the second floor hallway late one night. When they stopped near his office, he looked out into the hallway. It was empty. A few minutes later, he packed his briefcase and left, going down the staircase. As he reached the staircase's first landing, the *click-click-click* of high heels started descending the staircase above him. He neither saw anyone nor did he want to investigate.

"I didn't prolong my stay to find out what caused the . . . sounds."

Later, however, he demurred when he was asked to speculate on their source: "It could've been anything."

A decade later, another late-night Riverview worker, Judo Andersen, heard the same *click-click-click* of a woman's high heels along the second-floor hallway. Andersen was at the bottom of a staircase when the sharp footfalls again came down the steps, but this time they crossed the first floor and then went out the front door.

Andersen says he "saw the front door open and everything."

Perhaps she is a kindly spectral *Mrs.* Chips on her way home after a day with her young charges at the St. Cloud Model School.

ST. PAUL

The legislative session was running late at the **Minnesota State Capitol.** The young staffer in his small second-floor office was working on a project when he heard a soft rustling that seemed to come from inside an adjacent office. Both offices had once been part of the state supreme court complex. He got up and looked through the glass panel into the other room. His eyes widened at what he saw—a swirling white form was inside. He threw open the door and was hit by a dense mass of cold air that "scared the shit out of [him]."

That young staffer, Chris Cowman, now lives and works in Washington, DC, but has yet to forget that night in the haunted Minnesota capitol. He never saw the strange pale mass again, but he believes "something definitely" occupied the space.

"I'd be in the office . . . and just get the chills. It was something I've never felt before or since."

He is not alone. Over the years, reports have consistently circulated about ghosts in the capitol.

LeClair Lambert spent seventeen years there, most of them as director of the House Public Information Office. His office was in the same vicinity as Cowman's and was perhaps occupied by the same apparition.

Lambert had gone into an adjoining room to get a cup of coffee when a wispy, hazy form materialized and moved slowly across the room and then out a door into an inner hallway. It was like a "plume," he says, "very thin." It moved slowly in a curving sort of way. On another occasion, Lambert and an assistant found the oak double doors closed when they had been standing open moments before. The temperature near them had also dropped perceptibly.

The white smoky mass rolling through a doorway and then back out frightening a cleaning woman might be the same entity Cowman and Lambert saw. No one is quite certain, however, if the presence the men saw might be the same one that a legislative aide sensed when he thought someone watched him as he sat in his office, though he was quite alone.

But it's not only a wispy, white form that haunts the capitol. The tall man in a dark suit who has been spotted lingering near the famed cantilevered stairwell may be Justice Brown, a member of the state supreme court from 1909 to 1913.

STILLWATER

The 1853 **Warden's House Museum** in Stillwater began its storied existence as the primary residence of the Minnesota Territorial Prison's warden, just south of the old main prison complex, now a condominium development. When a new prison opened in Bayport in 1914, a deputy warden lived in the fourteen-room home. By 1941, the house was no longer needed by the state and sold to the Washington County Historical Society. It soon became the second house museum in Minnesota.

The last warden to live in the house was Henry Wolfer, but his daughter may continue the family's connection to the historic site. Her ghost may haunt one of the house's bedrooms. Wolfer's daughter was Gertrude Wolfer Chambers—whom her dad nicknamed Trudy. The Wolfers moved into the house when Trudy was nine. She lived there until she married and moved to outstate Minnesota. Her life was tragically short. Trudy gave birth to a son but just months later died of appendicitis. Her infant son was taken in and raised by his grandfather Henry. The Wolfers eventually moved west. House workers and psychics have sensed the presence of a young woman, especially in the upstairs bedroom, which may have been the boy's room.

Two other ghosts, both of them men dressed in the drab, gray uniforms once worn by prison trusties are said to roam the upstairs hallway and an area near the former carriage house.

Visitors can look for the ghosts in the house, which is decorated as it may have been for a nineteenth-century upper-middle-class family. Some rooms are devoted to Stillwater-area history, including the St. Croix River and the role the city and region played in the lumbering industry.

ACKNOWLEDGMENTS

This book could not have been written without the cooperation of the many individuals who provided information, sat for interviews, pointed me to possible resources, or in some other way helped to make this book possible. I extend my deepest appreciation to the following individuals and organizations for their assistance: Connie Amundsen, Decorah, Iowa; Jeanne Andersen, St. Louis Park Historical Society; Scott Anderson, Paramount Theatre, Austin; Nancy Bagshaw-Reasoner, Metro State University, St. Paul; Joan Bartell, Shoreview; Jeanne Bellefeuille, Sauk Centre; Stephanie Bellefeuille, Sauk Centre; Walter Bennick, Winona County Historical Society; Don Beuch, Lydia Area Historical Society, Jordan; Kelly Boldan, *West Central Tribune*, Willmar; Julie Bolos, St. Louis County Historical Society; Donna Bremer, Wabasha Street Caves, St. Paul; Jay Brisson, Sauk Centre; Greg Britton, Los Angeles; Maggie Britton, Los Angeles; Ken Buehler, The Depot, Duluth; Tom Campbell, The Fitzgerald Theater, St. Paul; Doris M. Claes, Shoreview; Jo Colvin, Alexandria; Steph Corneliussen, Hawley; Chris Cowman, Washington, DC; Cuyuna Lakes Trail Association; John Decker, Stearns County History Museum; Department of Natural Resources, State of Minnesota; Department of the Navy, Naval Historical Center, Washington, DC; Douglas County Historical Society; Lori Erickson, Minneapolis Institute of Arts; Tim Ericson, River Falls, Wisconsin; John Fellows, Eagan; The Fitzgerald Theater, St. Paul; Karleen Franklin, Goodhue Area Historical Society, Goodhue; Linda Fransen, Cottonwood County Historical Society; Jan Franz, Mora; Kelley Freese, Palmer House Hotel, Sauk Centre; Natalie Frohrip, Moose Lake Historical Society; Sharon L. Gammell, Thayer's B&B, Annandale; Gibbs Museum of Pioneer and Dakotah Life, Falcon Heights; Kathy Gill, Elmore Area Historical Society; Stephanie Hall, Pipestone Historical Society; Rev. Terje Hausken, Pine Island; Hennepin Theatre Trust; Historic Palace Theatre, Luverne; Elizabeth Hudson, St. Paul; Joe Jacobson, Dennison; Marcelin Jacobson, Dennison; Dorothy Johnson, Elmore; Erica Johnson, Harmony; Michelle Keim, St. Paul; Michael Klaers, Los Angeles; Kathleen Klehr, Scott County Historical Society; Della Dorn Klingberg, Jordan; Elmer Klingberg, Jordan; Greg Kneser, St. Olaf College; Tina Kockler, Elmore; Jacci Krebsbach, Shoreview Historical Society; Scott Kuzma, Ironworld, Chisholm; LeClair Lambert, St. Paul; Don Lawrence, Taylors Falls; Dr. Kurt Leichtle, River Falls, Wisconsin; Kathleen Lindenberg, St. Paul; David Little, *West Central Tribune*, Willmar; Mike Longaecker, *Red Wing Republican-Eagle*; Walter Lower, Moose Lake; Mark Lund, Moose Lake Historical Society; Amy Martin, Hastings; Elizabeth McCabe, Pipestone; Jean McFarlane, Todd County Museum; Carrie McShane, Minneapolis; Amy Merkle, Shoreview; Jodell Meyer, Mille Lacs Lake Indian Museum; Paula Michel, Harmony Area Historical Society; Minneapolis Institute of Arts; Minnesota Public Radio, St. Paul; Minnesota State University, Moorhead; Jude Mitchell, The Fitzgerald Theater, St. Paul; Marvin Oldenburg, Lydia/Jordan;

The Old Jail Bed-and-Breakfast, Taylors Falls; Tim Olmsted, St. Paul; Peggy O'Neill, Pipestone; Orphanage Museum, Owatonna; Susan Palmer; Jean Paschke, Melrose Area Historical Society; Sandee Hoiness Pates, Raleigh, North Carolina; Cheryl Pierre, Osceola, Wisconsin; Teresa Pistulka, Milwaukee; David C. Rambow, Pipestone National Monument; Ramsey County Historical Society; Red Wing Public Library; Richard Rewey, University of Minnesota; Doris Reynen, Heritage Huis, Hollandale; Eric Rhinerson, Harmony; Becky Risler, Taylors Falls; Harvey and Maxine Ronglien, Minnesota State Public School Orphanage Museum, Owatonna; Roseau County Historical Museum and Interpretive Center; Sam Rowan, Minneapolis; Jeff Roy, Summit Hill Association, St. Paul; Sue Samuelson, Norwood Young America; Stanley Sauder, Pine Island; Christina Schmitt, Minnesota Public Radio; Dr. William Seabloom, Shoreview; Cynthia Schreiner Smith, Wabasha Caves, St. Paul; St. Cloud State University; Prof. Thomas Steman, St. Cloud State University; Bernice Stenhaug, Dennison; Ray Stenhaug, Dennison; Shirley Klingberg Stier, Jordan; Bev Sviggum, Dennison; Jim and Peter Sviggum, Dennison; Tracy Swanson, Chaska Historical Society; Yvonne Thiele-Bell, Austin; Kevin Thomas, Richfield; Ethel Thorlacius, Marshall County Historical Society; Megan Tillmann, Boston; Lowell Tjentland, Windom; Leroy and Tyler Underdahl, Dennison; Nancy Vaillancourt, Steele County Historical Society; Alison Vandenberg, St. Paul; Marge Van Gorp, Douglas County Historical Society; Renee Vecing, Cass County Historical Society; Larry Vizenor, Detroit Lakes; Sharon Vogt, Kanabec History Center, Mora; Hazel Wahlberg, Roseau; Washington County Historical Society; Virginia Weston, Becker County Historical Society, Detroit Lakes; Annie Wilder, Hastings.

I also thank those who provided me with stories or information but who requested to remain anonymous.

My deepest gratitude goes to the superb Minnesota Historical Society Press staff who shepherded this book to publication, editor Marilyn Ziebarth and copyeditor Michael Hanson. To publicist Alison Aten, former press director Greg Britton, and former marketing director Alison Vandenberg go my deepest appreciation for originating this project and for early encouragement. Finally, thank you to my agent and friend, Mark Lefebvre, and to his wife, Marian, for their unqualified support over the years.

A special appreciation goes to my research assistant, Carol Ann Roecklein, who helped me track down some of these elusive ghosts, read most of the manuscript in draft form, and gently pointed out some of my least elegant English constructions. I will always be grateful for her invaluable assistance and indefatigable support.

SELECTED BIBLIOGRAPHY

Books

Anderson, David E. *Moose Lake Area History*. Moose Lake, MN: Moose Lake Historical Society, 1965.

Bardens, Dennis. *Ghosts and Hauntings*. New York: Taplinger, 1965.

Beuch, Don, and Pam Killian, eds. *Lydia Area News: The History of Lydia as Reported in Local Newspapers, 1870–1954*. Jordan, MN: Lydia Area Historical Society, n.d.

Chandler, V. W. *Minnesota at a Glance*. St. Paul: University of Minnesota, Minnesota Geological Survey, 1994.

Federal Writers' Project. *WPA Guide to Minnesota*. New York: Viking, 1938. Reprint, St. Paul: Minnesota Historical Society Press, 1985.

Ford, Antoinette E., and Neoma Johnson. *Minnesota: Star of the North*. Chicago: Lyons and Carnahan, 1961.

Koblas, John J. *Sinclair Lewis: Home at Last*. Voyageur Press: Bloomington, MN, 1981.

Lass, William E. *Minnesota: A History*. 2nd ed. New York: W. W. Norton & Company, 1998.

Moose Lake Centennial Committee. *Moose Lake Area History*. Vol. 2, *1918 to the Present*. Moose Lake, MN: Moose Lake Centennial Committee, 1989.

Moose Lake Historical Society. *Moose Lake Centennial Celebration Pamphlet*. Moose Lake Historical Society, 1989.

Norman, Michael. *Haunted Homeland*. New York: Forge/Tom Doherty Associates, 2006.

Potter, Merle. *101 Best Stories of Minnesota*. Minneapolis: Harrison and Smith, 1931.

Ronglien, Harvey. *A Boy from C-11: Case #9164*. Owatonna, MN: Graham Megyeri Books, 2006.

Rose, Arthur P. *An Illustrated History of Nobles County, Minnesota*. Worthington, MN: Northern History Publishing, 1908.

Schorer, Mark. *Sinclair Lewis: An American Life*. New York: McGraw-Hill, 1961.

Scott, Beth, and Michael Norman. *Haunted Heartland*. Madison, WI: Stanton and Lee, 1984.

Trenerry, Walter N. *Murder in Minnesota*. St. Paul: Minnesota Historical Society Press, 1962.

Wilder, Annie. *House of Spirits and Whispers*. Woodbury, MN: Llewellyn Publications, 2005.

Periodicals

Anderson, Ian. "Chronicles of a Ghost Hunter." *Manitou Messenger*, November 4, 2005.

Arnold, Joel. "Go Directly to Jail." *American Road*, Spring 2006.

Bell, Dan. "High-heeled Ghosts Could Inhabit, Haunt Hallways of Riverview." *University Chronicle* (St. Cloud State University), May 12, 1989.

Boyd, Cynthia. "Boy's Ghost Said to Greet Museum Visitors." *St. Paul Pioneer Press*, October 20, 1995.

Braaten, Matt. "Student Uncovers Some of St. Olaf's Ghostly Past." *Manitou Messenger*, October 22, 1993.

Carter, Perry. "John Weston's Ghost Is Still Famous Reminder of Early County Snowstorms." *Worthington Daily Globe*, n.d.

Corneliussen, Steph. "Skeptical about Spirits?" *Detroit Lakes Tribune*, October 31, 1991.

Crippen, Ray. "Trick or Treat: Nobles County Has Fair Share of Ghost Stories." *Worthington Daily Globe*, October 28, 2006.

"Detroit Lakes Horse Barn Was Once Known as 'Haunted House.'" *Becker County Record*, August 5, 1971.

Domaskin, Andrea. "Ghost Hunter Searches MSUM: Despite Rumors of Spooky Activity, Guest Spotter Doesn't Find Spirit." Fargo *Forum*, October 27, 2004.

DuBois, John. "Renowned Riverview." *St. Cloud Times*, September 26, 1989.

Evansville Enterprise, September 11, 1903.

"Ghost Story, A." *Cottonwood County Citizen*, February 16, 1894.

"Grant County Men Lay the Detroit Lakes Ghost." *Becker County Record*, June 8, 1934.

Gunderson, Becky. "Ghost Stories from West Hills." *Owatonna People's Press*, August 8, 2004.

"He Found Peace." *St. Paul Pioneer Press*, July 10, 1892.

Hoff, John. "Heritage." Douglas County Historical Society, October 26, 1988.

Hotakainen, Rob. "Adventure on Halloween Ends Tragically with Death in a Cave-in." *Minneapolis Star and Tribune*, November 2, 1986.

Hoyle, Steve. "'I Yelled; Then I Ran Like Hell': The Milford Mine Disaster, February 5, 1924." *Holmes Safety Association Bulletin*, January 2000.

"Is the Geyser Out?" *Jordan Independent*, October 3, 1940.

Janisch, Kris. "An Overpopulated Ghost Town." *Stillwater Gazette*, October 14, 2005.

Jenkins, Kathie. "An Old Haunt Gets New Owner, New Menu." *St. Paul Pioneer Press*, August 7, 2008.

Kammerdiener, Faith. "A Haunting of West Hills." *Owatonna People's Press*, October 31, 1999.

Leyden, Peter. "Minneapolis City Hall: Haunt Hangout?" Minneapolis *Star Tribune*, October 24, 1991.

Life and Times in Taylors Falls: The Taylors Falls Historical Society Journal, vol. 4, no. 2 (Fall 1997).

"Many Are Mystified by Soil-Blowing in Fish Lake Cornfield." *Jordan Independent*, August 28, 1940.

Marek, Patrick. "School Spirit: The Haunted Tale of Heffron Hall." *Winona Post*, October 28, 2001.

McAuliffe, Bill. "Developers Are Working to Restore Gangster Hideout in St. Paul Cave." Minneapolis *Star Tribune*, February 8, 1994.

Miller, A. P. *Worthington Advance*, January 13, 1881.

Minneapolis Journal, February 6, 1924; February 7, 1924.

Minneapolis Morning Tribune, February 6, 1924; February 7, 1924.

Molander, Swan B. "Interesting Article by Early Resident." *Kanabec County Times*, June 28, 1934.

———. "When Kanabec County Was Young: The Haunted Camp." *Kanabec County Progressive*, June 17, 1937.

Nelson, Rick. "A Forepaugh's That Refreshes." Minneapolis *Star Tribune*, August 14, 2008.

Ngo, Nancy. "Dining: Forepaugh's Has Been Sold." *St. Paul Pioneer Press*, April 5, 2008.

———. "Restaurant News." *St. Paul Pioneer Press*, July 23, 2008.

———. "Wabasha Street Caves." *St. Paul Pioneer Press*, October 26, 2006.

Oldenburg, Mike. "Cave That Claimed Student Being Filled at St. Olaf." *Northfield News*, n.d.

Olson, Dave. "Creepy Confessions." *Fargo Forum*, October 31, 2007.

Parry, Kate. "Good Spirits." Minneapolis *Star Tribune*, October 28, 1989.

Peddie, Sandra. "Haunted Houses: Several Homes in Twin Cities Tell Their Own Ghost Stories." *St. Paul Pioneer Press*, October 31, 1982.

Pohlman, Natalie. "Palace Theater's Ghost Stories Popular at Halloween." *Worthington Daily Globe*, October 31, 2003.

Readicker-Henderson, Edward. "The Most Haunted City in the World?" *National Geographic Traveler*, October 2008.

Richardson, Renee. "Like Time Forgot." *Brainerd Dispatch*, February 2, 2007.

———. "Milford Mine Disaster: It Started with Ill Wind and Left 41 Dead in '24 Tragedy." *Brainerd Dispatch*, n.d.

Rippley, LaVern. "The Northfield Brewery." *Northfield News* (Golden Nugget Supplement), April 20, 1977.

Ronglien, Harvey. "Unveiling the Orphan's Memorial." *State School News* (Owatonna), July 3, 1993.

"Some Changes on Pop Hill." *Manitou Messenger*, February 17, 1961.

Stockinger, Jennifer. "Milford Mine Memorial Park Project Gets Boost." *Brainerd Dispatch*, July 28, 2007.

Tieck, Sarah. "We're Not Alone." *Rochester Post Bulletin*, October 30, 2004.

Voxland, Phil. "Adventure and Mystery Ooze from Clandestine Corridors." *Manitou Messenger*, November 8, 1963.

Wahlberg, David. "Cave Adventure Ends in Tragic Death." *Manitou Messenger*, November 7, 1986.

Walsh, Jim. "Some Say Ghosts Stage Concerts at First Avenue." *St. Paul Pioneer Press*, October 31, 1995.

Xiong, Chao. "Mine Drama Brings Back Memories of 1924 Milford Mine Disaster on Cuyuna Iron Range." Minneapolis *Star Tribune*, August 5, 2002.

Unpublished Sources

Higley, F. M. "Reminiscence of the Cook Family Murder." Becker County Historical Society, n.d.

Selected oral history tapes. Iron Range Research Center, a division of the Department of the Iron Range Resources and Rehabilitation Center, Chisholm, MN.

"Vang's Vision and Victory: A Century of Christian Witness, Centennial Observance, September 29–30, 1962, Vang Lutheran Church ELCA."

INDEX to PLACE NAMES

The Nearly Departed was designed and set in type by Percolator, Minneapolis. The typefaces are Cyclone and Zingha. Printed by Sheridan Books.